Solomon's Grave

Daniel G. Keohane

Other Road Press
www.otherroadpress.com

Solomon's Grave

ISBN 10: 0-98373-295-7
ISBN 13: 978-0-9837329-5-2

Second edition published in January 2017
by Other Road Press, Princeton MA

For information, please contact: www.otherroadpress.com

Cover Design by Lynne Hansen Design

Printed in the United States of America

Other Novels

by Daniel G. Keohane
Margaret's Ark
Plague of Darkness

as G. Daniel Gunn
Destroyer of Worlds
Nightmare in Greasepaint

Short Story Collections

Christmas Trees and Monkeys

Solomon's Grave

Acknowledgements

Solomon's Grave, my first published novel, has had quite a ride since its inception. When I penned the first draft, my intention was to write a novel geared towards the then-burgeoning Christian fiction market (known as the CBA). It didn't take long before I realized this market was a tad restrictive content-wise (maybe more than a tad), so I reworked the book to fit the general suspense market. Before it found an American publisher, it was destined for a bit of globe-trotting. *Solomon's Grave* was first bought by a Russian publisher, only to have it shut down and remake itself into a military history house. In the process, I developed a great relationship with Italian literary agent Cristine Ranghetti (who has since retired), who sold the book to both an Italian and a German publisher. The book's still having a decent run in Germany to this day. In 2009, Canadian/US publisher Dragon Moon Press released the English language version. I like to tell people this book made its way to American shores via the ICBM route. It had a good first year, even garnering a nomination for the Bram Stoker Award for First Novel – an accolade I've since milked for all its worth.

Not long ago, I got the publishing rights back to this novel, and am rereleasing it myself so my backlist is still accessible to everyone. I went through the manuscript word-by-word before releasing this second edition. Overall, it's still the same story, but there were parts (as one would expect) that felt a bit... *first-novel-ish*. I deleted two entire chapters early on (which isn't saying much, considering how short each is). The end result, the book is a little tighter, a bit less in-your-face theologically, but still the same story which started this humble run of mine.

Most authors, if they want to be successful in this business, rarely work in seclusion. A number people contributed their time and talents in helping me bring this book to publication years ago, and I'm happy to have the chance to say thanks one more time (for anyone I might have forgotten, please forgive me, but thanks!).

Andrew, Amanda and Audrey for their bottomless enthusiasm for their Dad's little obsession. Mom & Dad for a lifetime of love and encouragement, you know I can never say enough to show you how much I appreciate what you've done, for all of us. My incredible wife Linda for her love and patience every time I run off and play in my head like this. Fran Bellerive, proofreader extraordinaire over the decades, for using your colored pens to decorate every page, and never—I mean, never—letting me get away with anything. I'm a better writer for it. Mark Lowell, proofreader extraordinaire number two, for never hesitating to ask the tough questions, and for picking this book apart and putting it back together in the right order. Janet for being the first to pour over the manuscript. Reverend David Switzer of Trinity Church in Northborough, who took the time to sit down with a complete stranger and discuss the life and times of a pastor, so many details which eventually found their way into Nathan Dinneck's life. Alton Gansky, for his willingness to mentor a struggling new novelist, and his support and bottomless knowledge of our little secret buried in Solomon's grave. Mario Kivistik for his Estonian translations (yep, those cryptic lines late into the book are Estonian). My agent when this book was originally published, Cristine Ranghetti who lovingly found a home for this book in the states after previously landing it Europe (you made my life very interesting, to say the least) and Sara Camilli for closing the original US deal. My original editor at Dragon Moon Books, Gabrielle Harbowy, for going through the manuscript more than once, and making it even better, and of course original publisher Gwen Gades for saying 'yes,' all those years ago.

Solomon's Grave

Daniel G. Keohane

"And God spoke all these words: I am the Lord your God, who brought you out of Egypt, out of the land of slavery. You shall have no other gods before me."
Exodus 20:1-3

"As Solomon grew old, his wives turned his heart after other gods, and his heart was not fully devoted to the Lord his God, as the heart of David his father had been. He followed Ashtoreth, the goddess of the Sidonians, and Molech the detestable god of the Ammonites. So Solomon did evil in the eyes of the Lord...."
1 Kings 11:4-6

Part One

Homecoming

Prologue

Constantinople, 1204 A.D.

Bishop Georgios Palaiologos stumbled on a raised stone as he ran the length of the torch-lit corridor. The top strap of his sandal broke loose. There was no time for mending it. He curled the toes of his right foot to hold the sandal in place and continued on. Even in this little-known passage he could hear the sounds of Latin crusaders crashing through rooms and halls on the main floor. The Church of the Twelve Apostles, God's most holy and majestic Byzantine cathedral, was now overrun by those who claimed animal violence in His name.

The courier, a young boy of barely seven years had given him the warning with terror etched on his small face. The message was from Georgios' fellow bishop at Hagia Sophia. *They are coming; the Latins are coming and you must leave with as many of the relics as you can carry. No one is being spared. No one.*

Then the boy's face crumpled. Before Georgios could reach out to comfort him he'd escaped out a side door, desperate to return home. Now, the bishop offered another prayer for the boy's safety as he opened a door hidden behind a tapestry at the end of the passage. He did so slowly, wary that perhaps he'd underestimated the preparedness of the knights storming up the church's steps only fifteen minutes after the courier departed. It would take time to find their way down here, but Georgios maintained stealth as he ran down the winding flight of steps and entered the large, cross-shaped tomb below the church. It was empty. For now.

No time to consider another plan. Even so, when he saw the

twelve caskets laid out in the chamber, relegated here centuries before by Constantius to hold the most sacred relics of Christ's original twelve apostles, the large man sagged to his knees.

"Dear God," he whispered, hands clasped together against his chest. "Please protect your church. Do not let these murderers destroy your temple. Guide my steps." He wanted to remain there, fall prostrate to the cold floor and beseech the Lord to lay his hand over the perfect and irreplaceable objects which lay within the sarcophagi. The sounds above him became suddenly louder. They had found the entrance to this basilica. He had to go *now*, since what he sought made even these precious objects insignificant.

Georgios was the caretaker, chosen by God. He mustn't hesitate. There were some, perhaps many among the invading hordes who were dark-minded men no more faithful to Pope Innocent III's holy Crusades than were the neighboring Turks. These hidden marauders, servants of the Dark One himself, were his true adversaries. He rose to his feet, curled the toes of his right foot into the broken sandal, and ran to the far corner of the chamber. He passed the Column of Flagellation, the very pillar to which the Lord Jesus was bound and whipped. He closed one eye, trying to pretend it was nothing more than a support column.

Nothing more.

Dear God, why does this have to happen?

The door was flush with the wall, save three indented holes into which he clumsily put the fingers of his right hand. He pulled. The door gave, though it tried to resist his efforts. The bishop leaned back, adding his own weight to the action, and the door swung wide. As soon as he released his handhold, the heavy stone began sliding back into place. He reached out and liberated the closest of the torches lining the room. They were lighted always, maintained by the nuns of his own order. *Those poor women...* no, he must think of nothing else but his mission. The door buffeted him as he passed inside, knocking him against the wall. Sparks from the torch dusted across his face. His right sandal, at last, broke free. He did not stop to reclaim it, but kicked off the other within the inner hall and walked barefoot along the passage. He held the torch's flame high to keep the heat and smoke out of his eyes.

Before he turned the corner into the chamber, the bishop felt its power. No matter how often, how constantly drawn he was to this secret room, the barely restrained power of God—both glorious and deadly—filled him with awe. But he did not slow; he *could not*. His bare feet slapped against stones which were regularly cleaned and washed by his own hand.

The relic before him seemed to suck the very light from his torch's flame, shining it back a hundredfold. Georgios was certain this was not mere reflection across the ornate gold. He had many theories on why this relic, as holy and historical as it was, was so coveted by both God and Satan. Why he and thousands before him had devoted their lives to its secrecy and protection. Someday he would need to write his theories down. He cursed his procrastination. He may not live out the day to write any more in his journals.

After inserting the torch into the nearest sconce, the large man climbed onto the platform. Voices now, behind him. How had the cursed knights found the apostles' chamber so quickly? Sounds of breaking stone. Georgios stumbled, closed his eyes and wanted to weep at the thoughts of what might be happening beyond the sealed door.

The sound of looting and destruction faded suddenly under an obscure hum. Music surrounded him. Chanting. No, not chanting, *singing*, a million voices collapsing into one, then back again to millions. He dropped to one knee, knowing in his heart the sound was of angels, just beyond the very doorway into Heaven.

He would consider such musings another time.

He looked up. The vessel was too large to be moved by one man, especially himself. After the boy left him, Georgios understood he'd been caught sleeping. He prayed that God would send a force to help him move it, but there was simply not enough time for help to arrive. Only one option left, which he must do alone.

Something crashed against stone at the end of the corridor. He heard voices, louder now, the grinding of the hidden stone door. It crashed closed. Even this most secret of places they had found with ease. It would not take long for them to realize how to handle the door and charge inside.

Georgios opened the vessel's lid, slid it sideways no more than a foot, and reached in with steady hands. He closed his fingers around them, the most sacred objects in existence. He lifted the bundle and held it close to his chest, feeling its power surge through him. This was the key. Without it, the door to Heaven would be locked against this violent, pathetic world.

Perhaps forever.

Chapter One

The sky above the desert glowed deep red, almost maroon. Toward the horizon it became brighter, lightening to a thin yellow where sand met sky. Nathan didn't know which direction this was, whether he was seeing sunrise or sunset. He prayed he was facing east, for then the dancing colors would imply the sun would rise and with it, the comfort of day.

Desert stretched around him as far as he could see, but he was not hot. No shimmering heat danced over the ground. The sand under his sneaker felt real when he kicked it. When he looked up again, his stomach tightened—a thin, acidic fear creeping through his body, filling his arms and legs with lead.

Where once there was only an eternal stretch of sand before him, a building now stood. Even from this distance, he could tell it was massive; two hundred feet high, maybe more. No definite delineation existed of *floor* or stories. It could have been a pyramid—its base wide, slowly tapering to a narrow girth at the top—or an Incan temple the likes of which he'd seen in old *National Geographic* magazines.

He was dreaming, a realization as familiar as the dream itself. Like before, with the introduction of the temple came the people marching past. They formed a long line on either side of him, hooded cloaks bathed in red hues of the surreal sky above. They marched in the sand like penitent monks toward the temple. Nathan did not want to follow. He wanted to run away, or wake up, or do whatever he could to escape. The sand pulled him forward like an undertow. The sand *did* feel hot, piling over his socks and sneakers. He tried to lean back, pull against the force.

Then he was in the air, flying toward the temple. He passed over the hooded figures as they trudged toward hundreds of steps leading up the building's face and to a single, massive door two-thirds of the way up. In the crowd that raced past below him, one face—just a quick glimpse—rang familiar before being lost in the ruddy shadows of its hood. The face eluded his memory, his thoughts too occupied on what lay ahead.

The doors of the temple swung inward. What remained was only a black square waiting to swallow him. Nathan spun, looked behind him to search under the cowls to glean any features of a friendly face. Someone to beg help from.

Nothing but lonesome darkness under each. If there had been someone he knew in the line of penitents, that person was lost forever. The twin formations faded into the distance. He was moving backwards, toward the open doors of the temple. Nathan ineffectually kicked his feet, tried to swim away in the hot, dry air. He remained caught in the undertow, sensing a heavy presence in the doorway behind him. He didn't want to turn around, didn't want to go inside. He closed his eyes, curled himself into a tight ball, tried to scream, tried to wake up, but his voice was mute.

"You are the sacrifice tonight," said a voice. It was the voice one would imagine belonging to God, but turned inside out, dark and amused. From everywhere and nowhere a hundred arms grabbed him, squeezed his skin, pulled him inside.

The desert faded to a square floating in darkness, growing smaller as he fell further inside the temple. Nathan thrashed in their grip. They pulled harder, hurting, drawing him down and ripping away his flesh. Another sensation now, an odor, something burning—

"Hey! Hey, pal!"

Nathan found his voice at that moment and screamed one long, desperate wail. He struck out, found his arms no longer pinned.

A large, burly man had leaned across the aisle and gripped his shoulder. "It's OK, man. You awake yet or what?" He pulled his hand away and leaned back into his own seat.

Nathan looked around. The steady vibration of the bus, rolling along the dark highway outside. *The bus.* He'd fallen asleep. Nathan checked his watch, pressing a small button to illuminate the dial. Two-thirty in the morning.

He took in a deep breath and exhaled. "I'm OK. Sorry. Bad dream, I think. I didn't hit you or anything, did I?"

The other man's body sagged with relief, and he nodded, moving his large frame back to the window seat where he'd apparently been sitting before coming across to pull Nathan from the nightmare. "It's OK," he mumbled, keeping a sideways glance trained on him. "Didn't hurt. Sounded like a bad one. I couldn't wake you up." He made this last statement almost to himself.

Nathan began to explain, but already the images and details were hard to remember, washed away in the real-life sensations of the bus's dimly-lit interior. Besides, the guy probably didn't want the details. He was being polite.

"I don't remember much of it, not really. Thanks, though." Three other heads were looking over the backs of the seats from scattered locations in front of him. Another advantage of taking such a late-traveling bus—aside from getting to Massachusetts quicker and without traffic—there were far fewer passengers spooked by his outburst. Nathan wondered if he really *had* screamed, or if that had been part of the dream. He didn't want to know, so didn't ask.

The man across the aisle extinguished the small overhead reading lamp, obviously trying to get back to sleep.

Nathan's left shoulder ached. The guy must have shaken him hard. Seeing nothing else to hold their interest, the observing heads moved out of sight behind their seats. Nathan was alone again.

He looked at his dim reflection in the bus window, broken occasionally by a passing headlight or street lamp along the edge of Interstate 95. He tried to capture details of the dream, to retain more of it this time. It was his second nightmare this week. Some details felt familiar, as if he'd experienced them before. Same dream, most likely. The temple itself was most vivid, because it was so alien. Maybe he'd seen it in a book, but couldn't remember. Its setting had a biblical flavor. Nathan had already checked the three versions of the Bible he owned and didn't see any illustration like it.

This time, though, there had been a familiar face in the dream. At least he thought so. His father, maybe? Other details, the red sky, the desert-scape... but again he returned to the quick glimpse of Art Dinneck—if that's who it was—walking with so many others, hooded, lost. But reverent. It almost made sense. Homecoming jitters. In a few hours, he'd arrive in Worcester. Then a cab ride to the small town of Hillcrest fifteen minutes north. Not to the house of his childhood, though he *would* visit his parents later.

Thursday morning—*this* morning, he realized after checking the time—Nathan Dinneck would step into Hillcrest First Baptist Church not as a parishioner returning to the fold, but as its new pastor. The prodigal son returning, as his mother enjoyed saying (and saying, and saying) since he'd first phoned with the news. Only the second minister to serve in the small church's thirty-year history. His assignment broke so many rules of a parish choosing a pastor, he half-expected a large

"April Fool's" sign taped to the door. Five months late for such a thing, granted, but a nagging uncertainty remained.

Maybe if he were older, more experienced, then his new job wouldn't seem so unlikely. But Jesus' words—that a prophet is never welcomed in his home town—weighed on him. In fact, those words were often a standard by which church elders based many decisions. Until now, it seemed.

Reverend Hayden himself had invited Nathan to interview. The old man had been looking forward to a long overdue retirement. His failing eyesight and chronic arthritis finally won out. Being the head of the search committee, he'd made the initial call. Nathan was serving as associate pastor in a large parish just outside of Orlando, a far cry from Hillcrest's smaller, more intimate congregation. Unlike the south, the Christian population in New England, especially Massachusetts, was predominately Catholic and Congregational. Many of his boyhood friends went to Saint Malachy's in the center of town, if they attended church at all.

Perhaps that would be an advantage. Running a small parish in such a sleepy town meant he could get his feet wet as pastor a bit more leisurely. In his experience, nothing too exciting ever happened in Hillcrest.

God had a plan for him, and that plan involved coming home. He closed his eyes, feeling the tug of sleep returning, and wondered if Elizabeth O'Brien still lived in town. If she did, he doubted she'd speak to him, big time pastor or not.

He *did* fall asleep, but did not dream. At least not that he recalled in the light of morning as the bus pulled into the Worcester depot.

Chapter Two

The Reformed Baptist church in Hillcrest was housed in a two-story saltbox on Dreyfus Road, once home to the founder of the long-closed Dreyfus Shoe Company in Millbury, and his extended family. After the prestigious clan's heyday in the late eighteen-hundreds and early into the following century, much of the sprawling estate had been bequeathed to the town. The large square home had stayed in the grasp of one family member or another through the mid-sixties until, falling too far into disrepair, it sat vacant for years. In the nineteen-seventies, Ralph Hayden and his wife Jean recognized that the population of their small parish in the city of Worcester had reached its limit. With the backing of fellow parishioners, the aging structure in Hillcrest was purchased from a grateful legal firm who had been acting as the Dreyfus Estate's trust company.

Two-thirds of the first and second floors were slowly refurbished into the main chapel, with the remaining area closed off and reserved as the new home of Reverend Hayden and his wife. The reconstruction had taken nearly a year and a half, a time of pot-luck suppers and other fundraisers held by the Worcester congregation. The money was raised, the mortgage approved, and the long, careful renovations begun. Hayden, ordained ten years before but never able to pastor full-time and still swing a mortgage, retired from his twenty-two year manufacturing job at Norton Company and, in his late fifties, fulfilled a dream.

Nathan had been only three when the maiden service was held. Since then, it was the only church he'd ever known until leaving for college. It was small, compared to the neighboring Catholic parish, but still listed over one hundred and sixteen registered parishioners from Hillcrest, its neighboring towns and the city itself. Its humbleness was an emotional anchor any time he returned home, second only to his parents' house.

The cab pulled onto Dreyfus Road and parked at the curb. Nathan climbed out and stretched, wishing he'd slept more. He lifted his two suitcases from the trunk before closing it, paid the fare. An old Chevrolet four-door, slightly rusted, sat in the lone parking space out front, marked with a small sign reading "Reverend Hayden." As for the man whose name still marked both the parking sign and the top of the weekly masthead, he stood slightly bent in the doorway, watching. Nathan waved.

The man had always looked *old*, gaunt with thin, white hair. Nathan tried to look casual as he walked to the door. He took Reverend Hayden's hand gingerly in greeting. The pastor may have appeared fragile, but his gaze was eternally young. Deep blue, Hayden's eyes scanned Nathan top to bottom as he returned the shake. *Looking for flaws*, Nathan thought, a little self-consciously.

Gesturing to the Chevy when he had his hand back, Nathan said, "I see you're still driving that old gas-guzzler."

Hayden waved the comment away. "Not exactly." He moved aside to let him enter with his suitcases. "I haven't driven in four years now, Nate. They made me give up my license. Too afraid I might run over a flock of schoolchildren or something. I don't know. Marcus O'Connor takes it for a drive once a week to make sure it's still working, God bless him. The parking spot—and the *gas guzzler*—are yours now." He said this with a sly grin as he closed the door. Nathan smiled back. The pastor enjoyed instilling terror in the hearts of the children with his mess-with-me-and-you-mess-with-God personality. Being his apparent successor (there was no "April Fools" sign on the door, Nathan was relieved to notice), he suddenly found this attitude amusing.

"What are you smiling at, Dinneck?"

Nathan's smirk disappeared. He stammered, "Nothing. Nothing, sir. Sorry. It's just good to be—"

But Hayden cut him off with another gesture of his thin hand, this time accompanied by a wide, slightly yellowed grin. The expression was warm.

"I'm sorry, Reverend Dinneck," he said, moving in front of him after a quick pat to his arm. "Old habits die hard, and," he coughed a little in what Nathan thought might have been a laugh, "you should have seen the look on your face." He laughed more clearly this time, and Nathan joined him, though slightly more guarded. *Old habits*, he thought.

Chapter Three

Vincent Tarretti leaned back in his worn recliner. He'd become a creature of habit over the years, falling into a set routine each night before bed. The chair was comfortable despite the occasional rips in the vinyl, having long adapted itself to his form. Johnson lay sprawled on the small rug in front of him, the large black Labrador content with his master's nightly patterns. Vincent ran his stockinged feet gently across the dog's back. Johnson wagged his tail in appreciation and stretched further out along the rug, eyes closed, already asleep.

Smells of grass from this morning's mowing drifted through the screen on the night's breeze and reminded him, as it always did, of the childhood he'd left behind twenty-six years ago to start a life with Melissa. Even *that* world had been taken from him before it had barely begun. For the last two and a half decades, Vincent Tarretti's life was this silent, simple substitute. Cutting the cemetery lawns in warm months, shoveling snow from the walkways or thawing rectangular patches of ground to bury the dead in the winter. His home now consisted of Hillcrest Memorial and Greenwood Street cemeteries, plus the two smaller, much older graveyards scattered across town.

Vincent looked at the Bible in his lap and wondered at the passage. He enjoyed randomly opening the book and reading whatever words he came upon. Tonight it was open to the new apostle Stephen's fateful speech to the council, discussing the tabernacle—the Ark which housed the law of Moses and the tablets upon which were written the Ten Commandments by the very finger of God. The ark resided in a temple designed by David but built by his son, Solomon. The same Solomon, Stephen explained in the passage, who eventually forsook the one true God in his later years to worship the local demons of the time, the deceivers.

This was the second time today that Vincent wondered if God's plan for him was beginning to change course. The first was during the call from Ralph Hayden, letting him know he'd be stopping by tomorrow afternoon with his successor, Nathan Dinneck.

Vincent did not know if Dinneck's arrival was related to his recent plague of dark dreams, details of which dissipated like the mist that hung among his cemeteries in the early morning. The only memory he could salvage on waking was a lingering, aching sense of misgiving. He used to dream a lot when he was younger. Not long after he'd moved to this small suburb, Vincent stopped dreaming altogether. At least he *assumed* he had. Maybe he'd only stopped remembering them. Their sudden resurgence worried him, now. He hadn't remained here, unfettered by anyone for so long by ignoring his instincts. He took no credence in *coincidence*. That was a word used by people too stubborn to see the hand of God at work in their lives.

A sudden gust of wind slammed against the house. Summer was winding down, but not without protest. He slowly rose from his chair and opened the front door. The sky was clear, a million stars above him. Wisps of clouds occasionally passed by, moving quickly as if driven by the wind; ghosts in search of rest they would never find. He watched their passage with growing apprehension, half-expecting the wisps of vapor to turn toward him, to form a claw reaching down.... He went back inside and closed the door, lest his fear be detected by whatever or whoever else might be out there, wandering around the cemetery looking for him. Looking for what he had sworn his soul to protect.

Besides, it was bedtime. Any change in routine might attract the attention of those who would eventually find this place, if not in his lifetime, then the next caretaker's. For Vincent, those people existed only in warnings from his predecessor and in the writings of those who came before. Faceless, nameless adversaries over the centuries, always searching. Never stopping.

Too much at stake not to stick to a schedule. Never stray.

Johnson lifted his head and offered a questioning wag of his tail. Vincent scratched him between his ears before sitting down at the kitchen table. The dented strongbox—circa World War II, if he wasn't mistaken—was open. He did not take out the four thick volumes, many older than the box itself. Rather, he turned to the spiral notebook on the table and re-read the small newspaper article clipped from the *Worcester Telegram* earlier this year. A small advertisement, one that Vincent would normally have glossed over if not for its local connection. He paid close attention to anything new to town—a store, a new family. Usually he gave more consideration when only one person was involved, or a pair of men or women moving in. Anything that indicated a change from the norm. The new organization, known simply as the Hillcrest Men's Club—HMC, for short—had been having an open house in a recently-purchased storefront in the town's lone strip mall. At the time, he'd examined the letters in the group's name for any indication of his enemy, an anagram or some such nonsense. If whoever these people might be ever came to town, they wouldn't raise flags to their existence. Still, Vincent had made a note of it at the time, just in case. The number "798" was written in blue pen in the corner of the clipping, in his own hand. The same number had also been written on the notebook's page, along with his scattered observations or concerns, always ending with the same notation he had written for his prior seven hundred and ninety-seven entries and the few that followed. The mantra, "Wait and see."

He flipped forward until he found a fresh page, on which he wrote the number "815" followed by, "New pastor in town. Nathan Dinneck—odd to choose someone so young *and* from town. Hayden retiring. Timing of this with onset of sudden foreboding— see entry 811—comes into question." He paused, then added, "Wait and see." He closed the notebook after tucking the newspaper clipping announcing Dinneck's new appointment inside, then laid it atop the older journals in the strongbox. He locked it with a small key attached to his everyday key chain before crossing the room.

"Come on, Johnson," Vincent said. "Bedtime. Big day tomorrow."

Johnson got to his feet and followed him into the darkened bedroom. Before heading into the bathroom to brush his teeth, Vincent lifted a loose board under the edge of the bed and laid the strongbox below the floor. He replaced the board and dragged a small rug, coated in dog fur, across it. Johnson waited until his master went into the bathroom, then circled twice before settling down for the night on the rug.

Chapter Four

Peter Quinn was not a tall man, standing just over five and a half feet. Beneath his loose fitting black shirt, however, his chest and arms were disciplined ribbons of muscle. This attribute was only noticeable when he was alone, naked before his private altar in the supply room at the back of the retrofitted storefront on Main Street. His public physique was masked by loose clothes and a humble, almost stooping posture. His face, groomed to look more like an accountant's than an athlete's, served as additional camouflage. His stark white hair was short and slightly curled and matched the finely clipped moustache.

The contrast of his hair against the black shirt—all of Peter Quinn's shirts were black, worn with well-fitting pleated Chinos of varying blues or browns—gave him the look of a preacher. Such was how he often thought of himself, the pastor of the hidden church he'd established in this little town. Of course, most of his congregation were unaware of the true, spiritual nature of their new club.

Discretion was important with his profession—his *calling*. Prior to opening the Hillcrest Men's Club this Spring, he had moved among the streets and towns of central Massachusetts, an anonymous face among the populace, never drawing attention. All of that changed one fateful day as he wandered among the tombstones and monuments of Greenwood Street Cemetery. He expected to find nothing more interesting there than anywhere else since he'd been relocated—*banished* would be a better choice of words—from Chicago.

The trouble in Chicago had been a miscalculation on his part, but the memory of it never failed to send a thrilling jolt through him. The absolute terror on that pathetic man's face as he knelt, bound, in the center of his burning home, facing Peter who leaned against the frame of the back door. The fool could have saved himself if he'd simply told him where the prize was. The man died pleading his innocence. Granted, in the end, Peter had to admit he'd been telling the truth. Again, a slight miscalculation, a misinterpretation of comments made in the gym one morning as Peter reluctantly spotted for his bench press routine, but one which required the Elders to send him off to this uneventful little corner of the country. They did this with a fair share of warnings and chastisements. They accused him of being a firebug, of being too obsessive. *Obsessive? Devoted* would be a better word. Over time, most of their ranks had forgotten their purpose, focusing on business, on whatever gains the material world had to offer. To them, the Mission was nothing more than background noise, an interesting historical footnote. To Peter Quinn, it was his life.

In the end, his absolute devotion to the master proved fruitful. An assignment born of shame, now showed itself as *Providence*. He'd discovered John Solomon's grave.

Destiny.

This time he would not act rashly, would walk with careful, slow steps. By establishing his base of operations here, he hid himself behind the men who came each night to drink, play cards, waste their lives. Over time, carefully, he searched out the minds and hearts of each, looking for weaknesses to exploit. Everyone had them. It was a matter of looking closely enough. With the exception of his unofficial protégé, Manny Paulson, most of them never knew they were anything but happy members of the HMC. In truth, that's all most were. Until they were needed. Then, he would use only those necessary to move toward the prize—if any would be required at all.

One such puppet stood before him now. Quinn spoke quietly, keeping the controlled cadence in his voice from reaching anyone else's ears lest they sense something more than a quiet conversation between two men.

"Is there something wrong, Arthur?" Peter said, locking his gaze onto Art Dinneck's face, not reading his thoughts but able to pick up strong emotion as clearly as a blush. *Empathic* was the word his uncle often used during training. Still, the Voice, long trained and the most important tool of his ilk, was Peter's true power. The Voice gave him a charismatic aura, an innate ability which he'd always possessed but never truly understood before joining the Order.

Art smiled weakly and shrugged his shoulders. "No, not really. In fact I have good news. My son has come back to town. To stay, it looks like."

Quinn nodded. "I've heard. He's the new pastor of your old church, I believe."

Art nodded. Quinn sensed the man's pride and did not like its implications. He'd worked hard to pull him far from his faith, a necessary requirement in order to control him. The arrival of his boy, a minister no less, could undo everything Quinn had orchestrated. People of strong faith were not easily controlled, too much holier-than-thou garbage filling their heads. A distraction, nothing more, but enough to occupy their minds and make them harder to manipulate.

Harder, but never impossible.

This recent urge to focus so much of his energy on Dinneck, rather than letting the prude wander away from the club's ranks out of guilt or sheer *boredom*, still puzzled him. The inspiration came from outside Quinn's will, as if the master himself had chosen this man. Once Peter learned of Dinneck's son taking over the Baptist church, he began to see that perhaps there might be a good reason. Not that it would make his job any easier. More interesting, perhaps, but far from easier.

A change in leadership in the church the same year as his own discovery was worrisome. He would need to keep the new pastor's father on a short leash, learn what he could every day. Knowledge was power in this war.

"I'm sure your Beverly must be proud."

"Oh, she is, she is." Another wave of pride from the man. Quinn focused his will on what he would say next.

"You will not resume attendance at that church, however." Spoken as a statement, though Peter raised his eyebrows as if having done nothing but ask a casual question.

Art looked confused a moment, and Peter felt his command sink slowly into the sand of the man's brain. "No, no I'm not." His brows furrowed, confused by his own admission. Something cleared in his face, and he added, "Sunday's his debut service, though. Bev's all but threatened me if I try to get out of going." He smiled and shrugged.

Quinn returned the smile. "Arthur, that's wonderful," he said, keeping his voice even. "Of course you have to attend. Besides, you don't have to go to any others after that. That is not something you wish to do, ever again." This last sentence was spoken without inflection, a narrow spear thrust forcefully into Dinneck's mind.

The clarity in Art's face washed away. "No, that's right. I don't."

Peter again forced a casual tone, one with no trace of the Voice. He laid a hand on Art's shoulder and gave it a pat.

"Please pass along my best wishes to him. Nathan is his name?"

Art nodded.

"After all," Peter continued, "he's your first born. That makes him special."

A slight worried look, then Art shrugged and said, "I guess you're right."

Quinn left his hand on Art's shoulder a moment longer. "Go on back to the group and have a beer. Relax; have some fun."

The paleness which had been creeping into Art's face during the conversation washed away, and he excused himself. Peter watched after him, knowing the man would only remember snippets of their conversation, and then only what was spoken in a normal tone. It had been close, though. A parent's love was a dangerous bit of baggage. The homecoming of Art Dinneck's son was significant. Best keep a close eye on this man's family, and their little church.

Chapter Five

The coffee was instant. Hayden apologized for the inconvenience, as he was a tea drinker and never had the need for a coffee maker in the rectory. "And no matter who you are, don't think I'll drag up one of those missile silos they use downstairs after services just for one cup."

They sat in the pastor's small but comfortable living room, adorned with photos of Ralph and Jean Hayden, highlights of the couple's life together. The Haydens had no children. Nathan never knew if this was by choice. Seeing the many tributes to his wife around the room, Nathan felt a pang of sorrow that the man had no other family now except for the people of the church. It appeared to be more than enough for him.

Over the course of the day they'd gone through the books in the office, his new pastoral schedule and a quick background on current patients who needed visitations at hospitals and nursing homes. Hayden wanted as much minutiae covered before news of Nathan's arrival spread. They'd have less private time after today.

After a supper of meatloaf, broccoli, and potatoes heated in the microwave—precooked meals were supplied each week by two elderly parishioners—they'd settled upstairs. Hayden's eyes drooped. It was nearing nine-thirty. He was obviously an early sleeper. He sipped his tea and said, "I've been blessed these years to have such a caring congregation, especially since Jean passed on. Having a new pastor after so long with the same shepherd isn't an easy thing for people to adjust to. Shakes up the parish. Seeing as how you're someone a lot of people know, the transition might be a little easier. Just try to forget that some in your flock have seen you wearing diapers."

Nathan smiled and sipped his coffee, hoping no one pictured him that way when he gave his sermon.

"I have to say," Hayden continued, "I was always proud of your decision. Today's kids get so caught up in the world, even when their faith is strong. Choosing to serve God as you have seems rare."

Nathan agreed. All his life, his own calling had never been questioned, neither by his parents nor himself. He'd always felt a burning to give his life to the church. Maybe he hadn't always known in what capacity that would come—who *did*, when they were young? By high school, he knew his direction. His classmates made college plans, having only vague images of what they'd do with their lives. Whenever Nathan was asked what he planned after graduation, his reply never changed. *I'm going to earn a Masters of Divinity and become ordained, run my own church someday, somewhere.*

Most would laugh and say, *No, seriously*. Except for his best friend Josh Everson who would nod, expecting no other answer. Even Elizabeth, aside from an occasional but loving jab, never tried to convince him otherwise. In those years she had enough influence in his world that questioning his decision could have changed his path forever. The fact that, in the end, he took this path without her, was a hurt only slightly lessened over the past few years.

The old man was staring with his usual intensity. Nathan raised his eyebrows inquisitively as he sipped the last of his coffee.

Hayden's gaze softened. "It's good to see you again, Nate. It's a rare thing to have a pastor emerge from one's own parish. I couldn't have asked for a better way to retire from God's service." He looked down then, not saying what Nathan assumed he was thinking. Retiring with the woman he'd loved beside him would have been one alternative. For the first time, Nathan saw vulnerability on the old man's face.

He cleared his throat and whispered, "Do we ever truly retire from His service, Reverend?"

Hayden chuckled. "No. No, I suppose not. Even so, over the next couple of weeks, I trust you'll pay attention." Back to business, his voice stronger. "I've reserved a cell in the Christ The King monastery a few towns away, in Leicester, a sort of devotional vacation for lack of a better term." He smirked. "Basically getting myself out of your hair for a while to let you get established. I think after whatever introduction I can offer you or the parish these next two weeks, I'll just be in the way."

"You won't be in the way," Nathan said. "Please, stay as long—"

Again the hand cut off his words. "I already have. Time for me to step aside before I start drooling all over the pulpit. You'll have enough to keep you busy without worrying about me every day. Besides, this old place isn't big enough for both of us. When we go over the books in more detail, I'll show you the separate account the elders set up for me. It covers rent of a room on Grazen Street for when I get back from the monastery, plus a stipend for food, et cetera. And the fine ladies who fed you tonight have already insisted on continuing to cook their wonderful meals for me."

Nathan laughed at the man's smug grin. "So," he said, "you're taking the cooking staff with you."

Another dismissive wave of his hand, and Hayden used the ensuing lapse in conversation to excuse himself to bed. He directed Nathan to the couch in the living room where a pull-out bed was hidden beneath the cushions. It would be his bedroom for the next two weeks.

Nathan returned downstairs alone. He quietly wandered among the rooms, eventually finding himself at the entrance to the church-proper. This section of the house—taking up two-thirds of the overall building—was the reason for Hayden's abbreviated living quarters. Here, the church hall rose the full two stories, looking too big to fit into the house when viewed from outside, an illusion caused by the tall stained glass windows in the front and outside walls. A spacious, calm setting. Standing with the hallway leading into the kitchen behind him, Nathan reached out and touched the edge of the sanctuary railing on his right, but did not step all the way into the church. Everything smelled and looked as he remembered from his childhood. The small altar resting against the back wall, the similarly understated podium nearer the pews. With only the light from the hall behind him, he could not make out any details of the stained glass. Come morning, the room would glow with an inspiring brilliance.

Tonight, empty rows of dark benches. His view of services would be from this perspective from now on. During the selection process for the new pastor, he was required twice to preach from this pulpit. He'd been a guest on those occasions, an amusing spectacle to those who saw him only as little Nate Dinneck, all grown up. Things felt different now. He was pastor.

Nathan stayed in the doorway for a while longer, mind blank, taking the room in, feeling it, then finally turned and walked back through the kitchen and climbed the narrow staircase to the living room. The mattress had already been pulled from the couch, a sheet and heavier blanket folded neatly atop it. He made the bed, knelt beside it and prayed that for whatever reasons God chose to bring him home, he would serve Him with everything he had. In any way He chose.

Chapter Six

The dream was different this time, as details of those which came before returned with sharp clarity.

The sky was still the red of an eternal sunset; the sand still blew across his shoes. Nathan stood on a hill, looking down into a valley through which the long line of hooded worshippers marched toward the temple. They were close to their destination, nearing the steps leading to the massive, open doors. In past dreams, the monk-like figures had always been traveling toward the temple, but had never reached the steps. Each time, they drew closer.

Nathan was wearing the black vestments of a Jesuit priest, black shoes this time, not sneakers. He dug these into the sand in anticipation of the inevitable pull from the distant structure, waited to be lifted into the air toward the horrifying darkness inside. It did not come. Maybe he was far enough away.

Smoke rose out of the door, swirling into a tempestuous but almost familiar form. Cloud-like arms stretched from its amorphous body, collapsed back, stretched out again. It was like seeing a birth, the emergence of a demon revealing its shape in dust and smoke. It rose above the temple, dwarfing the structure with its own formidable size.

The glow of the sunset burned through the demon's body in a red aura. The light focused, reformed into molten eyes. These eyes cast a burning light across the hooded procession, further back along their ranks. Traveling, searching for something. Drawing closer.

Nathan understood, as one could only understand such things in a dream, that the eyes were searching him out. He tried to turn and run down the opposite side of the hill, hide from the searching gaze of the monster floating above the temple. He couldn't move. The demon's light moved past the worshippers, up the sand dune, then shone across Nathan's face. He raised his hands to shield himself. His arms literally burned in the heat. His sleeves burst into flame. The paralysis ended. Nathan threw himself backwards and rolled down the sand dune.

The smell of burning flesh, like overcooked bacon, overpowered his senses. He felt no pain. Nathan buried his arms in the hot sand to extinguish the fire. A voice called to him—his father's voice. *You are the chosen*, it said, *the first born. You are the sacrifice.*

He wanted to scream, but dared not open his mouth. His hair was on fire. Rather than extinguish the flames, the sand fed them, and they spread down his back. He rolled down the dune, burning, still feeling no pain but sensing his body blackening to ash.

He reached the bottom of the hill, curled and thrashing, unable to scream. The smoky demon passed overhead with a tail made of wind, roaring with ethereal laughter. Nathan shielded his face and prayed for God's protection. For the dream to end.

Coolness. The smell of damp grass, freshly cut.

He lowered his arms. They were bare, unburned. He looked down at his naked body. Around him, impressions of trees towered overhead like sentinels, blocking out the starlight. He was safe here. Shapes were slow to reveal themselves, more as outlines and suggestions.

Above him, massive wings came into focus. The light of a moon which he could not see revealed the calm faces of two angels standing guard overhead.

No, he realized, that wasn't quite true. The angels didn't notice he was there. They stared without seeing, facing each other in silent, intimate communication.

A voice, different than that of his father's, more powerful, deep and without malice said, *You are the caretaker.*

"What?"

A wind picked up behind him. Nathan turned. The demon of smoke emerged from the blackness, its bright eyes covering him with fire and pain and his flesh bubbled and burned away—

He jolted awake, sitting upright on the crooked mattress, hoping he hadn't shouted as he'd done on the bus. Reverend Hayden had enough on his mind without worrying about the nightmares of a grown man. Nathan breathed quickly. Sweat dripped across his face, but he did not wipe it away. He waited for any sounds coming from the bedroom. Nothing. He took in a deeper breath, held it a moment and exhaled.

Why was he still having these dreams? He'd arrived in town. No more worried anticipation. They should have stopped.

Slowly, reluctantly, he lay back down. This time the details of his nightmare did not fade. In his memory, he stared at the shadowy outline of the angels' wings—each stretching toward the other's—

thankful for the comfort they offered amid such a vivid, horrific vision. *Dream*, he corrected himself. *Dream, not vision.*

Chapter Seven

"**N**athan!"

Beverly Dinneck swallowed her son in a hug and did not let go until Nathan pleaded for the right to breathe. His mother was a large woman and, as far as Nathan could remember, always smiling. She backed up a half step but continued holding him by the shoulders. "When you said you were chosen, I refused to believe it until I saw you in person!"

She finally released him and brushed at his shirt and tie. Nathan had decided this morning to dress his best, especially these first few weeks. He'd slowly work himself back into jeans and sneakers as he became more established in the parish.

His mother tried to restrain herself a moment longer, but could not. She attacked him with another choking hug.

From behind them, a man's voice said, "I hope you've got more than one suit. By the time your mother is done with you, that tie's going to be twisted beyond recognition."

Nathan gave his mother another, albeit quick hug, then pulled himself free. He walked up to his father who was leaning against the counter, and gave the man time to put down his coffee mug before embracing him. Art Dinneck's hold on his son didn't last as long as his wife's but was nonetheless longer than usual. Before he gently pushed Nathan back a step, he whispered, "Welcome home, Nate."

"Thanks, Dad." With great relief he realized the warmth of this place, his home, had not changed with the fact that he was now his parents' pastor. It was a good feeling, something secure to hang on to. He added, "How come you're not at work?"

Art fished out a second coffee mug from the cabinet as he answered. "Took the morning off. Left a message with them as soon as you called this morning. You almost missed me. Had my briefcase in hand."

"Hope I don't get you in trouble."

"Naw."

His mother rinsed out two cereal bowls in the sink—they'd been finishing a late breakfast when Nathan arrived. "Is Pastor Hayden giving you the morning off?"

"No, not really. We're going to meet with the elders and a couple of committees. Some quiet introductions before my Grand Entrance on Sunday. I've got to be back at the church in about an hour."

Art poured the coffee for his son and gestured for him to sit at the table. Nathan did.

"So, how is the old guy? He's got be almost a hundred by now."

Nathan smiled. "Not quite. In his eighties, though. He's doing all right. No different than when you saw him on Sunday."

Beverly made a noise at the sink and turned around. "Well, maybe if your father came to church more often, he would know that. Pastor Hayden asks about you every Sunday, Art."

Nathan looked at him. "You're not going to church? Since when? The only time I can remember you missing services was when you had your gallstones yanked out. Even then, you insisted we record the entire thing so you could listen to it in bed."

Four slices of bread popped from the toaster. Nathan had already eaten, but his mother insisted he have *something*. She buttered them with the speed and efficiency born of routine and cut the slices diagonally the way Nathan liked them. Art made a dismissive gesture with his hand, much like Reverend Hayden, and took a slow sip of his coffee before answering.

"It's not as easy at my age to get up early on Sundays."

"You're not that old, Dad. You're only fifty... something."

"Fifty-eight," Beverly announced as she delivered the toast, two slices on each plate, and gave one to him and one to her husband. She went back to her small pile of dishes and said, "A little too old to be out all night with his new buddies, that's for sure."

Art gave his wife an irritated look. Nathan wasn't sure what to make of that. His parents rarely argued.

"Forgive a man for wanting to socialize a little."

Nathan finally sipped his coffee. It was strong, the way he remembered coffee in the Dinneck house. He took a bite of his toast. "Did you join the Shriners or something?"

Art shrugged. "No. Well, not really. It's a group kind of like that, but less *religious*."

Nathan tried to ignore the edge in his father's voice when he said the word. As long as he could remember, the church was a cornerstone of the family. His father—and Nathan, too, when he was old enough—worked every spring and fall at the church fair. Art served as an usher when needed, and rarely missed Wednesday night Bible studies.

"What changed?"

Art raised an eyebrow over his mug. "Changed? How so?"

"What's wrong with going to church?" He tried not to sound defensive, but he truly wanted to know. Apparently, so did his mother, for she turned around and waited for his answer.

"Well, I guess," he sighed, gaze darting back and forth across the table—an Art Dinneck habit as he tried to think of just the right words to say. "To be honest, I don't know. It occurred to me at some point earlier this year that sometimes you have to step away from something, get some air, in order to know if you truly belong. Truly, well, believe. Besides," he added, his smile weak, almost nervous, "you know how I hate to be predictable."

Nathan *didn't* know that. Until now, his parents had been the most predictable people he knew. Creatures of habit. It was a trait he recognized in himself, some genetic aversion to change passed on through the Dinneck bloodline. He looked to his mother for a reaction. Her expression had softened to one of worry. It came to her easily, like a well-practiced habit.

Something was wrong. Maybe his father was drinking. This idea would not have occurred to him years ago, but in his short tenure in Orlando, he'd seen it happen more than once. *All too common*, as his Florida pastor Ron Burke would say. His father did look thinner, but not unhealthy. His eyes weren't bloodshot or webbed as an alcoholic's sometimes were.

"Sorry," Nathan said finally, and forced a smile. "Professional curiosity. I assume you'll come this weekend, though? Reverend Hayden wants to wait until Sunday before formally introducing me to everyone."

Art didn't reply right away. His expression tensed, almost looked like confusion. Beverly stepped forward and put a hand on the back of Nathan's chair.

"We are *absolutely* going to be there. Tell me, does the mother of the pastor get a special seat with a brass name tag?"

Nathan reached up and took her hand. It was soft, and wet from the dishes. "I'll work on it, Mom." Looking back to his father he added, "Well?"

Art finally smiled. "Wouldn't miss it." His smile never quite reached his eyes. Nathan had a feeling that this Sunday would be the only time Art Dinneck would attend, regardless of *who* was presiding. He wanted to ask more, but it was almost time to leave and he wanted the visit to end on a friendlier note.

They finished their coffee and toast, speaking of people in town. Some Nathan remembered, others not. It didn't take long for his mother to mention—a hopeful note in her voice—that Elizabeth O'Brien was still living in town. She was an RN now, working at Rosenberg's. Perhaps he might run into her there?

Rosenberg Senior Care was a low-ceilinged white complex, an old, but well-kept nursing and elderly care facility. Nathan's stomach tightened with the certainty that he and Elizabeth would run into each other next week, Tuesdays being the scheduled day of their pastoral visits. The thought sent conflicting emotions through him—apprehension, and not a small amount of relief. He kept his expression neutral as his mother spoke. Any idea of rekindling that relationship had to be squelched. He needed to focus on his new job, and Elizabeth's parting words before he left for his final year of seminary—over five and a half years ago, he realized with a shock—still reverberated in his mind.

He and Elizabeth had been friends in school as long as each could remember. She was an only child, like himself, and they found a kinship in that. As they grew older, their relationship shifted slowly, comfortably, to something more. In many ways they were symbiotic. Nathan was never one for spontaneity. He preferred to plan things out, research the best movie or place to visit before stepping out the door. Elizabeth, on the other hand, enjoyed walking into the Showcase Cinemas and buying a ticket for a film she knew nothing about, on the lookout for *something new to jump out at me*, as she liked to put it.

He often recalled one particular Saturday during their senior year of high school. Elizabeth drove them in her ten-year old Subaru to the annual Woodstock Fair in Connecticut. She noticed a small sign at the side of the highway, *Quilt Museum, Next Exit*, and turned off the highway. Much to Nathan's initial chagrin, they spent the next hour searching the back roads for the museum. It turned out to be an oversized barn in the back of an elderly woman's yard. The woman was small but full of an excited energy. She gave them a tour of the barn, lighted by a single bare bulb and whatever sunlight streamed through the wide barn door. Nathan and Elizabeth learned the history of every quilt that hung from the walls and beams. The museum was started, the woman explained, as a way of breaking the routine of her solitude after her husband died, and of sharing her work—all of the quilts were her own—with as many people as possible before she was gone from this world. Eventually, they said their goodbyes and continued on toward Woodstock. But the fair's crowds and noise couldn't compete with the simple quiet of that barn. Without Elizabeth's impulsiveness, Nathan would never have known that lonely women existed, or shared her life for those couple of hours. Nor would he have experienced so many other memories of his teenage years.

With Elizabeth. Always with her.

There was only one aspect of their lives they did not share, try as he might to do so. Elizabeth was not a practicing Christian, though her family belonged to Saint Malachy's. They'd attended mass, though irregularly, until two weeks before her thirteenth birthday when her father died in a car accident on the way home from work. After the funeral, she and her mother stopped going to church, except for an occasional Christmas or Easter service. Nathan never wanted to push, wanted to live his life in his faith and hope to draw her to the Lord with whatever light he could offer. Casual invitations to attend services at Hillcrest Baptist were always declined.

Six months before that fateful evening prior to his return to the university, her mother had died of a cerebral aneurysm, ten years to the month after her father's death. Nathan noticed a growing distance in Elizabeth's voice during the funeral, when talking on the phone from school and in person during that final summer.

As he packed his bags, Elizabeth watching quietly from his desk chair, Nathan had felt a sudden urgency to ask her to attend services with him the next day, before he left for school. She'd become cold, and with too much conviction for Nathan to write off as merely an angry outburst said, "There is no God. There never has been, never will be. Don't be so naïve, Nate."

He'd been stunned into silence. He finished packing, trying to think of how to respond. No words came. Even now, whether it was her avid declaration of the nonexistence of God, or the fact that she had called him naïve, that had hit him the hardest, he didn't know. Perhaps both. The night had ended early, both knowing a hurt had been done but neither knowing what to do about it. Something had fallen between them, an expanse too vast to be bridged. He never stopped praying for her, but after a couple of unreturned phone calls from his dormitory, he simply stopped calling.

He tried dating on and off with schoolmates, but nothing ever came of it. The link, the comfortable connection he'd always felt with Elizabeth, wasn't there. Without her influence, his life became a map clearly laid out and always predictable. He threw himself into the final preparations for his Masters of Divinity, and his life of ministry. Tried to let *time* be the salve which would keep the hurt and memories at bay. Moving to Florida was a shock in itself, a turn in the road that made him begin to think he would be OK. A chance to make his own path, his own changes.

Now, suddenly, he was back home to stay. It didn't feel like a step backwards. It had been his choice to accept. He could have stayed in Florida, far away under its sun and heat. He chose to come home, and would build his life here.

In order to change the subject from past to present, Nathan told his parents of the twenty-three hour bus ride the day before, leaving out details of his night terrors. When he finally stood and said goodbye, the mood in the Dinneck kitchen was decidedly lighter. For that, at least, he was grateful.

He'd worry about Elizabeth, and his father's sudden lack of faith, later.

Chapter Eight

Greenwood Street was a long, tree-lined avenue on the far western edge of town, one block from the church. Nathan walked with a forced casualness, keeping pace beside Ralph Hayden who stepped with strong, but achingly slow, confidence. The church's property abutted a small section of woods separating it from the older town cemetery. It was a warm day for mid-September, almost eighty, and he enjoyed the green tree shadows as they flashed over them. Cooler weather would be coming soon. A refreshing change from Florida's year-round heat. For now, Nathan walked to the entrance of the cemetery with his sport coat draped over his shoulder, hooked by the two fingers of his right hand. Hayden was good company, not offering unnecessary small talk and expecting none in return.

The cemetery looked ancient. The surrounding wall, most likely laid down as pasture demarcations in the late eighteen-hundreds, consisted of moss-laden stones, interspersed with a dangerous mix of blueberry bushes and poison ivy vines. The stones themselves were chipped and dark with age. Hayden muttered, "Here we are," as they entered a gravel drive at a narrow break in the wall.

Like the wall, the nearest headstones were stained with time, chipped in corners. Some leaned precariously to one side. Many of the graves in this area bore the name "Dreyfus". A hundred years ago, when the family owned most of this land, they likely had exclusive use of this place for their dead.

The cemetery was kept up well, considering its age. He made a mental note to comment on this when they met Tarretti. According to Hayden, the groundskeeper had worked here for over a quarter century, almost as long as the man's own tenure. Tarretti lived, and spent most of his time, at the newer property near the center of town. On Wednesdays and Fridays he did the rounds at the older graveyards and so had asked them to meet him here.

"He's a stickler for routine," Hayden had said this morning before leaving. "You'll find it easier to work around his schedule than the other way around."

A rusting white Chevy Blazer was parked in a small shaded lot fifty yards from the road. Vincent Tarretti ambled toward them.

"Reverend Hayden." The groundskeeper was probably in his early-to mid-fifties, Nathan guessed. His long blonde hair had slight gray tinting around the temples and a peppering in his thin beard. He had the tanned, weather-worn skin of someone who spent most of his time outdoors.

"Vincent, always a pleasure." Hayden gestured to Nathan. "May I introduce my able young protégé, Nathan Dinneck."

Vincent made a point of shaking Hayden's hand briefly before turning to Nathan. He said, "Your name sounds familiar. Do you have family here?"

"My mom and dad," Nathan said, shaking hands. "Unless you mean *here*." He gestured to the cemetery. "Not yet, thank God, though my parents own a plot in the main cemetery. At least, I *think* they do."

Vincent offered a noncommittal nod and turned to walk between the two men. Having no real destination, they simply followed along.

"Could be," he said, "I've met your mother once or twice around town over the years." He held a clear plastic bag in his hand, partly filled with various flotsam—papers, wrappers, a couple of cans, dead flowers and sticks. As they walked, Tarretti occasionally snatched up some driftwood litter or an aged pot of flowers.

Since the gist of the meeting was mostly to get the two men acquainted, Nathan gave him a quick synopsis of his time in Florida. Vincent spoke solely of his life here in town. The only reference to his past was one mention of "back in California" when comparing the weather.

Though this cemetery was smaller than the newer one across town, it was deceivingly large compared with the view from the road. They walked downhill, moving between headstones in what Vincent explained was a random pattern of travel to avoid marring the grass. Nathan thought that might be going a bit beyond whatever mysterious Rules of Grounds-Keeping might exist.

At the base of the hill, the property opened up. The bordering stone wall broke away to their right. Between two trees, far ahead, Nathan saw the far border. Past that was more woodland. He commented on the size. Vincent nodded.

"Five and a half acres, all told. There're two older, much smaller lots across town. All of them are dwarfed by the new one, though." He looked around. "This place was the primary cemetery for seventy years. It's pretty big. The Dreyfus family donated most of it, with the stipulation they get exclusive use of the section closest to the road."

They turned right and were now walking north, toward the deepest part of the property. Ornate statues loomed over some of the gravesites. Weeping angels, mischievous cherubs, a great many depictions of the Virgin Mary.

They were a hundred yards from the farthest corner when Nathan stopped. Vincent and Reverend Hayden continued on, the caretaker asking the pastor what his plans were after he left the church. They didn't notice the younger man staring transfixed over the tops of the tombstones.

Two stone angels knelt upon a raised pedestal, wings spread in a glorious and time-stained image of prepared flight. The tips of one merged with the other to form a stone canopy over the gravesite. They were bathed in soft shade from the trees looming over the wall from the woods behind, but he recognized them as the ones from his dream. Had he been here before, maybe as a child? He didn't think so. Nathan had never been a boy who found graveyards fun places to visit.

When he realized the other men had turned and were regarding him, Nathan forced himself to look away and catch up.

"Everything all right, Reverend?" Ralph Hayden asked.

Vincent Tarretti followed Nathan's earlier gaze, then looked intently back at him.

"Fine," Nathan said. "Just admiring the statues in this section. Some are very elaborate." Try as he might, he found his gaze returning to the far corner, to the twin angels. "Who—I mean, how old are the graves in this area?"

Tarretti continued staring a heartbeat longer before answering. "Oh, quite old," he said at last. "Most around the turn of the century... the twentieth century, I mean." He nodded toward the back of the grounds. "Any statue strike you in particular, Reverend?"

The question was unexpected. Nathan was unable to answer at first, feeling like a kid caught stealing candy. Tarretti's eyes locked on him. But he hadn't done anything. No one knew about his dreams; they *couldn't* know. Nathan shook his head. "No, not really. No."

Vincent sighed and looked at Hayden. "Well, if you two will excuse me, I have a few more things I need to do here before heading back. It was very nice meeting you, Pastor." He extended his hand, and Nathan took it only after realizing he'd been addressing him, not Hayden.

"You, too."

"I'm sure we'll be seeing each other again."

Nathan figured he must be tired. Not sleeping enough because of the nightmares. He nodded and shook the man's hand. "I'm sure."

The three men walked back to Tarretti's Blazer in silence. After a final round of goodbyes, the two ministers continued on, leaving the cemetery and turning right along Greenwood, heading for Dreyfus Road.

Chapter Nine

Vincent watched the two men disappear around the corner, then walked back among the tombstones, deciding to do a perfunctory inspection of the grave to assure there were no signs of tampering. The young minister had given it too much interest for his liking. He had no reason to think Nathan Dinneck knew anything more about this place than he'd said. Still, the unquestionable fact remained that his secret, revealed to the wrong person, risked that knowledge finding its way to his enemies.

Then what?

It was a question he'd asked himself on and off for years, a question his predecessors over the centuries must have asked themselves. A question, he knew, that could never be answered. The Lord didn't play to lose. It wasn't His style.

He walked around the base of the statue, below the angels' dispassionate faces. The grave was, in fact, a crypt built nearly a hundred years ago. It was the only one in this corner of the property. Even so, its nature wasn't immediately obvious. Vincent wiped a stray hair from his face and looked at the name on the placard. There was no one named John Solomon buried here, save for the legacy of his famous namesake. The groundskeeper thought it was a foolish name to use, too much a beacon to those in pursuit of the treasure.

He thought again of the impending doom that had settled on his heart lately. Change always set him on edge, made him look for the menace behind every new face in town. All this time, and no one overtly paid any attention to this distant corner of this forgotten cemetery in this nothing town.

Until now.

Even so, he needed to be careful. Such an isolated life, even one as self-imposed as his, brought with it too much of his own imagination. At some point, however, his time would run out. Vincent was caught in the midst of a cat and mouse game played over the millennia. He didn't plan on being the one to finally lose. God wouldn't abandon him. Every change around him promised danger, but there was always hope.

Diligence Always, was his motto. It had to be. In this morning's case, much could be implied in the changing of the guard at the neighboring church. The old minister's departure, local boy Dinneck beating the odds and getting such a position.

Maybe.

Vincent squatted and picked up a broken piece of branch, probably fallen in the heavy winds of the night before. He walked to the far wall and tossed it over, then hefted his trash bag and moved slowly back toward the entrance. He threw the bag into the back of the old Blazer before climbing in and heading home.

There were moments, sometimes entire days, when Vincent had doubts about his calling. Times when he made the mistake of looking at his life, with its lack of any substantiality, since leaving California. Every day he woke up, got out of bed, showered, ate breakfast and read the *Worcester Telegram*. He would then set out to work tending the grounds in the cemeteries with Johnson following faithfully behind him. Today was an exception, since he knew he'd be meeting Hayden and Dinneck and didn't want to have to listen to the dog barking in frustration from the car. Otherwise, Vincent and the dog worked together, he talking to the animal as he would any human being and recognizing that many in town thought he was a bit *daft* because of it.

Maybe he was. A man doesn't isolate himself from the rest of the world, guarding something of such significance, and not get a little nutty. One night, a few years ago, he rented a movie called *A Beautiful Mind*. The concept of a man so lost in his own hallucinations— supported by the fact that this was a true story—had terrified him. Was this what he'd been doing all his life? Was there nothing in John Solomon's grave but a long dead body of a real man?

That moment had been especially difficult. Until he'd fallen to his knees and asked God for some kind of clarity in his mind, praying until he could barely keep himself awake. He felt a little better after that.

Then, as now, he understood the answer that God put into his heart. Since coming to Hillcrest decades before, hiding even from other people of faith, he'd not attended church services. He'd not sat among those who also believed with all their hearts and souls. The Sunday after watching the film, he drove aimlessly among the neighboring towns. He passed a small, non-denominational church tucked among the trees in the town of Boylston, when something settled on his heart.

He turned the car around and pulled into the parking lot, joining the small crowd filing into the rows of seats. Many realized he was a newcomer and greeted him warmly. Vincent was skittish, as he always was whenever someone gave him too much attention - never knowing whether they were being friendly or if he'd been discovered, if the smiling old woman offering her hand was ready to cut his throat for the relic buried under his adopted hometown.

That first morning he had sat in the back of the church. By the time the service was over, he felt the Spirit renewed within him, proud of his calling beyond words. He wasn't crazy. Yes, his situation was like none other save that of his predecessors, but if he was nuts for following God so blindly, then so were all these fine people. None of *them* seemed crazy to *him*. Though he continued to avoid the churches in his own town—he doubted anyone in Hillcrest even knew he was a Christian—since that first Sunday, he never missed a service in Boylston. Always a reminder that, though he worked and lived by himself, he was never alone.

Lonely, yes, sometimes achingly so, but never alone.

Prior to his arrival as caretaker, Vincent Tarretti had not been so lonely. As a child, he'd been dragged to church, sat listening to the ranting preacher talk about sin and redemption. Mostly he concentrated on the raven-haired Melissa Alvaraz sitting with her family in the front pew.

During his junior year of high school, Vincent, who at the time insisted on "either Vinnie or Mister Tarretti, there ain't nothing in between," learned to his delight that Melissa spent those same Sundays thinking about him. They were soon inseparable. The relationship was purely platonic at first, a mutual evangelical upbringing having at least *some* effect on their behavior. But after two years, they could no longer restrain their feelings for each other and broke away both from their celibacy and the church.

They left home, sneaking away in the night, and found a tiny, roach-infested apartment thirty miles north, just outside of Hollywood. While she looked for a modeling job, Vinnie worked the grill of a diner two blocks from the Strip. He would have taken any job, as long as it paid the rent. They married. Not in the church, but in a small chapel in Las Vegas following a grueling day-long drive. A Justice of the Peace performed the ceremony. Melissa's modeling career ended before it ever began, when she learned they were going to have a baby.

Vinnie took a second job. They found a place slightly bigger and with smaller cockroaches. Even now, Vincent wondered what his son would have been like had he been born. He wondered what kind of a mother Melissa would have been—a fantastic one, he was certain—had a man named Simon Ellison not taken one drink too many before trying to drive home.

Vinnie had been home from work only twenty minutes when the police came to his door and told him his wife was dead. The officer, sent to inform the next of kin, had not been at the scene. He simply took the report he was given and told Vincent Tarretti that his "wife and son had been killed in an automobile accident."

In the strongbox hidden under two loose floorboards beside Vincent's bed, sandwiched between his notebooks and the short stack of other yellowed clippings, was the single newspaper report of the accident. A small number "1" was written in the corner, but with no corresponding notation in any book. It was the only thing he kept from those long-ago days, aside from his cheap, gold-plated wedding ring which he also kept in the box.

His memory of life after the funeral, held in the town in which they'd both grown up, was a blur of alcohol. He had died in every sense of the word in that accident with his wife and son. Afterward, he was simply *waiting for the van to arrive*, as the song went. He was certain, thinking about it in retrospect years later, that death was waiting for him one particular night as he washed his third shot of Jack Daniels down with his ninth beer. If not that night, then soon. He'd sensed his personal limit had been reached, a signal to return upstairs and pass out on whichever piece of furniture was easiest to reach. That night, he'd hesitated, ordered another shot and beer. Once crossed, it was a line that would continue far into some desperate darkness waiting only for him.

While he slouched in a booth, twirling the now-empty beer bottle on the table top and considering without much resolve about going back upstairs, an old—no, *ancient* was the word that came to him that night—woman slowly slid into the bench across the booth from him. She had garnered a lot of looks from the brooding regulars at the bar. As soon as they saw with whom she sat, people kept their comments to themselves. They'd watched Vinnie's deterioration and short temper long enough to know not to make any comments about someone who was most likely his grandmother.

She wasn't his grandmother.

"Is your name Vincent Tarretti?"

"Yea…" he'd said, trying to focus on her face, but not succeeding very well.

"My name is Ruth Lieberman," she said. "I'm dying."

Vinnie rolled his eyes. "Well, too bad for you," he said, and raised the empty beer bottle, trying to catch the attention of the bar's only waitresses, a thin girl with tired eyes. She seemed to be looking everywhere but in his direction. He lowered his arm and said, "Everyone is dying. I'm dying; you're dying."

"In a way," she said, never breaking eye contact, "you're already dead. You've made up your mind to choose oblivion. Now," she said, laying her aged hands flat on the table, "forgetting the obvious repercussions of such an act, God has need of you. You will have to stop drinking, forever, and come with me."

In his state, the fact that this woman was echoing the thoughts blurring through his mind only a moment before did not carry any surprise. He simply smiled and said, "Yeah? Where to?"

"Massachusetts."

The answer was spoken so assuredly that Vinnie sat up straighter in his chair. Hollywood was full of more kooks and weirdoes than he could ever count, but they never failed to entertain him.

"Mass-a-what?" He chuckled, a gesture that felt alien in those days. "And why would I do that?"

"I told you—because I'm dying, and God has sent me here to find you." She looked around then, and for the first time Vinnie saw the calm certainty in her expression waver for a moment. "Everything I see, including you, is exactly as in the dream. There's no question."

"Yeah, and what exactly am I going to be doing in Massachusetts? Selling flowers at the airport?"

She smiled. "No, sir. You're going to be the new caretaker of the cemetery in town. Hillcrest, Massachusetts to be exact. It's a pleasant little place a few miles north of a city called Worcester. It's very nice."

He leaned over the table. The wrinkled hands remained flat on the surface. He whispered, "Go away now or I swear to God I'll—"

And then her hands came up and touched his cheeks.

And the bar disappeared.

Vinnie Tarretti saw the face of God as flames, burning His commandments into the stone tablets… a terrified old man carrying them down the mountain and in anger shattering them on a stone at the sight of the idolatry before him; returning from the mountain a second time with new tablets, placing them in a tabernacle adorned with the gold from destroyed idols, carried across the desert for forty years; then King Solomon, tall with a knitted beard and flowing robes and riches beyond match, building the temple of God, the placing of the golden Ark of the Covenant beneath angelic wings of gold and....

He vomited across the table. In the days that followed, he never found out—and dared not ask—if he'd also thrown up on the old woman. But as Vinnie fell into unconsciousness, he felt his life and whatever remained of his soul burn away. The world he thought he knew blew apart like ash in the light of God's vision.

When he awoke, he was in the hospital. "Alcohol poisoning" was how the medical report read. He was released as soon as he could stand under his own power. No insurance. Vinnie walked outside, into painful sunlight and thick, dirty air. An Asian man waved to him from a cab waiting at the curb, running to open the rear door without waiting for a response. Reflexively, Vinnie climbed into the back seat. Before he could get back *out,* the cab pulled into traffic.

The old woman from Massachusetts patted his hand and said, "It's time to go, Vincent."

Twenty-six years later, Vincent pulled his Blazer to a stop at the back of his small caretaker's house. Johnson barked from inside. The dog's bark sounded different this morning. An angry, warning tone. Whether he was still pissed for being left behind or because of the short man standing on the front porch, he didn't know. But he could guess.

The man stood with hands folded calmly in front of him, as if in prayer. He wore a dark suit with a black shirt and white tie. The outfit matched his clipped moustache and short white hair.

As Vincent mounted the single step, the man extended his hand.

"Mister Tarretti, I presume? So glad to finally meet you." Vincent took his hand in a perfunctory shake. "My name is Peter Quinn. I was hoping we could talk."

Chapter Ten

Nothing about the man standing on his porch, neither his neat appearance nor his quiet, affable manner, was threatening. Yet as Vincent shook his hand, the disquiet plaguing him these past few weeks re-ignited.

Bad Guy, the feeling said.

Perhaps it was his eyes. Blue and clear, but with a mocking gleam in them. A knowing, half-smile on his lips. Vincent shook the feeling off and silently cursed his paranoia. No wonder people thought he was nuts.

Johnson continued barking his displeasure through the door as Vincent muttered, "Mr. Quinn. A pleasure. Can I help you with something?"

Quinn nodded toward the front door. "Maybe we could discuss this inside?"

Vincent gestured to a pair of wicker chairs crowded onto the small porch. There was a reason Vincent insisted on meetings with clergy and the town's funeral director on the cemetery grounds. Allowing anyone inside the house, stepping into his refuge so close to the secret box with its records and history felt too much like opening himself up for scrutiny. He didn't like scrutiny. The man before him had nothing but good intentions, most likely, but that didn't change matters. Vincent was too old to change much of *anything* of his life.

"Obviously, my dog seems a bit uptight at the moment. Best we talk out here."

Quinn nodded and without objection sat in one of the chairs. Vincent pulled the other a slight distance away, sat and waited.

"As you may or may not know, I am Grand See—a rather silly title I suppose, when it comes down to it—of a fairly new organization in town called the Hillcrest Men's Club."

"I've heard of them." *Entry 798*, he thought absently. Already he was yearning to get free of this man, open his notebook and make entry 818: *strange man from Hillcrest Men's Club visits me.*

Quinn leaned forward, elbows on knees, and occasionally cast an annoyed glance at the door, behind which Johnson was busy trying to dig a hole through the wood. "Yes, well, we feel it's time, having been officially in town for half a year, to give a little something back to the community. We thought perhaps to place flower arrangements on the graves of local veterans." He opened his hands, palms up. "It's the least we could do."

If he noticed Vincent's startled look, he did not show it. He merely sat back, eyebrows raised, and waited for an answer.

They know, Vincent thought. *Who knows? A bunch of drunks? It's a nice gesture. He doesn't seem like a bad guy, honestly.*

God, give me clarity of thought again.

He composed himself, forced his breathing to a measured rhythm, then mirrored Quinn's act of leaning back in his chair. Whether or not his paranoia was finally boiling over, Vincent couldn't afford to let down his guard. More so, he had to act normal!

"That's a kind gesture, to be sure." He felt his face flushing and hoped the man didn't notice. "But, I mean, the Boy Scouts generally do that. It's a merit badge requirement." After a pause, he added, "I think."

Quinn looked thoughtful, nodded his head once. "Yes, I'd thought that might be the case. However, they usually do so on Veterans Day. That won't be for another two months. By then, any tokens we might leave would need replacing anyway." Another smile. There was something odd about the man's voice. Vincent's ears itched. He was just being stupid.

The man's argument had some merit. Saying "no" would make no sense under normal circumstances, and asking too many additional questions would be a risk, especially if his long-feared enemies were close. He doubted it. How could they know?

The grave is marked John Solomon, *not* Enrique Jorgenson, *don't forget. There are twin cherubim hovering over its crypt. Of* course *they could figure it out, if they happened to stumble upon it.* He wondered, not for the first time, at the thinking - or *lack* of thought - behind such an obvious clue left in public.

Forgive me, Father. I do not want to question you.

The man before him was patient. He sat, hands on his lap and open like the sacrificial statue of Molech....

Stop it! Vincent scolded himself.

"819" coming right up.

"That's very kind of you," he said quickly. "Any chance we have to honor our veterans is welcome. Was there a particular day you were thinking of?" He wanted this man to *leave, leave, leave* and let him go inside.

Calm. You're doing fine. I am always with you.

He couldn't place the verse, if it *was* a verse. Its effect was soothing nevertheless.

Quinn finally moved those placating hands off his lap and said, "Thank you. There is a bit of planning, ordering the flowers, et cetera. Why don't we just leave the date open-ended? Sometime this month, make it a surprise."

Was that a threat? *No, everything is fine. I'm doing fine.* Vincent offered another neutral nod and got to his feet.

"Fair enough. Thanks for coming by."

"It was my pleasure." Quinn stood and offered a perfunctory hand shake. After walking down the two steps of the porch, he turned around as if having remembered something.

"Oh," he said, "I also understand the minister of the Baptist church is leaving town the week after next. Retiring, is he?"

Vincent furrowed his brows, feeling the weight of the statement. *Leaving town.* Was Hayden leaving so soon? He nodded, but said nothing.

"A pity to lose such a holy man, as I understand from Mr. Dinneck. *Art* Dinneck, I mean. I understand Reverend Hayden will be spending time in a monastery."

In fact, Vincent had no idea *where* Hayden was planning on going. He'd thought the man was moving into an apartment somewhere in town. "What Reverend Hayden does is really none of my business."

Quinn nodded and looked down for a moment, muttering, "No, I suppose it's none of my business, either. Still," he added, looking back up with those clear blue eyes, "he deserves a rest after such a long time serving the town. I should offer my congratulations on his retirement but, well, I don't really know him." He shrugged, smiled, and gave Vincent a perfunctory wave before walking to his car. He didn't look back toward the house.

As the car drove down the road, Vincent felt exhausted, like he'd just caught the flu. At least his ears had stopped itching. Their short discussion about the flowers had shaken him, but this last part of the conversation—added more as an after-thought by the stranger—was confusing.

Hayden was leaving town. If there *was* a threat to what lay under Greenwood Street Cemetery, it would need to be moved. The words of the prior caretaker came back to him. *Neither you nor I*, Ruth had said, *are allowed to move it. We are caretakers only. Even from the earliest days of Moses and Solomon, only the Lord's priests may touch it, move it to a new location.*

He had stood within that musty, claustrophobic crypt only once, but he had felt, almost *tasted*, the power emanating all around him. His skin had crawled with goose bumps, the air vibrating into his bones. It was enough of a demonstration to prove that his charge was the genuine article. Not so much the vessel itself, but what it contained. Enough to keep him almost thirty years above ground protecting them from a millennia-old group of demon worshippers who still, on occasion, referred to themselves as Ammonites.

Only priests could move it to a new location. Men and women ordained by God. *Baptist ministers, for example.*

Peter Quinn had made a point to mention Reverend Hayden's departure. The man's tone implied that Vincent should have known the date. Again the words *leaving town* struck him as significant. Vincent had focused on Dinneck; his arrival coinciding so well with the sense of doom pervading every corner of his life. Now the young man had taken a sudden interest in John Solomon's grave, or at least the statue. His arrival in town may have, in fact, meant nothing. What was significant was the departure of Ralph Hayden.

It didn't *feel* like the right explanation, but logic pointed there. Not that logic always played a part in the Lord's plan. Only truth.

Regardless, the time may well be at hand. He would make his entries, right away, then pray on them. He needed to be sure, certain in every respect. When the time came, it would be made clear to him. Until then, there was not much he could do but wait.

Chapter Eleven

The basement of Hillcrest Baptist Church had long ago been converted to a hall for church functions. It was wider than the church itself, running under the full length of the house, with a two-foot high stage for the occasional children's play and group meetings. This room was as familiar to Nathan as his parents' home. Every other Sunday for eighteen years, the Dinnecks joined other families of the parish here for fellowship dinner, a community breaking of bread and discussion on everything from the morning's sermon to the Patriots' chances that afternoon. The tables usually filled quickly, though today many chose to stand and mingle among the larger-than-normal crowd. According to Hayden, the last time Sunday service had been this crowded was Easter.

The room filled with the scent of brewing coffee, orange juice, meatballs, pasta and pies. Children wandered toward the dessert tables, only to be pulled away by a parent who forced them to fill their plates with "good food" first.

Both of his parents came, though his father had fidgeted more than usual during the service. Nathan had also spied his friend Josh Everson smiling at him from the last row of folding chairs. Like Elizabeth, Josh was never a diligent churchgoer. Nathan had always been more forward about inviting him, but had also known when to back off. Nathan often wondered why he'd hung out with so many people who weren't believers rather than with more kids from his parish. In life you didn't always get to pick your friends, not that Nathan had complaints. Josh was one of the good ones. They hadn't seen each other since Nathan came up for his last interview, but the two were in constant contact online or the occasional phone call.

When their spot in the receiving line reached him, Nathan embraced his parents. He'd tried to get them to come forward and greet him first but Beverly insisted on waiting her turn. Pulling away, he said, "It's good to see you today, Dad. What did you think?"

Art Dinneck offered a sheepish grin and said, "You did well, Nate. Kept your mother awake; that's the important part."

Nathan gave his father's arm a squeeze in conjunction with the playful slap from Bev. Before he could stop himself, he said, "See you again next week?"

Art's smile faded and his face lost much of the healthy color it had begun to show. He looked away. "We'll see. I'll try." But Nathan knew he'd overstepped the line his father had drawn between them the other day. Art glanced across the room and behind him, hesitating for a moment before noting with another wave of his hand the length of the waiting line. "We'll move over there," he said, nodding to one of the tables. "Catch up to us when you're done here."

They moved on. Nathan greeted the next person, a shy older woman with thin gray hair. Pastor Hayden conversed comfortably across the room with a small group of people. This was a welcome reception for the new pastor, but next week would be the send-off for the only other minister many of these people had known. Nathan felt a pang of guilt at all the attention he was getting this morning.

Josh Everson had his turn and Nathan embraced him with as much vigor as he'd given to his parents.

"Father Dinneck, I presume," the young man said with a flourish.

Nathan laughed. "It's Reverend Dinneck, Buddy."

Josh smirked. "Close enough."

"I see you got my email."

"Yep, I replied, but never heard back."

"A few minutes after sending you the note, I was in a cab heading for the bus station. How's work going?"

"I tell you, Nate, the *Greedy* would surely fold without my stellar management." The *Greedy Grocer* was the town's only convenience store, tucked into the end of the strip mall a half mile away on Main Street. Both Nathan and Josh had worked there at various times in their teenage years. Josh continued part-time as he attended Wachusett Community College to earn a two-year Associates in Business Management. A few months after graduation, he was offered the job of manager at the store. Lately, their banter across the Internet had focused on the parallels between them. Nathan returning after college to his hometown church, Josh to the *Greedy Grocer*. Of course, his friend was quick to specify which was more significant a homecoming. *You can't get milk at church at ten o'clock at night*, he'd explained in one letter. Josh said, "Good to have any kind of a job these days. Nice service, Nate. I admit I couldn't help over-examining the fact that my best friend was the one talking, but I got used to it after a while."

"Come again next week."

"I just might." Nathan hoped that was true. Josh gave him a rap on the shoulder and moved on with a "Talk to you later." Any longer a reunion would have to wait. The man who greeted Nathan next introduced himself as Manny Paulson.

"I'm a friend of your dad's. He said a lot of nice things about you." At his father's mention, Nathan looked across the room. Art Dinneck was staring back at them, with what Nate could not mistake as anything but apprehension. When his father caught Nathan's gaze, the look was replaced with a smile and a perfunctory wave. Paulson nodded in return and turned back to the minister.

"A good sermon, Pastor," he said. "I'll admit I'm not much of a church-goer myself, but when I heard Art's first born was the new pastor, I just had to meet you."

Nathan thought *first born* was an odd way of putting it, but he thanked the man and perfunctorily said he hoped to see him more often.

"Careful what you wish for." The man laughed at his own joke and moved in Art's direction.

When Nathan turned to greet the next person in line, the church hall disappeared. Two stone angels towered over him, their faces dripping with a lightly falling rain. He watched them, expecting their heads to lower and stare at him, perhaps take flight like gargoyles. He stared, unable to collect his thoughts, feeling the rain across his face.

"Pastor? Are you alright?"

The scene spun around like dirty water. He closed his eyes, fought down a sudden nausea. When he opened them again, a woman was holding his hand. He was in the church hall again, still standing and greeting a young mother with two bashful children hiding behind her dress. He felt himself sinking. His knees buckled but he caught himself. "Reverend!" the woman shouted.

Nathan waved away her concern with his free hand. "I'm fine," he said, his voice only a whisper. But he wasn't fine. He was exhausted. Perhaps he *had* just been in the cemetery, looking at the angels, then run back into line. No, that made no sense. It had been raining. He looked out the window, which was now very far above him. The world outside was clear and sunny.

Someone yelled. He was on the floor, the children hiding further behind their mother's skirt. "I'm OK, really," he murmured, before the world went dark.

Chapter Twelve

The soup was hot, but its burn sharpened his senses. Nathan took three spoonfuls before looking up to face Pastor Hayden. The old man sat at the far end of the small kitchen table, leaning back in his chair. Beverly Dinneck sat in another, her hands trembling as if to catch Nathan's spoon arm should it suddenly drop.

"Feeling a little better, Reverend?" Hayden asked. Nathan tried to find a hint of anger or frustration in his voice, but heard only concern.

He nodded, and took another spoonful of soup. He cleared his throat a moment later, when he realized the others were waiting for him to say something.

"I'm sorry," he said.

Beverly grabbed his arm. Small drops of soup spilled back into the bowl. "Don't you dare apologize, Nathan. You were exhausted. Mrs. Stanton said so. That is, after she calmed her boys down." She smiled, though it was a sad expression. "You gave them a scare."

"Gave us all a scare," Hayden said. "We thought we'd lost our new pastor after only one day." He leaned forward in the chair. "Have you been sleeping well?"

Nathan shrugged. "I think so. I'd been having some vivid nightmares lately, but I wrote them off to nerves. In fact, I've had only one since arriving here. Except... well, nothing. Felt like I was dreaming at the reception before I... fainted."

Hayden nodded and thought for a moment, the wrinkles in his face twisting. "Well, the EMTs said that you were fine. It looked like simple exhaustion, so there's a good chance you *were* dreaming just then. Passed out on your feet."

Nathan grimaced in embarrassment and tried to hide it behind another spoonful. He'd awoken, vaguely, soon after blacking out. Those moments—*were they hours or minutes?* he wondered now—were a mix of images and unreality. As if waking from a dream but not quite coming all the way to the surface. By the time the EMT began packing up his bag, Nathan had begun to feel better, but allowed his mother to lead him to the bed Hayden had pulled out from the upstairs couch. He'd slept the rest of the afternoon away. Nathan visibly cringed every time he wondered what the rest of the reception was like.

"Do I really need to go in for tests? I'm feeling a lot better, physically at least. I just needed to rest."

The older man shrugged. "Your call. They wanted you to get tested for epilepsy, tumors..." He waved his hand across the table as a way of finishing the sentence.

Beverly gasped. Nathan winced at the pain of her grip on his arm. Hayden smiled. "I have a very strong feeling it is none of those. As it is, I agree with Nate. I assume you slaved all night on that sermon, Reverend? It was a good one, by the way."

"Thanks." He appreciated the change in subject. After another spoonful of soup—some chicken noodle left over from the botched fellowship dinner—he added, "Yeah, I was up pretty late."

"That's what I thought. I hate the dentist. Get all nerved up before going in. He makes me sit there for five minutes before I get out of the chair. Says patients like me get so worked up that when the appointment is finally over, they collapse in relieved exhaustion when they try to stand." He looked at Nathan's mother and pointed at his yellowed teeth. "Have I mentioned, Bev, that these are all the originals?"

Beverly allowed herself a relieved smile.

Nathan put the spoon down with a clink. He looked up pleadingly. "Even so, I'm afraid I made a pretty poor impression. New pastor collapses after his first service."

Hayden nodded. "I won't lie and say that's not true. At least you have something to start next week's sermon with."

Nathan nodded. The man was never one to sugar-coat things. He remembered something that had bothered him since Hayden suggested he lead this morning's service. "I assumed you would want to be lead minister next week, Pastor, seeing as it's your last."

Hayden looked down for a moment, then said, "Yes, well, I suppose I should, shouldn't I?" He slapped his legs and slowly rose from the table. "I'd better start working on the sermon soon, then, so I'm not wearing myself out with worry the night before." He looked sideways at Nathan, a half smile implying the comment was only *half* in jest. "But you will handle the announcements at the start of the service, and can say what you wish about the events of this morning."

"I'd like that; thanks." He didn't like it, would rather visit Hayden's dentist than face anyone after today.

His mother insisted he go back to bed. It was dark outside. He tried to calculate exactly how long he had actually slept. It was almost eight o'clock now. Hayden would be going to bed soon. Part of Nathan wanted to stay up, drive to the cemetery as he'd planned last night after polishing up his sermon, but his body refused to cooperate. His mother busied herself downstairs straightening the kitchen and washing the few dishes while he changed, then came upstairs to make sure he was actually going to bed.

"Mom," he said, already feeling sleep overtake him.

She stopped at the top of the stairs and turned around. "Yes?"

"How's Dad?"

"I don't know."

"Is he home?"

She looked away, down the hall, as if searching for his father. "No, probably not. But today's Sunday and he still has work tomorrow. He won't be out too late. You get some sleep, and don't worry about him."

She looked back, and saw that her son was already asleep. She turned off the light.

Chapter Thirteen

The rain began near midnight. It slashed against the narrow, painted-over windows of the storefront's back room. Peter Quinn knelt before the altar—an area on the floor designated by flickering black and red candles. In the center stood a cross-legged statue of a man with the head of a bull. Its bronze skin shone in the firelight. A steady stream of aromatic smoke issued from its open mouth and through small holes at the end of long tapered horns. Human-shaped hands reached palm-up, as if waiting for an offering.

Long ago, the statue would have risen twenty feet into the air, the hands large enough to hold its squirming, sometimes screaming, sacrifice. Like this small representation before him, the idol's body would be hollow and the furnace within would illuminate the open mouth like the entrance to hell itself. When the offering was placed in its palms, the arms would rise on gears and pulleys, dropping the child into its mouth to feed the dark god's hunger.

Quinn's resources, and his required discretion, prevented him from establishing a true temple for Molech, but soon he would have enough power to build a massive sacrificial statue wherever he desired.

Then the *true* sacrifices to his dark god would resume. Sacrifices to his master, the most powerful of demons, had always been—always *would* be—the first born of a chosen follower. Quinn thought about the report given to him by Paulson this afternoon - the incident with Dinneck's son, the weak minister. His first day of official service and he'd fainted like a schoolgirl.

He smiled. *The good are weak*, he thought. If a sacrifice would soon be needed, he wondered if he could make Art give up *his* first born. A *Baptist minister* as an offering. That sounded delightful. Its body bathed in candlelight, the small statue seemed to smile back in agreement.

All in all, it had been a productive couple of days. Until the other day, Quinn had some doubts as to Vincent Tarretti's role in this grand game of hide-and-seek. The caretaker played his cards very close to his chest. No amount of research into his life turned up much more than the obvious fact that Tarretti was an eternally dull man. But Quinn saw the fear in his eyes on Friday afternoon when he suggested his group lay those flowers down. Any lingering doubt that he was involved in some way, dissipated during the conversation.

Still, Peter had to remain cautious. The Elders would be reading his weekly reports with a deserved grain of salt. They would not stand for another Chicago incident. He would not survive another blunder. His uncle would make certain of that.

Peter had stopped at Greenwood Street Cemetery earlier this week, a trip which had cemented his resolve to visit Tarretti. He'd wandered among the grave markers, moving circuitously deeper and deeper into the far section of the old graveyard. It was his third visit since arriving in town. He stared for a long time at the angels standing guard over the grave's placard. The name Solomon so clearly engraved. As before, elation had filled him, nearly causing Quinn to fall to the ground and dig with his bare hands.

He did not. If he was as close to the prize as he suspected, he needed to be careful. Instead, he walked around, moving leaves and dirt with the toe of his shoe, always kicking them randomly back into place so as not to reveal someone had been there. It *was* a crypt, no question. Crypts were used to store things, though usually just bodies. Peter was certain no human lay inside. It had been so long, for him and those who came before including his own uncle.

They were not destined, it seemed, for the great discovery. Only him.

Long ago, a young Peter Quinn had been slowly, methodically, taught the ways of the sect by his dear Uncle Roger, beginning as early as the boy's tenth birthday. Peter's internship into this holiest of priesthoods began with casual questions, odd remarks made at family gatherings at the Quinns' home in Indiana. Comments designed to pique the boy's interest in the unknown, in the darker side of the world outside Muncie. Uncle Roger was a large man, nearly as wide as he was tall. When he spoke, his voice came from somewhere deep in his belly.

When Roger suddenly packed up the studio apartment he maintained two blocks from his brother's family, and prepared to move to Chicago, he invited his twelve-year-old nephew to join him. Peter's parents refused, wanting him in school and not trusting Roger to be strict enough with the boy. Max Quinn was a distracted man, working long hours in the tool shop and bringing home too few dollars to show for it. He made no bones about the odds of Peter ever being able to go to college. But a high school diploma was one thing he *could* offer his son, something he himself never earned. The night Uncle Roger left Muncie Indiana forever, he came to the house and had a quiet, whispered conversation with his brother and sister-in-law. Peter waited anxiously in his room, already packed.

Max and Abby Quinn were sitting on the couch watching television when Roger called Peter's name and said it was time to leave. His parents looked up sleepily when Roger waved his nephew toward the door. "No need to say goodbye, Peter. Your mother and father are too immersed in their show. They have, however, agreed to let you come with me." The last he saw of his parents was the slow turning of heads, in perfect unison, back toward the television set. It was then that Peter Quinn had the first true glance at his uncle's power. Over the next ten years, the man phoned Peter's parents often, lying about a school his nephew never attended, each time lowering his voice to a whisper before hanging up.

Peter Quinn eventually learned everything about his uncle's true mission. His, and others'. Dozens, perhaps hundreds—their numbers known only to a few—of disciples like himself scattered across the globe, servants of Molech. They were modern Ammonites, an association reflected only in the dark god they served rather than any lifestyle. They were bloodhounds. Sniffing, searching. Always cautious. Funding their covert activities through other, more conventional means, including an extensive drug cartel and occasional prostitution ring. The Quinns' specific line of business was mostly a respectable one, loan collections and money laundering. Any occasional drug-running was done as a cooperative effort with the many pre-established channels in the city.

Uncle Roger and his people preferred to keep low profiles. Waiting for the day that their adversaries, who hoarded the prize like frightened children, made a mistake.

The general consensus among the worldwide Ammonite movement was that these zealots were well-organized, both Christians and Jews, able to communicate quickly and discreetly among themselves. Peter Quinn's people were patient. The prize was rightfully theirs. To appease his many wives, old King Solomon himself had pledged servitude to their gods, to the point of building temples in their honor. Most of these other gods were weak, at times nothing more than cheap clay monuments. But Molech—when one declares devotion to the master, he does so *forever*. As such, the king had given up any rights to property. All he owned was an implied offering to the master. Among all the treasures of that ancient age, there was one they desired most. The Ark of the Covenant. Its mere presence offered the power to destroy any enemy. There were other reasons, as well, why the relic was so precious, reasons which Peter didn't think warranted too much consideration. Echoes of a superstitious time, best put behind them if they were to focus on the present. Talk of it being an actual *gateway* into Heaven, a door through which the very *God of the Israelites* would move when he deemed to do so. And like any door, it could swing both ways. Ludicrous, in Peter's opinion, but a concept that served to drive his predecessors with more force than the obvious wealth such a possession would promise.

But until this age, it was not to be. If rumors and legends were to be believed, a handful of priests in Solomon's court discreetly smuggled it west into the land of Ethiopia. They never returned. Other theories pointed to Josiah, one of the last kings of Judah. Even with his obsessive destruction of the altars to Molech and Baal—including the priests who served at them— he knew the end would come, eventually. He chose to have the Ark stolen away to safety before his death. Regardless, when the Babylonian army finally swarmed into Jerusalem, the relic was gone.

Quinn's predecessors came close in their search many times, felt its power at their fingertips. The experience of such proximity was chronicled in official documents preserved for centuries—even, in a few cases, for millennia.

Peter spent his early days with Uncle Roger studying these accounts, watching as the man traced theoretical travel routes over the centuries on a well-worn wall map. From the African continent, to the Mediterranean and an extended stay in Greece during the Middle Ages, the wastelands of Russia, back to a small village in what was currently called Uruguay. Eventually to the self-proclaimed *Free World*. The last time a confirmed sighting occurred was a year before the turn of the twentieth century, in Arizona. The desert landscape was a mirror image of its original homeland. But the Ark was gone when his predecessors found their way into the recently-abandoned cave once belonging to a relocated Yavapai Indian tribe. Twin wooden carvings of angels stood sentry, their crude renderings of wings crossing each other over the cave's narrow entrance.

Then nothing. Year after year after year.

Until now.

When Peter arrived in Worcester, Massachusetts he began a slow, methodical search of the city and its surrounding towns. He often wondered if he would end up like so many others who came before him, his life spent in fruitless search, never feeling the prize brushing so close to his fingertips as it had been these past few months. When he discovered the existence of John Solomon's grave, he felt a rush of certainty that *his* mission was going to be different—glorious perhaps. The misunderstanding in Chicago was not a blunder, but a necessary step taken by his master to send his Chosen One here, to the very doorstep of heaven's power. It was a drug a thousand times more potent than any he'd taken in his youth.

Still, training taught caution. This town was a reflection of a much different world than where the relic had ever before resided. He must move slowly, establish a small cadre of followers, aides for when the prize was uncovered. Those whose minds and souls could be controlled. Except for Manny Paulson who, by his nature, was self-obsessed enough that he could be controlled simply with the promise of power. He and the others could be eliminated or left to themselves if the location proved a ruse, a red herring planted like so many others in the past.

The angels and the name of the gravestone, after all, were *too* convenient.

Still, the grave had sat here almost a hundred years without being discovered. The United States was a big country, this town an insignificant speck. So easy for it to remain unnoticed.

His next steps were clear—stir the pot as he'd done on Friday with Tarretti, then wait for someone to make a move, reveal whether Solomon's grave was his target. In the past, false locations were more than simple diversions. They were death traps, man-sized *Roach Motels* luring the unwary inside and devouring them. Best keep an eye on the prize, but with an open mind and cautious step. Paulson was keeping the caretaker under casual observation. If Tarretti made a move, Peter would hear about it.

What of Hayden? Rules set down centuries ago would be no different today. Their God was like that, big on *tradition*. Too many corpses lined the streets of the past, men and women foolish enough to test it.

But wasn't Peter, himself, a priest serving a much mightier deity than their silent God? When the time came, he was certain he could carry it to the feet of Molech, to the new temple which his people would finally build.

The fabled yet very real Ark of the Covenant, the ornate chest housing the stone tablets on which Yahweh Himself scrawled his Commandments to the Israelites—and at one time containing the budding staff of a man named Aaron, the Book of the Law and even some manna which had supposedly fallen from Heaven—would finally be delivered to its true owner. And, if those crackpots of yesteryear were to be believed, the very portal into Heaven would be opened. A doorway through which Peter Quinn's dark master and his legions of damned would pass and wreak long-awaited vengeance on those who cast them out. There were some in their group who believed this latter part very much. These were the true elders of the Ammonite organization, reclusive people whom Peter hoped never to meet. Unlike his Uncle Roger. The only time the man had shown the smallest sign of humility, or fear, in front of his nephew was the one time Peter asked about these people. Of course Roger told him nothing. Why waste his breath on his own nephew?

Peter Quinn took a cleansing breath and leaned back onto his heels. There were final preparations needing attention, including some flowers to personally deliver in a week. Not to the cemetery. The flowers would be for Hayden, to greet him on his arrival at the monastery. An excuse for Peter to learn where in the complex the man was staying. After that, he and Pastor Hayden had much to talk about.

Chapter Fourteen

Nathan met and spoke to a dozen-plus parishioners Monday morning. They had stopped by the church to see how he was feeling, or used some other pretense. Always the same questions, but asked with genuine concern—at least outwardly. He'd gotten his explanation for yesterday's collapse down to a reasonable, but condensed, rhetoric. He spoke with an easy smile, but inside he squirmed with embarrassment. The dread he'd felt about facing the group at Wednesday night's Bible study and next weekend's service slowly dissipated. Everyone seemed to understand, more so perhaps because he was already one of them, someone familiar and given more slack than an untested newcomer.

He'd slept soundly last night and did not dream. Nathan felt better, but the nagging continued in the back of his mind. If he didn't face it soon, the same thing might happen all over again.

The agenda for Monday afternoon, planned out by Hayden, was lighter than usual. He'd apparently decided to play it safe and give Nathan extra down time.

Upon returning from the Spring River nursing home in West Boylston, a warm-up of sorts for his visit to Elizabeth's place tomorrow, Nathan had a wide break in his schedule between one and three o'clock. Hayden gave the pretense of needing to pack more items and suggested Nathan take a nap.

It had begun to rain, but this didn't keep Nathan from taking a walk. The weather kept most people indoors, and no car passed him along Greenwood Street. He could just as easily have walked through the short patch of woodland separating the church from the cemetery, but after yesterday's incident he didn't want to be caught wandering in the woods alone. It wouldn't help his already shaky image.

No sign of Tarretti's Blazer. That was good. The fewer questions from him or anyone else, the better. The large umbrella Nathan had found in the back closet, smelling slightly of mold, and the long black slicker his parents sent him two years ago when he was in Florida were good protection from the rain. He would likely wear the coat more often now that he was in a climate better suited to its purpose. He walked into the heart of the cemetery, along the same route they'd followed last week.

He did not stop when he saw the twin angels.

Just get this over with and move on, he told himself. The ground was soft, the damp air crisp with the smells of early leaves beginning to turn. Cold water leaked into his shoes when he stepped in a puddle. His attention, however, was riveted on the statues' faces, as much as theirs seemed to be on each other.

Rain dripped off stone noses and chins. Small details had worn thin by weather and time. Their wings stretched up from their backs and touched at the tips, blending into each other to become one solid piece. Nathan supposed this was deliberate, in order that one or the other did not tip too much to the side.

This was what he'd seen yesterday, and also in the dream his first night here. Was it a premonition, or could his imagination be strong enough to associate weather predictions with his plans to come here today? The only aspect of what he was seeing felt undeniably true, as much as he could be certain of anything in this moment: prior to arriving here last week, he had never seen this statue before. No familiarity at all in what he was looking at. He'd grown up here, spent so much of his life at the church through the woods on the other end of the cemetery. Not once did he remember wandering around this place, not especially wandering this far back to where he now stood, out of sight from the road. He must have, at some time.

As much as he tried to rationalize, standing here in the rain, no reason felt like the truth. Except one, a rationale which felt too contrived and too easily taken by those who shared his faith for him to accept completely. He was sent here. But sent by whom? God? He reflexively shook his head and examined the gravesite.

The headstone was a wide, square base supporting the stonework. Like the faces above it, the inscription was worn by seasons.

John Solomon, it read. *1852 – 1909.*

Reading the name sent an electric buzz through his body. That feeling of something missing, of a detail lodged in his brain slowly coming loose.

Solomon. The name was biblical, of course. Nathan tried to recall any Jewish families in town by that name. Of course, this was a very old grave. He looked at the angels, tilting the umbrella back only enough to give him a clear view. The association between their posture and the name on the inscription was obvious. Solomon's temple, housing the Ark of the Covenant. Two golden cherubs standing guard atop the mercy seat, or lid, of the box protecting the tablets of the ten commandments. The association was likely an artistic interpretation of the deceased's name. The missing detail, perhaps, but its significance eluded him.

Nathan wondered, not for the last time, if he was simply going mad.

He walked around the base looking for additional writing, some sort of epitaph other than a name and dates. Nothing. Concrete scraped under his shoe, partly buried beneath years of dirt and leaves. The base was massive, more so toward the front.

Not just a simple grave, then, but a crypt?

He walked around the statue one more time, rain dripping from the umbrella down his back. No sign of an entrance. Judging from the dates, if one existed, it was buried under a century of sediment.

Like Peter Quinn the previous day, he had an urge to fall to his knees and dig, uncover the entrance, expose the truth.

If he did that, he surely *was* insane.

He stood a moment longer, staring down and listening passively to the rain above him, then turned and walked quickly away. The water-soaked ground was soft under his feet. He had faced his dreams, but felt no closer to a resolution. Maybe he *should* see a doctor. He emerged onto Greenwood Street and looked around. No one coming either way. That was good.

On the walk back to the church, Nathan again tried to find an association between the elaborate headstone and everything that had happened. He'd dreamt of a temple. It wasn't anything like Solomon's as far as he could tell.

He sighed. It would come to him eventually.

He hoped.

Chapter Fifteen

"**S**ystems, Art Dinneck."

"Hi, Dad. How's work going?"

"Nate! How are you feeling?"

"I'm fine, Dad, honest." He reiterated what the EMTs had told him, keeping to the basics. His mother had likely covered the details with him the night before. He'd been back from his *walk* only a few minutes but couldn't relax. It seemed like as good a time as any to check in with his father, try to learn a little more about what was going on. "I'm just getting to a few bits of paperwork Pastor Hayden left for me. He says anything to do with red tape has officially been passed on to me."

"Very generous." From his voice he knew his father was smiling.

Nathan asked, "What have they got you doing these days?" He wanted to jump in to the topic of the men's club, but instincts told him to move slowly, keep his father from getting defensive.

"Oh, same old, same old. I'll be a mainframe dinosaur until I retire. I'm too old to learn any of the object-oriented stuff the kids work on today. Besides, someone's got to keep the lights on in this place."

Nathan only understood half of what his father just said, but he didn't care. Understanding the *working world* wasn't something he'd ever have to worry about, save for its effect on his parishioners.

"The pastor's last service is next weekend; then I officially take over."

"That's good." Then, as if Art couldn't think of anything else to say he repeated, "That's good, Nate." No *I'm proud of you*, his trademark line. It seemed the right time to broach the reason he'd called.

"Listen, Dad. I know I've been away a lot with school, then my stint in Florida. Been kind of out of touch lately."

"Naw," Art said. "You called more than most children probably ever would in their lifetime. Don't worry about it."

"Well, OK." Nathan fiddled with a blue and white Bic pen he'd lifted off the desk. "Still, you've joined this new group in town and I don't know anything about it. I have to admit it's got me a little curious."

The pause which followed made Nathan wonder if he'd already gone too far. His suspicions were confirmed when Art finally said, "Your mother put you up to this?"

"No, not at all. She doesn't even know I'm calling. I'm just curious. You're an adult; you can do whatever you want. I'm just wondering, like I said. I—"

"It's just a bunch of us guys from town getting together, shooting the breeze. Nothing to get uptight about." His voice was terse, without the comfortable warmth of a minute ago. Nathan knew he should just let it drop, but something pushed him on. Whatever his father was involved in suddenly felt bigger. Nathan wondered again if this change in behavior had less to do with the men's club, than with something in the man himself. Drinking? God forbid, another woman? The latter seemed too out of place. Too much to swallow.

"Well," Nathan said, hardening himself for a possible argument. "Let's just say I like to know what my new congregation is up to."

"I'm not part of your congregation, Reverend. I'm your father. Don't forget that."

The statement, and its cold, unfamiliar tone hit Nathan as if his father had physically punched him. He found himself without anything to say.

Art continued, "Listen, I have to get back to work. If there's nothing else?"

Nathan moved his lips, feeling the emotion, the *rejection* creep along his skin and settle in his chest. He finally managed to say, "No, I guess not."

"Thanks for calling. I'll talk to you later."

The line disconnected. Nathan continued to hold the phone, even when its warning klaxon bleated in his ear.

On the other end of the severed connection, Art Dinneck buried his face in his hands and leaned on the cubicle's desktop. He took a deep breath through closed fingers, willed himself not to start sobbing. Why had he spoken like that, to *Nate* of all people? Why did he do the same thing to Beverly every time *she* asked the same question? It was as if some switch in his head turned on whenever someone pushed him for answers. *They're intruding*, a buried voice said, *How dare they ask you about us? You're a grown man—you can make your own decisions.* At times it sounded like an actual voice, but when he tried to place it, the sensation passed.

Beverly must suspect more than he originally thought. If Nate was so quick to see the guilt in his father's eyes, surely Bev saw much more. One night. One stupid drunken night, and everything changed. What had he been thinking? He loved his wife, loved his family and God. But if that was true, why feel such a strong desire to keep away from the church? If anything, he should be falling to his knees and begging for forgiveness, from both the Lord and Beverly; two absolutions which would quickly pull him from the confusing spiral he found himself in these last few months. Instead, he returned to the men's club, night after night, pulled there like an addiction.

Waiting for the woman to return, perhaps? the voice asked.

"No," he whispered through his hands, and hoped no one heard. Too much to drink that night, that was all. For him, who normally had no more than an occasional beer or glass of wine, he must have passed whatever limit his body could handle, so much that later events blurred in his memory. The odd thing was he didn't *remember* having more than one beer. Still, if it wasn't for Manny Paulson filling in the blanks as he drove him home that night, Art likely wouldn't have remembered any of it. Maybe that would have been better. Ignorance is bliss, as the saying went.

Art leaned back in his chair, absently tapped the space bar on his keyboard to keep the screen saver from kicking in. Even now, he had trouble visualizing details about the woman. She had frizzy red hair, he was sure of that. White blouse, big smile. He remembered talking to her after she'd entered the club, something about a car broken down, stranding her for the moment. She decided to stay, "and party". Those two words were clear. The club hadn't been crowded that night— Paulson, Quinn, and a couple of others who'd already begun to drink themselves into a quagmire and became lost in their usual poker game. Art did recall that first beer, at least. He wondered, not for the first time, if something had been added to the drink. That implied someone there had done it, and...

...everyone in the Hillcrest Men's Club can be trusted, the voice in his head said. *It is safe there.*

No, it couldn't have been anyone there. Why would they lie about that? After all, he'd come to his senses in the back room, the woman lying beside him with a contented smile. The memory sent a pained revulsion through him.

He leaned forward to pray for forgiveness, for clarity in thought. And, like the other times he'd tried this, he felt only a hesitancy, an unwillingness to give this burden over to God. An invisible hand seemed to fall over him. He grew angry...

...weak man, can't depend on his own strength....

He cursed his weakness. Was this the man he'd turned out to be? So what? He was drunk that night. Nothing wrong with that. If something happened with the woman, he wasn't to blame. He couldn't even remember it except in quick flashes, as if he'd been watching rather than participating. He loved his wife, and would not feel guilty the rest of his life over one mistake.

...if the church tries to make you feel guilty, you should forget all about it....

He looked at his computer screen, focusing through the reflected overhead lights on the program he'd been working on. In the reflection, he could make out the edges of the cubicles behind him. A man with short white hair stood there, watching him.

Art spun in his chair. No one was standing in the aisle outside his cubicle.

There never *had* been, of course. The building was secure enough in that regard. Peter Quinn would not have been allowed in without an escort. He was seeing things again. The need to go to the club tonight—*just for a little while, for crying out loud*—came over him like a junkie's need for a fix.

Not that Art thought of it that way. To him, it was a perfectly natural desire for a man to have.

Part Two

Departure

Constantinople, 1204 A.D.

Everard of Dampierre had only a few minutes in the cavernous room to consider the proper direction to move. Already the remaining crusaders, all of whom were well-acquainted with this "secret" basilica under the Church of the Apostles, were regrouping above. Everard could divert them only temporarily, giving their troop leaders directions with his sacred Voice. Scattered among the city and other corners of the cathedral, they would not immediately stumble upon the passage which would lead them here. The knights of the Crusade, dedicated and loyal to their leaders for the past two years, could maintain ranks only so long. For most, the promise of riches beyond their feeble imaginations was the primary incentive for leaving their families in the first place. So close to such wealth and treasures, they would soon be uncontrollable in their lust. Nothing was sacred. Everything profane.

It was a wonderful day.

The six men under his command were carefully chosen over the past year from ships off the Byzantine coast, as they angrily watched this city's bloody politics unfold. Their financier, the newly reinstated emperor Alexius IV, and his son—who had successfully rerouted Pope Innocent's troops to Constantinople in the first place—managed to get themselves decapitated only a few short months after regaining power. For Everard, the turn of events proved advantageous. Father and son had outlived their usefulness. Rumors of wealth, and more importantly ancient relics, below both this church and Hagia Sophia drew him to the city and its surrounding islands. His ability to control others allowed eventual visits to this fabled, cross-shaped room to be possible.

His men now stared in wonder about the basilica. The riches in this place were beyond counting. Everard spoke to each man individually, telling them all of this belonged to them provided they did what he asked of them *right now.* In truth, mobs of their fellow knights would be here soon, but they did not need to know that.

They followed the knight to a spot beyond the Column of Flagellation. Thankfully, none of the others knew its significance. There were already enough distractions were about to make the task of controlling them difficult.

"Sire," called a squire named Marcus, no older than sixteen. He held up a broken sandal. "I found this on the floor. Over there." He pointed to a section of wall just beyond the Column. To the others, the discovery meant nothing. To Everard, it meant someone had beaten them down here.

"Quickly!" He felt along the wall, as he had done the last time he'd visited this room. Now he knew what to look for. Had, in fact, entered the next chamber only one week earlier. Everard had stood before the very Ark of the Covenant and wept with joy, an uncharacteristic display of emotion but one which he allowed himself just that one time. Then, he had dared go no further. Haste killed. Everard had returned to his ship to begin the too-easy task of influencing the Crusaders to finally take matters into their own hands. Alexius V, the anti-Rome replacement to the headless former emperor, was refusing any trade negotiations with Rome. Things then moved along of their own accord. The men were eager for battle, among other more immoral pleasures available in such a vast city. The invasion of Constantinople by the forces of the Fourth Crusade was the culmination of Everard of Dampierre's master plan. *And* of the great god Molech, known by many names over the centuries: Bringer of Chaos and Death, Loki, Lucifer.

Now, finally, the prize his master had sought since the days of Solomon's fall would be his. No flea-ridden priest or knight or whoever was inside would stop him. Everard had stood beyond this stone passage, seen with his own eyes, heard with his very soul the power of such a relic. He understood more clearly now than perhaps the thousands before him why the master sought it so. Never mind the mindless other rumors or theories held by the Elders and so many of his predecessors. To him, it was simply... *perfect.*

"Prepare to storm inside as soon as the door is open." The men drew their swords, expecting a siege of defenders beyond. Everard removed a studded glove from his left hand and inserted fingers into three holes that were angled to make them invisible to the casual observer. He pulled. His hand was damp with sweat. His fingers slipped free and the door crashed closed. He cursed, wiped his hands on his leather wrist shield and tried again. This time he kept his body leaning hard into the gesture. The door opened.

"You," he indicated the squire, focusing his voice since the lad was beginning to consider their surroundings a bit too hungrily. "Stand here and hold this door open. If anyone other than us comes along, in either direction, cut them down."

"Sire!" The boy named Marcus leaned against the door. Everard led his men down the long hall, turned the corner. He stopped, knowing what he would see. The others continued past him but soon they, too, froze in their tracks at the realization of what stood before them.

"My God," one of the men said, and fell to his knees.

Everard shouted, "You shall not utter that name here! Do as I say and the world shall be yours to command!" There was enough controlled cadence in his voice to get their attention. Time was running out. There was no one here. Another, narrower passage opened on their right. It had not been there the last time.

He gestured to two soldiers armed with long, crooked staffs. They believed they were carrying lances. The staffs were actually well-trimmed branches of acacia wood.

Then Everard realized two things simultaneously. The first was that the Ark's lid was partially open. Someone had defiled it! His blood boiled; his face burned in rage. A moment later, all color drained from the expression.

A fat man—a bishop if his attire was any indication—appeared in the entrance to the side passage. Something was clutched against his chest, glowing softly in the darkness. With his free hand, the bishop gripped a wooden lever beside the doorway.

Something in the fat man's eyes told the knight he had to run *now!* Before he could do anything, the bishop pulled down on the lever. The room filled with the sound of grinding stone. The holy man was gone as quickly as he'd appeared. Everard of Dampierre wondered for half a second if the man had escaped down a trap door; then the ceiling crushed down upon him and his men in a deluge of boulders and stone.

When the remaining horde of crusaders charged into the cross-shaped basilica of the Apostles, they found a young squire digging at a mound of rubble filling a doorway. Two of the newcomers eagerly joined him, assuming riches lay beyond. They soon lost interest for easier pickings among the sarcophagi. A moment later, even the squire

Marcus stopped digging. He joined the others in search of spoils.

Chapter Sixteen

Nathan gently brushed a gray strand of hair away from Margaret Conan's forehead. When he finished speaking a prayer to comfort her in her pain, she opened her eyes and smiled. The gesture dropped a decade from her sunken, wrinkled face.

"Thank you, Pastor, and may the Lord bless you and your work as well."

Nathan sat back in his position at the edge of the bed, careful not to brush against her thin legs under the sheet. As advanced as Mrs. Conan's diabetes had become, she never complained, but he knew enough about the symptoms to be cautious. As always, she was overjoyed to share prayer and scripture, even asked about his parents. Margaret Conan had once been his neighbor, three doors down from the Dinneck home. She would babysit him as a toddler, and in later years, he'd visit for no other reason than simply to share her company. Her house had the air of freshly baked cookies and spice candies.

Reverend Hayden suggested he visit the nursing home alone, having to make a trip himself to the monastery to make final arrangements for his arrival. On the drive across town, Nathan worried about being too distracted— about running into Elizabeth. Seeing her was inevitable, though. If not today, someday soon. There would be no avoiding it. Whether she would want to speak with him, after such a long time without any communication save secondhand reports from Josh Everson, was another question.

He closed the old woman's Bible and unconsciously ran his hand across its familiar, threadbare cover. When she had asked him to choose the reading earlier, Nathan picked the opening chapters of Paul's first letter to the Thessalonians. His parents had often read scriptures aloud to him when he was younger, so they never complained when Mrs. Conan did the same when he was in her care. Nathan remembered many afternoons in her living room, eating oatmeal raisin cookies while she occasionally read short passages for the sheer joy of sharing in the Word with such an eager audience of one. When Nathan was old enough to stay home alone while his mother was out, he would still wander up the road now and then to visit. She always seemed pleased to see him, to discuss and debate passages from the same Bible Nathan now held in his hand—less worn and frayed back then, but not by much.

If he was ever asked when his calling to the ministry first occurred, Nathan could think of no stronger moments than those afternoons in Mrs. Conan's living room, eating cookies.

He felt moved to explain this to her, but she suddenly looked past him toward the door, smiled wider and said, "Looks like *you* have a caller, Nate."

Nathan turned, already knowing who was there.

Elizabeth O'Brien looked exactly as he remembered. There was a more determined set to her face, one that came with the level of maturity they both had reached over the past five years. The face still had the round, cherub-like quality which never failed to pull him to her. She wore jeans and sneakers, a blue pullover sweater and a pinned name tag that read "Elizabeth O". She was tall, not quite his own height, but taller than the average woman, with the slightly-rounded figure of someone always fighting off extra pounds, winning some but never all of the battles. Her blonde hair was as thick and unruly as ever.

The smile on her face filled his heart with an unexpected happiness.

"Hi," she said, and stuck her hands in her jeans' pocket. All she would have to do, Nathan thought, would be to lean her shoulder casually against the door frame to complete such a perfect picture of *coolness*.

"Hi," he said, knowing it was the lamest response he could have given. Mrs. Conan's thin hand nudged his arm. He looked back. She nodded in the direction of the door and said with a sly grin, "Bye, Nate."

Chapter Seventeen

The coffee in the employee break room was surprisingly good. Nathan took another sip as Elizabeth returned from the vending machine with a can of ginger ale. She sat next to him at the table, not in the seat opposite as he'd expected.

His head was spinning. He wished it would stop.

Nathan wondered if maybe his feelings for this woman were still as strong. The thought brought a jolt of pain, not a physical hurt but a wrenching ache of the heart that showed as a nervous rumble in his belly. He couldn't *love* her. He was a minister and she was a self-proclaimed atheist. No, he never truly believed that last part, not with five years to replay that infamous conversation in his mind. She simply did not *want* to believe.

Don't press, an inner voice said. It was sage advice, and the thought sobered him.

She said, "I thought Reverend Hayden wasn't leaving until next week."

Nathan raised an eyebrow. "You're right. I think he's making me try out my sea legs. How did you know when he was leaving?"

Elizabeth smiled. "Mrs. Conan keeps up on all the gossip. She shares it with me whether I want to hear it or not."

It occurred to him that Mrs. Conan must have known about his episode Sunday. Since the first thing out of Elizabeth's mouth wasn't *How are you feeling?* his old neighbor probably hadn't mentioned it. *God bless that woman.*

He asked, "Are you a nurse now?"

She nodded and looked down at her soda can. "I finally went back to school and finished up. Couldn't let you have more degrees than me."

Reflexively, Nathan said, "Yeah, but I'm ordained as well. Technically that means I'm one up on you diploma-wise."

She laughed and said, "They give a diploma for that?"

"Well, they give us," he made a box-like gesture with his two hands, "a thingy. You know, whatever they're called."

"Certificate?"

"Yeah, that's it," he said.

A short black woman, hair pulled tightly back into a bun, poked her head and shoulders into the break room. "Lizzie, Mr. Gansky needs some... oh, hello," she said, seeing Nathan.

Elizabeth, whose comfortable smile never wavered, swept her arm with a small flourish. "Serena, meet Nate. Oh, sorry, I mean Reverend Nathan."

"Ooh, so this is the—"

"I'll be right there," Elizabeth interrupted, her composure at last broken. Her neck flushed red. "Sorry, Nate. Got to see what Mr. G. wants."

They stood at the same time. "That's OK." He hesitated, and hoped Serena, as nice as she seemed to be, was no longer there. "Seeing you again was, um, really great."

Elizabeth began to speak, caught herself, then sighed. She stepped forward, hesitantly; then the two embraced in a gentle, quiet hug.

So much time had passed since he'd held her like this. The sensation of her in his arms felt strange. No, he realized, not strange. It felt *new*. They were two different people, now.

In that moment, he was certain of one thing. He did still have feelings for her. Strong feelings. If he had his doubts before, now they were no more.

Another dilemma to deal with in the little town of Hillcrest.

They reluctantly parted from the embrace, and Elizabeth was again flustered.

She put her open soda into the refrigerator and dumped his half-finished cup of coffee in the sink. "Maybe we can get together some place where we can talk more than just a few minutes," she said.

"I'd like that." His heart was racing. He needed air. This wasn't a good idea.

She walked beside him into the hall. He began to reach for her hand, but caught himself. That would be too intimate. When they reached the front doors, she looked sideways at him. He caught the gaze, and as usual, something unspoken passed between them. They both began to laugh at the same time.

"Look at us," she said.

He reached over and this time did take her hand. "Look at us."

"What about Saturday?"

"Sure," he said, then released her hand to reach for something in his sport coat. "Wait. Have to check. The pastor's had a pretty full plate between us, but it's been lightening up lately." From the coat's right inside pocket, he pulled out a Palm Pilot, tapping with the stylus across the screen's calendar.

"Hey, lookie here. The church is in the twenty-first century."

When he got to Saturday, he looked up and smiled. "Got me a *gen-u-ine* cell phone, too." He tapped the left coat pocket with the edge of the PDA. "Mom and Dad figure these sorts of Christmas gifts get more use than new socks." He quickly scanned the calendar entry. "Yep, as long as it's after 6:30, Saturday's cool."

"Don't you have to drop that word now that you're a priest?"

"Minister," he corrected for the second time that week, and tucked the small organizer back into his pocket.

"Same thing." She reached out and lightly touched his cheek with the tips of her fingers. Then she turned around and hurried down the hallway.

He wished he could see her face, assumed it was blushing as much as his own.

Chapter Eighteen

The next few days progressed without incident. Nathan and Hayden continued their dissection of the church's paperwork, and various other miscellany. Now and then someone paid a visit and Nathan offered his pre-established explanation about Sunday's fellowship dinner dramatics. This had become so repetitive that he soon answered their concerns with a genuinely confident smile. More importantly, he was picking up the regular order of things. Hayden joined him for Wednesday's visit to the three hospitals in Worcester, but let Nathan do most of the talking. Bible study that evening, led by Pastor Hayden one final time, was crowded and boisterous. Hayden was a man of many passions, but his strongest was discussing the Bible with young people who usually—and that evening was no exception—comprised more than half the attendees. By Thursday morning, the pastor looked more relaxed and admitted feeling better about leaving the flock in Nathan's hands.

"As long as you promise not to fall down too often," he said as they drove to the main cemetery.

Nathan grimaced. "If I *do* fall down, I promise to at least stay conscious."

Hayden nodded. "Fair enough."

They were in the fifth car of a modest funeral procession convoying from the church. The deceased was a ninety-one year old man named Karl Gipson. The man had passed away in his sleep at the nursing home Tuesday night, less than twelve hours after Nathan visited his bedside. Nathan remembered Gipson as quiet, perpetually tired and mumbling. It surprised him to think of how close he'd been to death. Even in his exhausted state, the man had laid a withered hand on Nathan's Bible to pray silently along with him. Nathan felt a momentary wave of euphoria at the memory. Sadness and exaltation—the contradictions of a Christian's life.

Gipson's family followed the hearse at the front of the procession. In his rear view mirror, Nathan counted five other cars behind his. Not a large group of mourners, but then he'd had a small family, many of whom were either dead themselves or living in the southwestern part of the country. Elizabeth was in the last car, representing the Rosenberg Senior Care Center. In their only, and brief, conversation at the church before setting out for the burial, Elizabeth mentioned that Mrs. Conan had wanted to attend. But she explained that the woman could barely stand. "Besides," she added quietly, "and I hope this doesn't sound bizarre or anything, but this is the last place I'd want her to see considering how advanced her own condition is."

When she paused, Nathan had put a hand on her shoulder, told her that was probably a wise move. He'd removed the hand quickly. Too familiar, too soon.

The green sprawl of the newer Hillcrest Memorial Cemetery came into view. He assumed Tarretti would be waiting at the gravesite, standing off at a respectful distance. When the funeral plans were made Wednesday morning, Hayden remarked that Tarretti never failed to have everything ready for the procession's arrival. As far as he knew, the man rarely left the grounds, and remarked that he probably "had nothing better to do, anyway." Hayden said this with his characteristic grin, an expression Nathan was only now able to detect in the otherwise stony face.

As the hearse entered the grounds, Nathan asked, "Pastor, my dad's involved with some new group in town. I don't think I've heard the name yet. Not the K of C. Something more recent. Spends a lot of time there."

Hayden made a noise of acknowledgement and nodded his head. He said nothing.

Nathan turned the car into the wide stone gates and pressed, "Do you know the group I'm talking about?"

"I believe so. A small lot from what your mother has told me. Call themselves the Hillcrest Men's Club."

"My mom thinks he's been going there too much, might be drinking..."

Hayden didn't comment right away, but as Nathan pulled to the curb behind the last family car and parked, the old man said, "I really don't know. I've tried to talk to your father about it, but he gets very defensive. Lately, all I've been able to do is keep tabs on him via your mother." He opened the passenger door and paused. "You don't mind if I lead the graveside ceremony this morning? I've known Karl for a long time."

"Not at all." Nathan decided to drop the subject of his father for now. He'd forgotten Hayden's feelings again. Gipson was a friend. Besides, it didn't sound like he knew much more about the club than Nathan did.

Though the sky was overcast, the weather remained calm and dry at the graveside. The chill of autumn floated teasingly in the air. Nathan kept two paces behind the pastor and tried to blend into the background. Hayden read apt passages from the Bible before the mourners took turns stepping onto the artificial grass laid over the grave and laying down flowers offered by the funeral director. As they did so, Vincent Tarretti slowly moved closer, trying his best to be discreet. His graying blonde hair was tied back in a ponytail and tucked inside a flannel shirt. While Hayden spoke softly with the family, Nathan moved from the group and shook Vincent's hand.

"Reverend, good morning. How are you feeling?"

"I'm fine," Nathan said, and hoped that was enough. "Pastor Hayden has a lot of praise for your work here."

Vincent smiled and nodded. "We've done a lot of these over the years. He's a good man. Ready to take command?"

Nathan shrugged. "As ready as I'll ever be." A thought occurred to him, and after checking that Hayden wasn't giving him signs that he was needed, added, "Listen, Vincent—do you prefer Vincent?"

"That's my name."

"You've been around for a while. Ever heard about a new men's club in town?"

A surprised expression crossed the caretaker's face. A moment later he masked it with a look of indifference. "I've heard of them."

"What have you heard?"

Vincent stuck out his lower lip and slowly shook his head. "Not much. Why?"

"Nothing serious. Just my dad's been spending a lot of time there lately and my Mom's worried." When Vincent said nothing, simply continued his faux-disinterested stare, Nathan tried another approach. "Any idea what they're all about? If there's a religious background? I suspect it's mostly just a bunch of guys hanging around, something like that."

Now, the other man looked at the minister directly, and for a moment Nathan thought he was angry. When he spoke, his voice was subdued, cautious. "I learned long ago that some things look one way to the public and another in private."

"Meaning?"

Vincent nodded to the dispersing crowd. "I think your boss wants you."

Hayden was looking in their direction, and when he realized he had Nathan's attention gave a short wave, fingers wiggling in a *come hither* gesture.

"Can I—" Nathan said as he turned back, but Vincent was walking toward the gravesite, casually putting on a thick pair of work gloves. He was either in a hurry to lower the casket, or running from the conversation. Nathan moved into step behind Hayden as the minister walked with Gipson's middle-aged daughter toward the line of cars. He tried to get his bearings, keep his mind on the somber event, but he kept wondering what Tarretti's answer meant.

Vincent hovered near the gravesite, but not so close as to look impatient. He would make no move to lower the casket until the lead cars in the procession had rounded the far curve.

Waiting gave him time to calm down. He didn't like people asking him questions about anything not related to work. Dinneck asked about the men's club, of all things. The timing of the kid's question less than a week after Quinn's visit was troubling. Still, all Dinneck wanted was information. To help his father. It still bothered him, though. Vincent thought of his notebook. His notes were his own; they were between him and God. Let Dinneck get his answers somewhere else.

Last week the young preacher had reacted oddly when he saw John Solomon's grave (*Entries "816" and "817"* he thought reflexively)—and now this.

The cars moved on, rounding the corner and passing out of sight. Vincent carefully pulled away the Astroturf to reveal a small winch at one side of the hole. He offered his own prayer for Mister Gipson, then slowly lowered the coffin. He worked steadily, but was unfocused. He thought again of his notebook. He did not like it when so many entries crossed paths.

Chapter Nineteen

"I still think he might not be ready." The gray-haired woman leaned against the kitchen counter and took a long sip of tea. Ralph Hayden knew that Gabby Zawalich had more to say on the matter than that single statement. The pause was simply a way of collecting her thoughts. Gabby was one of the few parishioners who still referred to Hillcrest Baptist as "the new place". Most younger adults in the parish were too young to remember a time when the church wasn't here. Gabby and Hayden's wife had been as close as friends could ever be. After Jean's death, the woman standing in front of him had taken it upon herself to be Ralph's self-appointed guard dog. She was also one of the church elders, the only one who continued to express reservations about their newly-appointed pastor.

Hayden waited, hands loosely clasped behind his back. The few remaining mourners sat on Karl Gipson's living room couch, pouring over a yellowed photo album spread across the lap of his daughter. They took turns pointing to pictures and relaying stories about the man.

No sooner had Nate Dinneck excused himself and returned to the church to finish the paperwork, than Gabby ushered Ralph into the kitchen. He knew what was coming.

"It's not that I don't think he's technically qualified, mind you. His grades in school were exceptional, and Reverend Burke couldn't say enough good things about him. Emotionally, though, given his age...."

"Gabby, Sunday shook a lot of people up, but honestly I think his little 'spell' was an aberration. I haven't seen anything since to worry me."

Her teacup was a delicate china piece with intricate roses etched along the lip, now with a blotch of red lipstick. She placed it on the counter atop its saucer.

"All last week, Ralph, he seemed so, I don't know, distracted. You must have noticed." She cast a quick look into the living room and lowered her voice. "First Art stops coming, won't talk to anyone about it, not even Beverly. Now Nate has that episode during the reception. I don't want to start comparing the sins of the father to—"

"I wouldn't call Art taking some time off for personal reflection a sin, Gabby."

She waved her hands in front of her. "I know, sorry. If that's what it's about. But you'll be leaving Monday. Do you really think Nate Dinneck is ready to run the church on his own? I'm serious," she added when Ralph was unable to suppress a grin. "Another incident like this weekend's and I won't be the only one wondering if...."

She hesitated again.

Ralph's smile faded. "Wondering what?"

"If we hadn't made a mistake in choosing him. It's a big move for someone so young, so much going on with his father and all."

Ralph took Gabby's small hands gently into his. He gave them a squeeze. "Honestly, I think he'll do fine. I'll stay in touch while I'm at the monastery. If I sense anything wrong, I'll cut my visit short and move back to town a few days early. You have the number. Call me any time you want."

She nodded.

"Then let's keep this between us, for now at least. Give Nate a fighting chance. Don't forget that when I began this church I wasn't the flawless specimen of liturgical perfection standing before you now."

She smiled. A good sign.

He said again, "Nate'll do fine."

He wondered, however, whether he really believed that himself. Dinneck *had* been less distracted this week. There would be bumps. No one should expect otherwise. It might take some time, but they had plenty of that.

He squeezed Gabby's hands again and together they returned to the living room to rescue Karl's daughter from the photo album.

Chapter Twenty

Nathan stood at one end of a massive blue room. Like the walls, the ceiling and floor were also painted a bright, sky blue, with no clear delineation between them. Looking too long in one place made him dizzy. The sole object in the room anchored his vision. The door. It stood opposite him, painted black, twice as big as any door should be.

He squeezed his hands into fists and thought, *Not again. Please. No more nightmares.*

He knew this was a dream, or maybe another waking vision like he'd had on Sunday. He didn't remember going to bed, couldn't recall *what* he'd been doing—before this room appeared.

Something pressed into his left palm. He opened his hand, saw the key. Like the door, it was the right shape but oversized, a child's toy rendition. There was no door knob. Rather, the keyhole was built into the black wood where the knob should have been. Light shone through it. Wherever the door led to, it was bright. Another room? Outside, maybe.

He turned around. Maybe he could walk out of this dream of his own free will. He had expected to be paralyzed, rooted to the blue floor, but he was able to turn. There was no other door. Just a wall. It might have been blue, like the others, but he could not tell because it was covered with monsters scrabbling along its surface. Ugly, horrible things, some brown, others white with red splotches, others still darker or stained green. They had two arms and legs, or only one, or four, or six. He stepped back. They swarmed over the wall like wasps on a hive. Their heads were pocked, scarred, misshapen. Some of them had the distinguishable features of eyes and noses, other less identifiable orifices. All of them, though, were *wrong*. They were terrible, misplaced. And laughing.

They were laughing at him.

As a group, they scurried to the floor, flowing like mud around and behind him. The now-exposed wall was streaked with grime, smelled of old garbage and excrement. Nathan dropped the key and covered his face. As he sank to his knees, he felt their horrid presence pass by but never touch. They were so close to him.

"*Nad ei tohi seda võtit saada!*" shouted a woman's voice. The voice was young. He didn't recognize it. "*Nad avavad ukse!*"

She must have been speaking to him, but what she said made no sense. The language sounded familiar, maybe Russian, but the voice was urgent.

He pulled his hands away.

One of the creatures from the wall stood less than a foot away. Its brown and yellow face was malformed, looking like it had been pounded out of clay by an angry child. One milky eye considered him for a moment; then the bottom of the face split. More rotten garbage smell. It had opened its mouth to make more of that laughter-noise. Two chipped teeth were visible before it closed again and the thing reached down and grabbed at something in front of Nathan. It moved quickly and with the caution of a dog snatching food from its master's plate.

It had the key. The mouth opened again, more laughter and more awful stench. It scuttled away, out of sight behind him.

Nathan pivoted on his knees and faced the black door again.

"*Nad ei tohi seda võtit saada!*" The young woman screamed at him from her hiding place.

The wall where the door had been was gone, covered in the squirming, giggling bodies. Were they demons? In the past few moments, Nathan had forgotten that what he saw wasn't real. If this was another dream, and it was, had to be, demons would fit in well with this recurring theme.

He shouted, "I want to wake up, now. I don't want to see any more!"

The creature with the key slapped and punched at the others, forcing them to clear an area around the keyhole.

"*Peatage nad! Nad avavad ukse!*"

"I don't know what you're saying!" Nathan stared at the blue ceiling and stood. He was arguing with a nightmare! He didn't even know what the woman was telling him.

The laughter in front of him changed to screams and shouts. He looked down in time to see the door swing inward.

Everything that happened after, happened in seconds.

Every detail etched in his mind one moment, to be lost in the next.

Beyond the door was beauty beyond beauty beyond beauty....

Nathan screamed. It was too much; the light beyond the door spilled over them, pushing the creatures back. They huddled in the center. Something moved behind Nathan, but his eyes were locked on the world beyond the door. No single detail could be grasped. Trees, then they were gone; hills traveling on and on forever with no horizon, also gone in a blink; light so, so, so bright; colors, figures beyond the door, standing twice Nathan's height. He tried to focus on them.

These figures stood in rows stretching away as far as he could see, standing in twos and threes. Hair long and flowing, they disappeared, returned, women, men, bald headed with beards, naked, clothed, wings? No, yes. Anger from them, savagery, love, armed with swords that burned white with flame.

Too much. More sounds behind him. More of the demons filled the room. Nathan forced himself to look away from the door. Behind him the wall was gone. A long shadowed hallway, stretching to eternity like the world beyond the door. But in this direction was only black, with bodies of thousands of millions of creatures racing along the walls and ceilings toward him, around him, filling the room with their stench. Too many, they couldn't be—

When he looked back toward the door, the army of monsters poured through it, tarnishing the perfect light beyond. The tall men/women/angels fell onto the creatures and smashed them from existence. But more came. More and more. Beyond the door was a war not seen in this universe since—

Nathan opened his eyes.

Windshield.

Reverend Hayden on the sign.

He was in his car. Staring at the church. Staring at the sign.

A sob hitched in his chest. Nathan reached up and wiped cheeks wet with tears. He wanted to get out of the car and start running because his heart was racing.

The engine idled. A song played on the radio.

His hand shook as he reached forward and turned the radio off.

Details of the blue room and the universe beyond the door flared in perfect detail one more time; then the dream began to fade.

He hadn't fallen asleep. He had just parked the car. Couldn't have simply dozed off. He remembered pulling into this space. Just a second ago.

But he *had* dreamt... hadn't he? Another vision. A room. No, a light, along a hillside. Something terrible. Something beautiful.

He couldn't remember. It had been frightening. At least, he thought so.

Nathan's pulse slowed. He must have drifted off for just a second, gotten confused when he realized he was still in his car. He rubbed his face, remembered the tears. He'd been crying? Sleep tears, maybe.

No, he didn't have another vision. Definitely not. More like an extended blink. Details of a large room came back to him. Must be thinking about the funeral parlor. Relief. Not a dream. That would've been the straw that broke the new pastor's back, wouldn't it? He turned off the car and got out. When he put the key into the lock of the side entrance, a pang of fear jabbed at him.

What if it had been a seizure? No. He was just tired. Maybe take a quick nap, set the alarm for an hour later, then finish up Mr. Gipson's paperwork.

By the time he closed the door, Nathan had forgotten the vision entirely.

Chapter Twenty-One

The Eastside Mall was a low-lying strip of five businesses, side by side along a narrow parking lot on Main Street. Like the rest of Hillcrest, this section of town was primarily residential, but the road's small-town semblance of traffic served enough of a justification for the plaza's existence. The large sign, embedded in the sidewalk along the road, sported distinctly-tailored logos of each company, one atop the other. The topmost advertised the town's one small convenience store *The Greedy Grocer*, followed by the lace-adorned *Hair U Doing?* salon. Below the hair salon's name was a blank sign, then *Thames Carpets* and *Breaker Mortgage Group*. The signs cast the parking strip in a multi-colored hue, though with the exception of the men's club set in the middle of the strip, *The Greedy Grocer* was the only establishment still open this time of night.

Josh Everson slid the door sign to its *Closed* position as the last customer pulled from the lot with his emergency milk ration. He flipped a switch beside the door. The outside light above the entrance turned off. At the same time, the large marquee at the side of Main Street went dark. It was wired to shut off once the final store killed its overhead light. The Hillcrest Men's Club had theirs off all the time. Just one more quirk of their bizarre little troupe. Now that the *Greedy Grocer* was closed, the neighborhood fell into darkness for the next nine hours, at which time Josh would drag himself back to start another day.

Not that he minded. He was never much of a late sleeper and all he had to do was open the place until Shirley Riggalaro showed up after her kids got on the bus. Then the day was his own, until the closing shift.

He checked his watch. Five minutes past ten. Before moving back to the register to cash out, Josh looked outside, pressing his hands against the glass to see past the inside glare. Aside from his own rusting Toyota parked out front, three other cars sat bathed in the filtered white light spilling from the men's club two doors down. Every night, with few exceptions, *someone* was over there. Granted it was Friday, but it could as easily have been a Tuesday or Wednesday. Having to get up for work didn't seem a priority for them. Including Nate's dad. Mr. Dinneck's car had arrived sometime in the past hour.

For some reason, the fact that Mr. Dinneck frequented the place never seemed odd until now. He never came into the store when Josh was working, not even for a last minute loaf of bread. The guy in charge of the club came by often enough. Perfectly coiffed white hair and clipped moustache like some displaced English gentleman. The few times he and Whitey (a private nickname Josh tagged for him since he never caught the guy's real name) exchanged pleasantries, Josh invariably got uncomfortable. Something very weird about the man. For some reason, he never felt the need to mention anything to Nate about any of this during the past few months. Now he wondered why. Not until Nate swung by this evening to grab a few necessities like soda and microwave popcorn, did Mr. Dinneck's nightly sojourns to his little club take on significance.

During their brief conversation at the counter this afternoon, Nate kept looking out the window. When Josh asked what was up, Nate explained about his dad. Not much, but enough to let him know that all was not well in Dinneck Land.

The discussion took a U-turn when Josh bagged the groceries and asked, "Any big plans for the weekend, Nate?" He assumed his buddy was planning some wild night of reading the Book of Moses or something equally enthralling. When Nate beamed and shyly mentioned his date with Elizabeth, Josh couldn't suppress the sudden fear slamming into his belly.

Not that he'd done anything wrong. Not really. Well, maybe a little. He'd never told Nate about what happened. Not once in the years between the *then* of his dirty little secret and now. He tried to mask his worry as surprise. Josh's instincts screamed to tell his friend the truth, *now*, before Elizabeth did. But, well, Nate seemed to have somewhere to go.

If E told him tomorrow, so be it. No big deal. It was over now, anyway. Still, Nate was his best friend. Friends don't keep secrets.

Josh hunkered down behind the counter and locked the canvas money bag. He dropped the bundle into the safe and spun the day's cash into the floor. He preferred not to do any bank drop-offs at night; too many stories of ambushes to make it worth the risk. Muggers didn't usually work the morning shift. He shut off all lights except for the few needed for security, and left the store.

He hesitated in front of the Toyota. To his left, an occasional shadow passed across the men's club windows. No details, though. The glass was covered with some kind of white paint, or soap. Why they didn't get drapes or curtains instead of smearing goop all over the window was beyond him. Then again, that would be something a woman might think of, not a bunch of chain-smoking Bud drinkers playing poker.

Maybe he could take a peek, if there was a gap in all that paint. Let Nate know what his dad was up to. He felt a sudden sense of déjà vu. Hadn't he done this once before? It sure felt that way. He'd have remembered it, of course. More and more the fact that he hadn't been keeping tabs on Mr. Dinneck until now, nor even mentioning anything to Nate about the place bothered him. There *was* a reason, a good one, but right now he couldn't remember what it was.

Maybe he should mind his own business and head home, or go back into the store and grab a movie from the increasingly spare rental shelf.

Just one peek...

As he thought this, he was already moving down the front walkway. His reflection in *Hair U Doing?*'s front window followed. He stepped lightly, stomach tight as if he was spying into a neighbor's bedroom, then paused. He was just taking a peek.

The paint/soap was fairly consistent across the windows. The place reminded him of one of those campaign headquarter politicians set up during election season, taking up residence in an abandoned storefront only to abandon it after the votes were cast.

He tried not to venture too close to the door—another soaped over glass job. Someone might decide to leave. Wouldn't be very cool to catch the *Grocer*'s manager spying on their secret games. *There.* A scrape, no more than a few inches long at roughly waist height. He could see old floor tiles from his current vantage.

Go home, he scolded himself. He suddenly needed to go to the bathroom. *Just look*, then *you can go, you chicken.*

Josh hunkered down until his left eye was level with the clear spot. The only light around him came from inside so he shouldn't cast any shadow on the window. He leaned forward, stopping when his forehead rested soundlessly against the glass.

Someone at the bar. The guy who came in now and then for a six back of Sam Adams. He liked to glare at Josh when he paid. Typical *crowbar to the wallet* dude. The guy also liked to park in the back alley next to the owner's car. Someone's knee just to his right. Josh rolled his head, careful not to bump the window, and Mr. Dinneck came into view.

The guy looked wasted. He sat in a folding chair and stared across the room at a point to Josh's left. At least the guy wasn't looking at *him*. He didn't seem to be looking at *anything*, in fact. Mr. Dinneck just sat there, hands flat on his legs and stared. Behind him, some kind of card game was going on. No one inside seemed concerned about the way the guy was acting.

Very creepy. He wasn't drunk. Drunks wouldn't be able to sit that still. Drugs, then? Yeah, maybe. Mr. Dinneck's eyes were open, so he wasn't asleep. What was he looking at?

Josh did the roll-thing with his head, trying to see what—

Everything went dark. Something blocked his view in that direction. He looked back toward Nate's dad.

Still dark.

Uh-oh.

He stood up. Where his face had been was now a hulking shadow on the other side of the window. The shadow rose.

A man... who was now walking toward the front door.

OK, folks, time to leave. Josh looked back at his car. He'd only make it halfway before the guy came out. That would look worse than what he was doing now.

The front door opened. *Be cool. I was just heading home and thought I'd take a peek. That's it. Nothing else.* It was the truth.

He turned back to face Whitey himself, holding the door open. He said with that bizarre voice of his, "Mister Everson, I presume?"

Josh's ears suddenly itched. He ignored the feeling and put on his best *Oh, hey, how you doing?* look, hands in pockets. His right hand felt car keys. They represented escape. Just in case. "Heya," he said. "Just locking up for the night."

Whitey let the door close behind him and walked forward. "See anything interesting?"

Josh took a breath, let it out. "Just Mr. Dinneck staring off into La La Land, not much else." *Why did you say that, you moron?!?*

"You didn't see anything inside," the man said. "Surprisingly, for a Friday, there was no one here. In fact—"

...Josh began to pull out of the parking lot when he hesitated, pressing the brake harder than he needed to. He blinked. How'd he get here? He looked over his shoulder. The *Greedy Grocer* was closed up, security lights on inside—always the last step in closing. Yeah, he remembered doing that. Then he took a peek into the Weirdo Club. No one home tonight, though. First time that had happened on a Friday. He looked over his shoulder at the club's soaped-over windows. Dark and lonely.

Josh rubbed his eyes. Driving home was getting too routine. He was doing it in his sleep. Not good. He pulled onto Main Street, only then remembering that he wanted to grab a movie from the rack. No, better get home and catch up on his sleep.

Peter Quinn watched the car drive away. He stood silhouetted against the club's lighted window. His experimental prodding into the store manager's head on the previous occasions they'd spoken paid off well tonight. According to Manny Paulson, he and the new minister were close. Now the boy was snooping around. Checking up on Art, no doubt. It wasn't the first time, either. Controlling him was becoming easier. Peter thought he might prove useful to him someday. Maybe. It was good to have options.

Chapter Twenty-Two

Elizabeth O'Brien looked one more time into the mirror over the fireplace mantle, pushing a stray hair back into place and inadvertently releasing three others from captivity. It was no use. Keeping the mop on her head pulled back was the only way to manage some semblance of neatness. Before the night was over, though, she'd be ripping the scrunchy out in exasperation. Her unruly mane would be free to fall back into her face and her food. Some impression that would make.

She wondered again why she cared. Five and a half years and he hadn't sent one letter, one email or Christmas card. Of course, neither had she. She'd learned Nathan was back in town both from Mrs. Conan, and in a call from Josh Everson. All morning Tuesday she'd walked on pins and needles, expecting the inevitable confrontation. When she walked by Mrs. Conan's room and saw Nate sitting at the bedside, her first reaction was to turn around and hide in the break room.

Then she heard his voice, the voice that sounded so much like *home*. She stopped and listened to him work. He was reading from the Bible, of course. He was *always* reading from that book.

She envied him his unwavering faith, but felt frustrated at how pointless it was. She'd reconsidered her convictions only once, six years ago when she'd prayed for the first time in her life. There was never the need to ask Nate's God for anything before. Even that one night, leaning exhausted against her mother's hospital bed, she felt like she was whispering her prayer to the walls and nothing else. Still, was it so much to ask? Her father was gone. All she had left was that woman. Nate was only around for short intervals before jaunting back to school. If her mother died he *would* come home, but not to stay. His plans to become a minister had always been stronger than what he and Elizabeth had. That much she couldn't deny.

The summer after the funeral, after her pleas were ignored and her mother was stolen away, she sat in his room as he packed for his senior year and thought, *it's time to move on.* Nate knew she was alone, knew she needed him, but still was packing up to serve a God who didn't give any thought to her. Then Nate had the *gall* to ask her to come to his church again.

After returning to her empty house that night, she'd cried, knowing it was over. For a long time, the loneliness felt *too* strong. She'd lost her father, her mother, and Nathan Dinneck forever. It occurred to her that there was nothing else to live for. She could end it, walk away from life and maybe, if the New Agers were right, come back as someone else. Get a second chance. Elizabeth was usually smart enough to ignore thoughts like that, but one night the urge was so strong she filled the bathtub. Standing there, fully-dressed beside the tub, she began to plan the best way to die.

Since her mother passed away there had been two conflicting voices in her head, both of them her own. Both had their own opinions. One was quiet, whispering, telling her that things would be OK, time heals, all that *yadda yadda*. The second had darker thoughts which she'd eagerly been nurturing. Nothing was going to get better, the second voice said. Thinking otherwise was pointless. She deserved better and if she couldn't get it, why continue?

With uncharacteristic assertiveness, the first voice chimed in with, *If you take your life in this way, what will be waiting for you on the other side will make today's problems glorious in comparison.* That night, standing by the tub in a moment of indecision, she chose to listen to this other voice. It wasn't Nathan's, though it did sound like something he might say. It got her thinking. This might indeed be her only chance to live in this world. What *was* waiting after death? She never held much stock in the concept of Hell. What if there was nothing at all? The idea sent a wave of fear through her. She put her hand on the lever to open the drain, ready to forget the whole thing. Still, she hesitated. The voice, once so subtle but in that moment more insistent than ever, said, *Use the life you have, if not for yourself then for others. Be patient, believe in yourself. There are other people, with their own trials. Help them....*

It was an idea filled with inspiration. She thought of Nathan. He was giving up so much for his own calling. He was a smart kid, would have succeeded at anything he tried, but he chose a path of service.

Elizabeth understood then, her hand lingering on the lever, that this was an option for *her*, too. Obviously not the same as his, but if she was so ready to throw her life away, why not... *recycle* it? Since it wasn't doing much in the way of helping her own situation, change it to one that helped another's.

She'd thought often about going to school for nursing. She'd inherited the house from her parents, and its mortgage had been paid off with the money from her father's life insurance policy. She had enough money from her mother's insurance and bank accounts to carry her. And there might be financial aid out there. She supposed she could give school a shot.

And if the voice was right, it might be the only chance she had left.

It was odd, thinking these thoughts as if they'd come from someone else. She was alone in the world, in the same small bathroom where her mother used to sing while baby Elizabeth took a bath, where her mother would wash her hair, pat her dry.

She knew the tub would still be there if this new idea didn't pan out. A disturbing thought, and one which had prompted her on that lonely night to push the lever down and send the water swirling into the drain.

Now as she waited for Nathan, five years later, Elizabeth thought about that night again. She was a different person from the one crouched by the tub. At least she hoped so. Over time she had dated other men, including Nathan's best friend Josh—though she often worried about revealing that bit of news to him. Josh never had. He'd said as much when he called to tell her Nate was coming home. The relationship had lasted almost a year, then fizzled out. He and Nate were too close, his presence always lingering between them. They'd started as friends, and ended their romance the same way, though with more distance between them afterwards.

Headlights on the street outside, pulling to a stop in front of her house. Her heart raced with a mixture of fear and apprehension. The more she thought about this date, the more she wondered if this was taking a step backwards. She'd built a life for herself here, and she was happy. Alone, but happy.

Nate got out of the car and walked the path toward the door. Maybe, she thought, adjusting the scrunchy in her hair and opening the door, it wasn't so much falling back as stepping forward. They'd taken time to become their own people. Maybe they were ready to try again.

Yeah, right, she thought. The Atheist and the Pastor. Would make an interesting movie-of-the-week. Perhaps not all her cynicism had been washed down the drain that night. The idea worried her.

"Hi," Nate said after walking onto the porch.

In her mind, she dropped the tub's lever again and sent that dark inner voice swirling away. She moved forward and held him in a long, quiet hug. She was showing too much weakness, but at the moment she didn't care. She needed to be held, by Nate and no one else.

"I missed you," she said.

He must have understood she needed this closeness since he did not move away. Instead he whispered, "I missed you, too."

Elizabeth stopped thinking then; simply breathed in the comfort and love which she thought was lost forever. Maybe it still was. For the moment, though, she was happy.

Chapter Twenty-Three

The Sole Proprietor in Worcester had tripled in size since he'd last been here. In a way it was a relief to Nathan that this visit - to what had always been their mutually favorite restaurant - didn't feel like "the good old days." It felt new; *she* felt new. Over the years of their separation, he'd come to realize how dependent he and Elizabeth had become on each other. Sitting with her now in this landmark of their past, Nathan understood the time apart had, in a way, benefited them both.

They talked of events in town over the years, who was still around and who wasn't. Conversation never dragged, never became uncomfortable. If any sore spots were hit, Elizabeth was quick to change the subject with a quick, "Let's change the subject" preface. That was one attribute which had not changed about her. Elizabeth O'Brien was never one to mince words.

They were seated at adjacent corners of the small table, much like they'd been in the break room. It was how they'd always sat together at restaurants. Tonight they fell naturally into their respective positions, no uncomfortable hesitation. The food was delicious. It always was. Seafood always tasted fresher in a New England restaurant. Everything in Florida tasted *shipped in*. A fallacy, he knew. The state was surrounded by ocean. When he mentioned this to Elizabeth, she laughed, and told him food always tastes better at home.

She fell quiet then. Nathan assumed there would always be lingering pain, a sense of loss somewhere in her. It was a place he might be able to fill. He chided himself for being too optimistic. *Revel in her company*, he thought, *and make no assumptions*.

He said, "I saw Josh at the store last night. You two still keep in touch?"

She shrugged, "Not as much as we used to." She took a bite of her scallops. Nathan could feel some *other shoe* hanging above her answer, so he waited. Finally, Elizabeth looked up and, blushing, said, "We dated for a little while. Did you know that?"

She never broke eye contact, wanting to catch his reaction. A weight dropped into his stomach. He started to speak, stopped, broke a piece of fish off with his fork but did not lift it to his mouth. "Um, no," he said finally. "No, I didn't know that."

Why didn't he know? How could he not have? Josh never said anything about it. Never!

"Well, it wasn't like he was sneaking around behind your back or anything. You and I weren't..." she caught herself and stopped. This was a dangerous moment. Elizabeth put down her own fork and laid a hand on Nathan's. His arm twitched, but when he realized that he had almost pulled his hand away, he turned it palm-up and closed his fingers around hers.

"Sorry," he said, not sure what he was sorry for. Unfamiliar pangs of jealousy. It was a strange feeling. More than once over the years he wondered if she was dating, serious about someone else, and this same stomach-turning, dry-throat panic would hit him. Not as strong as this moment, having to face the reality so directly.

She said, "I'm sure he kept it quiet because we were never sure if anything would come of it."

Nathan looked at her, willed himself to be rational. Still, the idea of Josh and Elizabeth being together felt like... betrayal. "I'm being selfish," he said, "feeling like I am right now."

Elizabeth smiled that wide, real smile which always—this moment included—made him feel special for reasons he could never fathom. She squeezed his hand and whispered, "Yes, Nate. You are being selfish." With her free hand she held her thumb and forefinger close together. "Just a little. If you were in his shoes, you'd have stayed quiet, too."

He wasn't sure about that. But not being in that position, he accepted it. "What happened? I mean, why did you stop?" He had to force the words out.

Elizabeth speared another scallop with her fork and chewed, her eyes looking sideways. Finally, she said, "We both...." She never finished the sentence, instead speared another scallop and popped it in her mouth.

"Both what?" he said.

She signed, finished chewing, then waved the fork between two fingers for emphasis. "Both... decided it wouldn't work out. Let's leave it at that." He didn't think that was what she was going to say, but let the answer be. Elizabeth released his hand and punched him hard in the arm.

"Ow!"

"Oh, stop complaining and eat your veggies. They're good for you."

And that was the end of that. The remainder of their meal continued amiably. Elizabeth asked about his parents. Finding himself in a somewhat more somber mood, he talked about his father's situation, the uncertainty around the men's club. He struggled to keep the growing emotion from his voice.

Even with her many whimsical adventures during their childhood, Elizabeth had always been the practical one. She suggested he simply pay the Hillcrest Men's Club a surprise visit. Granted, his father would be upset, but he sounded upset already based on their phone conversation. Nathan nodded his agreement, thinking he could use his new role as pastor as a viable excuse for the visit. Learn more about local town groups and such. No one would buy that line, but it gave some rationale other than merely checking out his father's new friends. He told her it would have to wait until the following week. Hayden's last service as pastor was tomorrow, then Monday he was leaving. Too much to do at the church before that happened.

Perhaps because the conversation finally led to the subject, they talked about his new job, moving closer now to more fragile ground. She was genuinely interested, though, especially when he mentioned the fainting spell. He *had* to tell her. She'd hear about it eventually. Nathan used the opportunity to explain about the strange dreams he'd had, though did his best to downplay their impact. Sitting with her in this place, finishing their meals and debating on whether dessert was really such a good idea, these issues didn't seem worth dampening the mood any more than had already been done. He was content for the moment, and wanted to remain so.

Apparently, so did Elizabeth, since she accepted his noncommittal shrug when she pressed the issue, and moved onto another topic.

The evening eventually wound down and he drove her home. During the fifteen minute trip from the city they talked some more, but they were approaching the inevitable goodnight portion of the date. Both wondered about the next step.

When they stood on her front porch, Elizabeth didn't offer to have him come in. He wouldn't have accepted anyway. This particular date felt over. God willing, they had plenty of time.

Nathan took her hands in his and said, "Thanks. I had a good time."

"Me, too."

There followed a brief moment which, looking back on it later in the quiet of the living room above the kitchen, Nathan could not successfully recall. A moment between her reply and the ensuing kiss. He must have crossed the two feet separating them, but he did not remember doing so. He was simply there, kissing her, realizing how new it felt, how comfortable. It ended with a prolonged embrace. Try as he might not to say anything to break the moment, he eventually pulled back and said, "I've always loved you, you know."

He winced when he said it, but once spoken, he could never take the words back. He didn't regret what was said specifically, as much as feel it was the wrong time to say it.

Elizabeth still knew him better than anyone, even after all this time. She had proved that more than once since their reunion at the nursing home. At his proclamation, she smiled and laid a hand on his face.

"I know," she said, then gave him a pat on one cheek. "Good night, Sweet Prince."

She opened the front door and stepped inside.

"Good night," he said, and turned to leave.

Her voice stopped him mid-stride. "Are we still going to go on dates like this when you become the official Grand Poobah over there?" She nodded her head in the general direction of the church.

Her implication that his feelings for her might, in some way, be reciprocated lifted a hundred pounds off his shoulders. He almost laughed with the joy of it. "Absolutely. Just remember I'll be pretty much on call twenty-four-seven starting Monday." He shrugged embarrassedly.

Before she closed the door she said, "Such a popular boy, my man is."

Nathan's walk to the car, and the drive home, were lost in a turmoil raging in his head.

My man, she had called him.

She wanted to see him again.

Try as he might to suppress his excitement—he was a grown-up now and shouldn't be acting so love-struck—he couldn't stop grinning, picturing himself as Rudolph the Red-Nosed Reindeer in that Christmas animated special, jumping through the air yelling, *She said I'm cute!*

The kiss was unplanned. He assumed Elizabeth understood that any future dates would not go any *further* than that, at least until—

Until what? Could he possibly be thinking of marriage? She didn't even believe in God. History showed that preaching the Word to Elizabeth was a sure-fire way to send her running. Besides, she might not be considering anything long-term. Not anymore.

But they *belonged* together. Aside from his own calling to the ministry, nothing else in his experience ever felt so right. He needed to be patient, trust God's plan for them.

Whatever that might be.

Chapter Twenty-Four

Monday morning brought a cool breeze and the smell of changing leaves. Autumn had arrived at last. The dramatic changes in New England seasons were an aspect of home Nathan missed most during his tenure in Orlando. Standing on the sidewalk in front of the church, Reverend Hayden consulted a well-worn list. The sheet was wrinkled from constant handling. He looked from the list to the suitcases and bags on the sidewalk.

"Have you got everything, Pastor?" Nathan asked. Hayden waved away the question with one of his dismissive gestures then tucked the list into the back pocket of his chinos.

"It's amazing," he said. "All these years, and what do I leave with? Two suitcases and two bags of books. You'd think I'd have accumulated more stuff, eh?"

Nathan smiled. "You always said we should accept whatever God offers and want for nothing else."

Hayden grumbled, "Is that what I said? All those sermons and you just remember that one. I suppose it's true. Jeannie was the pack rat of the family. Over the years, all that bric-a-brac found its way into church fairs, charity or what-not. She would have liked it that way. I was always more of a minimalist."

He screwed up his face, doing his best to maintain an impatient, almost cranky façade. This church had been his home, serving the parish was the meaning of his life for over thirty years, and he'd been alone doing it since Jean Hayden went to the Lord thirteen years before.

Today it was over.

Nathan wanted to put a hand on his shoulder, offer some comfort. It would be the wrong thing to do, to knock down the emotional wall Hayden had built.

"I'll make you proud, I promise."

A rusted SUV approached. Its directional light came on and the car pulled to a stop in front of them. Hayden ignored it. "You make sure no more fainting spells. Life can be traumatic enough without the pastor adding any drama."

"I promise. You sure you don't want to leave some of this here until you're back in town?"

Hayden shrugged and said simply, "No, no."

Vincent Tarretti emerged from his Blazer and walked casually up to the two men. His face was its usual emotionless mask.

"Reverend," he said, nodding his head to Hayden, then turned toward Nathan. "Reverend," he repeated, with a slight trace of a smile.

"Vincent," said Hayden. "I'm sorry. I should have told you what day I was leaving."

He shrugged. "Not to worry. I heard about it. Wanted to catch you before you left, see if you have everything you need."

A car drove by slowly, but did not stop. Nathan looked up and saw his father's friend Mr. Paulson, watching them from behind the wheel. The car rolled past. Nathan felt a tightening in his stomach he couldn't explain. Why did that man make him nervous?

"No, I'm all set, but thank you just the same. Just showing my young protégé here how few items I have to take along."

Tarretti looked down at the luggage, then back up at Hayden. To Nathan, he seemed distracted. "Well, if you think you have everything. Nothing I can help you with?"

The old man patted Tarretti's shoulder and lifted a suitcase. "No, Vincent, but thank you for the offer. I have everything I need right here."

A blue sedan arrived, pulling to the curb in front of the Blazer. "Besides," he added, "my ride's here, and they don't appreciate too many material goods in the monastery. Too much of a distraction."

Tarretti nodded. "The one in Leicester?"

"The one and the same."

The man who emerged from the other car looked younger than Nathan, wearing long tan robes tied at the waist with a rope sash. The monk's attire was a stark contrast to the modern world. He introduced himself as Brother Armand. After perfunctory introductions, he proceeded to load Hayden's luggage into the trunk of his car. Vincent and Nathan helped, and by the time the trunk was closed, Hayden was already in the passenger seat.

He rolled down the window and shook their hands. Brother Armand got behind the wheel and started the motor.

"Take care of your flock, Pastor," Hayden said. "Above all else, there is nothing more important than them."

"Agreed, Reverend. Good luck."

"Vince...."

"Goodbye, sir. It was a pleasure. If you need anything, just—"

But Hayden had pressed the window switch and there was suddenly glass between them. Tarretti and Nathan watched the blue sedan pull from the curb and followed its progress until it wound around a corner out of sight.

*   *   *

Vincent had made it a point to check the weight of the old man's bags, try and feel some of the power he remembered from so long ago. No indication that he was leaving with anything more significant than socks and underwear. The grave had not been opened; he'd set his alarm for three o'clock this morning to check. He'd left Johnson in the house, much to the dog's displeasure, and quietly crept along the grounds and into the woods, unseen by anyone who might be stationed nearby to keep a watch on him. It had taken almost an hour to reach Greenwood Street Cemetery via his pre-planned route through the back streets of Hillcrest. Only when he was at the base of the grave did he risk turning on the flashlight from his backpack and examining every detail around the site. Nothing looked disturbed; no more than small burrowing signs caused by a chipmunk or mouse.

He now looked askance at Nathan Dinneck, who seemed uneasy with Vincent's silence. Obviously the preacher wanted to get back inside and start his first official day in charge. Vincent had been silent for twenty-seven years, cautious and careful for almost half of his life. Now, he wanted to grab this young pup, shake him, ask if *he* was the one, the "priest" to carry the lost contents of the Ark to a new, safer place. His tongue was stayed by twenty-seven years of walking among the headstones of the town's cemeteries, of blending into the background like a chameleon, never drawing attention to himself. He continued to stare, until finally Dinneck broke the silence.

"Well, I guess I'll be heading inside now. Lots to do." He laughed nervously, started to offer his hand, but withdrew it, realizing the gesture would not be reciprocated. Vincent finally forced himself to blink and look away.

"Yep," he said, "me, too." He walked to his car. "Call me if you need anything."

"I will."

Chapter Twenty-Five

The silence of the night permeated everything. His cell, the hall outside. Ralph Hayden shifted uncomfortably on the bunk. The dark was so complete he couldn't see his own hand held in front of him. The normal nighttime sounds of cars along Dreyfus Road, the occasional barking dog, voices of walkers passing the church, these had been the background noise of his life for thirty years. Already he missed it... that, and the extra thick mattress which he assumed Nate Dinneck would now be using. A bed Ralph and Jean shared in their glorious, if too brief, time together. Living their dream.

The dormitory where he lived, for the time being, was nestled in the midst of the sprawling monastery in the rural town of Leicester, southwest of Worcester. Surrounded by over one hundred acres of private property, the room's daytime view consisted only of what could be seen through the narrow window, now closed tightly against the outside chill. He was already looking forward to the day when he came home, albeit to the Grazen Street apartment. He would attend services not as pastor but as a member of the congregation. But not just yet. His presence would prove intimidating to Nate. Best lay low, as he'd planned; let the boy stake his place in the parish.

So quiet, here; time to think and pray, look for answers on how best to spend the rest of his life. At the moment, there was no sound but his own breathing and constant shifting on the unfamiliar bed. The walls were concrete, looking like a stage version of the medieval castles they were built to represent, blocking all sounds including, he assumed, any snoring from the brothers sleeping in adjoining cells. The bouquet of flowers on the nightstand, sent by the parish according to the small card inserted among the stalks of off-season tulips, filled the room with the sweet odor of spring. It helped lighten the weight of his solitude.

He raised his left arm to what he hoped was a position in front of his face and pressed the illumination button on his watch. Ten-thirty. And he was still awake.

Give it time, he told himself. *This was not a mistake.*

He released the button but the dial's after-glow hovered before him. The cell door opened and closed. The outer hall was as dark as the room, so he could not see any details. Any fatigue he'd been fighting this night washed away.

Propping himself on one elbow, he whispered, "Hello?"

"Good evening, Reverend. I trust you're comfortable?"

Hayden struggled to place the voice. He could not. The brotherhood spoke so infrequently, he wouldn't recognize their voices anyway. The fact that this man had entered his cell so late in the evening, in the dark, set his heart beating in fear.

Then the light clicked on. He closed his eyes to the sudden glare, but opened them as quickly as he could and blinked away the sudden brightness.

The first thing he noticed was that the man standing before him was definitely not from the monastery. Though he wore all black, including a black knit hat, he resembled more a businessman than a burglar.

Then he noticed the gun held unwaveringly in the stranger's right hand.

He sat up and swung his legs over the edge of the bed, conscious that he wore only pajamas.

"Who are you?"

The man raised the pointer finger of his left hand to his lips and whispered, "Quietly, now. I've come to take back what is ours."

Hayden's mind was spinning. Had this man stayed in this same cell once and left something behind? No, he was holding a *gun* after all.

"You're a thief?"

"I'm a priest of Molech, the one true god. I've come for the Ark, old man. I don't have time for discussion. Did you really think we would let you simply waltz out of town with it?"

The man was insane. If Hayden called for help, would he be shot? Not that his frightened voice would carry through the walls. From the determined look on the other's face, being shot was highly possible. He had to stay focused. This turn in events made him dizzy. All he could think to say was, "What Ark?"

The smiled without humor. "The Ark of the Covenant, Reverend. You know what I mean. I want it. I want the tablets containing your pathetic commandments, and whatever else might be hidden inside. I want the power. *He* wants the power, that which has belonged to him since the time of Solomon. He wants the doorway to heaven opened wide." He smirked, but said nothing else.

The old pastor tried to stand, but fear drained the strength from his legs. What could he say? He knew with dreadful certainty that this man would not believe anything he told him.

"I don't understand, really I don't. I have nothing like what you describe. No one does." He realized suddenly that simple reasoning might work. Just give the man facts. "The tablets and their holy receptacle disappeared thousands of years ago. They're lost, forever. Very likely they no longer even exist. There were so many wars, it is unlikely it remains. I'm sorry."

The intruder's unsmiling face dropped completely. It flushed with anger.

"You are a minister. We are close. You know it, and so do I. You will tell me where it is—*now*—or I will kill you."

Hayden closed his eyes, and prayed for strength. A certainty filled him that he would die by this man's hand. There was nothing he could do, except ask for courage to face it. There would be so much wondrous beauty on the other side.

Some semblance of strength returned to his legs. He stood. "I don't have what you're looking for." He involuntarily winced, waiting for the bullet.

The man stepped forward and grabbed his arm. "Oh, no. Not here. You will walk out with me, and you will not say a word. I have so many more questions for you, but in this moment you will not make any noise. If any of your new friends see us, I will kill them. Do you understand?"

Hayden nodded. The man led him into the dark hall, their path illuminated only by a narrow beam of light from a penlight produced from his pocket.

Hayden wondered how he'd found him among the many hallways and rooms of the four buildings in the estate. Perhaps he was not looking for him specifically, but only chose a random cell. It was possible. As he was led through a side door and out into the chilly night, he hoped he would have a chance to find out.

In his heart, however, Ralph Hayden knew that he would never be coming back.

Chapter Twenty-Six

"**I**'d say it was a mutual agreement," Josh said, and took another sip of Coke. Nathan guessed his friend would have preferred to bring along a six-pack of beer as a church-warming present instead of the soda, but Josh knew him well enough to know the strongest thing he ever drank was black coffee. Beer and wine were tastes Nathan had never acquired, nor wanted to. They sat in the small kitchen, the church hall beyond dark and silent.

Tuesday evening, the end of his first full day as pastor. When Hayden was here, his presence had never been overpowering, but now that he was gone, the place felt empty, as if the house mourned his departure.

Josh had called earlier to see if Nathan was busy doing "church stuff." Nathan invited him over, looking forward to the visit, but harboring some dread, too. As soon as he'd received the call, he wanted to shout *Why didn't you tell me about you and Elizabeth?* and that same feeling in the pit of his stomach returned. He didn't say it, but early on into Josh's visit, the subject needed to be broached. If nothing else, it might exorcise the demon of jealousy, which kept rearing up over his shoulder—or in his stomach, as the case may be.

"You could have told me, you know."

"Yeah, I suppose. Almost told you the other day at the store but...." He trailed off, took a sip of his drink and shrugged. "Hindsight is twenty-twenty and all that. I just couldn't help thinking I was doing something wrong. I knew how you two felt about each other and, well, Kaila and I had broken up a few months before. Elizabeth and I, well, we started spending more time together. After a while, it seemed like we were dating, so we just decided to play the role. We didn't; I mean it was *almost* platonic."

He winced, obviously regretting where his words were leading. He continued, "Anyway, after me and Elizabeth called it quits, Kaila and I got back together. As you *do* know, that didn't work out too well in the end."

Nathan knew that story—sans the interlude with Elizabeth. Kaila recently married a man named Roderick (that was his *first* name, Josh was quick to point out with a roll of his eyes), and Josh hadn't been seeing much of anyone for the past year. That was another surprise. He tended to be a ladies' man, with natural good looks and half-day beard growth that never seemed to shave completely off. It added movie-star charm to his appearance.

Nathan didn't want to press, but he wanted to know more about Josh and Elizabeth's breakup. It was human nature, he supposed, the need to *know*.

He hadn't seen Elizabeth during his rounds at the nursing home this morning, and missed her all the more because of it. Nursing schedules rotated to assure weekend coverage. It would have been nice knowing they had another date planned. If nothing else, it would have been a mental anchor during this conversation.

"So," he pressed, "it just wasn't working out, you and Elizabeth?"

Josh put the can down with too much force and said, "Oh, for crying out loud, Nate." Though he spoke with an overlay of exasperation, he tried to suppress a grin. "You two were made for each other. I mean, if I had to pick one reason out of many for why she and I weren't compatible except as friends, it's that we both love the same man." He blushed, lifted the can and pointed with one finger. "Now don't go getting any ideas. I'm not that way."

Nathan laughed, but said nothing. How could he open up, even to his best friend, about his feelings for Elizabeth when that same friend once dated her, short-lived as the relationship had been? Then again, Josh had just said it himself, hadn't he?

As if reading his thoughts, Josh added, "You still love her, that much is obvious; and seriously, Buddy, she digs you just as much."

"Digs?"

Josh shrugged. "Yeah, hippie talk is coming back, didn't you know? We get to say *dig* and *groovy* like we did when we were six."

"So what about you? Seeing anyone now?"

"Naw, taking a sabbatical from the opposite sex for a while. But I'm keeping busy."

The kitchen phone began to ring. Nathan stood and cleared his throat, knowing that most of the congregation used the main church line. "Pastor Dinneck," he said, realizing with a start that this was the first time he'd answered the phone this way. *Feels kinda good*, he thought, not without a little shame.

"Pastor, hello. This is Brother Armand. I'm sorry for calling so late."

"Not at all," he said. "How's Reverend Hayden settling in?"

"That's just it. They suggested I call you, to see if he's contacted you."

Contacted? "No," Nathan said, drawing out the word. "Last time we spoke was yesterday morning. I could check my machine, though."

"Could you?"

Something was wrong. Nathan wanted to question the monk further, but if Hayden did leave a message it would explain everything. Even as he walked into the office, he didn't expect to see the answering machine's light blinking. Nathan had listened to all the messages when he came home this afternoon.

There were three messages on the machine. The light wasn't blinking, which implied none of them were new. Still, he pressed PLAY and listened to the first. When he was sure he'd already heard it he pressed NEXT, then again to the third. He returned to the phone with the last message—Josh asking if he wasn't busy with his church stuff—still playing behind him. As he reached for the phone, he heard Josh mutter, "I really sound like that?"

"I'm sorry, Brother Armand. Reverend Hayden hasn't called. Isn't he there?"

"I'm afraid not. This morning he missed breakfast. When I went to his cell, he was gone. No one has seen him all day."

"He moved out already?"

"That's the odd thing. His belongings are still in the room, including his coat and shoes, even the bouquet of flowers your parish sent him." Nathan didn't remember ordering any flowers, but likely one of the elders had taken it upon themselves. Armand continued, "We assumed he might have gone for a walk, if he brought a second pair of shoes. But we've covered the grounds as best we could. They suggested I check with you."

"They?"

"The police."

"The police?" At these words, Josh looked up. Nathan gave his friend's raised eyebrow a shrug in response.

"Yes. They say it's too early to file a missing person's report, and to be honest, I don't think there's any real need to worry, but...."

Nathan swallowed, suddenly feeling in his heart what the unspoken words of the monk were. "But... what?"

The voice on the other end sighed heavily. "Well, Ralph has been pastor of your church for so long, perhaps this might have been too much of a change for him. I've seen men who have worked hard at their job for decades come apart once they retire. Sitting at home, not having direction. I don't want to speculate. I'm not a psychologist, but the thought is troubling."

Nathan suddenly had an urge to end the conversation. "Tell you what," he said. "I'll call around to some other people he was close to, see if he's called them."

The monk's voice took on new hopefulness. "Yes, exactly. If you know anyone he might have called, that would be the thing to do right now." He gave Nathan his phone number and asked him to call if he learned anything. Nathan agreed and gave Armand his cell number, asking him to call anytime day or night if Hayden should return.

When he hung up, his grip lingered on the handset. He tried to brush away a pervading sense of dread. Again, he wondered how selfish he'd been, worried about himself and his own acclimation to this place. He should have given more thought to Hayden. He might have had a harder time moving away than anyone had suspected. *Here's your watch, Reverend. Your life is over.*

"I assume that was about your old boss?"

Josh's voice startled him and he let go of the phone. "What? Oh, yeah. He's gone."

Josh got up slowly, put his empty can on the counter. "Gone?"

"Yeah, as in disappeared. Listen, I hate to cut this visit short, but I think I'd better call some people." He looked up at the clock on the kitchen wall. "It's late, but the sooner I find out—"

Josh raised his hand. "Say no more, Nate. Give me a call if you hear anything. Not sure who the guy knows; otherwise I'd offer to make some calls myself."

Nathan walked him through the church to the front door, since his friend had parked his car beside Nathan's. He put a hand on Josh's shoulder. "Thanks. I guess this is going to be par for the course, though maybe not this kind of incident—*hopefully* not. But, calls will come in at all hours."

Josh smiled, then hesitated. "No hard feelings about the Elizabeth thing?"

"None," Nathan lied, and opened the door. So many mysteries had been passing under his nose lately, it bothered him to have to deal with the fact that his oldest friend had been keeping something from him. Jealousy, he knew. It would fade in time.

He stood by the door watching Josh's car pull onto Dreyfus Road. He tried to recall names of those closest to Hayden. Mrs. Zawalich and Mrs. Lewis, of course, but he shouldn't call them so late. If they had nothing to report, his call would only keep them up. Best make a note to call them first thing in the morning.

Vincent Tarretti. The name came to him and immediately made sense. The two men at least *seemed* close. Even if Tarretti hadn't heard, he might be able to supply more names for Nathan to call.

Decision made, he went into Hayden's den—*his* den now—and pulled the address book from the top left hand drawer. It was an old, well-worn leather volume, phone numbers of parishioners and church offices written in neat, boxy handwriting, sometimes crossed out and replaced with new ones where they would fit. Nathan made a mental note to computerize the list first chance he got. He couldn't find Tarretti's phone number at first, not until he had inspiration to look under "C". An entry for "Cemetery", and Tarretti's name written below.

Nathan punched in the numbers on the desk's squat black phone. It was answered after three rings.

"Hillcrest Memorial Cemetery, Vincent Tarretti speaking."

"Mister Tarretti, hi. Nathan Dinneck here. Hope I didn't wake you."

"Reverend Dinneck, how are you? Call me Vince, please. No, you didn't, though I *was* making motions. Hang on a second." A thunk-thunk sound of the phone being placed down onto a table, then shuffling papers. His voice returned. "OK, go ahead. Deceased's name?"

"Um," Nathan whispered. "What?"

"Decea— oh, sorry. Pastor Hayden and I never minced words when he called to plan a funeral. I assume someone has passed away?"

"God, I hope not," was all Nathan could say, but now that he had the thread of conversation back, he decided he'd better try and recover from his *Um, What?* remark. "Sorry, Vince. That's not why I'm calling."

He heard the unmistakable sound of papers landing on the table. "Oh. OK, then what's up?" His voice had changed from professionalism to irritation. Nathan had to remind himself that he might have, indeed, woken the man.

"It's about Pastor Hayden. Has he contacted you since leaving?"

The subsequent pause was long enough to give Nathan some hope. Then, "No." Like Nathan's answer to Armand's question, the word was drawn out, almost a question in and of itself. "Why?"

Chapter Twenty-Seven

Nathan explained the call from Armand and the pastor's disappearance.

Another long silence followed. Nathan didn't wait for Tarretti to speak. "Listen, Vince, I'm sorry for such a late call, but I thought even if he hadn't called you, you might know other people he might have contacted."

"No one at the monastery saw him, you're saying? No word, no note?"

"No."

Then Vincent cursed, loudly, and Nathan felt that omnipresent mystery close around him again. It was an irritating sensation. So much so, that he responded with a louder, less careful tone to his voice.

"What's going on, Mister Tarretti?"

"Nothing."

"That's a lie." Nathan was gripping the phone, his exasperation and confusion suddenly too much to hold in. "It's like you aren't surprised Hayden is gone."

"If there's nothing else, Reverend, I'd like to—"

Nathan shouted, "You will stay on this phone and tell me what is going on! I've had enough of mysteries to last me the rest of my life. Ever since I've come here, it's been one strange thing after another, and now I can't help thinking you might know more than you're letting on. Where is Reverend Hayden?"

"Strange things like what?" Tarretti asked. Nathan felt his irritation growing with every nonsensical turn of the conversation. This man was ignoring everything he said. He took a breath, decided to ignore the caretaker's questions just as the man was doing to him. "Where is Pastor Hayden?"

"I don't know."

"Why didn't you sound surprised that he went missing?"

"I *was* surprised. Sorry for not acting the way you expect me to. I've a lot on my mind."

"Like what?"

"That's none of your business."

"I'm afraid it is my business. Ever since we first met, I sensed something strange about how you've acted toward me. Why is that?"

"Maybe you're paranoid."

Nathan took a breath, realizing he *was* starting to sound that way. *Lord give me strength. I feel I'm near something, but what is it? Why am I carrying on like this?*

"Reverend?"

"I apologize for snapping. Between getting ready to take over the church, concerns for my father, I haven't been sleeping well. I'm afraid with this new situation I might simply be taking out my frustration on you." He didn't mean these words, wanted to scream into the mouthpiece, but he forced himself down a notch.

"Apology accepted. Sorry you're not sleeping well. Bad dreams?"

Nathan took in a reflexive breath. The question had been asked innocently enough, but in his current state of hyper-alertness, it struck him like a rock. *Don't wig out now. He was only trying to make nice.*

"Reverend?"

"Nothing to worry about. If I *was* having nightmares they've stopped. Anyhow, can you think of any place Pastor Hayden might have gone?"

An extended silence again, but Tarretti's voice returned sooner than the last time. "I really don't know. I wish I did. What were your nightmares about, when you had them?"

"Why do you keep turning the conversation around?" He didn't understand why, but Nathan suddenly wanted to confide in this man, tell him everything. It made no sense. Nathan was calling about Hayden's disappearance, not for a therapy session. "Never mind about my dreams. If you hear of anything, or think of something, please let me know."

"I will."

"Thank you."

"Please call me if *you* hear anything."

Nathan said he would and hung up. He sat back in the desk chair and covered his face with his hands. The conversation had gotten away from him. Tarretti was only being polite, maybe trying to calm a panicked minister. The man couldn't maintain a single thread in a conversation, but it was late, and he'd probably woken him up. His heart beat quickly, as if he'd just sparred with the caretaker in a boxing ring.

He lowered his hands and took in another breath, felt himself calm. Confrontation was never an easy thing for him. What, exactly, this particular confrontation had been *about,* he didn't know.

Not really.

His nerves, his nightmares, had nothing to do with the disappearance of Reverend Hayden. Somehow the discussion seemed to lead that way. Not for the first time, Nathan wondered if he was ready to head a church on his own.

He held off calling anyone else. The news had obviously disturbed him more than he'd realized. Hayden would be OK; likely wandered away in confusion inspired by his new surroundings. He'd turn up. He had to. Nathan would make as many calls as necessary in the morning, until he found out the truth.

He sat a while longer, letting his jangled nerves settle, then got up and turned off the light on the desk and the one in the kitchen before heading upstairs. He thought of Vince questioning his dreams. The day in the cemetery, wondering if any particular monument caught his eye. He knew more than he was saying. Nathan's strange visions of the stone angels. Hayden's disappearance.

There was no logical connection. These events were not related.

Chapter Twenty-Eight

Vincent Tarretti remained seated at the kitchen table long after he and Dinneck ended their conversation. He was shaking. Something was happening. Whatever it might be, it was happening.

Hayden had disappeared.

Ruth Lieberman conveyed many scattered facts to him decades ago, before her death to cancer eight weeks after Vincent's arrival in town. There were certain rules God had ordained for the handling and transportation of the Ark; rules that even today must not be broken. One in particular was that it could not be moved by anyone except priests, those ordained by God. There were examples in the Bible of men who ignored this. They died instantly. Vincent didn't know if, in this modern age, any of these rules had changed. Not according to the sometimes-ancient writings kept in the box under the floorboards. Many, especially the older ones, were not written in English. They were scribbled notes in French, Russian (at least it looked like Russian, he couldn't be sure), Hebrew and Latin. Once in a while, Vincent would buy a translation dictionary, convert random sentences to something he could understand. Most were day-to-day notations, like his own. Others chronicled, as best he could tell with his rough interpretation, the sudden uprooting of the Ark's long-secluded resting place. He kept his translations in the books, thinking to convert all the texts, but time and routine kept him too busy. Maybe the next person, whomever God chose to replace Vincent someday, might give it a try.

One recurring theme, however, was that it would be best not to tempt fate. Doing so might question God Himself. Vincent was no priest. That left only a few in town who qualified. Father Carelli from Saint Malachy's, Nathan Dinneck, and Ralph Hayden.

Now Hayden was gone. Vincent had an overwhelming urge to race across town to Greenwood Street, verify—again—that the grave had not been opened. If Hayden was chosen by the Lord to move the treasure, it wasn't up to Vincent to stop him. He was so old, though, and the grave hadn't been opened, at least not Monday morning.

Vincent thought of Peter Quinn's interest in the pastor's departure. It was this interest that prompted Vincent to check on the grave in the first place.

Hayden is a red herring.

The thought felt so true that a renewed sense of urgency took hold. Vincent had spent so long marking every occurrence in town that struck him as out of place. At times, his notes covered nothing more bizarre than the Stop 'N Shop repaving their parking lot. Not once could he remember anything out of the ordinary with Ralph Hayden's behavior. The man never looked at the gravesite more than any other, never mentioned visions or nightmares.

He looked up suddenly, like someone hearing a sudden noise. But there *was* no noise save the constant chirrup of the crickets and late season peepers outside, the distant roar of a jet on its way to or from Logan Airport.

Nathan Dinneck. Noticing the grave, his dreams—whatever they might be about. So many oddities about this new minister. But Dinneck was coming, not going. Maybe the time for change was not as close as Vincent feared. The looming sense of danger might only be a sign of the final stage. Maybe Dinneck *would* be the one, but not for another twenty years.

The new men's club wanted to plant flowers. The white-haired accountant type, Quinn, asked after Hayden. The old man disappeared.

Vincent pounded a closed fist against the table, scattering the forgotten interment forms he'd produced from their folder when Dinneck called. He wished he could pry the nightmares out of that young preacher's head and examine them. Faith was important, but after having spent so many years protecting what lay in the grave, any new step felt dangerous.

He got up and turned off the lights on his way back to bed. Johnson looked up from his rug and offered a concerned wag of his tail. Vincent would pray for the safety of Reverend Hayden, and wait. There was nothing else to do.

Chapter Twenty-Nine

Try as he might, Nathan could not sleep. He sat on the edge of the bed, then slowly slid from this position onto the floor. He knelt, using the mattress as an ad-hoc prayer bench.

God, he thought, *please help me. Am I going mad? This should be a time of great joy, a culmination of everything you've given me.* He leaned further forward until his forehead pressed against the rumpled comforter. *Nothing feels right; it's one of those bad dreams where everything goes wrong. Please.*

He remained prostrate against the bed for a few minutes more. No rumble of thunder, no sudden inspiration in answer to his questions. He was tired, as tired as the day he'd collapsed in the church hall. Nathan pulled himself up and sat back down on the edge of the mattress. He reached to turn off the bedside lamp, then hesitated.

There were a few Bibles scattered throughout the house. He'd placed his New International Version on the bedside table last night— the first night he'd slept in this room. Nathan always liked having the book handy. Good reading to fall asleep to.

He didn't know what to look for, what passage might help him see this insane situation in a new light. He pushed his pillow against the headboard and leaned back, staring unfocused and flipped the pages. The word "Solomon" caught his attention, then disappeared in the blur of passages. Nathan stuck his thumb inside, turned pages backward, then forward again, no urgency in his motion.

Solomon's Wives the heading read.

Tomorrow, Nathan thought.

Read, whispered an almost instinctual voice in his heart. *Just this chapter. Closure, then sleep.*

Nathan took the suggestion and read the chapter. It was the story of Solomon's fall from grace, when the Israelite king chose to worship the false gods of his many foreign wives. In Jerusalem, he built a "high place for Chemosh the detestable god of Moab, and for Molech the detestable god of the Ammonites" and other demons which had their own, unflattering adjectives.

Solomon's actions had been the final straw. This had become the king's fall from grace, how he'd lost his throne to God's wrath. Solomon had put other "gods," the popular demons of that time, before Him. And paid the price.

Nathan looked up, thought of John Solomon's grave. He thought of Tarretti again, of his father. Hayden. Too many threads blowing across his mind, not seeming to be related but somehow all feeling as if they should be.

Long past midnight, the questions still raced like gnats, landing just long enough to bite, then vanishing again. The lamp remained on as he slid into sleep, the book open on his lap.

He did not dream, save vague recollections of flashing images as his brain tried to sort things out while his body regenerated. When he opened his eyes, the sun was shining through the windows. He lay on top on the comforter, never having gotten under the sheets. What day was it? Wednesday. Perhaps he should stay here, not face the day. It seemed a good idea. He'd overslept anyway. The clock read nine thirty-four. He must have appointments for the day, *but stay in bed*, he told himself. Maybe it would all go away on its own.

A muffled shrill broke the reverie. The cell phone, still in his pants pocket. He considered ignoring it, but knew he could not. He was pastor now. He was *responsible*. The thought gave him enough motivation to reach down and fish the phone out before the caller disconnected.

"Hello," he said, staring at the ceiling and realizing too late that he should have answered with "Pastor Dinneck". The salutation hadn't become routine enough yet.

"Well, good morning," a familiar voice said. "Sounds like you just woke up."

"Elizabeth." Hearing her voice, saying her name, washed everything away, cleared his mind. It was a temporary reprieve, but he relished the feeling and sat up on the bed. "Sorry, yeah. I forgot to set the alarm. I was up late reading."

A small laugh. "Must be a good book."

Nathan smiled. "The best."

"Oh, *that* one." Her voice lost none of the mirth, however. "Well, I won't keep you. You probably haven't even brushed your teeth yet."

"Nope."

"I'd forgotten I was off yesterday, so I didn't see you at the nursing home. We never made a date."

Thank you, he thought, *for Elizabeth at least. Whatever else is happening, she is an oasis.*

"Right," he said, and walked from the bedroom. "Hang on a second, I've got to go downstairs to check the calendar." Down the steps like a child on Christmas morning, he turned into the den and opened his desk calendar. "OK, let's see. Tonight's no good, as we've got Bible study. Care to join us?"

"Nope."

"Didn't think so," he said. "I'd say maybe after that, but I have a feeling I'll be a bit pooped. Should get to bed early to make up for last night."

"Everything OK?"

"Actually, no." He told her about Hayden.

"That's pretty bizarre."

"You're not kidding. Let's pick a night, and I might even tell you some more bizarre things."

"Deal," she said. "Tomorrow night, then? I'm off Friday, so I wouldn't have to turn in too early."

"Thursday sounds good."

"Great. I've got to go; break's over."

"Say hi to Mrs. Conan for me. Listen, could you, you know, discreetly ask around today, see if anyone's heard from Reverend Hayden?"

She said she would. They picked a time to meet and Nathan disconnected. Her call was a Godsend, perhaps literally. He checked his calendar for today. Less than forty-five minutes before he had to drive to the city and make his rounds at the University of Massachusetts Medical Center, then downtown to Saint Vincent's. He'd make a few calls about Hayden first, then rush through a shower. It would be a full day. There didn't look to be a break to make it back to Hillcrest until the late afternoon.

Even with everything else going on, Elizabeth's earlier idea of checking out the Hillcrest Men's Club still felt like a good one.

Any answers he might garner from a visit would have to wait until tomorrow. He had inked in breakfast at his mother's house for Thursday morning. Maybe she could give him some ammunition before he drove across town to confront whatever waited for him behind the club's front door.

Plans made, he opened the phone directory and looked up Mrs. Lewis' number. He didn't have the time to dwell on any more mysteries today. Tomorrow he could dredge it all up again.

Chapter Thirty

"**So**," Nathan said before taking a mouthful of scrambled eggs, "I'm going over there today. See what's up."

Beverly Dinneck took a quick sip of coffee and got up from the table. "Here," she said, "let me get you more eggs."

He raised his hand and waved her back to her chair. "Ma, please! Relax. If I eat any more, I'll burst."

She hesitated, her eyes darting as if running through a list of chores to be done and trying to decide if anything else needed attention. Finally, almost reluctantly, she sat back down. Her large fingers played absently with her coffee mug, never quite gripping it, never able to completely release it.

Nathan sat back and put his fork down. "Why so restless?"

Beverly looked at the table, at her mug, the refrigerator, anywhere but at him. "I need to keep busy. I'm so worried about Pastor Hayden, and everything else."

He leaned forward. "Why didn't you come to the Bible study last night? Would've taken your mind off things for a while."

Beverly shrugged, then let out a long, almost wailing sigh. "Oh, I don't know, Nate. I had thought to go, actually, but this was the first one you were attending solo, and I didn't think you wanted your mother hovering."

Nathan smiled. "You wouldn't hover."

"Still, you need to make a place for yourself as a man, not as my son."

What she said made sense, but troubled him. "Mom, the last thing I want is for you to stay away from church because of me."

"There were other reasons." When she said this, her visual scan of the room began again in earnest. Nathan thought he could guess what at least one reason was.

"Dad?"

She nodded. "He was home last night, all night. It was wonderful, not that he's much company. So depressed lately, and exhausted. I've stopped worrying that he's drinking and started to wonder if he's doing some kind of... drugs." She whispered this last word. Nathan thought to tell her that his suspicions weren't much different, but she was worried enough.

"Well, we'll know soon enough what the big mystery is." He rose from his seat and, grateful to be moving about the room again, his mother did likewise.

"Be careful, Nate. Art keeps saying there's nothing bad about that group but I know there is. You've noticed it, too, haven't you? And you've only been around a couple of weeks."

"I never said I thought there was something bad."

For a wonderful moment, Beverly looked at him with her full motherly stare, the one that said *don't try to kid me, Mister. I know better.* "But there is something strange about them, and you *have* noticed it." It wasn't a question.

Nathan smiled. "Yes, I have. And I'm off to see what it is." He hugged his mother, and her arms crushed him into her. She whispered into his ear, "You be careful. I'll be praying for you." He felt his mother's tears land on his cheek.

"That'll be the best thing you can do, Mom. More than you know."

She finally relented and separated herself from her son. Straightening his shirt and wiping her tears off both their faces, she whispered, "I'm going to call Nadine, ask her to pray, too. Help your father, Nate. If you can."

Nathan said he would try, then cleaned up the table, against her vehement objections before leaving. He had an eleven o'clock visit with a parishioner who'd broken both legs courtesy of a skiing weekend in Colorado. That gave him a two-hour window for his sojourn to the men's club. The sooner he did it the better. Not for the first time, he wondered what his father's reaction would be when he found out. It wouldn't be pretty, if their phone conversation the other day was any indication.

Chapter Thirty-One

Nathan parked directly in front of the storefront's glass door, then waited in the driver's seat, tapping one finger absently on the wheel and looking for any activity inside. The only movement was someone entering *Hair U Doing?* next door. He got out of the car, gaze always on the door as if afraid his father would burst outside in a rage. Of course, his car wasn't here. He'd be at work now. Josh's Toyota was outside of the *Greedy Grocer*, however. Maybe he'd swing by for a sanity check if there was time.

He walked up to the club's soaped-over door. There was no name visible anywhere, not at first. When he reached for the metal door handle, he noticed a plain white sticker above it with the letters *HMC* drawn in orange marker. Nathan never considered knocking, no more than he would entering any other store. He pushed the door open and stepped inside.

He had a sudden recollection of himself and Josh, thirteen years old, riding their bikes along Route 12. They'd ridden all the way to the neighboring town of West Boylston. Once there, they passed a row of nondescript but clean brick office buildings. The boys had parked their bikes in front of one and simply walked inside. The "apartments", as the directory in the lobby called the various closed-off rooms inside, contained one anonymous and generic company name after another. Nathan and Josh made it an adventure to walk among the silent halls, drinking from the water bubbler, using the rest rooms, sitting in the chairs lining the disinfectant-smelling hallway and reading outdated magazines. Trespassing in a place that, in retrospect, could care less they were there. At last, though, someone from a small lawyer's office told them they needed to leave.

They ran from the building with hearts racing, mouths and eyes laughing hysterically. Their "escape" was so frantic that they had gone two blocks before remembering they'd left their bikes behind. They had to sneak back to get them.

A half hour, maybe forty-five minutes in the life of two bored kids.

Now, stepping uninvited into the men's club, Nathan recalled the smell of that long-forgotten place, dusty couches and stale air.

Letting the door of the Hillcrest Men's Club close silently behind him, he smelled the aging soap smeared along the inside of the windows and door, the lingering presence of beer.

The room measured roughly thirty by forty feet, devoid of people. At the back right-hand corner stood a small bar, a tall narrow thing one might get for a basement room. Atop it lay an empty Marlboro cigarette box and two beer bottles containing about an inch of old Budweiser. *Bud and Marlboro,* he thought, *can't get much more old-fashioned American.* The sight of these items offered some ironic relief. If the worse he had to deal with was a few beers and second-hand smoke, Art Dinneck might not be in such bad straits after all.

Nathan observed all this without moving any further than two steps into the room. He moved his head slowly, side to side, taking in the rest of the room's innocuous details. Against the back wall, beside the bar, was a closed door, its green paint peeling near the upper hinge. It likely led to a back storage room. This *had* been a store once. *Which* one he couldn't remember. Maybe a hobby shop, but he thought that might have been next door in what was now the carpet place. The furnishings—some cushioned and others simple folding chairs surrounding various-sized tables—were gathered in three groups, not counting the bar and its two stools. One low-riding table had a telephone, its cord running under a section of carpet whose sole purpose, apparently, was to make the area trip-free. Three magazines adorned another table, the topmost being the required *Sports Illustrated.* Across the last was scattered a discarded deck of playing cards.

There were some decorations on the wall, mostly stock paintings which he didn't pay much attention to. The place didn't look like anything more than an abandoned storefront taken over by a bunch of guys drinking beer and playing cards. Not his father's style, but not as bad as Nathan had feared, either. The "HMC" looked like the Little Rascals' *He-Man Women-Haters Club,* but all grown up.

He remembered the frightened, childish fear he felt the other morning when he'd sensed the tension between his parents. Maybe all of this wasn't about Art and this club. Maybe it was always about Art and Beverly. The thought of his parents falling out of love was ludicrous. He shook his head involuntarily. That couldn't be it.

Still, their personal life was as much removed from him as his own was from them. More so. It was an ingrained habit of parents not to confide too much in children.

"Oh, Ma," he whispered. Needing something to do, he walked across the floor, toward the bar and the closed storeroom door. He began to sweat. It happened so quickly and with such force he thought the overhead sprinklers had gone off. His arms and legs felt weak.

Run, run, run, run, his body suddenly screamed. He continued forward, trying to will away the sudden sense of... what was it? Like moments when he'd gone too long without eating, the sudden light-headed craving for food. More than that, though, almost flu-like in its intensity. A sudden, overwhelming *terror*. Blood rushing from his extremities, his body's fight-or-flight reaction kicking into overdrive.

But the room was empty. It made no sense. When he finally stopped walking the room tilted. He turned back toward the door, had to find some way out of the place.

There! Run outside; hurry.

Nathan looked at the peeling green paint on the door at the back. Something was on the other side, out of sight but no less visible to the screaming part of his mind. Something... *heavy*, the word making no sense but fitting with a nightmare logic. *Bad things here*, a panicked voice in his head screamed. He smelled something, a stinging in his nostrils, incense mixed with paint thinner mixed with oranges. Heady, putrid, sour. He walked toward the back door, reaching for it.

RUN!!!

The knob was locked. He leaned forward, finding it hard to stand upright. When he glanced behind him, the front door stretched miles away. He couldn't fall, not here. He let go of the knob, leaned forward, nauseous. It was like the other day after his first service, only much, much worse. He splayed his hands across bent knees, body pressed against the green door.

Please, God, whatever this is, help me deal with it. I need to know.

You need to leave, a voice screamed, more instinctual than concrete.

Please help me get through this.

The smell faded, a little at first, but losing even a fraction of its intensity was like a breeze across his face. The nausea passed, lingering in the back of his stomach should he try anything foolish like trying to open the storeroom door again. He took three cautious steps into the middle of the room. Sweat ran like melting ice under his shirt. It matted his hair. Even his shoes felt wet. The *Bigness* of the back room diminished, like a nightmare dissipating with dawn.

A man's voice behind him said, "I agree this place needs more decorating, but surely it's not that bad." Then the man laughed.

Chapter Thirty-Two

The only thing that kept Nathan from screaming at the shock of hearing the voice was his complete lack of energy. He straightened carefully, not wanting to resurrect the nausea, and faced the speaker. There was nothing immediately worrisome in the man's appearance, only that he'd come out of the back room while Nathan was having what felt like a minor nervous breakdown.

The man was sweating almost as much as Nathan. This was reassuring. Maybe the heater was set too high in here. Whatever it was that had struck him so suddenly seemed to be dissipating. Nathan reluctantly offered his hand.

"I apologize for intruding," he said. "Nathan Dinneck. My dad comes here a lot."

"Indeed he does. I'm Peter Quinn." Quinn took his hand. Nathan had a sudden craving to see what was going on in that back room. The door was still open, just a crack. From where he stood, Nathan could see nothing of what lay beyond except darkness.

Realizing the direction of his guest's stare, Quinn turned and closed the door. "Well, you have my undivided attention. What can I do for you, Reverend?"

Nathan's skin was cooling uncomfortably. He wiped the back of his neck then put his hands in his pockets. "Nothing, really. I just thought I'd visit the place where my father spends so much of his time." He said this with a twinge of irritation, remembering his mother's desperation this morning, and this man's condescending smile.

"An admirable mission for a son. You are interested in joining our humble group?"

"No. Not exactly. Is my father here now?"

At first Quinn simply raised an eyebrow and offered an unspoken answer, looking around the deserted room. "No," he finally said. "I believe he's at work."

Nathan's irritation became stronger, broiling to anger. He didn't understand why, but perhaps seeing this place, this man who had likely played a hand in corrupting his father, at least *changing* him in some way, made the whole situation more tangible. Quinn was someone Nathan could blame. Sin always followed temptation. He tried to remind himself that whatever problem plagued his father, Art Dinneck was ultimately to blame. Not this guy.

"Looks like this place gets a lot of use," Nathan said, trying to sound casual. "Is it usually crowded every night, or just weekends?" He wanted to ask *does my* father *come here every night, or just weekends?*

Peter Quinn laughed, a full, hands on flat stomach guffaw. "Ah," he said at last. "It's very heartening to see how roles between children and parents switch over the years. We're a men's club. That's all. A place for like-minded people to get together and talk outside of their sometimes mundane and restrictive homes. An escape, if you like."

"Maybe I'm wrong," Nathan said slowly, "but I never thought my home, or my mother, were overly restrictive."

He *was* angry. This rage felt wrong, however, forced. He didn't like it. A few minutes ago, he felt sick and terrified. Now he'd swung to the opposite end of the emotional spectrum. He was furious with everything around him. Maybe this was a defense mechanism, but defense against *what?* Nathan took a step forward, uncertain why he'd done it. Quinn's smile faded. His gaze darkened.

"Many things can restrict a man from being what he wants to be, Reverend. Marital strife, even outdated religious beliefs."

He was being goaded, needed to step back and calm down. It wasn't the first time someone tried to find chinks in his faith. But this was so sudden, out of context. And it was said with a victorious gloating. *I shattered your father's beliefs, young Dinneck,* the man's voice implied.

"My father chose his faith, of his own accord. Like everyone." What was the point in arguing like this? As he stood in a posture that could not be mistaken for anything but "squaring off" with Quinn, his thoughts were too jumbled to remember any specific goals he might have had in coming here today.

Quinn nodded. "And everyone has the right to choose for themselves if they want to learn other ways, serve other gods. Even if such a god proves to be nothing but their own wants and desires."

The statement struck Nathan mute. Quinn's voice had taken on a cadence, much like many evangelical preachers he'd listened to in the past. There was a *power* behind it. Sweat broke out again across his back, down his arms.

Speaking slowly, running his words through his own head before speaking, Nathan took a step away, then two. "So, is there some religious or faith-based background to your group?"

He looked at the old paintings on the wall, not focusing on them but needing something other than Quinn's challenging stare to take up his field of vision.

"Any faith or religious beliefs we might have are merely those carried into the doors by our members. We do not condone any specific creed."

Nathan felt a physical strength in Quinn's voice, a charisma to his speech. He tried to ignore it. Before him was a woodland scene, creek running through, a flat reproduction but still powerful in its motion, the name *Robert Gilbert* clear in the corner. Quinn moved with him, matching his slow steps but keeping two paces behind. In the corner of his vision, Nathan detected a trace of a smile.

Another painting, snow-capped peak rising above a vast plain, not as powerful as the Gilbert, but pretty to look at.

He said, "And what about you, Mister Quinn? What do you believe in?" He continued moving slowly, almost sideways across the room, trying to convince himself he was pulling Quinn along rather than being pursued by him. Nathan had gained some control in the short conversation.

"Do not try and convert me, Reverend. My beliefs and yours could not be further apart." Any trace of amusement in Quinn's voice was gone.

Nathan stopped finally and looked at him. More as a statement than a question, he said, "You're an atheist, then?"

Quinn laughed. It was a shallow sound, without mirth. "Hardly. I believe in your God very much. I simply choose not to serve him."

Nathan knitted his brows. The connotation was undeniable. He resumed his slow trek across the room, needing to focus. The way this conversation was heading, he could imagine his father's angry reproach. *How dare you come and preach at my club*, he might say. A week earlier he would never have imagined his father scolding him for such a thing. But now... *Dad, I don't think you understand the nature of this place.*

And you do?

Nathan was beginning to think he did, at the very least the nature of the man who was behind him right now.

He stopped in front of another painting. Unlike the others, this had an ornate dark wood frame. It looked quite old, but the colors were striking, dimensional in their fiery hues. Nathan began to say, "What do you—" but then could no longer speak.

The painting before him was of a desert, deeply colored in oranges and browns. The burning red sun had fallen behind a pyramidal structure. It was a temple, a massive backdrop when compared to the minute hooded figures marching away from the viewer, toward the temple's dark red stone. All were washed in the hues of the dying sun. The walls rose up in stepped tiers, a slightly skewed rendition of an Incan temple.

Nathan knew this place.

Chapter Thirty-Three

The pilgrims were no more than slight, impressionistic dots along the bottom, dwarfed by the structure's magnitude and presence. He imagined them moving as he watched, felt himself pulled forward, lost in the nightmare which had once again invaded his waking world.

He needed to look away, pretend this painting meant nothing. It was too late for that. Seeing this representation of his own private nightmare was too much of a shock. Its impact was not as it might have been, had there not been so many *other* enigmas these past few days. Just another mismatched jigsaw piece dropped in front of him.

"A lovely painting, isn't it?"

Quinn had moved beside him and gazed at the picture.

Nathan's voice was a harsh whisper. "What is it?" Any cards he'd hoped to play close to his chest had just been scattered across the floor. The best he could do was feign indifferent curiosity.

"If you don't mind my saying, Reverend, you look a bit shaken."

His confusion melted back into anger, or maybe this was simply what abject terror felt like. It filled every corner of Nathan's body. The wall around the dark frame, the room itself, was crinkling away. Only the painting's sharp colors offered any clarity. He needed to focus elsewhere, turn away. Instead he whispered, "What is that, that building in the painting?"

The other man said nothing, not right away. Instead he looked alternately between the temple image and his guest.

Nathan wasn't sure if he'd answered. He didn't think so. He closed his eyes, and the pressure around his head lightened a little. He turned to his right before opening them again, no longer trying to keep his composure. He wanted to run screaming into the parking lot but also grab this man and shake the answers out of him.

"Tell me," he said again, with a voice only slightly louder than before, "what that is. Now." This last word surprised him. He didn't like threatening anyone, even subtly. But it was too much. Too much to take in. Too much to accept.

Something changed in Quinn's eyes. They had opened wider and his face softened in some unspoken understanding. An understanding which brought with it a slow, but genuine smile.

"I could say," Quinn said, "that I do not know. But that would be a lie and we both know it." His new stature, both physically and vocally, brushed away any assertiveness Nathan may have been building. In its place was defensiveness. The urge to leave was stronger now, but he was close to... something. Some answer which this man seemed about to give.

Realizing he would get no response, Peter Quinn continued, "It is a rendition of an ancient Ammonite temple, built for the great god Molech." His voice took on a hushed reverence. And something else, a vibration that tickled Nathan's ears. "The greatest of all gods of those days, more powerful than any other. He demanded constant sacrifice and worship. Those pilgrims," he nodded to the painting, and his smile grew, "are celebrating the Feast of the Wind, one of many celebrations in honor of the master."

Quinn walked closer to the picture, leaving nothing between Nathan and the door.

Nathan needed to speak, take back control of the conversation. Quinn, however, was not finished. "At least, I believe that is the festival depicted, based on the depictions of swirling wind in the background, kicking up sand devils among the followers." He laughed at some hidden joke in the statement, but said nothing else.

"Are..." Nathan began, then caught himself. He was going to ask if this man was such a worshipper, a pilgrim like the dots at the bottom of the painting. Of course he was not. A Satanist, perhaps, an avid researcher of old world religions, but the Ammonites were centuries gone and forgotten except by historical and Biblical scholars. He swallowed. "You know quite a lot about this. You've studied the old religions?"

Though he kept an outer calm, Quinn's face belied an inner excitement about the subject. "Studied... yes, I suppose that's one way to put it. Quite extensively. Tell me, Reverend, as you are a scholar of such things in your own way, do you know when the worship of dark gods of such great power was at its peak?"

Nathan knew only of what he'd studied in the Old Testament. The Ammonites—at least the demon Molech, whom they worshipped—were referenced throughout Scripture, as far back as Genesis.

A name, perhaps the most prominent in those biblical chronicles, occurred to him. Nathan felt the room began to spin again. Quinn answered the question for him, moving a step closer.

"A few thousand years ago, during the reign of many famous Jewish kings. David, for one, though he did not pay much attention to the other sects of his time unless they were a threat to his small but powerful little nation." Another step closer. "His *son*, however, ah, he was a different story. Displayed quite an interest in the Ammonites, did he not? Took some rather beautiful wives from among their ranks." He was standing in front of Nathan now.

I want to leave, Nathan thought. *God, please, what is happening?* As had happened when he stared too long at the painting, the room blurred around the face of Peter Quinn. Nathan was in trouble. Every pore in his body that was not sweating screamed at him to leave... *now!* But he was frozen, paralyzed. It was too late to run. He'd had that chance earlier and did not take it.

"David's son," Quinn said, almost in a whisper. Nathan could almost *taste* the power in the voice wrapping around his head. "Solomon. I have studied your book, the stories of his time almost as much—more, in some cases—as your contemporaries. I know details most of your kind choose to ignore. Solomon was enraptured with his Ammonite wives." His breath was sweet across Nathan's face, like incense. "He understood the power of their master, of the true god of that time." He chuckled. "Irritated your little *Yahweh* to no end."

God, help me.

"Does anything I say strike you in particular, Reverend Dinneck? Why did you react so excitedly to this painting? To this story I'm telling you, now? Tell me."

The voice, barely a whisper, a breath, was a vice he could not escape. He had to tell Quinn about his dreams, about John Solomon's grave, the angels. Had to tell him everything. More than that, Nathan realized that he *wanted* to.

When he opened his mouth to speak, a voice across the room shouted, "Hello? Anyone home?" The room came into focus so sharply Nathan gasped and stumbled back. Quinn had such a sudden rage about his face Nathan thought he was going to snarl and leap upon the newcomer.

Josh Everson took another step into the store, his hand still holding the front door's handle.

"Nate? God, Nate, what's wrong?" He ran into the room. From the look on Josh's face, Nathan figured he must look as bad as he felt.

"Excuse me," Quinn said, raising a hand. "Mister Everson is it? We were having a private conversation."

"Excuse me, yourself," Josh said without looking away from Nathan.

Quinn's composure slipped a little, and he said with a more conciliatory tone, "Please, you are trespassing. The reverend and I were having a—"

"Nate, you OK?" Josh asked.

Nathan nodded, but couldn't remember ever feeling less OK in his life. "Josh. What... what are you doing here?"

He shrugged. "To be honest, I'm not really sure. I mean, I saw your car, and..." His voice trailed off. He looked as confused in that moment as Nathan had been a minute earlier.

Nathan looked over at Peter Quinn. He had moved a few paces away, his mouth a tight line.

Nathan remembered with a shock how close he'd come to telling this man everything. He'd been powerless *not* to. The voice... no, an ability like that was reserved for stage tricks and vampire movies.

Of course, so were a bunch of other things that had already happened. All he wanted was to get outside.

Quinn's demeanor was all business again, but a trace of sweat had broken across his forehead. "I apologize, Reverend, but I have other business to attend to soon. Thank you for stopping by. I'll tell your father I saw you. He'll be pleased."

Nathan doubted that. Still, for some reason he didn't think Quinn *would* tell his father. Why he thought that, he couldn't say, but so *many* things were occurring to him in the frenzied state of mind that he decided not to question it.

He said to Josh, "I'll head out with you." His friend looked relieved. Nathan took one last look at the painting of the Molech temple, assured himself that it hadn't been a mirage. He shuddered visibly and turned away. Peter Quinn was watching him, and the same half-smirk returned to his face. He called after the men as they walked to the door, "Perhaps we can continue our discussion another time, Reverend." *Back in control*, his voice said. *A minor setback only.*

"Maybe." Nathan grabbed the door handle. Josh kept a loose grip on his arm as if preparing to catch him if he fell. Nathan had no intention of falling down, or ever speaking to Quinn again if it could be helped.

Chapter Thirty-Four

Nathan barely felt the cool air against his skin as they stepped outside. His legs were heavy, filled with clay. *Too much*, he thought. *It's all too much.*

His world had always been clearly defined. Even his faith was a straight-edged resolve that never wavered. Now, he found himself in a place where mystery heaped itself upon more mystery. *Supernatural* was a word he never cared for in the past. Now it fit too neatly. Nightmares scratching their way into the real world. Daylight becoming more and more a dreamscape, not a solace to wake up to.

Should talk of demons and ancient religions really be alien to him? The Bible spoke incessantly on the subject. God Himself warned the Israelites to worship only Him. Why would He bother acknowledging such dark creatures in the universe if they didn't exist?

Peter Quinn certainly believed in them.

Dad, what have you gotten yourself into?

When they reached his car, he wanted to fall to the sidewalk and pray, for God to clear his mind and open the thickening gray clouds in his head.

Of course, if he fell to his knees, Josh would probably call an ambulance.

"What was all *that* about?" His friend leaned against the hood of Nathan's car, beside a large paper shopping bag.

Instead of answering directly, Nathan gestured to the hood. "That yours?"

Josh craned his neck to look beside him, and said, "Oh, yeah, right." He picked up the groceries as he said, "You looked like you'd just seen a ghost or something."

"Or something," Nathan conceded. "Your timing was impeccable."

Josh scratched the back of his neck with his free hand, looking suddenly uncomfortable. "Pretty *weird* timing, more like it. I don't even know why I'm here." He looked into his bag. "I mean, chips, soda and a loaf of bread... oh, man, Shirley put the bottle on top of the bread."

He nodded toward *The Greedy Grocer*. "I've really got to send my employees to Bagging School or something."

Nathan looked at the club's closed door. He turned and leaned against the driver's door and stared at the convenience store. "Why are chips and crushed bread weird?"

"Just that I was done with my opening shift a half hour ago. Cashed out; Shirley cashed in. She's good enough that I don't need to hang around. Instead of leaving, I decided to get some stuff I needed. Like a craving or something." He slapped the bag. "Don't even need chips. I mean, isn't this the same stuff you got the other night?"

Nathan nodded at the shopping bag. Not exactly the same, but close enough. "Craving? You pregnant or something?" Their apparently pointless banter had a strengthening effect on him. He took a breath and leaned his backside against the driver's door.

"That's just it. I've got plenty of bread at home. Half a loaf at least. Why I needed to stick around to get this," he pulled the crushed bread out of the bag and laid it gently back in beside the bottle of soda, "is beyond me." He sighed. "Anyhow, I saw your car when I was leaving and figured I'd poke my head in to see if you were, well," he nodded toward the store, "in there."

Slowly, the implications of what his friend was telling him registered. One thing Nathan had learned in life was never to believe in coincidence. He had been about to confess *everything* to Quinn—a man who had pretty much *admitted* to being a demon worshipper, then Josh arrived just at the right time to stop him.

He considered explaining all this to him, but decided against it. When he sensed God had intervened in some way in his or others' lives, it usually filled him with joy, a sense of confirmation. This time, it scared him to death.

"So," Josh said, "what was going on with Whitey in there? About your dad, I assume?"

Nathan nodded. "Figured I'd stop by to check it out."

"The place gives me the willies. Looks like a college dorm room inside—well, not yours, but Marty Connolly's, definitely."

"You ever see my dad in there with anyone?"

"No. After you came by Friday, I took a peek. Dark outside, and the lights were on," he spoke with a mock Bela Lugosi voice, "but no one was home..."

Nathan smiled. The expression felt alien to his face in light of everything that had happened.

"So," Josh pressed. "Why did Drac look like he was going to bite you in the neck just now?"

Nathan felt infinitely better. A conversation of any length with Josh Everson made anything seem humorous. He wanted to tell him about his dreams, about Hayden's disappearance, Tarretti and the cemetery. Even more so, the painting on the wall just now. It felt more and more like his only chance at mental salvation, the only way to put things in perspective. They could hash it out together and Josh would let him know that he wasn't losing his mind.

Because he'd come so close to saying it all to the wrong person, however, he was reluctant. He needed to sit in silence, in prayer, before anything else passed his lips.

"Nate? What's up? You're looking all *ghosty* again." Josh wouldn't let him get off without some tidbit to make his shopping madness worthwhile.

Nathan shrugged. "Not much. Quinn's a little crazy I think, and he might be into some bad stuff."

"Bad stuff?"

Nathan shrugged again, not knowing what to do with his body. "I thought drugs at first, from the way Dad's been acting. But I'm suspecting something a little more dark, now."

He got a raised eyebrow in response.

Nathan whispered, not wanting his voice to carry too close to the door. "I don't know, really. I think it's some kind of cult. Quinn's into something nasty, maybe demon worship."

Now it was Josh's turn to go pale. He wasn't normally one to have a dark complexion as it was, so the simple fact that Nathan actually *saw* the blood draining from his face was unsettling. He raised a hand, "I really don't know. Just a few things he said and all." He hoped Josh wouldn't ask what "and all" meant.

A thought occurred to him, and he slapped his friend's arm. It felt good to have something concrete to suggest. "Listen, Josh, you've got Internet access, right?"

"Sure. I don't suppose old man Hayden had a computer at the church? I assume he's turned up, by the way?"

Nathan needed to change the subject, get Josh focused on something other than what had happened here, or to Hayden. He needed information. "Listen, maybe you can look something up for me? No, there's no computer at the church and they still don't know where Reverend Hayden is. People are looking."

"Sure, anything." As he said this, Josh pulled a dirty pen from his *Greedy Grocer* shirt pocket and folded a section of the paper bag down as an ad-hoc writing tablet.

"Do some research on the name Molech. It's an Old Testament name. If I'm not mistaken it's spelled M-O-L-E-C-H, or might be -O-C-H. Depends on what version of the Bible you read."

Josh looked up, "You want me to read the Bible?"

"No, I'll handle that part. Already have the degree and everything, remember? You just do some surfing and see what comes up. I'm going to give you two other names to include. Don't ask why."

"Cool, a man of mystery."

Nathan told him to include "Ammonite" and "Solomon."

"Also, I suppose anything on a men's organization which might revolve around any or all aspects of this. I doubt a search on the name itself would show anything, since it has the word 'Hillcrest' in it."

Josh was a little less pale at this point. As he backed away to give Nathan room to open his door, he said, "Man, a cult in our town. Not cool."

"Nope, not cool at all," Nathan agreed, getting into the car. "But it's just a theory right now. Anyhow, 'Knowledge is Power'."

More and more it felt like his imagination had simply gotten carried away. He tried not to dwell too much on details because when he did, a new wave of terror washed over him. Now was the time for action, to get something concrete under his feet. Josh would help. He made a mental note to sit down with him someday and offer up the whole story, but it would be good if he did his research with an unbiased eye.

In the meantime, Nathan had other matters to attend to. The parishioner with the broken legs, for starters. Hopefully, there would be word about Pastor Hayden when he got back to the church. And, he remembered with a brief flash of joy, his date with Elizabeth O'Brien tonight.

Nathan backed from his spot. Josh had reached his own car, dumping the grocery bag unceremoniously onto the passenger seat. With a sudden pang of guilt for getting him caught up in his personal mystery, Nathan pulled left onto Main Street and drove away.

Chapter Thirty-Five

The Cabel Grille was named after the family who had opened the establishment fifteen years ago. It was sold after only two years, the Cabels deciding not to spend their retirement years tied to a restaurant, even with the healthy influx of customers. The Grille had become *too* successful in relation to the amount of effort they were willing to put into it. The newest owner was a young woman who lived a few towns south in Auburn. She was allowed to keep the restaurant's name as part of the deal, to avoid scaring away established diners. She also left the menu pretty much as it was, except for the addition of more vegetarian items to the list.

Coming to the Grille had been Elizabeth's idea, and Nathan was thankful for the gesture. It showed, at least in his mind, that she did not want to hide whatever relationship they might be cultivating. With the events of the past few days—this morning's in particular—still swirling in his brain, and the congregation increasingly agitated over any lack of substantial news about Hayden, he felt more comfortable staying close to home. All through dinner, he suppressed the urge to cut the date short and call Josh, to see if he'd been able to uncover anything.

"Did you pay a visit to your father's little gang?"

Elizabeth had ordered a Caesar salad and punctuated her question with a jab of her fork into a piece of chicken. Their conversation had so far been light, but she seemed to sense Nathan had something more on his mind than the missing preacher.

He nodded. "This morning, in fact. It was very weird, too."

"Weird how?"

Nathan paused, waiting to see if the instinct to stay quiet returned. It didn't. Since leaving Josh this morning, the thought of confiding in Elizabeth had blossomed. As with Josh, however, he wondered how wise it would be to tell her too much.

He decided to take it slow, gauge her reaction. "Well, it's kind of strange."

"Weird and strange," she said. "My kind of story." She lightly touched the back of his hand with her fork and left a miniscule drop of dressing on his skin. He found himself smiling, feeling the loving meaning behind such an innocuous gesture. Forget caution, he decided. If he was going mad, best she knew about it early.

"Where do I start? Before I came here, and for a little while after, I was having these really bizarre dreams." Without waiting for her to comment on yet another interesting adjective on his part—he saw her mouth move as if to speak and knew exactly what she was going to say—he jumped in with a detailed description of the nightmares, focusing mostly on the temple.

When he was finished, she took another bite of her salad, chewed, and said, "Pretty creepy."

The simple fact that she said this before bothering to swallow, muffling her words with the lettuce still in her mouth, made Nathan want to jump from his chair and embrace her. He couldn't decide why, just that she was so utterly there, all the time, listening to him, interested. It was with this simple moment and his reaction to such a nondescript thing as talking with her mouth full, that he accepted how absurdly in love with this woman he still was. When he was not with her, he questioned any potential for their relationship, but when they were together like this, he wanted to be nowhere else.

"Then you'll love this," he said. "There was a painting on the wall inside the place this morning, exactly like the one in my dream."

She thought about that for a while, then suggested, "Maybe you'd seen the painting somewhere before?"

He hadn't thought of that. The idea didn't sound right, though. "No," he said at last. "No, I don't think so. If I'd forgotten it, I would have probably remembered on seeing it today. To be honest, I think it was an original. But I'm no art expert."

"Any idea what it is?"

"Kind of. I mean, the guy who runs the place told me." He looked at her sideways while he lifted his cooling cheeseburger and took a bite. It tasted funny, and not until he chewed and swallowed did he realize what it was. "Garden Burger doesn't mean it comes with lettuce, does it?"

Elizabeth laughed and slapped her leg. "Nope. It's a veggie burger. No meat. For a while there, I thought you'd gone all New Age on me."

Intrigued, he took another bite. It wasn't bad.

She said, "Well, finish your Tasty Tofu and tell me what he said."

He finished chewing, but his cell phone rang before he could say anything. He'd worn chinos and a sport coat over his white dress shirt (no tie, though—Elizabeth would've mocked him severely if he'd gone that far). He reached into the inside pocket of the coat draped over the back of his chair, and took out the phone.

"Sorry, one second." He pressed TALK. "Pastor Dinneck." He tried not to smile when he caught Elizabeth doing a lip-synch of his salutation, eyebrows raised in mock snobbishness. He listened for a moment, then said, "Yes, Claire. Yes, that's a good time. See you Saturday... no, it'll be my pleasure. Good night." He disconnected and put the phone away.

"Sorry. I'd asked her to call back when she knew what time her mother was being released from the hospital. A small stroke. Claire's husband is in Florida so I agreed to lend a hand."

"Don't let the hubby know his mother-in-law's moving in. He might not come back." She said it with all seriousness on her face, but Nathan smiled.

"You're evil."

She leaned forward, jutted her chin out. "Then ex-or-cise me!" she said, and growled.

He reached for his burger. "Don't tempt me."

She touched his arm. He put down the burger and held her hand in both of his. Her eyes were clear; a deep Irish brown, bordering on hazel. "I wouldn't dream of it," she said. The affection in her words—words which in any other situation might have been misconstrued as a rejection—touched his heart. He knew what she meant. She was serious, and had given him an unspoken promise. It was an agreement made years before, but it was reassuring to hear it repeated now, with their new lives.

His cell phone rang again.

In the nightmare that followed, he would look back often to this one moment in his life, the moment before he answered the call. He would see it frozen like a snapshot, play the last few seconds of normalcy over and over in his mind. Her hand in his. Before everything changed forever.

He didn't reach for the phone, never broke eye contact with her. "I've got voicemail," he said.

She playfully slapped his hands away. "You have to answer it, Nate. It's part of your calling now—pun fully intended. I'm going to have to get used to it."

He pulled the phone out reflexively, basking in the glow of the implied promise in her statement.

"Reverend Dinneck."

Elizabeth whispered "*Pastor* Dinneck, you moron..."

He smirked.

"Reverend, this is Brother Armand." Something in the man's voice told Nathan that the call was going to be a bad one, even before the monk said, "I'm afraid I have some terrible, terrible news."

Part Three

Solomon's Grave

Constantinople, 1204 A.D.

Sister Danelis Raoulaina emerged from the lower-level Chapel of Saint Mark with silent, hesitant steps. Voices of men, some distant, others frighteningly close, wound their way along the corridor from every direction. For a moment it seemed as if the laughter and angry shouts, sounds of breaking glass and other unidentified objects were almost upon her, only to recede again. Even from a distance, the tenor of the voices and savagery of their inflection made the small woman shake with terror. She and her sisters had watched, briefly, what transpired in the streets outside. When the crusaders arrived, the eighteen nuns in her order had been reciting late morning prayer in the main cathedral. Before that moment, there had been blessed silence, save the penitent whispers of the nuns, the occasional click of rosary stones against the marble benches and the background clop of horses along the main square outside.

Then *they* arrived, like a tempest blown in from the sea. A storm no longer content to stop at the breakers. A heavy wave of violence, of men lost to their animalistic natures pulled forth by Satan himself.

It happened as it had in her dreams, in the Lord's vision. The devil had come to the Church of the Twelve Apostles. Sister Danelis berated her lack of faith, for she had hoped the visions were in truth only nightmares. Still, she'd taken the steps outlined for her by the Man of Light, the one who spoke to her in the Holy visions. He instructed her how to prepare. Two months, long enough to carry out His wishes and to hope that God's will would not have to be done.

But they came, and the evil tempest now rampaged above her in the holy cathedral. Demons, taking everything within reach of their bloody fingertips. Defiling the women of Constantinople, sparing no one, not even blessed nuns. This they had seen from the large windows above the square, but only for a moment, until the Mother Superior's face went rigid and she instructed them to move into the catacombs. They would follow the route known as the Path of Saint Peter toward a secluded dock on the rocky shoal below the church. It was a path taught to all sisters, in the event the Turks should attempt yet another siege of the city.

This time, God forgive them all, the invading hordes were their own soldiers in Christ.

Sister Danelis had twelve novices under her direct charge. Early on she chose five from their ranks who were most suited for manual exertion. When the soldiers moved into the square, she and her sisters, led by the Holy Mother, moved as one toward the Path of Saint Peter. Danelis held back, gesturing to the five to stay at her side. After sending the remaining novices along the Path with prayers for their safety, she moved along a different corridor. They needed to reach the Chapel of Saint Mark three levels below, retrieve two objects, then follow a path she had traveled only in her dreams.

At the moment, the hallway outside the Chapel of Saint Mark was deserted. She waved her sisters to follow, then heard the footsteps. She whispered, "Back, quickly," and joined the five horror-stricken faces as they faded into the room's darkness. The footsteps slapped along the corridor. Danelis prayed that whoever was coming would pass by and not see their shadows cringing in the doorway.

Bishop Georgios Palaiologos ran past so quickly he had nearly rounded the far corner before Danelis could step from the room and call, "Your Eminence!"

Georgios spun at the sound of her voice and almost stumbled. His large face was bathed in sweat, his very pores bleeding with the effort of escape. She noticed that his feet were bare.

When the bishop saw who had spoken, he managed a relieved but brief smile. The expression lifted her heart. He gasped, "Oh, thank God you're still safe. Please, Sister, leave here now."

She took a step toward him. "Father, there is something I need to tell you." He was the bishop, after all. Certainly they were meant to cross paths in this moment. He would help them. The heavy man clutched something against his chest, stumbling sideways as he prepared to continue along his chosen path. Surely he would not leave them here alone?

"Your Eminence, wait. We need to—"

"You need to leave now!" he interrupted. "Come this way; you can reach the Path of Saint Peter if the way is not already blocked."

Please, God, don't let him leave us. "I cannot, Father! There is something we must do first!"

Bishop Georgios Palaiologos did not wait to hear. He disappeared down the corridor, calling, "Forgive me, Sister, but I must go *now*. I cannot explain. God pro—" The words faded into the distance, blending with those of the demon crusaders drawing ever closer.

She found it hard to breathe. They were alone again. Completely alone.

"Sister?" A voice behind her. Novice Rhea peered from under her pale blue habit. "Sister, what should we do?"

Danelis cursed her weakness. These were children of God. They needed her faith. They were not alone. They would *never* be so long as she followed His command.

No longer whispering, she said, "Come, this way. You have the staffs?"

Two other novices stepped forward, each holding long smooth poles before them. Danelis had ordered them carved to the angel's specifications weeks ago and laid them in the corner of the chapel, trusting they would not be tampered with. He had promised as much. Surely if this was possible, so too would be the rest of her task.

"Follow me," she said, careful to show only confidence in her voice. "We have much to do for the glory of the Lord."

She grabbed a torch from its sconce outside the chapel door and turned in the direction from which the bishop had come. She did not look back to see if the others followed. The sounds of their steps and the occasional rap of the staffs along the stone walls told of their obedience. Down more flights of stairs, the way at times so narrow they were forced to travel in single file, walking nearly sideways. They did not stop. She had seen this way dozens of times in God's vision. The further they went, the more sure she became that they would succeed.

Even so, as they reached the end of one corridor and saw what lay beside a rock-filled entrance to a chamber that had not been in any of her visions, the shock was too much. The women froze. Like the crusaders whose bones lay crushed beneath the stones spilling into the passageway, they fell prostrate before the Ark. It was tilted at an awkward angle, as if carried into the narrow hall by the very stones themselves.

Slowly, Sister Danelis raised her face. She shouted at the novices to get up, move quickly. She knew where they needed to carry it, to the end of the next passage where one last boat was waiting for them at Saint Peter's dock. There would be no one to steer it to safety but she and her sisters. After that their lives, and the safety of their burden, would be in God's hands.

Chapter Thirty-Six

Elizabeth watched Nate turn sideways in his chair, phone pressed against his ear. Regardless of the rift which had opened between them in the past, she never failed to marvel at how strong his convictions were. The word commonly used was "faith", but that was just a word. He *believed*, and would follow that belief all his life. Now and then, she had considered giving herself over to the God he served, become "born again" to coin an over-used and, she guessed, often misunderstood phrase. Do it for Nate, give him some hope that she wasn't going to burn up in the netherworld when she died. In a way, she'd considered acting as a wife might, supporting her husband in his passionate ventures.

Of course, she knew it would be the most hypocritical thing she could do. Nate had freely given himself to the Christian life. Because he believed. Her faith would be a sham, a charade. If Nate's God wanted her to believe in him, then he would know her nature required something more tangible than words in a book or preachers crying on an altar, begging her to come forth and receive a mysterious holy spirit. Those might be extreme examples, but they were part of Nate's world. Concrete evidence wasn't necessary for him, outside of his own consideration for how God works. He was someone who believed—who *needed* to believe—in things in a certain a way. She was certain if God ever tried doing anything tangible like speak to him through a burning bush, Nate would have a nervous breakdown on the spot. She smirked at that image.

A burning bush, however, or a quick parting of the Wachusett Reservoir, was exactly what Elizabeth needed. She didn't think she deserved it, nor was she asking for anything of the sort. All she wanted, right now, was Nathan Dinneck by her side. She knew this, all of it, was a mistake. Sly comments across the table tonight, pledging her love without saying anything specific. The overwhelming pull she felt for this man, after all these years, was too strong to resist. Strong enough that she'd broken up with Josh over it. Stupid reason to do so, considering Nate had been out of her life at that point, presumably forever. Now, she was glad it happened.

Maybe they were meant to be together, she and Nate. Or, maybe this evening together was nothing more than the work of fate. Not the three-hags-toiling-over-a-cauldron kind of fate, but simple *good fortune*. Nate, of course, would call it an act of God.

The phone call didn't sound like it was going well. Nate was pale, looked like he was going to start crying. Not sure if she was stepping over some invisible line—he *was* doing church business, after all—she nonetheless reached over and took his hand. He did not look at her, but squeezed her hand in return and did not let go. A lone tear dropped from his eye. This definitely wasn't good. She decided to pay more attention to the conversation.

"Thank you," Nate whispered into the phone. "I'll come over tonight. I'm sorry, what? OK, then. I—" He paused, closed his eyes tightly, sending more tears down his face. "I'm sorry. That's fine. I'll come by first thing in the morning."

With a shaking hand he thumbed the cell phone off. Teardrops fell onto the number pad before he closed the cover. He let go of her hand and fumbled to return the phone back to his coat, apparently thought better of it and flipped it open again.

"Nate, what happened? What's going on?"

"I have to call someone. I'm not sure. I mean, oh God...." He turned until both elbows were on the table then put down the phone and covered his face. His shoulders shook as he cried. He made no sound. Elizabeth shifted her chair sideways and put an arm awkwardly around his shoulder. She wanted to shake him, ask what had happened, but didn't. He'd tell her. He'd certainly tell her before making any other calls. She lifted the discarded phone from the table and moved it out of his reach.

He was a minister now, the man in charge. He needed to get his emotions out with *her* first until his head was clear.

She thought all this reflexively, realizing with only a touch of irony that she was already falling into the role of Pastor's Wife.

Chapter Thirty-Seven

Nathan felt empty. When he thought he might be able to pull his hands from his face and talk rationally to Elizabeth, he pictured Reverend Hayden's face. The quiet, almost sorrowful look when the minister had gotten into the car and been driven off three days ago. Then the wave of sorrow was too strong, too painful. He cried again. He never was one to do this loudly, even as a child. He simply shook behind his hands. The dampness of his tears fell down his face and dripped into his open collar.

He lowered his hands and sighed, long and heavy. Elizabeth's arm, draped across his back, was more comforting in this moment than he could ever explain to her. He didn't have to, since she squeezed him harder.

Reverend Hayden was dead.

How could such a horrible thing happen? *Why* did it happen?

"Nate?"

He wiped his face with a handkerchief from his coat pocket. He kept one handy, used for various despondent parishioners with whom he might speak. He took another deep breath, then said, "Reverend Hayden was found this evening. He'd dead."

"What? Nate, what..." She didn't finish, only stared wide-eyed, waiting for further explanation.

And the explanation was simply too terrible to accept.

"The police are saying, um, well, that he was murdered. Someone shot him and left him at the edge of the property." Saying these words caused his body to seize up, assaulted by a renewed attack of shock.

The silence stretched between them. Once he'd spoken the words out loud, they didn't seem real. Ralph Hayden couldn't have been murdered. He was in a monastery, for heaven's sake. Nathan looked at the table top, feeling Elizabeth's arm on him, and tried to understand. His legs began to bounce up and down as if by their own accord. He had to do something.

"I need to call someone," he said finally.

"Who?"

He looked around the restaurant, hoping to see just the right person. At the table nearest him a family ate their meal in frenzied enjoyment, except for a little girl with a pair of braids who'd noticed his tears and stared with curious detachment.

The Hillcrest police had already been notified, according to Brother Armand. He would have to call everyone on the Board, the elders, Mrs. Lewis or Mrs. Zawalich. They would be devastated. *God*, he thought, *this will be too much for them.*

He sniffed, sat up straighter, stared at the table. There would be funeral arrangements, he knew. *Vincent Tarretti*. He could call the caretaker first. From their last conversation, Nathan knew Tarretti did not know many parishioners. He could speak with him, though, tell him the news so that if, in the telling, Nathan became lost again in emotion, those kind old women wouldn't be burdened with it.

And it was something to do. It was *action*.

Of course, that was what he'd thought last time. Why did he always think of *Tarretti*? He'd have to call him at some point, anyway. This fact only brought more grief.

He reached across the table but couldn't get to the phone. Elizabeth slid it closer to him. He flipped it open and looked up the number in its electronic phone list.

"Who're you calling?"

"Tarretti, the groundskeeper. He organizes, well...." He didn't finish the sentence, and didn't think he needed to. As he scrolled to the number, he gave her a quick summary of his reasons anyway. He spoke half-heartedly, wondering how much of his mumbling she'd understood.

When Vincent answered on the second ring, Nathan told him the news. He was surprised by the steadiness of his own voice.

Tarretti was silent for a few seconds. Nathan heard him take in a long breath; then, as he had done during their prior conversation, the man whispered a curse as he let it out. Tarretti added, almost to himself, "God, what is going on? Please tell me."

"I don't understand," Nathan said, more to remind him that he was still there. The man's words struck a chord with him. He'd prayed the same prayer recently himself. Some unseen connection came to light, one which seemed inexplicably to stretch between him and Tarretti. Until this moment, the other oddities of his return to town had been temporarily forgotten. Now they came flooding back, try as he might to push them away. There *was* no connection. How could he be dwelling again on his own problems?

"I'm sorry, Reverend," Tarretti said. "Obviously we'll need to talk about this right away. I—" He hesitated. "I'm not good with phones, not sure if you could tell that from our last conversation. Could you come by my home right away? Do you know where it is?"

Nathan said he did, and looked at Elizabeth. He had so many things to do, so many people to contact, he should not even consider accepting the invitation. But the sensation of a connection, of puzzle pieces falling together—this new terrible one included—was overpowering. He heard himself say, "I'll be there in a few minutes," before he could decide on any other reply.

Tarretti said that was good, and to hurry. "Call no one else, Reverend," he added before disconnecting, "until we've spoken. Please. I'll explain everything when you get here."

Nathan pocketed the phone, numb. A brief idea stuck him, like a car racing by as he stood at the side of the road. He may have just accepted an invitation to visit Hayden's murderer. But like a passing car, it made an impression only for a moment before he ignored it. The world around him had gone completely insane. If he did this, visited Tarretti right away, heard what he had to say then moved on to more urgent matters, maybe he could come through to the other side. The rational side. The way his life was before coming to town.

Or maybe he'd already cracked up but hadn't yet realized it.

He grabbed his jacket and stood. Elizabeth fumbled in her pocketbook for money to leave on the table. Though they hadn't gotten the bill yet, what she left seemed far beyond what it would have come to.

"Sorry," he said. "I'll drop you off—"

"I'm coming with you, wherever you're going." She got up and took his arm. He didn't argue. At the moment he wanted no one else at his side but her.

Then he remembered that fleeting thought about Tarretti.

"Maybe you should stay at home. I don't know if—"

"Don't bother, Nate," she said, and caught the waitress's attention to explain the money was on the table. They walked outside together. Nathan's tears had dried. He had too much to do. He'd mourn his old pastor another day. There would be the sorrow of others to deal with, now.

Chapter Thirty-Eight

Josh Everson clicked the "back" button on his browser and chose the next link on the Internet search page. He'd gone through seven so far and was getting a little nervous. Of course, there were a couple of pages that were so obviously the result of fractured minds that he didn't take them seriously. In one, a person—man, woman or kid, he couldn't tell—calling himself WFC-Guy (the WFC meaning Watchdog For Christ, the name of the website), claimed the existence of an international organization of neo-Ammonites who actively worship the demon *Moloch*. A slight variation on Nate's spelling, but he had said to expect that. The site claimed such followers were, in truth, aliens from an as-yet undetected galaxy who were slowly replacing top figures in world governments with replicants. If that was true, he'd voted a space creature for U.S. President in the last election. This last bizarreness aside, it did have the connection he was looking for, so Josh bookmarked the page and moved on.

Another site explained in gruesome detail the various modes of sacrifices to the demon-god. Here, its name was spelled *Molech*. This particular page gave him the willies. Descriptions of young children placed atop the hands of a large iron idol, cast in the shape of a sitting man with the head of a bull. Through the use of pulleys and winches, the arms were raised up. The demon's mouth was always open, "always hungry" as the description read, ready to receive the offering. In its belly raged a sacrificial fire. The flames grew so hot that the idol's iron skin glowed red, giving the impression of demonic life within.

He bookmarked that one, too. Much of the other information he'd uncovered was similar, or mentioned Molech only in passing with scores of other demons not a whole lot nicer.

He sat back and took a sip of his warm Coke. He refined his search. Alongside "Molech", "Ammonites" he added "United States" and "Massachusetts".

From the living room came a hard knock against the apartment door. Josh reflexively checked the time—nine-sixteen—then clicked

"Search" before getting up. He reminded himself to give Davy a call at the *Grocer* in a half hour. He'd convinced the kid to work a double shift tonight so he'd have time to get Nate his info. Davy had closed the place before, but he *was* a teenager and tended to forget little things like shutting off the outside light.

When he opened the door, Josh expected to see Nate's eager face. Instead, a familiar white-haired man stood in the hall. For a moment, he thought the guy might be one of the many neighbors he hadn't gotten around to introducing himself to over the past two years. Then he placed the face.

Looking much less menacing in the bright hallway lights than he had this morning, Whitey from the men's club said, "Josh Everson?" He didn't sound angry. That was good. Josh steeled himself for a barrage of insults for walking in on him and Nate. He recalled the details of Nate's suspicions and what he'd just read online.

Oh, man, he thought. *I'm toast.*

"Hi," he finally said, "that's me. Can I help you with something?" He wanted to slam the door and call the cops, but what would he tell them? That a demon-worshipping alien from Galaxy X was standing at his door?

The man smiled. His white moustache hardly moved, so little did the smile affect his mouth. "Yes, you will help me." His voice had a calmness and power that put Josh at ease. Why had he been so worried about the guy?

Quinn continued, "Let me in, Josh, and I will explain what I need."

Josh nodded, never looking away from the other man's eyes. Very clear. A smart man. He hoped he *could* help him, and backed up a step. Quinn entered the apartment and Josh followed his progress.

"Close the door."

He closed the door.

"Come and sit," the man looked around then pointed to the couch, "over there."

Josh walked over to the couch. He looked away from Quinn's face as he sat and suddenly wondered why he was being so agreeable with this loony.

"Look at me and listen carefully."

Oh, that's right, he remembered. *I was going to help him with something.*

Quinn sat beside him on the very edge of the cushion and said, slowly, "You talked to your friend Nathan Dinneck today, after the two of you left my store. Is that correct?"

"Yes." That was a relief. If this was about Nate, he knew everything.

"Tell me everything you discussed, from the beginning." He leaned forward. "Remember everything and tell me."

Josh walked out from the Greedy Grocer and saw Nate's car. He looked back through the store's window. They must have missed each other. Nope, not in there. He wondered if Nate might have actually had the gumption to check out his dad's new hangout for himself. He walked casually along the sidewalk, neither feeling the concrete under his feet nor thinking it odd that a moment ago he was sitting in his living room with the guy who ran this place.

As he told the story, his eyes remained unfocused. His visitor listened. When Josh finished, he simply stared across the room, like a robot who'd been switched off.

"Josh Everson?"

Josh's eyes refocused on Quinn's face.

"Hmmm?"

"Tell me everything you have learned on your computer."

"I can show you," he said, emotion now trickling into his voice.

"That would be wonderful." He followed Josh into the spare bedroom where the illuminated computer screen waited.

Chapter Thirty-Nine

Vincent Tarretti's house was mostly dark when they pulled into the driveway. From the front window issued the understated glow of a light shining in a room at the back of the house. Nathan and Elizabeth got out of the car without speaking, and walked to the front door, her hand in his.

The cemetery was quiet and deserted. No sound but the calls of crickets and frogs in the woods beyond the gravestones. Even these sounds would be gone soon as cooler weather loomed. A mosquito buzzed in his ear. He swatted it away with his free hand. Their footsteps on the small porch echoed in the near silence, as did his knuckles rapping against the edge of the aluminum storm door. It was answered by the heavy timbre of a dog's barking. Then a voice, hushed, telling "Johnson" to be quiet. The dog stopped, but Nathan could hear a low growl. Johnson apparently didn't like night visitors.

Elizabeth released his hand when they heard Tarretti's footsteps. Neither the porch light nor any lamp in the front room turned on. When the caretaker opened the door his face was masked by the interior gloom.

"Reverend Dinneck," he said quietly, then hesitated when he saw Elizabeth. "Oh, I'm sorry. I thought you were coming alone."

"Vincent Tarretti," Nathan said, "this is Elizabeth O'Brien." He nodded toward her with his head. Tarretti's outline turned to her with a glancing motion, then focused back on Nathan.

"Can she—" he began, then stopped. He pushed open the storm door and waved them into the house. They walked into a small living room, illuminated by the light spilling from the kitchen at the back. Nathan noticed a couch and coffee table, one chair. To his right was a short hall, which probably led to the bedrooms. The dog—a massive black Labrador with gray patches around its face—stood in the entrance to the kitchen, its tail wagging in short waves as if uncertain whether to be pleased with the visit.

"Come into the kitchen, please," Tarretti said, "and don't mind

Johnson. He's well trained." A hint of threat lined the statement, though Nathan was unsure why. Nothing about how the man reacted to the news was making sense. Nathan had seen grief externalize in many ways and would not have been surprised if, when they stepped into the yellowed kitchen light, there were signs Tarretti had been crying. However, his face revealed only a stony expression of... what? Suspicion? The man continued to eye Elizabeth with cautious glances. Nathan felt a strange obligation to explain her presence.

"Elizabeth and I were at the Cabel when you called."

She added, "I hope it's all right that I came." Only Nathan heard the tone in her voice which implied she really didn't care if it was or not.

"So you two are, I mean, dating or something?" Tarretti stopped beside a small table. There were only two chairs. No one made a motion to claim them.

Elizabeth smiled. "Or something. Does it matter?"

Tarretti's stare hardened, any pretense of hospitality gone. "It matters a great deal," he said. He turned back to Nathan. "I need to know if she can be trusted. What I'm going to tell you—*if* I tell you, that is—cannot leave this room. I've spent too long...."

He stopped, and looked down with eyes darting back and forth, as if trying to remember something.

As during their phone conversation when Hayden first disappeared, Nathan felt a wave of irritation toward him. Tarretti was playing some kind of guessing game and Nathan no longer had the patience for it.

"Vincent, I strongly suggest you tell me what you know about Pastor Hayden. If you don't, then we'll go to the police right now and—"

"You have no idea what's going on, Mister Dinneck!" He was shouting, and began his side-to-side glances again. "Don't tell me what to do and what not do. I answer to God alone." Johnson, who had lain under a table too small to hide his bulk, raised his head and growled.

This guy's nuts, Nathan thought. It was a hard thought to shake once he grabbed on to it. The possibility that he was speaking with Hayden's murderer took on a more ominous urgency. Nathan moved a half step closer to Elizabeth, as if preparing to launch himself in front of her should Tarretti move suddenly. Johnson followed him with his head, growling softly. The dog sounded more confused than angry.

"Mister Tarretti," Nathan said, following the caretaker's lead and turning formal in his speech. "Explain yourself right now or we're going to the police. Even if I have to knock you down and drag you there myself." As he spoke, he stepped forward. All the confusion and anger of the past few days began to boil over. He spoke in a measured tone, but he found himself hoping this man would defy him so he could do exactly what he'd promised. Johnson stopped growling. That probably wasn't a good sign.

Vincent stared at him, gauging any bluff in the threat. His gaze softened, and he gestured to the two chairs.

"Please sit," he said, softer now. "And listen. I don't think we have much time. I do not know why I feel this so strongly, but the Spirit is driving me to move, of that I'm certain. Please." He pointed again to the chairs.

Nathan remained standing, as did Elizabeth. She held a stony look of determination, which Nathan hoped was an echo of his own.

Vincent shook his head at last and muttered, "Fine. Just stand there," and walked across the small kitchen to lean on the counter. Nathan did a quick scan of the area, relieved not to see any knives handy. "But before I explain anything to you I need to ask you a question. And you need to answer me truthfully. If you don't, then you can leave now. Call the cops if you like, but I have nothing to tell them."

Nathan crossed his arms across his chest. "Ask."

"You mentioned some dreams you'd been having since coming to town. What were they about?"

This question was the proverbial straw. Nathan dropped his arms and walked across the room, stopping only when his face was a hair from Tarretti's. Johnson scrambled to move out from under the table but Elizabeth made a quick "Shut!" sound and raised her flattened palm toward the dog's nose. Either from surprise or the uncompromising tone in her voice, Johnson sat back down. He looked up at her, then back at the two men.

Nathan said, quietly at first but building to a shout, "I don't know what you're playing at, but my dreams have *nothing* to do with Pastor Hayden!"

Tarretti did not flinch. "They have *everything* to do with him."

"Why?"

"What were your dreams about?"

"Why?" This time Nathan grabbed Tarretti's shirt. He didn't know what else to do. He was angry, but as well the question terrified him.

Not so much for the answer it begged, but for the fact that he was asking it at all.

"What was in your dream?" Tarretti's voice rose to match Nathan's. Both men looked ready for violence.

Nathan was frustrated, so much so he truly *wanted* to punch this man. He didn't want to tell him anything, wanted to continue this posturing until Tarretti broke down and told him why he cared so much about his stupid dreams.

The temple, its appearance in the painting on the wall of the Hillcrest Men's Club. The sick, terrible feeling he'd had walking into that place this morning. Solomon's grave. The vision in the church basement still so clear in his memory like a photograph in the paper you don't want to look at but do anyway. Unable to turn away.

He closed his eyes and took a deep breath, held it, then made a decision. He was a man of God, and as such should be the first to back down in a quarrel. Without letting go of the man's shirt, but forcing himself to at least loosen his grip, he whispered, "It was nothing. A dream about some temple in the desert. And some angels."

Tarretti's reply was immediate. "What kind of angels?"

Nathan suddenly *knew* that the answers to everything plaguing him these past two weeks were either with this man, or nowhere at all. He was falling, losing any last vestige of hope that his world would soon come back into focus.

He retightened his grip and actually shook Tarretti back and forth twice. When he shouted, drops of spittle landed on the man's cheek. "The angels above John Solomon's grave! Are you happy?" He shook Tarretti one more time. He sensed more than saw the dog rise back up and Elizabeth's renewed reprimand. The animal settled onto its haunches, barking angrily across the room. "Now tell me what's going on! Tell me or so help me I'll—"

He didn't finish. As quickly as it had changed a moment before, Vincent Tarretti's stance sagged, and his eyes closed. Nathan saw droplets of his own spit on the other's face, and was filled with self-loathing. He let go of the caretaker's shirt. The material was bunched in a three-dimensional handprint. How could he have lost his cool like that? He needed to hang on. Needed to remember who he was.

Still, he was close to something. Close to answers.

Elizabeth's hands landed lightly atop his shoulders. He felt a final urge to lunge at Tarretti, but held himself back—or was held back by Elizabeth's soft contact. Tarretti sagged further against the counter.

"Then you *must* be the one," he breathed. He opened his eyes and wiped his face with a sleeve. He stared at Nathan, at Elizabeth, back again. "You are the new caretaker, and my time is over. Nothing else makes sense. But there might not be enough time left for any of us."

For a moment Nathan thought he was resigning his position. Much later, in retrospect, he realized that this was exactly what Vincent Tarretti was doing.

Chapter Forty

Peter Quinn felt conflicting emotions when he saw what Josh Everson had uncovered on the Internet. Part of him was amused at the way rumor and overactive imaginations could twist the truth into nonsense. *Aliens*, of all things.

But not *all* of what Everson showed him was rubbish. There were just as many sites accurately describing some aspects of Quinn's group and their activities as those which accused them of coming from a comet. *Too much* accuracy, even when buried in nonsense, to give him comfort. Peter wondered how much of his people's cloak of secrecy would be lifted when the Great Molech, at last, had his prize. If the power it held would be enough to emerge from the shadows and into their own light.

If not, then he would need to show these pages to his uncle Roger and the other elders.

His cell phone rang. Josh blinked rapidly.

"Remain here," Peter said, "and do nothing until I say."

He moved a few feet away and answered the phone. "Quinn."

"Hi. Manny Paulson. Something's up."

Peter raised an eyebrow. "Something's up," he echoed, irritated with Paulson's habit of not getting to any point immediately. "What kind of something, Mister Paulson?"

"Tarretti has visitors. Guess who?"

"No."

"OK, OK. The new preacher-man. Dinneck. Art's boy. And he brought his girlfriend."

Peter checked his watch. A bit late for a visit. He decided not to ask about the "girlfriend".

"Details please."

Paulson's car was parked in the access road running alongside the main cemetery, out of sight from the street. The road was used for driving in the town's backhoe when digging new graves. He told Peter about the arrival of Nathan and Elizabeth, and how they were quickly ushered in to Tarretti's dark house. The fact that the house remained mostly dark rang a warning bell in Peter's head. *Secrecy*, it said. *Clandestine meeting.*

Perhaps the authorities had finally found Hayden's corpse. Peter had left the old man's body where it had fallen, far into the woods at the edge of the monastery's property. He did not want to carry it in his trunk, too much risk of leaving DNA traces. When the preacher was found, Peter hoped it would send a signal to Tarretti, perhaps make him move.

Apparently it had.

The time was close.

Or, he thought, *the time is now.*

"Manny, stay there. If they leave, call me. No matter what, stay on Tarretti. Don't move unless he moves. Got it?"

"You're the boss."

"Yes, Mister Paulson, I am. I'm going to head over to Greenwood Street Cemetery. If they make a move tonight, it'll be to go there."

"You ever going to tell me why that grave is so interesting?"

No, Peter thought. *Or maybe I will, before I put a bullet into your head for your disrespect.* "If I'm not mistaken, you'll find out soon enough. Stay put and watch the house."

He disconnected. An idea occurred to him. He hit the speed dial for the Dinneck house. As the phone rang, he looked down at Josh Everson. He thought. *Everything's coming together.* Everson might prove more useful than he had already.

"Hello?" Beverly Dinneck's voice. Peter silently cursed.

"Mrs. Dinneck," he said. "I apologize for calling so late. This is Raymond George from operations. Art's program has a problem and I need to speak with him. It is a very important program; otherwise I wouldn't have bothered you." He was uncertain if he'd used the correct jargon, but this woman likely wouldn't understand it any more than he. He had to get her husband on the phone.

"One second," she said. "Art...?" The phone was placed onto a table, the sound clunking in Peter's ear.

"Disconnect your computer," he said to Josh while he waited, hearing the couple's conversation in the distance over the phone line. "We're going out."

Josh clicked his browser closed as Art Dinneck's tired voice came onto the phone. "Art Dinneck."

Peter moved into the apartment's living room as he spoke, so the boy beside him wouldn't overhear and think the words were directed at him. Using the Voice over the phone took a somewhat more focused control. Over the years, it had become second nature when talking in person. Now, even with such clear phone reception, it took more concentration and control.

"Art Dinneck, listen carefully. The person you are speaking to is Raymond George, who works with you."

Chapter Forty-One

As Tarretti told Nathan and Elizabeth his tale, adding as much detail as possible, save a few important facts that needed to wait a while longer, the couple moved back across the kitchen and sat in the two chairs. Johnson returned to his perch under the table and worked his long legs between their feet. When Vincent realized his constant pacing was a distraction, he paused in his story long enough to pull a metal folding chair from the closet at the front of the house. He sat near Nathan, chair turned backwards so he could lean forward.

The woman's presence still bothered him—he'd gone over this conversation in his head hundreds of times but imagined it being with only one person. The recipient of the tale was always a faceless being in his mind, his eventual successor. But she seemed genuinely close to Dinneck. In any event, she was involved now, and he would have to trust her. He would have to trust God. *Especially* now, when time no longer seemed on their side.

He told them of his past, abbreviating only those facts not applicable to the moment or still too painful to discuss. He felt naked before these two. Was he failing in his mission by sharing this? Was he saying the right words? What if he couldn't convince them?

When this doubt crept in, he remembered his *own* attitude decades before, and Ruth Lieberman's frailty. He remembered how in the end the Lord stepped in to make her words too strong to refute. The vision in the bar.

And now, Reverend Dinneck's dreams.

There couldn't be any doubt. The fact that Dinneck was also a minister emphasized the urgency of their situation. Vincent was healthy, at least he thought so, and there would be no use in choosing a minister-successor unless the prize needed to be moved to a new location.

He told them about his flight back to Massachusetts with the old woman, settling in, and answering the ad that had been placed for the new caretaker. Ruth had explained her health issues with the town selectmen before leaving for California, and asked them to place the ad as soon as possible. His timing was good, and came with a reference directly from her. She claimed Vincent as a distant, and reliable, cousin. The selectmen had been willing to put the issue to bed quickly, and there had been no one in the wings waiting for the position. They appointed him with no objections offered at the next selectmen's meeting.

In the following weeks, the two shared this house. Vincent took possession of the couch much like Nathan had done in the church. Ruth handed over the strongbox and its contents. Three days before her declining health forced her into the hospital, she brought him into Greenwood Street Cemetery. It had been after midnight when they opened the crypt and she revealed what lay inside.

Nathan Dinneck seemed affected by this part of the story especially, though the caretaker could not help noticing the mocking smile his girlfriend had been trying to keep from her face.

Vincent stood up and stretched. "I need to show you—both of you, I guess—something important. I'll be right back." He walked from the room, around the corner and into his bedroom. He left the light off, becoming more certain as the night progressed that someone was watching the house. The feeling had begun around the time Hayden had left town. At first he'd written it off—and written it down in his ledger, *entry 819*—as paranoia. The night Dinneck called to say Hayden had disappeared, he no longer thought it was just his imagination.

He knelt beside the bed after moving Johnson's rug aside and worked a finger into the slight indentation in the boards where once there had been a knot. He hesitated. Next to the treasure in John Solomon's grave, the strongbox had been his most secret possession. Bringing it out, letting eyes other than his own see its contents, seemed such a final act of transition.

He removed the board, but folded his hands against his chest.

God, please guide my hands and my mind. Everything is happening, everything seems right. After so many, many years, how can I be certain? What if I go back there and they're gone? What if they're the enemy?

No answer. Of course not. He'd made his conclusions already and there could be no mistake. Maybe he was dragging his feet because he didn't know his own role in the coming events—if he had one. If he could convince these people of the truth, they might take the treasure and leave. Vincent could move on. Maybe go back to school after all these years, earn a degree, become ordained and serve in some new capacity which did not require so much seclusion.

It was a joyous proposition, one that made the act of lifting the strongbox from its hole easier to bear. Still, he shouldn't be so eager to end his ministry. Such eagerness would only open them up to mistakes. Right now he needed to tread carefully. Quickly, but carefully.

He left the compartment open and walked back into the kitchen. *Could* he convince Dinneck? The young man seemed to be listening. And there was the matter of his dreams. But the girl. He'd been trying not to look at the mocking way her eyes squinted at certain details. She laughed at him with those eyes.

She held the same expression when he returned to the table. They'd been whispering to each other. He'd heard the sounds but not the words.

The box *thunked* on the table. He undid the latch and opened the lid, turning it toward Nathan.

"You do not need to read the contents now," he said. "But here are all the notes I've taken over the years. There are also ledgers from Ruth, and many others who came before her. It's not complete, and I don't admit to knowing everything they say since many are in different languages, some pretty archaic. But the story is there if you're willing to take the time."

Elizabeth snorted derisively. "Oh, come on, Tarretti." She nudged Nathan's shoulder. "I think we've heard enough for tonight."

Nathan looked at her. "I told you, we're staying until he's told us everything." He turned back to Vincent.

She leaned forward, whispering though she had to know Vincent could hear. "You don't believe this. He just told us that the Ten Commandments are buried in our town cemetery. The same ones that Charlton Heston carried down the mountain!"

With a calm that belied his growing anger, Vincent said, "Moses carried them, Ma'am. You'd do well to show some respect for—"

"For who? You? A nut who lives like a hermit with his delusions and then takes notes about them? Delusions that God's buried the Ark of the Covenant in a graveyard in a backwoods town like ours?" She stood. "Nate's going through some tough times right now. He has enough to worry about with Pastor Hayden dead and his father involved in some weird group in town. Now you bring us here and tell us that he's got to start guarding some dead guy's tombstone!" She leaned forward and jabbed a finger at him. Johnson growled. "Oh, shut up, you mutt."

Johnson lowered his head and whimpered.

Nathan said nothing. Like Vincent earlier, his eyes were unfocused, his face set in concentration. Vincent decided to ignore Elizabeth and looked at him.

"Reverend," he whispered, and the use of the title made Nathan look up. "This *group* she's talking about—is it the same one you asked about the other day?"

Nathan nodded.

Vincent said, "Tell me everything you might have learned about them since. And do it quickly."

Chapter Forty-Two

As Art Dinneck spoke with the computer operator on the phone, he tried to picture Raymond George. He thought he knew him, but for the moment the man's face eluded him.

"You will need to leave tonight, and go to the storefront. There might be a few men there if the card game isn't over. If not, there is a key hidden under a stone in the back alley. I have just told you that a computer program you wrote is not working. Do you know which program that is?"

Art looked across the kitchen where Beverly was putting detergent into the half-full dishwasher and eyeing him suspiciously. The operator mentioned a program he'd written that had just gone down. He concentrated, trying to remember the name.

"Do you mean FBB714?"

"Yes," the controlled voice of Peter Quinn / Raymond George said. "That is the program. You need to come in and correct the problem."

Art looked at the wall clock and sighed. "Can't it wait until tomorrow?" He wondered why Raymond was making such a big deal out of a report program.

"No, and you do not think so either."

"All right. I'll be there in fifteen minutes."

Beverly slammed the dishwasher door and turned the knob to start the cycle. From her expression, however, Art knew she would accept it. It was work pulling him away from her this time, nothing else. She wouldn't like it, but at least he wasn't going out to... where was he going again?

"Mr. Dinneck?"

"Yes, I'm still here. I—" he hesitated. He didn't *know* any computer operator named Raymond George.

"You have to go now. Go to the men's club, and when you get there you will *want* to be there. Mingle. You have something very important to talk about with Peter Quinn. Wait there until he arrives.

You will believe you are going to work until you are about to reach the highway. Is that understood?"

The man's voice sounded strained. Art decided he must be a new hire. Hopefully the visit wouldn't take too long. "Fine. See you in a little bit." He hung up. "You heard?" he asked Beverly.

She was wiping her hands on a dish towel. "I heard. Will it take long?"

Art grabbed his sneakers beside the back door and sat in a kitchen chair to put them on. "Not at all. The guy's just new, doesn't know what he's doing, or which jobs have what priority, I guess. I should be back in less than an hour."

"Promise you'll come right home?"

He pictured the HMC storefront. He needed to tell Quinn something. But at the moment he couldn't remember what it was. It could wait until tomorrow, worst case. He got up and grabbed a jacket from the closet.

"Promise."

Before he could leave, Beverly was beside him and touching his arm. He turned around and found himself in her strong embrace. He returned it, wishing for a moment that he'd told the guy to ignore the problem and wait until morning.

He could still do that.

No. This was important. He'd be back soon. He gave his wife another prolonged squeeze, then kissed her slowly on the lips. "I'll be right back." He patted his coat pocket, felt a bulge. "I've got my cell if you need to reach me."

Beverly looked like she was going to cry. He thought he understood. He'd been spending so much time at the men's club, and for what? The rift between them was only getting larger. That would change. He walked outside and got into his car. Backing from the driveway, he wondered why he was spending so much time there. A bunch of guys, some no older than Nate, playing cards and drinking. What was the point?

He drove street to street, heading for Interstate 190. As he neared the on-ramp he flipped on the directional. What was he doing? He wasn't going to work, not at this hour. He drove past the ramp and continued across town. He needed to get to the club. It would be the last time, though, for a long time. Maybe ever. Beverly needed him home. He would swing by and talk to Quinn. This was important, and had to be discussed tonight. Then he'd come home and *stay* home.

Maybe this weekend he'd go with her to church, watch Nate.

The thought filled him with immeasurable pride.

The strip mall loomed ahead. The lights of the convenience store shone two doors down from the ethereal glow of the HMC's whitewashed windows. The rest of the storefronts were dark. He tried to remember what it was he wanted to tell Quinn. No matter. It was important and it'd come back to him, in time.

Chapter Forty-Three

Nathan kept his face calm, but inside he was screaming. His mind reeled with so many facts, Tarretti's fantastic story among them. It fit too neatly, especially in light of how his dreams seemed to suddenly have a shocking association with what was happening to his father.

If Tarretti's story was to be believed, he and his predecessors had been hiding the actual Ark of the Covenant from a group of Old Testament Ammonites—a name which Peter Quinn made a point of dropping in their earlier conversation.

To the apparent disgust of Elizabeth, he told the caretaker about his visit with Quinn. When he was done, Tarretti was pale. The man stood so abruptly, Nathan leaned reflexively back in his chair. Johnson rose and moved to his master's side, assuming something was about to happen.

"The flowers in the graveyard," Vincent said, turning in a half circle toward the front room then, as if remembering something, turning back. He picked out the topmost notebook from the stack in the box. "Entry 818," he mumbled. "Here, see?" He held it out. Nathan caught a quick glimpse of messy hand-scratch in blue pen before Vincent pulled it away to look at it himself again, running his fingers along the edge of the page. "They know. They know where it is. Reverend Hayden. Oh God, I'd suspected it myself but I checked..." He pinched the bridge of his nose, sounding and looking as if his tether had finally come loose.

Nathan got up from his chair, slowly, and stood beside Elizabeth. She gave him a look that said, *See? What'd I tell you?*

"Quinn," Vincent continued. "He or someone working with him. They killed Pastor Hayden."

Nathan's heart skipped a beat. All he could think to say in reply was, "What?"

Again, Vincent turned the notebook toward him. "See? Here. I wrote that Quinn made a point to mention Hayden was leaving. That's how I knew to stop by the church that morning. I wondered how the guy knew... he knew because he thought Ralph was leaving with the Ark. Only a priest can move it. Don't you see?"

Elizabeth lashed out with her right arm and knocked the notebook away, sending the pages flapping and the book tumbling against the wall beside the back door. "That... is... enough!" Using the same hand, she backslapped Vincent's face. He stumbled back. Johnson, already cowed by Elizabeth's earlier assertiveness, simply watched and whimpered.

Tarretti put a hand to his face and glared. Nathan steeled himself, knowing he was now going to have to fight to protect her.

"I don't expect you to believe what I'm saying, Miss. You were not the one to whom God has given the signs."

Elizabeth was breathing hard, trying not to cry—but in rage rather than sorrow. His last statement had unwittingly struck a nerve with her.

Nathan stood between them. He had to balance what Elizabeth stood for—worldly rationale, logic—and what Tarretti was saying, which in anyone else's mind, including Elizabeth's, would sound like madness.

It was time, right now, to take a stand one way or the other. He hoped Elizabeth would understand.

He faced Tarretti. "Those people you told us about, the ones you say have been hunting this thing for thousands of years. You're telling me they're the Hillcrest Men's Club? The group my dad belongs to?"

Still holding his cheek, Tarretti nodded. "It's the only answer. And no, they are not the whole organization. I can't imagine they're a very large group. Maybe a couple of hundred people around the world, all told. For the most part, they're nothing more than common thugs. Well-connected, but petty criminals when it comes down to it. More organized crime than any sort of established religion. But that's the crazy part." When he said this, Elizabeth offered an exasperated laugh. "After all this time, neither side knows very much about the other. Knowing anything would mean getting too close. They may number a dozen, or a thousand. But for our side, as far as I know, there's only been one at a time."

Looking for a moment at Nathan and Elizabeth, he added, "Three, now."

"Don't you dare count me or Nate in your little delusion."

"My father is not a demon worshipper."

"Perhaps not." Vincent lowered his hand to reveal a fading red blemish on his face. "He might only be part of the camouflage Quinn has laid around himself. It's their usual MO." He gestured to the box. "It's all in there."

"Nate..."

"Wait. Vincent, you want me to drop everything I'm doing, turn my back on my calling, my church, and... do what?"

Vincent stepped forward. When Elizabeth moved to intercept, he stopped her with a look filled with such loathing she stopped. She was temperamental and protective, but she wasn't stupid. Tarretti was not going to let her get in his way again.

"Reverend Dinneck, I believe God wants you to take what is hidden and leave this town. Forever. You must disappear, trust in the Spirit to guide you to a new location. Of the three of us, only you can even *touch* the relic. This has been the case throughout history. Many have died testing it."

Nathan looked at the strongbox. "You're saying Quinn went after Pastor Hayden because he thought an eighty-year-old man was running away with a gold-laden chest the size of a hatchback car?"

Vincent began to speak, caught himself, then only said, "It's not that big."

The kitchen was quiet. The three of them stood facing each other. Johnson hunkered warily between them. Nathan took in a deep breath and said, "Take me to the gravesite and show me what's inside. I'm not agreeing to do anything you say, but if what you're saying is true, then this would be the next natural step."

"Agreed." At that Tarretti became more animated, bending down to pick up his notebook from the floor. He straightened a bend in the cover then placed it reverently into the box.

If what Tarretti said was true, Nathan would never see Elizabeth again.

No. She could always go with you.

He shook his head reflexively. What was he thinking? Elizabeth was probably right. The man was crazy and Nathan's own problems were clouding his judgment.

"Nate, you can't go with him. Think about what you're going to do. Go into a graveyard in the middle of the night with someone who thinks he's Indiana Jones." Her hands were on his shoulder. Tarretti stood in the kitchen doorway with the box in his hand, waiting. "Nate," she continued, "listen to what I'm saying. A graveyard... in the middle of the *night*." She lowered her voice even further. "He's nuts. You have to know that. He killed Hayden and now he's going to kill you."

"Maybe," he whispered back. "But you haven't seen what I've seen. You didn't have those dreams or experience what happened this morning."

She turned away and said, loudly, "Oh, just forget it. You two are going to run off and play Hardy Boys no matter what I say. And you!" She walked up to Tarretti and jabbed a finger into his chest. He did not flinch. "I'm coming, too, and if you try anything—anything!—I'm going to kill you with my bare hands. Do you understand?"

"Yes, Ma'am."

She jabbed him again. "I'm serious!"

He reached up and bent her hand back so quickly the pain didn't reach her brain until he said, "And if you jab that finger at my chest one more time, I'll break your wrist. Do *you* understand *me*?"

He didn't wait for her reply. He released her and said to Nathan, "Sorry, Pastor. Please follow me so I can show you where I hide this. Just in case."

He turned and walked toward the bedroom. Nathan, despite the terror and confusion of the night, walked past Elizabeth and whispered, "You're cute when you're angry."

She swore in reply, but stayed in the kitchen absently scratching Johnson behind the ears.

Chapter Forty-Four

"**R**oger Quinn speaking. This had better be good."

"Uncle Roger, this is Peter. Did I wake you?"

"Why are you calling me so late?"

Over all these years, Peter could never remember his uncle answering a call with a simple hello. He always made it seem your call was the most inconvenient thing that ever happened to him. Peter switched the cell phone from his left to right ear, as if to block the conversation from Josh Everson. The boy was sitting in the passenger seat staring blankly out through the windshield. It was a relief speaking to his uncle without worrying about controlling his voice. Of course, he expected the conversation to be unpleasant. It always was.

"Things are happening, Uncle. If I'm not mistaken, they're going to happen quickly."

Roger Quinn sighed over the phone. "You're often mistaken, Peter. What sort of *things* are we talking about now?"

Peter felt the familiar twinge of fear and guilt in his stomach. He felt this way every time his uncle spoke to him – always in a disappointed, mean-spirited way. He'd been the man's best disciple, learned quickly, eagerly, yet *never* had he received an actual compliment. Before the mess in Chicago, he hadn't thought Uncle Roger's derision toward him could be any worse. He'd been wrong.

Whether this man liked it or not, things were going to change. At the moment, Peter was grateful he'd kept the murder of Hayden to himself. He'd been wrong about the old preacher, and his tenuous standing in the organization would have been utterly destroyed if they found out what happened.

"The Ark, sir. I'm almost certain they're going to try and move it tonight."

"You don't even know it's there."

"It is." He used his shoulder to hold the phone against his ear as he took a sharp left onto Lexington Street. "And yes, I know that the gravesite might be a ruse. There might be nothing in there but a note laughing at our stupidity. But whether it's there or not, the new minister and Tarretti are having a clandestine meeting at the caretaker's house right now. I told you this afternoon how Dinneck reacted to the painting. Something's up. I'm driving to the old cemetery to keep an eye on the grave."

"It's the caretaker you should be watching."

"We are, Uncle. He won't make a move without me knowing about it."

A long silence over the phone. Peter drove past Greenwood Cemetery and glanced into the dark parking lot. In the passing glow of his headlights, he saw no car. That was good. He slowed and looked for an inconspicuous place to park.

"All right," Roger said at last. Gone was the weary tone of a moment before. It would be the only sign of encouragement Peter would get. "We have a person in New Hampshire. I'll give him a call, tell him to head down. You'll put him up in your place for as long as you need him. I'm not doing anything else until you call me back with more. I'm not wasting more travel money until you've got something concrete to show me."

Ahead, there were three houses in a row, all with their lights off. Peter killed the headlights and coasted to a stop at the edge of the first house's property, close enough to the driveway to give the appearance it belonged there.

"Thank you, Uncle. With any luck, I'll be calling you again tonight."

"I won't hold my breath. And, Peter?"

He turned off the engine, watching the curtains in the house's windows for any sign he was being checked out. "Yes, Uncle?"

"Don't kill anyone this time, please."

Too late for that. "Of course not." He disconnected and turned to Josh. "Mister Everson."

Josh looked at him sleepily. "Yes?"

"We're going to take a walk. Please follow me, and leave your door open when you get out." He reached toward the dash and deactivated the dome light. From the glove compartment, he produced a black knit cap. A bit early in the season, but better than letting his white mane be a beacon. It should provide enough camouflage. He got out of the car, closed his door, then Josh's as quietly as possible. He waited. Nothing changed with any of the darkened homes.

"Follow me, quietly." Together they walked back along Greenwood Street. Josh had to trot to keep up with Quinn's hurried pace.

Chapter Forty-Five

Vincent saw Nathan looking around the bedroom for a light switch and quickly said, "Keep the light off, please. There's a chance the house is being watched."

Nathan dropped his arm but remained in the doorway. Vincent had obliged him by at least turning on the small hallway light on the way in. Light spilled into the bedroom, casting the minister's shadow over the unmade twin-sized bed and dresser. There was enough light to reveal the opening in the floor. Vincent began to replace the box, then hesitated. Something else was in there, something he'd taken out only twice in thirty years. He reached down and lifted the item, wrapped in a light blue shammy cloth. When he laid it down on the floor beside the hole it made a metallic clunk.

"I keep the box here," he said, hoping to bring Dinneck's attention away from the other package. "The board is loose. You have to take the box with you when you leave town."

Nathan whispered, "I never agreed to leave, Mister Tarretti. You know that."

Vincent nodded in the darkness. "Yeah, I know, you said that. Still, don't leave it behind." He put the box into the hole. There was no basement in the house, only a foot-deep sub-flooring. Years earlier, either Ruth Lieberman, or someone living here before, had partitioned the sub floor, creating this makeshift "safe". Three sections of hardwood flooring were sealed together to make the door. He replaced it now and slid the dog's fur-covered bed over it.

When he rose, he left the second package where it lay, partially covered by the dog bed. Elizabeth already thought him a mad man; it wouldn't help her to let her know he was also armed with a nine-millimeter automatic. On the two occasions he'd removed it from the floor, he'd brought it to a pistol range in Worcester, making sure it still worked. Both times he cleaned it before returning it to its hiding place. Once a year he bought a fresh box of nine millimeter rounds and replaced the box in his bottom drawer. He'd prayed he would never have to use it, but he felt better knowing he'd have it tonight.

He waved the minister into the hall. Nathan did not move. Instead he said, "Vincent, listen. Let's say you're right about all this. When you said only priests can move the Ark, I assume you don't mean just Catholic priests. And we'd be hard-pressed to find any Jewish Levitical priests these days."

"Of course not, Reverend. In the days of Solomon, there was no such entity as the Catholic church, or Christians in any form. In this context, priest simply means one ordained by God. Like the Levites you mentioned. Today, well, priests come in all forms. Come on now, we should be moving."

Before they left the hall, Vincent took his windbreaker from the closet. In the kitchen, Elizabeth hadn't moved, except to continue giving Johnson scratches. The dog sat beside her, tongue hanging out joyfully. When he saw Vincent with his jacket he wagged his tail and ran to him.

"No, Boy," Vincent whispered. "We're not going anywhere yet, and when we do, you have to stay put. Going to be hard enough sneaking out without you jumping all over the place."

"So we're going to sneak out now, are we?" Elizabeth took Nathan's hand with the one she'd been using to scratch the dog.

"No, Ma'am. Just me."

She rolled her eyes, but before she could say anything in reply, Vincent raised his hand. "I don't want to hear any more arguments. Have your boyfriend drop you off at home if you have a problem with this. I can't be seen leaving here with you, or they'll know something's up. They already killed Pastor Hayden. If they realize Nathan is the one they're after, then he's in terrible danger."

For the moment that stopped her, but her stare became even icier than before. He had hoped that the two of them leaving without him would be enough to appease her. Give her a chance to convince Dinneck to change his mind. It didn't matter. Nathan had been chosen by God and there wasn't a damned thing she could do about it. He would be there, if for no other reason than to finally have answers.

Nathan said, "So, what's the plan?"

"Drive back to your church, Reverend. You know there's a hiking trail that runs alongside the properties? Go into the church, turn on one light then go out through another door. Use the trail to reach the cemetery."

Nathan nodded. Every child growing up in that part of town knew where the path led, not to mention Nathan's own jaunt along it just last week. There was a spot where the cemetery's bordering rock wall opened up.

"Wait at the gravesite if I'm not there. It'll take me a little longer since I'm going to walk. If I drive they'll see me. Best they think I've gone to bed."

Elizabeth muttered, "Can we go now?"

"Yes. Stay safe, and may God protect you."

"Sure, whatever." She headed for the door, stretching Nathan's arm between them. He held back.

"Don't take long," he said. "As much as I want to resolve this, we're not going to wait all night."

"Agreed. Go now."

When they were gone, Vincent reached down and patted the dog's rump. "Come on, Boy, bedtime." He turned off the kitchen light and walked in the dark to the bedroom, tossing the jacket onto the bed. He unwrapped the gun and loaded fresh rounds into the clip. He worked quickly in the light spilling from the hall, not wanting to be out of sight much longer. He put the gun into the front pocket of the windbreaker and went into the bathroom, turning the light on as he entered, and began brushing his teeth. Johnson had remained in the bedroom, eager for the routine to fall back into place. Vincent finished at the sink, used the toilet and turned the light off behind him as he left. He had to be careful not to break his pattern. Anyone watching him, *if* he was being watched, would notice. Bad enough Dinneck and the girl showing up so late. He turned on his beside lamp, knelt beside the bed and prayed. He stayed longer than usual, begging for strength, for the Lord to protect the two young people and not let the woman keep Nathan from doing what he was called to do.

He prayed also that he would be allowed to serve Him in some way even after the prize was turned over to new hands.

He rose at last, stripped and went to bed. He set the alarm clock, turned off the light then jumped out of bed and dressed again. In the dark living room he carefully put on the windbreaker, made sure the pistol was secure in the pocket with the Velcro-fastened flap. He opened the kitchen window, then the screen, and slowly crawled outside. The gun clunked once on the sill, but otherwise he emerged onto the grass without a sound.

Johnson tried to follow him out the window.

"I'll be right back," Vincent whispered, and pushed the dog back inside with one last scratch behind its ears. He slid the window as far closed as he could manage with one arm still holding back his oldest and best friend. "Stay. Good boy." He gave him another scratch, then withdrew his hand. "Good boy. I'll be right back."

The dog whimpered in protest.

Vincent turned around and waited, letting his eyes adjust to the darkness. Then he ran the short distance to the tool shed.

He knew the location of every tool, every unobstructed space, without needing the light. The crowbar was where it always was, on the lip of the second highest shelf near the door. His hand passed through a thick layer of spider webs to reach it. He'd had no use for this tool—he used much larger versions for working with gravestones—since Ruth last opened the crypt for him. He wiped off the cobwebs and a layer of rust all around it. He hoped it was strong enough to do its job. He reached behind him and slipped it under the jacket, wedging a third of it into the back of his jeans. Once its position had been adjusted enough to offer the least discomfort, he left the shed. The crowbar pressed painfully against his right buttock with every step. There would be no running, not without some painful consequences.

He got his bearings before moving across the yard, keeping to the edge of woods whenever possible. He walked silently, but quickly.

Chapter Forty-Six

For most of the ride to the church, Elizabeth remained quiet. She brooded beside Nathan, arms folded across her chest. He would have welcomed a distraction from his jumble of thoughts, even if the distraction was Elizabeth finally blowing her top. What he was planning to do felt *right*, the next logical step. Even if all this was pointless, even dangerous, at least it would be an answer. Either the dreams and Hayden's murder and his father's situation were all connected, part—or the result of—some overall plan by God, or he was letting himself be drawn into another man's delusions. Either way, it was coming to closure. It felt like he was moving along in another dream, unable to change what was coming.

He could stop it now, call the police and turn Tarretti in. Let them separate truth from fantasy. When he considered this, a tightness pulled at his stomach. It would be wrong, his instincts told him. Don't fight the current; swim with it to the end.

Then maybe Nathan could move on with his life, prepare the congregation for the shock of learning their former pastor was dead. There would be many, many people who would need him; his ear and his arm and his words for comfort.

Problem was, he couldn't see that result on the horizon. Not in the direction they were heading.

The intersection with Greenwood Street passed by on their right. Elizabeth followed its progress through her window but remained silent. Nathan took the next right onto Dreyfus Road and in a moment was turning into the church's driveway. The building was dark. He considered driving past the smaller lot in front, with its space still marked "Pastor Hayden", and parking in the back. It would be closer to the woods and the path leading to the southern edge of the cemetery.

That would be breaking his own routine. He parked in front. Seeing Hayden's name bathed in the headlights filled him with a renewed sense of pain. He pushed it down. Time for that later. There was something else, another sensation kindled at seeing the sign. A sense of urgency. *Nad ei tohi seda võtit saada!*

What did that mean?

It was going to be a long night. He needed to stay focused. Looking back to the road, Nathan saw no sign they'd been followed. Time to enter the church, then pass straight through and out the back door. If someone was watching, hopefully they'd think he was still inside.

With Elizabeth.

Let them think what they would. At the moment, it really didn't matter.

As soon he turned the car off, Elizabeth turned toward him, partly restrained by the seatbelt.

"Nate. I've given you enough time to think about this. Let's go inside, and stay there. Tell me we're not going to walk through the woods and wander into a cemetery. Please tell me that."

He stared out the windshield. In the dark, he no longer could read Hayden's name except for a veiled impression of the letters. He didn't dare look Elizabeth in the eye. Not yet. "I'll be willing to drive you home, E. I just—"

"I'm not going home! Especially if you're still going through with this!" Her voice fell soft, pleading. "Nate, let's go inside and call the police. I'm not saying Tarretti doesn't have some connection to all this. He might even be right about your dad's group being involved." She laid a hand on his arm. He flinched involuntarily, but she did not let go. "But Tarretti might be involved in a *bad* way. Have you thought of that? Reverend Hayden was found in the middle of the woods; you told me that yourself. Now some guy wants you to climb into a grave with him?"

She had a point. But the images from the dreams, the vision during the Sunday fellowship dinner....

What if they'd been warnings? What if God wasn't telling him to pay more attention to John Solomon's grave but rather to stay *away* from it?

He closed his eyes. Elizabeth, perhaps sensing she'd made ground with him, remained quiet. She left her hand on his arm, even offered a gentle squeeze in support.

He imagined the stone statues, remembered the second dream. An evil had been approaching. The angels offered an unspoken peace.

Protection.

Dear God, I have to know. Even if it kills me, I have to know. Tonight. Now.

"I'm going, but I'm not ignoring what you said. In fact, if you're right, one of us needs to stay. If I'm not back in a half hour, call the police."

He opened the car door and stepped out. She followed him up the walkway and into the residence's side door. Nathan felt her anger like heat against his back as he unlocked the door and stepped in.

He turned on the light in the small hallway, bypassed the stairs and proceeded into the kitchen. He left the kitchen light off. Elizabeth's outline stayed close behind. He said, "When I'm gone, turn on the light in here. Make yourself at home." He walked forward and kissed her on the cheek, not daring any more of a gesture for fear he would never leave. "I'll be right back."

Elizabeth held his shoulders with both her hands. She sniffed once, and Nathan realized she was crying. "I'm going with you, Nate. If you walk directly into hell, I'm walking there, too. Don't *ever* think otherwise."

She kissed him. It wasn't long, nor was it simply the quick, affectionate gesture he'd offered a moment before. Her tears ran down his own cheeks. When she moved back a half-step, both wiped their faces dry.

Between sniffles she said, "Got a flashlight somewhere?"

"In the broom closet by the back door." He nodded behind him. "I think."

"We'll grab it as we leave. Just keep it turned off until we're far enough into the woods." She groaned at her own words and followed him to the closet.

He hadn't been long enough in the house to know everything's location by rote, but after some fumbling with his fingers along the closet shelf, he found the flashlight. He closed the door partway and flipped the switch on and off quickly to make sure it worked. There was now a glowing white dot in his vision. Trying to blink it away, he opened the door and walked outside. Elizabeth followed, closing the door with a single click behind her.

The main parking lot took up most of the cleared property behind the church. Beyond, a large swath of grass spread between pavement and woods. It served as an elongated back yard for church functions. They walked across it without speaking, Nathan holding the darkened light in one hand and Elizabeth's hand in the other. There was no moon. Starlight was scattered among breaks in the dark clouds above them. He made his best guess as to the entrance to the path, wishing he *had* taken this route last week so it would be more familiar to him.

"You OK?" she whispered.

"Yeah, I'm fine. Here..." He gestured toward a patch in the bushes and trees which was slightly darker than the rest. When they passed into it, Nathan released her hand and held his arm ahead of him. Nothing blocked their way. They were on the path.

He kept the arm extended, face-level. Every now and then it would connect with a low branch. At these moments, he would bend it back to allow Elizabeth to pass, then let it swing behind him like a gate.

In this way, they moved toward the cemetery, alternating who led and held aside the next obstruction. They reached the bordering stone wall to their left sooner than Nathan anticipated. The darkness was impenetrable in most areas, but still he refrained from using the flashlight. His eyes were slowly adjusting in the pitch.

"Keep an eye for a break in the wall. Somewhere soon, on the left."

There it was. An old, gnarled shape of a tree rose before them, visible only because it blocked out the stars behind it. Past this, the land opened up. The cemetery. The tree's shape was so utterly black Nathan felt that if he reached out, his hand would pass straight through. The tree bordered one side of a small break in the wall. A smaller birch stood on the other end. Its spotted white bark was easier to distinguish.

Before he stepped between them Nathan whispered, "Shhh." He stood still. Elizabeth gripped one of his back belt loops as if worried he'd suddenly take off running.

Nathan listened. Slowly, he turned his head around and gazed into the impenetrable shadows of the woods to their right. Had he heard something, seen movement in the corner of his eye? He held the flashlight before him, wanting to turn it on and bathe everything into a comforting white glow. Part of him—his guttural, childlike fear of the dark perhaps—was certain that a monster stood there, waiting for the light so it could show its teeth and devour him.

The logical side of him also stayed the thumb resting on the switch. If the cemetery was being watched, what better way to give the two of them away than to light up the woods just before they entered?

The feeling passed. Best get into the open and over to the gravesite. There they could duck out of the way and wait for Tarretti. Maybe stay hidden even after he arrived, see how he behaved. Check out what—or who—he brought with him.

Nathan stepped through the opening in the wall. A slight tug on his belt loop told him Elizabeth was falling into step. He tripped over a stone and stumbled forward. The flashlight rolled out of his hands and across the cold grass a second before Elizabeth landed on top of him. His breath left in a dim cloud of mist.

Elizabeth scrambled off and laughed, suppressing the sound with her hand over her mouth. Nathan was too concerned with breathing to be embarrassed. She bent down and kissed him on the top of his head. "You OK, Sherlock?"

He took a tentative breath and nodded. "Yeah, yeah. I dropped the flashlight."

She crawled forward a few paces and picked it up. "Let's not hang around here too long. For all we know we're lying in a patch of poison ivy."

Nathan got up slowly. He took her hand. She kept the flashlight, but left it off. Nathan led the way toward Solomon's grave.

Chapter Forty-Seven

Peter Quinn held his breath the entire time Nathan Dinneck stared into the woods where he and Josh Everson were crouched. If his voice would not have given him away, he would have commanded Everson to hold his own breath. The boy would have obliged, then eventually passed out from oxygen deprivation. Instead, he stood motionless, and Peter hoped the kid didn't breathe too loudly.

He'd heard the two of them coming early enough to move off the path. They probably didn't realize how much noise they were making. Their ignorance was a blessing, for his eyes had been on the small parking lot waiting for Dinneck's or Tarretti's car to pull in. The fact that they might trek in through the woods this late at night hadn't occurred to him.

Of course, it also meant Paulson may have failed him. If these two were going through such an effort to come here, Tarretti mustn't be far behind. But Paulson had called only once to say that they'd left and the caretaker had gone to bed. As Dinneck stared almost directly at him, Peter assumed Paulson would choose that moment to call. His phone was set to vibrate-mode, but even that would be like a klaxon this close.

When Dinneck and his woman fell over each other just past the wall, Peter took the opportunity to let his breath out, slowly, and take another in. Josh made no motion whatsoever. At least he was breathing. Now that the couple was far enough down the hill toward the grave, Quinn whispered into the young man's ear, "Mister Everson, follow me, and make no sound. Move carefully."

Whispering in the Voice was tricky, but easier than using it over the phone. Josh followed like an obedient dog.

Peter stayed behind the large tree, keeping to its side enough for a view into the cemetery. At one point, someone had turned on a flashlight. He could hear voices. They carried far in the cool night air. He did not understand what they were saying, but soon the light was out again. The dark figures hid themselves behind a large monument not far from the cherubim. He guessed they would remain there until... what? Until Vincent Tarretti arrived, of course.

Realizing how far their voices had carried, he put his lips to Josh's ears and whispered for him to sit in the path. The tree would cut off any chance of being seen by Dinneck or the woman. Paulson still had not called. The implication was that Tarretti was laying low for a while, or that the man knew he was being watched. Not a good situation. If they knew Peter was this close, he'd have to move fast when the chance arrived.

He looked down to the path under his feet. He couldn't see it, but its existence sparked an idea in him. What if the caretaker really *had* left, snuck out and taken some back way as these two had done?

He'd know soon enough. He didn't want to call Paulson, afraid the dim glow of the phone would give away his position behind the tree. He made himself comfortable on the ground, making sure the couple's position was at least partially in view, and waited for something to happen.

Chapter Forty-Eight

Vincent Tarretti needed to get off this street as soon as possible. Even if he could run without skewering himself with the crowbar, he didn't want to draw any attention. The pistol bumped against his belly with every step. Vincent hadn't realized he'd forgotten to bring a flashlight until he'd already walked half way across town. He usually kept it in the front pocket. He'd become too much a creature of routine, never thinking outside of the box he'd built around himself. He would have to be sharper than that to get through whatever was ahead. Hopefully Dinneck thought to bring one. Going back to his house now, or to the church, was a detour he didn't think they could afford.

The sense of urgency plaguing him these past few days filled every muscle in his body, growing stronger the further he walked across town. Tonight's discussion—or confrontation, depending on how one looked at it—was its fuel. Dinneck and the girl might not be there when he arrived. They might have stayed at the church and called the police. What he'd said tonight certainly convinced Elizabeth he was a little under-stocked in the sanity department.

Vincent felt, with all his heart, that he'd connected with the young minister. Nathan Dinneck believed him, or at least hadn't completely ruled him out.

There was nothing to do but continue forward and trust that God would keep Nathan on the right path. Vincent kept mostly to the darker, residential roads, moving at a forced leisurely pace in the more populated corners of Hillcrest. It was the second time in less than a week he had traveled this route. Cutting through the woods at the end of the main cemetery was always difficult, and he wondered how the teenagers managed it so often during the summer without breaking their necks. His jeans were caked with mud up to the knees, the result of stepping in a soft section of the wetlands. Now as he walked along Hepworth Avenue, his sneakers squished with trapped water. He reached back and adjusted the steel bar under his jacket.

Hepworth intersected with the far end of Greenwood Street. Almost there. Headlights behind him. He looked in panic for a place to step off the road. Nowhere, not without looking suspicious. He continued on, hands in his pants pockets, keeping a steady pace. The pistol suddenly weighed a hundred pounds. He hoped the approaching car wasn't a police cruiser. Nothing like coming across a guy with a pony tail wandering through Smalltown, USA, carrying both a gun and a crowbar.

A minivan passed by. He made a point not to look into its windows. The van continued to the far curve in the road before pulling into a driveway. Its headlights cut out. Vincent slowed his pace, not wanting to catch up too quickly. As it was, he moved past the house just as the driver, a teenager obviously having borrowed his parents' van for the night, was walking up the front steps. He looked over as Vincent passed. Vincent waved absently and the kid waved back, probably assuming he was a neighbor taking a late stroll. The boy went inside.

Vincent let his breath out in a slow, cleansing sigh. He was nervous, edgy. He wished he could go back to the house and write in his notebook. Noting the events of his life gave him control over them. Or the illusion of control.

He reached the intersection with Greenwood. It was a long road, mostly wooded, with the old cemetery at the far end. As he turned onto it, something troubled him. When he brought Dinneck and the girl down into the crypt, what would they see? The vault held more than one secret. An amazing, terrifying thing. When Ruth first showed him, he was shocked. *Dazzled* wouldn't be far from a qualifying adjective. The Ark had been smaller than he'd anticipated, barely a yard long, two feet high and deep, but that fact didn't seem to matter. Not at first. It should have. There was so much power filling the small room. She made him look a second time, bringing him closer to what he'd assumed was the source of such pulsing energy. He saw something very different, as if a veil had been lifted inside his head.

At that moment, twenty-seven years ago, a much younger Vinnie Tarretti wondered aloud how in the world he'd seen what he'd seen the first time. Ruth had smiled, weakly, and whispered that *nothing* in the world had anything to do with it. More than anything else, that moment standing before the makeshift altar under the earth had convinced him. Of everything. This, more than anything, would be his ace when convincing Dinneck. It had to be.

Twenty-one paces past the last house on his right, he turned off the road and made his slow way through the mountain laurel and sumac, deeper into the woods. It didn't take long before he stepped into a clearing dotted with the muted outlines of dozens of gravestones at the far northern edge of the graveyard.

He was blinded by the glare of a flashlight.

"Who's there?" whispered Dinneck's voice.

Vincent raised his hand to his face and whispered back, "Could you please try your best not to blind me, Reverend?"

The light cut out. The dark cemetery was replaced by a white sheet.

Dinneck and Elizabeth had been hiding behind a statue of the Virgin Mary near the exact point of Vincent's arrival. They probably heard him coming as soon as he'd stepped off the road.

He blinked and waited for the night blindness to resolve itself. Two shapes walked up to him.

"Sorry," Nathan said.

"It's all right." He reached behind him and carefully pulled out the crowbar. The woman gasped. He said, "Oh, relax," and waved it in the air like a baton. "We need this to get inside." He pointed toward the grave across the way, then handed the bar to Nathan. "Let's get to work."

*   *   *

In that brief, second flash of light across the clearing, Peter saw Vincent Tarretti. Soon after, their voices reached across the distance to him. *Paulson*, he thought, *you are such an ass.* He needed him here now, but did not dare turn on his phone. Not yet. He needed to wait, at least until the trio were out of sight.

From the way things were progressing, he knew that meant when they'd lowered themselves into the grave. Even if they wisely left one of their number at ground level as lookout, he would have to make the call. There would be precious little time left. While he waited, he busied himself wiping the gun he'd used to kill Pastor Hayden. He used a new handkerchief, working at every corner. If everything panned out, this would be the last time he would hold the weapon.

*   *   *

"I'm glad you thought to bring a flashlight," Vincent mumbled. "I can't believe I forgot something so basic."

Elizabeth kept the light aimed at Tarretti's feet. She didn't trust much of anything he said, but *Nate* had chosen to trust him so she didn't have much choice.

"After you," she said, waggling the beam quickly across the ground. He took the lead, followed by Elizabeth, who tried to keep the light fixed at a spot just ahead of him. Vincent's shadow loomed over the angels' bent forms. Nate was being his usual quiet, introspective self. She wondered—not without a little hope—if he was suffering from second thoughts now that the moment of truth had arrived.

The caretaker wasted no time. He knelt down, occasionally directing her to point the light this way or that. He pushed aside the leaves and dirt like someone looking for a lost marble. An appropriate image, Elizabeth decided.

Tarretti worked his fingers along the concrete base, at first only pushing aside a thin layer of dirt, but shifting more and more as he worked his way to the edge of the platform. Here the dirt and sediment was at least three inches thick. Once he found what he sought, he carefully ran his fingertips back along the narrow groove he'd made, then stopped.

"Here it is," he said. Nate moved beside Elizabeth, gave her one quick glance, then continued to stare. All their attention was on the kneeling man as he slowly uncovered more and more of what was apparently the edge between the concrete base and a door of some sort.

"Keep the light here. Good." He straightened, then raised his hand to Nate, who handed over the crowbar. Tarretti worked one edge into the exposed rift between the two concrete sections, rocking the tool back and forth. Something shifted.

Vincent looked up and offered a tired smile. "Well, here goes nothing."

He pulled back on the crowbar, exerting a slow but increasingly intense pressure. The silence of the night was invaded by a subtle hiss, like someone slowly opening a bottle of Coke. The sound grew in intensity, a *sssssssssssssssssss* followed by what Elizabeth could only describe as a *sigh*. Air raced into the void under the concrete slab. Tarretti used the sudden release of pressure to lever the cover up and over an inch, enough so that it did not fall back into place. Once done, he relaxed, and the concrete slab settled back at a new, awkward angle.

The smell was of old dust, of clothes in her grandmother's attic.

Images of discovering a long-neglected trunk one weekend while her parents cleaned out Gram's house after her funeral. Elizabeth was young, five or six years old, but the memory of the trunk being opened and the smell of decayed fabric and stale air came back to her now. As did the image of herself as a child, lifting one thin, long white dress from the trunk. Then the stale odor passed up from the breach in the grave and was gone, merging with newer, fresher air. With it went the unexpected memory of the attic.

It occurred to her only then that in the hole they'd just reopened was not a pile of forgotten dresses and shawls, but a body. A decomposed, perhaps mummified corpse of John Solomon, preserved by the airless vacuum inside.

It was time to go home. No question.

"Seen enough?" she whispered. "Can we leave now?"

Nate seemed to consider the suggestion, then slowly shook his head. At least he appeared to, in the afterglow of the light still trained on Tarretti's hands. The latter was looking up with a worried expression. He'd apparently heard the question.

"Let's get this over with," Nate said at last, and Vincent nodded in undisguised relief. Using the crowbar, he wiggled it up and down slowly along the edge, until the slab was far enough off the base that he could move it with his own hands. He slowly dragged it clear of the entrance.

The three of them stood and looked down into the square black hole at their feet. The hole stared back like an unblinking eye.

Trying to keep out of Elizabeth's flashlight beam, Nate walked up and stood beside Tarretti. The light bounced as Elizabeth joined him. She was like a guard dog, not letting him get more than a pace away.

She shined the light into the hole. The three of them peered in. A wooden ladder reached from the dust-covered floor to the lip of the entrance.

"I'll go in first," Vincent said. "This ladder is built into the side, see? Last time I was here it held my weight, but that was a long time ago. If it can still support me, you can follow."

Without waiting for a reply, he sat on the lip of the concrete and carefully stepped onto the top rung. It creaked, but held. Using his hands to support himself on the edge, he stepped down two more rungs, far enough to grip the ladder. In the flashlight beam his fingertips were black from digging. This time, the ladder's protests were more a moan under the weight. Before his head dropped below ground level, he took one last, deep breath of the night air. Then he was down, standing with a slight hunch on the floor.

"Not a very high ceiling in here; watch your head."

Nate sat on the edge and mirrored Tarretti's descent. It was Elizabeth's turn, now. Using only one hand for support, she kept the flashlight trained always on some part of their host. Her first sensation as she moved lower was how much colder the air felt inside. When she stepped off the ladder, the floor of the room was, indeed, covered in dust an inch thick. From the way the chamber's seal had hissed, she didn't imagine much had fallen recently. Perhaps over the years, enough dirt and grime had settled into the cracks to effectively seal off any remaining source of outside air.

She took a tentative breath. Not as bad as she'd imagined, but then, it was the same air that had been outside a moment before. It tasted... older, though. Probably the dust kicked up by her feet, enough to remind her where they were. Elizabeth saw nothing in front of her, and kept Tarretti in her peripheral vision.

Then she felt it, like an electrical thrill in the air moments before a thunderstorm. Her imagination again, fueled by the cooler air.

Vincent whispered, "It's over here." He took a step forward into the darkness. Only then did Elizabeth shine the light in that direction.

Nathan grabbed Elizabeth's arm. She didn't react, but stared ahead and with a harsh whisper, said, "It can't be true. It is not true...."

Chapter Forty-Nine

Manny Paulson was constantly amazed how bright the world truly was at night, once his eyes adjusted. He'd had plenty of practice, lately. For the past four nights, Quinn had him sitting here in the graveyard's utility road, with no purpose but to keep an eye on the house of the weirdo who took care of the cemeteries. Manny had worked night shifts in a couple of different jobs. Those hadn't been very long-lasting, through no fault of his own. If the idiots running the bottling plant couldn't keep their heads above water, it wasn't his fault.

The last job he'd had, doing data entry at a small mail-order shop, was even worse than his assembly line gigs. He'd been forced to hunker over a computer all night, entering names and addresses into a glitch mail order program. The printing on the data entry sheets got smaller and smaller the longer the night stretched on. Heaven help him if he hadn't met his quota of contacts by morning. On that job, the challenge had been keeping awake without drinking so much coffee that he spent most of his shift in the bathroom. More than once he tried to convince the witch who ran the place that converting from mail order to a cheaper spamming venture on the web would be the way to go. She insisted on staying in the dark ages. The company closed down six months after he'd been laid off. Well, he assumed that's what happened. He never bothered to check.

Manny couldn't remember holding a job much longer than a year. Not that he wasn't qualified, with an associate's degree in business and a couple of older reemployment references he still managed to squeeze onto one more application. The time finally came when his luck ran out, along with the country's economy. He'd been living day to day as it was, but soon it felt more like *dying* day to day. The zombies at the unemployment office kept limiting his benefits because of sporadic work history. His options had quickly dried up.

At least the letters demanding child support for his son and daughter, usually from someone claiming to be an attorney (though he was certain it was just some guy Melissa worked with), had trickled to an occasional note venting his ex-wife's disgust with his lack of concern for "your children". She was an accountant and made plenty of money. Manny once considered finding a lawyer himself and suing her for alimony. But lawyers cost money, and money was tight.

As for his kids, fatherhood was never big on his list of goals. It was fun while it lasted, but now that he was free, Melissa could keep the headaches. Maybe if grandchildren came into the picture a decade or two from now, he might show his face again. He heard they were a lot less work.

Enter Peter Quinn, during one of Manny's rare purchases of beer at the *Greedy Grocer.* He never had been much of a drinker, preferring to avoid any habit that might suck more coins from the bare cupboard his bank account had become. Still, now and then he'd splurge on a twelve pack of Bud and rent a couple of movies.

His first assumption when Quinn caught up with him outside the store was that the guy was hitting on him. Manny had excused himself and headed for his car, but Quinn followed. He asked if Manny needed a job. Steady work, not very difficult, and the pay was good.

Sounded too good to be true. But Quinn hadn't been lying. The work was easy, and the pay was twice anything he'd ever collected before. Everything was under the table, too. Nothing for Uncle Sam, or Melissa, to lay claim to. All Manny had to do was not smirk when Quinn started chanting to the devil or talking about some *valuable prize* buried in town. The guy was seriously nuts, no question. But he must be rich, connected with the mob or something like that. The cash every week was real, and had to come from somewhere. Quinn was always calling someone in Chicago. Most like his connection was with the Mafia than a three thousand year old cult. Quinn and his goons were on some modern day treasure hunt, no more, no less.

Didn't matter to him. As long as they kept paying and he didn't wake up some day with a horse's head in his bed, he was more than happy to sit in the woods and stare monotonously at some dark house all night. The vigil wouldn't be half as hard, though, if he could read something. The boss had been very specific about no lights, and Quinn had an uncanny way of knowing when he was being lied to. So, Manny simply sat in his car, now and then pouring more coffee from his thermos when he felt his eyes closing for too long. Like they were beginning to do now.

His phone vibrated against his hip. *Thank God*, he thought. *A distraction.*

He pulled the cell from its holster. "Manny Paulson."

Quinn's voice was barely audible, so quietly was he whispering. "Where are you, Paulson?"

"The usual spot. Nothing to report."

A pause, then, "Obviously. Tarretti, Reverend Dinneck and his girlfriend are here at the cemetery on Greenwood Street, you blind, useless...." He stopped, let his breath out slowly before continuing. "Get over here, now, but be quiet about it. Do you remember where the grave is?"

"Pretty sure, yeah. And listen, I swear I didn't see—"

But the call had already been disconnected. Manny cursed and started the car.

*   *   *

Peter pocketed the phone, then lifted the gun in the handkerchief. It was a clip-fed nine millimeter, the same type carried by Vincent Tarretti, though Peter didn't know this fact. The rounds were small but effective.

"Mister Everson."

Josh looked at him. "Yes?"

Making sure the safety was thumbed to the "on" position, at least until he could see how the kid handled it, he handed him the weapon. He would be sure the safety was off before he sent the boy into the grave. "Take this and follow me. I have something I need you to do. Very important, and you will want to do this very much." He rose; the young man did likewise. Peter picked up the battery-powered lantern they had brought from the car, but left it dark.

He led Everson out of the woods, making sure to keep him slightly to the side as they walked toward the gravesite, in case he tripped. Safety or not, he didn't want to risk being shot in the back. As they came closer, the voices, which had faded once the trio dropped from sight, came back to him along with an occasional blink of the flashlight. Peter removed the black cap and tucked it into his back pocket, then worked his fingers through his hair, putting it back into some sense of order.

He forced himself to breathe steadily, clearing his mind. So close, but not there yet. In whispers, he used the Voice to instruct Josh Everson what he must do.

Chapter Fifty

In its entirety the room was barely twice as large as the area where the three of them stood. No furnishings, save one significant slab of concrete raised a few feet from the floor with matching slabs acting as supports. The setup reminded Elizabeth uncomfortably of an altar. Most of the room lay under the base of angelic statues. On either side of the concrete altar, from floor to ceiling, rose two cylindrical concrete supports like she had in her own basement.

What drew everyone's attention, however, was what sat on top of the slab.

In the beam of her flashlight, the gold trim of the Ark glittered as if freshly washed. The dust that permeated every corner of the room seemed not to touch it. It was a chest with elaborate gold designs of multi-faced figures staring out from the every side. The lid was trimmed with more gold, but was simple in design. She remembered again the memory of the chest in Gram's attic. The entire vessel was no more than a yard wide, rectangular, much smaller than the images she'd seen once or twice in pictures from her old Sunday school books. She thought there should have been something atop the lid, statuary or some such decoration. The word "seat" came to mind but she wasn't sure why. Overall, the structure seemed too small. Something occurred to her. She wasn't sure what that *something* was, but the Ark's size and details no longer seemed wrong. It was just, well, different than she'd imagined.

The gold reflected more light than could have come from her flashlight, though when she lowered the light experimentally, no additional glow emanated from that side of the room. She scratched the back of her neck with her free hand. The air felt... *itchy*, filled with static electricity.

Knock it off, she thought, trying to regain her composure. *It's a fancy box. Nothing more.*

Nate, however, must have thought otherwise. He slowly fell to one knee, with an expression of wonder and awe. He said, "How can this be? How can this possibly be?"

Tarretti shrugged. "It's God's will that the Covenant not fall into the hands of anyone but His followers. It's been a long race, a long struggle. We cannot understand the why of it, except for the reasons I've already explained. More than that, we'll never know. Not until we're with Him in paradise. Someday you can read some of my translations of earlier caretakers' theories. There are references to the Ark of the Covenant in the book of Revelations, but in those, it appeared within the glory of heaven. Nothing earth-bound.

"But the adversary is close, and it's time for the treasure to leave this place."

Elizabeth turned the flashlight onto the caretaker's face. Vincent squinted and raised one hand to block the light. She said, "What exactly do you want with Nate? If you want to take this thing away somewhere, just take it."

"Please take that light out of my face." When she didn't, he sighed and nodded in the direction of the altar. "I've already explained that only an ordained priest of God can transport the Ark." He looked at Nate. "You know what I'm saying is the truth, Reverend."

Nate rose up. One knee was caked in dust. Tarretti was somehow enchanting him, playing on his faith in order to manipulate him. She aimed the light back at the box. "This is getting ridiculous. What's inside that thing? And don't tell me the ten commandments or I'll hit you with this flashlight."

She walked up to the altar and reached out. Tarretti tackled her from the side, arms around her waist. She felt something else as well, but before she could think much about it she was in the dust with Tarretti on top of her and already struggling to his feet. The flashlight had rolled to the corner of the room.

"Don't," he said, almost pleading, trying to catch his breath and move away from her at the same time. "If you touch it, you'll die!"

Chapter Fifty-One

Nathan ran to Elizabeth and took her arm, helped her up. Tarretti's sudden move had broken the reverential spell he had fallen into when he saw the Ark. It looked much smaller than he'd expected, but the shape, the detailed gilding along its face and lid, was very much like what he had envisioned. His mood had shifted decidedly at seeing Elizabeth attacked, however, and for the moment, he let himself forget everything else except his own anger.

He turned toward Tarretti's rising form. "Keep your hands off her, Mr. Tarretti. Maybe what you're saying is true, but if you do something like that again, so help me—"

Vincent raised his hands. "I apologize, but you've read the Bible, Reverend. You know what happens to anyone who touches this vessel."

Nathan *did* understand. There were incidents in the Old Testament of people reaching out for the Ark only to fall instantly dead. Many scholars theorized that perhaps the structure was built in such a way that it was hyper-conductive to electricity, a battery built before such a concept was ever conceived. Nathan never bought into that theory. Batteries didn't win wars.

But something in how Tarretti said this made Nathan think, for the first time tonight, that he was lying. In some way. He looked back at the gold-laden chest.

"Is that why you need me? I'm supposed to be the only one who can touch it?"

A dust-covered Elizabeth walked to the corner and retrieved the flashlight. When she returned, she moved it alternately between the Ark and Tarretti. "Maybe you should try Saint Malachy's across town."

"Elizabeth, please," Nathan said, letting impatience slip into his tone. He pointed to the table. "Where do you think I'm supposed to take this? I have a ministry to support. People need me here, not hiding in some graveyard in Kansas or Missouri."

Vincent brushed dust off his sleeve and said, almost sadly, "God will lead you to the best place. This is your ministry now, Reverend. He will take care of your old flock somehow."

Nathan swallowed. The dust was beginning to make him choke. He couldn't accept this; even now, he needed to be certain. "Like Elizabeth said, is what's inside there the tablets of the ten commandments? The actual ones Moses brought down from the mountain?"

He thought, perhaps hoped, that saying this out loud would sound ridiculous. It didn't, not to him, not at this moment. Perhaps God was putting this acceptance in his heart. Or maybe he was just tired of fighting. Time to just go mad himself and live out the delusion.

Tarretti moved toward the altar, but did not touch it. Elizabeth shined the light into the center of his jacket. "I thought I felt something when you landed on me. What's in your front coat pocket, Tarretti?"

Vincent put a hand to the front of his windbreaker and sighed, like a man who'd just eaten something that did not agree with him. "It's a gun, Miss O'Brien."

Nathan and Elizabeth stiffened.

"Please," he continued. "I'm not going to shoot you. I didn't think you'd like the fact that I came here armed. Believe me, it is purely for our protection." He turned toward Nathan. "Reverend, I feel strongly that our time is running out, and I need to tell you one more thing."

A light thump behind them was followed by a man's voice. "Please do not move, or I will be forced to shoot you."

The words were spoken with a monotone, like a person learning lines in a play. The shock of the new arrival was so surprising, no one moved, except to shift themselves on the dusty floor to look back toward the ladder.

Before Elizabeth's flashlight beam landed across him, Nathan knew who that voice belonged to. Josh Everson stood at the base of the ladder, a small black gun in his hand. He held it with a steady assurance, though Nathan couldn't remember his friend ever holding one before.

Josh stared with sorrowful eyes, almost the look of a sleepwalker. He raised the gun toward Elizabeth. "Move the light away now, please." His voice grew in urgency as he said this. Everyone in the room came to the same conclusion. He was preparing to shoot someone. Elizabeth lowered the flashlight to a spot on the floor between her and Nathan. Josh stood no more than five feet from him.

To Nathan, it seemed a hundred miles. This couldn't be Josh. It was too much to accept that he was involved in this.

Then again, he hadn't known about Josh and Elizabeth's relationship either. He hadn't known this... thing... was buried in his home town. No, his best friend was not about to shoot Elizabeth.

"Josh," he said, almost sadly. Josh moved his head toward him in a jerking motion. Nathan continued, "Josh, what's going on? It's me, Nate. And Elizabeth."

Josh's head did a robot turn toward her. No recognition, in what expression could be seen in the dust covered light.

There was a sudden *scrunch!* from across the small room. Vincent had opened the front of his jacket and was reaching inside.

Josh aimed his gun at the caretaker's chest and did not hesitate when he pulled the trigger. The room exploded with sound and one bright, blue-white flash. Nathan put his hands to his ears, feeling pain in his head from the shot's reverberation. Elizabeth reached out and pulled him to the floor.

Josh did not fire the gun again.

Elizabeth whispered, "Vincent?" The fact that she used his first name, and in such a tentative way, filled Nathan with a terrible premonition. In the suddenness of what had just happened, the fact that Josh had shot the man hadn't registered until now. He added his own, "Tarretti? Vince, you OK?" He wanted to ask Josh why he'd done it, but now he didn't want to draw his friend's attention their way.

Elizabeth shined the flashlight toward where the caretaker had been standing.

Vincent Tarretti slid along the wall, the jacket bunching up behind him. His hands were pressed against his stomach, just above the oversized pocket. Blood spilled though his fingers. He moaned once, landing in a spread-eagle sitting position.

Vincent blinked rapidly in the flashlight beam, looking more confused than anything, then whispered, "I'm sorry." He closed his eyes and he fell sideways until his head tilted onto the dusty floor. He tried to reach out, managed to get his right arm raised, then it, too, fell to the floor. He did not move again.

Elizabeth's shaking hand aimed the flashlight's circle across the dark streak on the wall. It dripped a path to where the caretaker lay slumped and unmoving on the floor. The spot on the wall glistened.

Nathan looked away, his throat tight, fighting down a nausea building in his stomach. He tried to speak but couldn't. Everything was gone. Nothing was real anymore. Nothing.

Someone climbed casually down the ladder. Nathan could not see who it was because Elizabeth kept the flashlight fixed on the far wall.

"You did the right thing, Mister Everson. Remind me to give you a cookie later." The speaker laughed. The sound was tight and without amusement.

"Reverend Dinneck, I presume," said the voice—Peter Quinn's voice. "And his lovely sidekick, whatever your name is." Another chuckle. "Sorry about all the dramatics. But rest assured, Mister Tarretti will get a fine burial. In one of the nicest spots in the cemetery." The figure raised its arms to the room. He moved forward, crossing into the beam of Elizabeth's light, and stood before the concrete altar. Almost as an afterthought, he added, "If either of them try to move toward you or me, Mister Everson, shoot the woman. I need the good preacher." He never took his eyes from the prize before him.

The prize which was now his.

Chapter Fifty-Two

Elizabeth couldn't turn the flashlight away from the blood on the wall. *It's not blood. No one's blood.* She was causing it somehow, with the flashlight. An optical illusion.

She needed to aim the light somewhere else. But to do that would be to reveal what she knew in her heart to be true. That there was nothing left besides this one red streak, a starburst of color quickly darkening along the wall. Nothing left of the world, her life, of reality. If she were to move her right hand, even just a little, then this last solid piece of the universe would crumble and fall away.

The logical side of her brain reflexively tried to step in, take control, berate her sudden confusion. *You're an RN!* it screamed. *Help him; he's been shot!* ...shot by one of her dearest and oldest friends. That was *beyond* logic.

Josh had not just shot a man. He hadn't just killed Mister Tarretti. He hadn't. That would not happen in the world she came from. There was no one else involved in this little charade of Tarretti's. Just him, Nate, and her.

Someone walked past, temporarily obstructing her view of the last vestiges of the world. She gasped, waited for the ceiling and the sky to collapse on top of her.

Josh had not just shot a man. There was not a stranger now staring at the box on the table.

"Elizabeth...." A soft voice; Nate's voice.

"Elizabeth, are you OK? Look at me, but do it slowly."

Do it slowly? Why would he want her to do it slowly? What did he want?

Slowly, she turned her head toward his voice.

There he was, still with her, looking scared. Scared because they were in a crypt, underground, and Josh had just shot someone. *No, no, no.* She began to shake. A gasp caught in her throat, became solid, tried to work its way out of her, a moan, a scream. The darkness shifted as she turned, revealing Nate's features. Now he was fading. *No, nothing is fading, I'm OK. There's an explanation.*

Nate was holding her shoulders now. She expected him to shake her, tell her to snap out of it, but he did not. Instead he pulled her into a hug, held her close. She heard him say, as if from a distance, "Shoot her and you hit us both."

Another voice, the stranger's, "Hold your fire, Mister Everson."

Everson, she thought. *Josh Everson. He shot the caretaker. Vincent Tarretti is dead.*

She buried her face into Nate's chest, feeling the shock of what had happened clear a little, enough to let in the realization of their situation. She had to hang on, keep it together. Nothing was making sense, but Nate was here, holding her. And they were in trouble.

God, what have you done to me now?

For a long time she kept her eyes closed, face pressed into Nate's white buttoned shirt. The ladder creaked, and a third voice joined them. Nate gently nudged her. Time to rejoin the real—if completely upside down—world. She looked up.

The light was more intense than she remembered. Josh stood in the same position as before, gun held loosely in his hand but still pointing at her. On the floor beside him sat a plastic camping lantern, bright with twin fluorescent lights. Its glow washed away all remaining shadows. A man she recognized vaguely, perhaps from town, stood at the bottom of the ladder behind him and talked quickly with another guy with white hair. This latter individual was the one who had approached the altar a minute ago.

She tried not to look at the opposite wall again, but instead looked into her friend's face.

"Josh," she whispered. "Josh, what's wrong with you? Why did you do that? Who are these people? Why did you shoot him?"

Something changed in hi expression. The blank stare widened. He blinked. For a moment Elizabeth thought she had overstepped some boundary and tensed, waiting for him to pull the trigger. She stared at the open muzzle. The gun slowly lowered.

"Please, Miss," the white-haired man said, moving away from the ladder and walking up to Josh. "Don't talk to the help. Mister Everson, keep an eye on these two, and when they speak, you will not hear what they say."

Something turned over in Elizabeth's stomach. The last time she'd felt such a sudden rush of fear she was walking across the parking lot of the mall in Worcester, alone save for one other dark sedan parked two spaces from her car. As she approached, the front doors of the other car opened and two men stepped out. They simply changed positions—the one from the driver's seat moved to the passenger, and vice versa—and offered only a subdued nod to her as she approached, perhaps realizing too late the bad timing of their mysterious game of musical chairs. But that could not alleviate the quick and sudden rush of adrenaline that had filled her, realizing it was far too late to stop whatever madness was about to happen. On that occasion, the feeling, though justified by the events, proved unfounded. Now, hearing the man's voice as he spoke to Josh, feeling the power in its cadence, this same fear screamed its existence in her head. The man with the white moustache was *controlling* Josh with only his voice, even to the point of getting him to kill someone.

No, that made no sense, not in the normal world she once lived in. He must be drugged. But there *was* power in the man's voice. She had felt *something*. Seeing Josh's expression fall slack, the gun raised again toward her, she knew there could be no other explanation. That kind of thing just wasn't possible, was it?

The man turned to her and smiled.

Oh, God, help me, please help me. Her prayer was without substance. She did not believe in the God she was praying to.

"Tell me your name, Miss." His words issued from his mouth like a snake's tongue, reached out and clutched her face. The feeling was not a bad one. It was comforting, to know she could answer him.

"Elizabeth." She saw Nate look down at her. What was *his* problem?

"Elizabeth, I would like you to come here and stand beside Mister Everson."

"OK." She worked herself out of Nate's confused grip.

"Elizabeth, hold on." Nate's voice was powerful of its own accord, and for a moment it was stronger. She walked back to him, waiting to see what he wanted.

The white-haired man took a step in their direction. "Mister Dinneck, the two of you stand on a very narrow ledge. I need your services, your *brawn* if you will, but the woman is valuable to me only as much as I can use her to control you. If you wish to test me on this, I will have our mutual friend send her to your God right now."

Chapter Fifty-Three

Quinn's words hit Nathan more powerfully than any blow: the risk of Elizabeth being killed now, in a time of her life where she had denied God completely. To die without God in one's heart was to die for eternity. It wasn't a lesson he often liked to preach. The threat of damnation was both a glue holding many to their faith and a deterrent to so many others. In this moment, he realized that her life, both in this world and beyond, was in his hands. It had always been, and until now, he'd failed miserably.

He let go of Elizabeth. Quinn smiled, the smug expression of a victor. "Thank you, Reverend." He moved a couple of steps closer. "Miss... Elizabeth was it? Please come over here to stand beside this handsome man."

She looked at Nathan for a moment, with no sign of worry or fear. During the confrontation at the men's club, he'd felt the power of this man's voice. He'd been able to resist it, barely and perhaps only through God's own intervention.

But Josh and Elizabeth hadn't had the same shield. This... man... had been able to make Josh kill someone in cold blood. This thought, the despair it offered, was an ache in his chest. He needed to regain some control in the conversation, buy himself some time. He said to Quinn, "You killed Reverend Hayden, didn't you?"

"So, there *is* something going on in your head aside from abject terror!" Quinn's joy at winning was becoming barely contained hysteria. A school boy discovering everything he ever wanted under the Christmas tree.

No one spoke. Manny Paulson had ascended the ladder again, probably acting as lookout. Elizabeth and Josh stood quietly, barely moving. Peter Quinn had one hand to his chin, deep in thought while he looked at the Ark from various angles. At one point, he had stepped over Vincent's body, giving it no more attention than a piece of trash. He stared, brow furrowed in confusion for a moment, then smoothing out. Satisfied with what he saw, Nathan supposed.

In the glare of the lantern, the Ark looked different. Nathan couldn't place what it was at first; then, as if a magician's veil was lifted away, he saw. He looked down, not wanting to let surprise show on his face. He looked back, just in case. He hadn't imagined it. What had Tarretti said just before he'd been killed? He couldn't remember. Those last moments were a blur.

At last Quinn looked up, down at the caretaker's unmoving body, then over to Nathan.

"All right. Here's what we'll do, my young Padawan. I am certain that I, being a priest in my own right, could carry this out of here myself. It's much smaller than I'd expected, but I can feel its power. Do you feel it, too, Reverend?"

Nathan did not answer. He *did* feel it, but now that whatever power of illusion this thing had held over him was no longer at work, he realized that the energy seemed *not* to come from in front of him... but rather from behind.

Quinn was nonplussed at the silence. He continued, "However, just to be safe, and to keep my hands free to kill your girlfriend if you try anything stupid, I'll let you do the honors."

He bowed dramatically, waving one arm toward the relic. To Josh he added, "Mister Everson, Miss Elizabeth, I would like you two to climb the ladder and stand by Mister Paulson. He is waiting for you.

"And, Mister Dinneck, please come over here and lift my little treasure chest, hmm? Best we gauge how heavy this thing is." He smiled wider. "Not to mention how dangerous."

Nathan reminded himself that there was still hope. Bad things had happened, *were* happening, but there were other layers here that he was now beginning to sense. Quinn was seeing, atop the concrete altar, what they'd all seen. If that was the case, there might be a chance. Not at the moment, but soon. Maybe. All he could think to do was play this psychopath's game until an opportunity presented itself.

And if he died, well, it would be God's will. Everything else had been that way up to this point. Though this current wrinkle might not have been in the playbook.

He took a breath, let it out slowly. Quinn watched him with obvious impatience. Nathan took two steps forward and raised his hands to either side of the Ark. This close, he saw its true nature. This was not the Ark of the Covenant, couldn't be. It wasn't even a good replica. What had been gold a moment ago was long-faded paint. But he needed to play along. He put his hands against the wooden box's cool and dusty sides, and lifted.

"Don't forget to use the knees, young man." Quinn spoke without humor, too intently waiting for something terrible to happen.

If Quinn saw a gold-laden chest, Nathan needed to struggle. In fact, though the box was a bit heavy, it didn't weigh nearly as much as it should.

It must be heavy, he told himself. Slowly, bending his knees, though he was certain he could carry this thing with one arm if it wasn't so bulky, he laid it back down, giving it a slight push onto the concrete to mimic a sense of weight.

"It's heavy," he said, trying to sound out of breath.

Quinn smiled gleefully. "As well it should be. I apologize for not giving you enough notice, time to join a gym or something, but time is of the essence." He nodded to Vincent's body. "Wouldn't do for us to be found in here with a dead man. Time to go topside and give Mister Tarretti that decent burial I promised."

He walked around the room, always facing Nathan, and stopped at the ladder. "After you, Pastor. I'd offer to help, but I'd prefer you carry it until it can be properly consecrated on my own altar."

In his relief, Nathan thought of a few retorts, but he held his tongue. He couldn't show too much confidence. Quinn was smart enough to see through most deceptions. The question was, how long before he saw through this one?

He turned back to the box, took a deep breath, and prayed that he wouldn't overact. He lifted it, turned, and took half-steps toward the ladder. As he did, a rope uncurled itself from outside. It was long enough for Nathan to tie securely to his burden and, he assumed, pull it to the surface himself.

"You didn't think I'd make you carry it up the ladder? You may be young and strapping, but that might be asking a bit much. Lay it down here and tie it off."

Quinn backed up until he was standing with his back to the wall, allowing Nathan room to put down the box and begin looping the rope around it. Dust drifted from the floor and the box's lid as he worked. He had to stop more than once to cough. A taste like old, forgotten books lingered in his mouth. He worked the knots, silently thankful for his four years as a Cub Scout. When he was done, he stood and wiped dust onto his pants.

Quinn waved him up the ladder. "Up you go, please. And, Reverend? Don't drop it."

"I wouldn't dream of it," Nathan said, unable to resist.

Chapter Fifty-Four

Again, Peter Quinn chided himself for being too celebratory, too soon.

But he had it!

Sand, gripped too tightly in one's hand, spilled. Caution, slow and steady progress was his only option. He checked that Paulson was waiting at the lip of the opening as the minister ascended the ladder. Dinneck kept one hand on the rope as if never quite wanting to leave the treasure completely alone. Something the two of them had in common. There was more than enough rope, and he assumed Paulson had already secured the other end up top, maybe to the statue of the pathetic angels. He would see if the preacher could lift the vessel on his own. If not, he'd have Josh Everson help him. Though he might still serve a purpose—there was already blood on his hands as it was, and with the same gun used on the old minister—he was also the most expendable. Peter assumed the woman would serve as the best inspiration for Dinneck to play along.

Looking again at the glorious Ark before him, he was certain the preacher could lift it out, though not without some effort. Again, its size bothered him, and the lack of cherubim atop the mercy seat. Perhaps they'd been broken off, stolen ages ago during its many travels. He looked closer, trying to see if there were any other questionable features. The gold was radiant; certainly it was real. If that were so, however, how could Dinneck lift it? His smile faded a notch. Then he felt the power of the thing, like a wave washing across the room.

His smile returned. It was his. His!

No, he corrected himself. *Not mine*. It belonged to the great god Molech. Peter was only a servant. He forced the smile down, not wanting to sound too smug when he told Uncle Roger the news.

Let the man think he still had the upper hand. When their god chose leaders for his new temple on earth, Peter would have his day. He reached into his pocket and produced the cell phone. The signal was strong, even down here. Yet another positive turn of events. He pressed the speed-dial labeled RQ.

The phone rang on the other end of the line. As he waited, Peter felt something like a ball of clay grow in his stomach. What if his uncle didn't believe him? He needed to be calm but confident. Play it cool, but assertive.

"Quinn speaking," a gruff voice answered. Peter wanted to take a deep breath before speaking, but what sort of confidence would that imply?

"Uncle Roger, good evening. I have some news."

Roger Quinn's sigh crackled across the connection, which had a tinny quality to it this time. Maybe the energy emitted from the slowly rising Ark was causing interference. "Peter. I should have known. Is the chase off, as I expected? Another false alarm?"

Curse you, old man, he thought. *I wish I could see your face in person when I say this.* "Actually, Uncle, quite the opposite. I—we, I should say—are now in possession of that which we've sought for so long. The Ark of the Covenant is ours. It's being lifted out of the crypt right now."

Dinneck was making slow progress, pausing to catch his breath. Peter heard Paulson's voice from above but ignored it. "One moment, Uncle. Be careful, Reverend," he said louder. "Damaging it now will cost you and your girlfriend dearly."

Roger still had not responded. Peter remained silent. He could wait. The Ark was nearing the concrete lip. Dinneck was saying something. Again, Paulson's voice, clearly saying, "No way, Man. I ain't touching that thing."

"Just the rope for heaven's sake. I need both hands."

Uncle Roger's voice finally returned. "How can you be sure it is real, Peter?" Not a mocking tone, but not entirely convinced.

"I can't be, Uncle. Not yet. But the vessel is covered in quite ornate gold leaf. It would be an awfully expensive forgery to be sure. We're moving with caution, though." He wanted to mention the power he felt emanating from it, but could not decide how to describe it accurately without sounding foolish.

Paulson must have conceded to hold the rope, for Dinneck was now standing on the second-to-top rung of the ladder and trying to lift the chest above his head. Then it was up, and resting on the surface. Dinneck disappeared from view.

Peter felt a wash of relief. Closer now than ever before, he thought.

Roger was speaking again, and he tried to focus. "...man I sent down from Maine's name is Lou Hautala. He should be there by midnight. Where will you be?"

Now, he noticed, Roger's voice was tinged with excitement. Considering how excited he felt himself, how much more breathless must his aging and overweight uncle be?

"We'll be at the storefront, in the back room. We'll arrive in the alley and I'll be sure to send home any loiterers out front before we examine the contents."

"Send them all home, yes, but don't do anything else until I arrive!" Roger's voice was strained toward panic. "This may be nothing, but I'd be a fool to let you do anything further without our people there. If it is the true Ark... if it is..."

His voice trailed off. Peter imagined his uncle's eyes darting across the room, lost in swirling thoughts. Even with the apparent insult just given, he was overjoyed at the reaction. But how long would it take for him to get all the way to Hillcrest?

"Uncle Roger," he said, tentatively, "it's quite a long trip from Chicago, and no telling when you'll find a flight. I'd be happy to wait for your man from Maine, but I feel strongly we should at least do more to validate the find before you waste any money or time on such a trip."

"I'm closer than you think, Peter. I should be over Providence by the time Hautala shows up at your doorstep. Expected arrival in Boston at one-fifteen. I have a car lined up when I get there."

Peter rolled his eyes. Roger hadn't been as skeptical as he'd sounded during their previous discussion. He'd booked a red-eye into Logan.

"Well," he said, trying to keep the growing disappointment from his voice, "that's good news. It's an hour drive from Boston to Hillcrest, so I should expect you by, what, two-thirty?"

"Secure the Ark, wait for Lou and do nothing else until we arrive."

Roger disconnected.

We? How many were coming with him? Peter flipped the phone closed with a loud snap. The man was coming to take the glory. Peter may have redeemed himself but his uncle wouldn't let him get any credit.

He swore under his breath, trying to regain the calm he'd need when he went up to join the others. At the foot of the ladder he looked up at the corner of the Ark visible from his vantage point. He was suddenly much more worried about how this evening would progress.

What if it wasn't real? What if this was a diversion, like so many others in the past?

He lifted the lantern and stepped onto the ladder, feeling the old wood creak under his weight. He remembered Vincent Tarretti. He waved the lantern in the man's direction, like a conductor hanging from the edge of a train's caboose. In the shadows, the caretaker still had not moved. From the amount of blood on the wall and puddled about him, Tarretti was definitely a corpse. Another bullet in him would be good insurance. Still, they'd be lucky if no one heard them the first time. Best not risk it.

He clambered out of the hole, carefully avoiding the Ark, and moved to where the slab rested at a cockeyed angle on the far side.

"Move the Ark away from the opening."

Dinneck hesitated a moment, then lifted the chest and laid it back down a few feet away with a dull thud. The man was young and strong, but he seemed to have worn himself out pulling the thing up. Peter gave a renewed command to Everson and the girl, then with Paulson's help slid the slab back over the hole. They moved slowly, careful not to let it drop through the hole and shatter, leaving the evidence inside open to the world. Most of the potential noise from moving the slab was muffled by moss and soil lining the edge. When it was back in place, he stepped on it to make sure it was secure, kicking dirt and leaves over the edges. He would send Paulson back here later to do a better camouflage job.

For now, they needed to leave. He checked his watch. Ten-thirty. Time was running out before the prize would be taken from him.

"Mister Paulson," he said, straightening and wiping the dirt from his hands. "Take the girl with you in your car. The reverend will return with me and my able-bodied assistant." Both Josh and Elizabeth made no reaction. He noticed the minister staring intently at the girl, as if his will alone—feeble as it was—could break the spell. "If we do not arrive at the back of the store within five minutes of your own arrival, bring the girl back here, shoot her, and drop her into the grave with Tarretti."

Manny Paulson smiled gleefully. In that moment, Peter became certain that he was too much a sociopath to leave alive once this was over.

"It would be my pleasure. Do I have to shoot her right away, or...?" He nodded in her direction and let the implication linger.

"For now I'd suggest you curb that imagination of yours. Besides, Mister Dinneck will be the epitome of cooperation. Won't you?"

Nathan glared at him and said, "Let's just get this over with."

Peter glared back at him and thought, *Impudence will kill you all the more quickly*. He said nothing. Let the boy think he's strong, until he dies in the flames as the first sacrifice. He felt a luscious wave of arousal at the thought.

He told Elizabeth to go with Paulson, then waved the group on. Manny and the girl headed for the parking area. Nathan lifted the Ark, with Josh and the gun close behind. Peter Quinn followed his ad-hoc parade out of the cemetery, toward his car parked down the street.

Chapter Fifty-Five

Vincent Tarretti wasn't sure if he was dead or alive. The voices in the room faded in and out of his consciousness. After he'd fallen to the floor, he remembered nothing at first, just a vast empty darkness. Then voices came to him, distantly as if he was sleeping in bed and they talked quietly in another room. He didn't open his eyes, wasn't sure if he could. He knew he wasn't dead. Death was not that emptiness from which he'd just emerged.

He dared not move. His body hurt everywhere, especially his chest. A small fire burned inside him, flaring up and dying out with every shallow breath. He was no use to Dinneck and his girlfriend now. He remembered being shot, maybe even in the chest. Whether his survival was luck or the will of God, he would make no supposition. They thought him dead. Every part of him screamed to stay still, not to let them know they were unsuccessful. If they knew, the boy who shot him might finish the job. The longer the others lingered, the less focused his mind became. He felt blood spilling from his body, out his front, down his back. At one point, it felt as if he was drowning. Panic set in. He needed to sit up, let someone know he was alive or he'd choke on his own blood.

But there was the Covenant to think about. He never had a chance to finish his warning to Nathan Dinneck when the shooter dropped in. Dinneck did not know the truth. Maybe that was good, now that the adversaries were in control. He wondered if the power veiling the chest's true nature would diminish the further it was moved away from its source.

He waited, taking shallow breaths, hardly breathing at all. He needed to seem dead to the invaders, and it was the only kind of breath he could manage. One of his lungs might have collapsed. He wasn't sure. The flow of blood from his wounds had not stemmed, weakening him almost beyond hope. Almost.

The impression of light he'd detected through his closed lids was suddenly gone. Sounds of concrete on concrete above him, echoing in the small chamber. They had sealed him in.

God, he prayed, *give me strength for just a little while longer. They'll be back. I need to do one final act for You. If it's Your will, help me.* There could be only one reason the Lord hadn't yet taken him.

He opened his eyes, just a crack. The darkness was so complete he had to blink a couple of times to be sure his eyes were open. Everyone was gone. He waited to see if his vision would adjust, but there was no light to latch on to. He rolled from the position he'd held during those eternal minutes after regaining consciousness. The fire in his chest spread to every corner of his body, even the tips of his fingers. He opened his mouth to scream and shoved the heel of his right hand into his mouth. It had not been long since they'd left. They may still be above him. *Quiet. Have to be quiet.*

What did he think he could do? If they came back, they would search the room, look for signs of the treasure. If they were diligent, they would find what they were looking for.

Using his elbows and arms, he pulled himself across the floor, toward the opposite side of the altar. The gun in his coat pocket pressed into his stomach, dragging along beneath him. It was no use to him now. Maybe that was a good thing.

He had to take the Covenant from this place. Ruth Lieberman had shown him the compartment in which it lay. He shifted again; the fire burned through him. Even if this motion didn't kill him, what he was planning to do most certainly would. He was not a priest. He was not a minister or rabbi. He was wearing Levi's, but he didn't think that counted.

Drag.

His chest felt heavier on the right side and he listed in that direction. It felt like a sack of water had been shoved inside him. He hoped this short trek across the room wouldn't cause his other lung to fill with blood.

Was he forcing himself along only to die at the end? Ruth had been adamant about following God's law. He mustn't touch them. No, the rule was he mustn't touch the Ark. There was nothing saying anything about the tablets of the Commandments themselves. He'd find out soon enough.

Two more lengths across the floor. His left foot had drifted outward and now hit the base of the altar. That meant the majority of him had already moved past it. He was close. Dust smeared his face, coating his mouth and nose. He wanted to cough, or sneeze. Doing that would probably be the last thing he ever did.

Lord Jesus, help me. Forgive me for what I'm about to do. Make me a priest of your teaching. A minister for these last few moments of my life, so that I might end my oath to your Father by serving him in this last way.

His head bumped into the wall. His left hand became caught underneath his body. His fingers opened, and he felt the small hole just above his belly. He panicked. *I've been shot. I should be dead. God, please.*

He worked his wet hand free and felt along the wall. Focus. The wall was smooth, caked in dust. Cobwebs of it stuck to his fingers. He wiped them on the wall and felt for—there! Three small indentations. He felt further and could make out the outline of the brick, pushing aside more dust from the cracks.

He could barely gasp in enough oxygen with all the dust, and was now going to try to pull this cinder block free from its resting place; move it from the spot where it had lain for almost one hundred years, with a hole in his chest and probably his back. One working lung.

Vincent laughed, then caught himself. He couldn't risk that first and fatal cough. Still, it energized him. This was *not* how he thought it would end. Almost dead, lying on the floor of John Solomon's grave, planning on pulling a forty-pound cement block from the wall.

Entry 823, he thought. *This one's a doozy.*

He worked three fingers into the indentation. The inward curve of the holes allowed him a reach up to the knuckles. A good grip, well-designed by the caretaker before the caretaker before Ruth. He'd been a mason, that one; and, he assumed, a good man. At the very least, a good mason.

Here goes nothing.

He moved away from the wall, rolling onto his side and ignoring the resurgence of pain and fire inside, and pulled.

The stone slid free a couple of inches. He pulled his fingertips out to feel the distance. More than he'd expected. It gave him incentive to try again.

Gripping again with his fingers, Vincent moved himself back, pulled and rolled, using his body's momentum. The stone followed. He didn't check on the progress, but shimmied away and pulled again. And again. His head began to tingle. He closed his eyes. The lack of any change in the blackness gave him vertigo and he opened them again.

After a rest, Vincent slowly felt along the block, further, further. His fingers reached around and touched the far side.

It was out. He could see now, vaguely, a steady green light beyond the brick like an afterglow of a flashbulb. It illuminated nothing; in fact, it was only there if he turned his head to look with his peripheral vision. But it was there.

He rolled onto his other side. The bag that was once his lung shifted with him. He fell flat to the floor and moaned loudly, not caring if anyone heard him. He lay there and sobbed. It wasn't the pain—it had all faded to a steady throbbing ache, everywhere—but the mental image of what his body was going through. The fear that a wrong move would cause it to open up and fall apart.

Just a little more, Lord, then you can take me home forever.

He moved forward until his head bumped the cinder block. He had to push it aside a few more inches, felt its sharp edges scrape across his skin. He touched the wall until the wall was no longer there. He couldn't pause. *Lord in this moment I am your priest.*

He hoped.

He reached inside.

And closed his fingers around old, coarse cloth. The word *sackcloth* came to mind, but he knew that was from years of Bible reading. He didn't even know what sackcloth felt like. This bag had the rough texture of a potato sack, maybe thicker.

The sacred tablets of the Covenant had been separated from the Ark for centuries. The actual chest had been lost a long time ago. It had housed these very tablets—the second unblemished set carried down by Moses from Sinai, the Lord's mountain—for longer than any historian had imagined. In the end, according to Vincent's own feeble translations of his strongbox's contents, the Ark was sacrificed to a group of Ammonites who had come too close to victory in the Greek capital of Constantinople. There hadn't been time to construct a decoy. The caretaker at the time had left it for discovery while its contents were carried far, far away.

The ironic part, however, was that the Ark never *was* discovered. If the enemy had possession of it, there would be no need for this elaborate duplicate in Hillcrest. The old Greek caretaker—a bishop, if Vincent's translations were correct—had written of his hopes to return to the site and learn of the Ark's fate. Vincent never discovered if he'd ever succeeded. If the bishop ever managed to return, he mustn't have found it. Instead, God's written Covenant with His people moved around the world in the roughhewn sack at Vincent's fingertips, or one very much like it.

To end up in the unsteady grasp of a middle aged man dying of a gunshot wound. But he wasn't dead, not yet.

"Thank you," Vincent whispered, and pulled the bag free. The stone tablets slid silently from the hole. Compared to the cinder block, this weight was manageable.

He risked a closer touch, coarse fabric between smooth stone surface and his fingers, feeling for any damage. They felt intact. An electric tingle worked along his fingers, up his arm. Vincent pulled his hand away. Its energy, this close, was like a lamp against his face. Best not to actually touch them for too long. The sensation gave him the willies. The glow was there, indistinct at the edge of his vision, offering no tangible light in the room but still... there.

He rested, and considered. The tablets were just under a yard in length. Two yard-long slabs of stone which together seemed to weigh at least as much as the cinder block which had given him so much trouble. And he had to get them out of this place.

He began the long trek toward the bottom of the ladder, moving forward, dragging the sack to his side, moving a little further, repeating the process. After a couple of misdirections, he found the rungs.

He wanted to rest, to sleep, but knew he would never wake up. They'd be back soon. They were *bound* to be. Where would he go? At once, he knew that he could not hide from these people. Even if he lived long enough to find a place, he was going to leave too obvious a trail.

He'd go to the only place that made sense. If he died there, before or after they found him, at least he would do so in God's house. It was the most he could do. Before then, however, pushing aside the concrete slab above him would be like moving a mountain.

He would make it to the church somehow. Then it was up to God, and maybe Nathan Dinneck. If the young minister was still alive.

Chapter Fifty-Six

Nathan *was* alive, and struggling for some plan to get them out of this mess. Josh hadn't turned against them out of any sense of free will. Quinn's hypnotic trick could be used, with apparent ease, against anyone.

Almost anyone. Nathan wondered again about the incident in the store that morning. Quinn's voice had been a third arm reaching for him, *almost* taking hold near the end. But he'd resisted, if by no other way than leaning on his faith and finding a sliver of strength. Was that it? He frowned on others mentioning faith as some sort of magical force field. It wasn't, at least not in the way that people liked to think. It wouldn't stop a bus if you chose to test it in the middle of traffic.

God didn't like to be tested. Nathan had to remind himself that he'd almost lost the battle this morning. His defenses had been knocked down when he'd seen the painting. Quinn had pounced on that weakness.

Faith—not in oneself, but in God alone—was the only way to resist the devil. That was whom this man represented. Even so, Quinn either wasn't able to control him now in the same way as the others, or chose not to. He controlled Nathan by his power over Josh and Elizabeth. What about his father? Art Dinneck was more faithful a Christian than most people Nathan knew. Art falling so far from the church was no more realistic than Josh aiming a gun and shooting a man in cold blood.

If Nathan had become prey to Quinn this morning, perhaps the same was true for his father. Maybe Quinn was threatening his mother, holding her safety against Art's cooperation.

The man sitting behind the wheel was crazed. *Obsessed* was a better word. Nathan never thought he was afraid to die. Such an event was only the next logical step toward spending eternity with Christ. Regardless, the instinct for survival was strong. If not for himself, then for Josh and Elizabeth.

The influx of questions dogged his thoughts and kept him from focusing on the present. He was crowded in the back seat of Quinn's sedan with the artificial Ark beside him. Even in the light of passing streetlights, the craftsmanship of the box was solid, but such a startling contrast to what Nathan had first seen.

He sat back and watched Josh, who, in turn, watched him over the back of the passenger seat. Nathan stared at his friend, focusing on his eyes. *God give me the strength to reach him. Open your eyes, Josh. Use your mind and see what's going on.*

Josh reacted, a little. The gun resting on the top of the seat lowered in his grip. His gaze softened.

"Mister Everson, please focus on the task at hand. Maintain your vigil over the prisoner."

Though the words were not directed at him, Nathan could feel the car fill with their power. The voice was unearthly. Demonic. Nathan believed demons were real, with strong persuasion over a person's heart. They never had any physical presence. Feeling this man's voice, seeing Josh's gaze become steady along with his grip on the pistol, Nathan began to reconsider that assumption. Fear, the slow, relentless enemy of men, worked a handhold on him again.

Chapter Fifty-Seven

When Matt Corwin said his goodbyes and left the men's club on shaky feet, Art Dinneck looked around to see who else he might talk to. He thought again of Beverly. Did she expect him home? No, she knew he was coming here. He'd told her as much. Granted, he didn't remember exactly what he'd said, but she seemed to be fine with this visit. He'd only been here a little while. It was too early to go home.

As he walked toward the table to watch the remaining four men race for the finish in a boisterous game of cribbage—he never thought of that game as being *boisterous* until he watched these four play—he checked his watch.

Almost eleven o'clock.

That was late. The lights in the room seemed to dim. For the first time, he saw how faded the furniture was. The walls were a drab color, redeemed only by the colorful oil reproductions hanging unnoticed at various points. Even so, with the exception of one which gave him the heebie-jeebies for some reason, they hung old and uninterestingly around them.

What was he doing here?

He was supposed to be at work. It was work that called him, wasn't it?

"Oh, God," he said aloud. Steve Arruda looked up after counting his peg down the home stretch on the cribbage board.

"What's wrong, Art?" He squinted, as if seeing something for the first time. "Man, you're looking pale."

Art looked at him, trying to focus. Why on earth did he come here? Someone from work called. There'd been a problem.

No, *Peter Quinn* called. Not someone from work.

Art staggered to a chair and sat. He gripped his right arm with his left hand, trying to calm its shaking. Steve scrambled drunkenly up from his chair and ran over.

"You OK, Art?"

Steve's cribbage partner laid the stub of a cigar he'd been smoking into an ashtray and swiveled in his chair, not rising, but looking over with no less concern. "You should maybe head home, guy. You don't look so good—hey! Leave those pegs where they are until Steve gets back!"

Next to him, a tall skinny man with a long, dropping moustache laughed and raised his fingers from his peg with dramatic flourish.

I'm going mad, Art thought. He leaned forward, barely hearing Steve's *that's right, Man, take it easy and breathe. Want me to call your wife?* and tried to calm down. His breath came in short gasps. He wondered if this was what it was like to have an anxiety attack. Maybe it was his heart.

The past months swam past unbidden, revealing truth in its unforgiving clarity. Night upon night, coming here, spending less time with Beverly, avoiding church. The call from Nate the other day, when Art told his son to leave him alone. He'd been acting like... like what? A man in a trance. How could he have moved so far...?

The woman, of course. Here, one night; a voice that sounded so much like Peter Quinn's speaking quietly, like the voice of Satan himself, *You cheated on your wife with her, and enjoyed it. Don't you remember?*

Yes, he did remember. He'd had too much to drink... so unlike him, at least the *him* before all this. A beer now and then, maybe, rarely more than a couple at one time... but yes, he did remember, one night, the woman. The details were sketchy. Memories without substance, like a movie.

Like a movie playing on a television.

What was he remembering?

"Steve," he said suddenly, the exhaustion and confusion washing away. Even as he looked up to the man crouched in front of him, he imagined lost pieces of his life falling into place.

"Yeah, feeling better?"

"Do you—" what would he say? Did he remember Art having sex with some strange woman?

A movie playing on a television.

He wasn't drunk that night. He couldn't have been. He'd remember at least drinking more than one beer before getting fuzzy. Then what—

The phone rang in his pocket. Steve and the man with the moustache rose simultaneously, each thinking the call was on theirs. Such was the curse of portable phones, Art always thought, generally with more amusement than now.

Art knew it was *his* phone. Could remember other times, coming clearer, when he had reached this level of understanding only to answer the phone and then... nothing. That moment after Nate's call at work, any doubt washed away as if some buried instruction in his brain had kicked in, shutting his thoughts down. Again.

Steve's cribbage partner broke his own rule and counted out his hand on the board. He said happily, "Ain't mine. *Mine* plays the *Star Spangled Banner* when I have a call. Does it better than most versions I've heard at the Red Sox games." He laughed, and slipped his peg a couple of unearned notches ahead.

Art's phone rang again from his coat hanging over the back of an empty chair. Steve said, "Art, it's your phone."

Of course it was, he thought despondently. He rose and grabbed his jacket, but not to answer the call. He headed for the door, needing to get home, talk to Beverly, try and save their marriage before it was too late. He was confused still, but more and more details fell into place in his mind. He hadn't been unfaithful, he was almost certain of that now. But the thought that he'd been drugged and shown a pornographic film, made to think... no, none of it made any sense.

The phone stopped ringing. Art didn't have voicemail, so whoever it was must have given up. If it was Beverly, it didn't matter. He'd be home soon enough. He took the phone from his pocket, turned it off, and put it away again.

Someone else's phone began to ring. The man with the *Star Spangled Banner* ring guffawed and said, too loudly, "Looks like the wives are calling you boys home!"

Steve pressed a button on his own phone and said, "Hello?"

Art opened the door and stepped outside. The cool night air opened his mind further. More and more understanding, some of it dark—almost frighteningly so—but clearer than it had been in a long time. It made him giddy with relief.

"Art!" Steve's voice. Art turned and waved goodnight to him. His hand froze mid-air when he saw the man holding out his phone. "It's your wife. She's worried sick, says you didn't answer your phone and figured she'd check with me." In a low, conspiratorial voice, he whispered, "If she's calling *me* she knows where you are, so no sense hiding." He grinned.

Art wanted to say *Just tell her I'm on my way home*, but remembered that he wasn't supposed to be here in the first place. The message would sound too much like a brush off. He'd tell her he would explain everything when he got home, then hang up before Quinn arrived. The sooner he was out of this place the better. In fact, once he got home, he'd remove the battery from his own phone. Maybe go so far as change his number.

He reached out to Steve's proffered hand, too late wondering how Beverly had known this man's cell phone number.

"Hi, Bev," he said, "Listen, I—"

"Mister Dinneck," said Peter Quinn's smooth voice.

The world crinkled around him, faded to black.

No, no! God hel—

And he was no longer anywhere but in the world created for him by his master. He listened to the instructions, handed the phone back to Steve and returned inside.

It was still early. He could wait a little longer. He saw Steve heading directly for his car through the closing front door, heard the *Star Spangled Banner* begin to play from somewhere in the room. He was content to simply sit in the chair and wait for Quinn to show up. He had something important to tell him.

After *Star Spangled Banner* listened to the call without speaking, he passed the phone to the next, who listened then passed it on to the third. All three men at the cribbage table rose as one and went to get their jackets. They said, "Goodnight, Art." Art Dinneck waved absently to them.

He was trying to remember something important. It was just at the tip of his memory, if he could only remember....

Chapter Fifty-Eight

"**Is** the girl inside?"

Manny Paulson nodded. He stood in the open doorway leading from the alley into the store's back room. Peter Quinn closed his car door and said, "Is Dinneck the only one out front?"

Another nod. Nathan, who'd been pulling the Ark from the back seat and trying to make the action look more like a struggle than it truly was, looked up at the name. He couldn't have meant *him*, so his father was here!

What did Dad have to do with this? More insurance?

Quinn moved around the front of the car, the fingers of his right hand grazing the hood absently. "Leave him there for now. He won't disturb us." He turned to Josh. "Mister Everson, please follow our Holy Man into the building."

Nathan straightened and gave Josh a look. His friend stared back blankly. What was he was seeing? Nathan followed Quinn into a long rectangular room, dark save for a row of short red candles burning along the far wall. There was a lingering odor of sulfur, from the matches Paulson likely used to light them. Nathan remembered the sudden welling of fear this morning, a sense that something evil lurked inside this room. The fear returned, though not the overwhelming terror of earlier. Nathan thought, *Lord, protect me. Give me strength to face what's in here.*

Bathed in the candles' red glow and drifting among a thin line of sweet smelling incense, sat a small altar. It reminded Nathan of a Japanese Zen shrine, minimal adornments, set low so one had to kneel before it. The incense stick's tip had only a small bit of ash.

Seeing what adorned the altar gave him a start. The small statue had a body of gold, though the gold was likely no more real than that which adorned the Ark in Nathan's arms. It was difficult to tell in the dim light. The idol had the head of a bull, outstretched arms waiting for an offering.

Forgery or not, he did not want to put the Ark on the floor in front

231

of such a desecration. He looked away. Elizabeth stood near the wall on his left, not far from the door leading to the front room where his father was apparently waiting. Her expression was less blank than Josh's now, and when he looked her way she blinked and returned his gaze.

Quinn said, "Ah, welcome back, young lady. I trust you had a pleasant sleep."

She was wild-eyed now, looking around the room in a panic. Only when she tried to move did she realize her hands were tied behind her back.

"Nathan, what—"

Quinn raised his hand. "Do not speak." She stopped talking like an obedient servant, but Nathan was glad to see her expression remained alert. She looked at him, mouthed *where are we?* Then her eyes fell on what he was carrying. Her look of shock changed to confusion. Maybe she saw it now for what it truly was. She mouthed something else, but Nathan was too preoccupied to interpret it.

Quinn stood in front of him, closely inspecting the Ark without actually touching it. His expression moved slowly from one of awe, to curiosity, to something else. Something darker. He looked up with his eyes only.

"Getting a bit heavy to hold, Reverend Dinneck?" Nathan didn't like the tone of voice. Sarcasm?

"A little."

"A little," Quinn repeated. He reached out, as if to touch the lid, hesitated, then waved his arm instead toward the altar and the Molech icon. "Please place it on the floor, there, just before the altar. Do not try anything stupid or one of your friends will die. I haven't decided which yet. Just know that I am very serious."

Nathan put the Ark down, deciding to curb the pretension of it being a struggle. He assumed the charade was about to end. Had Vincent Tarretti known the Ark was not real? Maybe. The man had sounded so convinced, beyond any doubt. A sudden thought, a realization that... he quickly put it out of his mind. Deal with the present. On the altar the statue's eyes stared up, its bull-head drifting in and out of clarity with the thickening smoke from the incense stick.

Nathan felt renewing tugs of irrational terror return, as if seeping from this idol. Drifting like mist along the floor to his knees. He found he couldn't pull his face away from the dark animal-face with its wide, open mouth. His fear grew.

God help me, he began to think, before his thoughts became muddy. It was hard to focus. He was aided unwittingly by Quinn, who grabbed the back of his jacket and pulled him away.

"Please step back, Dinneck."

Nathan stumbled, wanting to swing out, to keep the man from touching him. He was pulled back ten steps. Quinn's white hair and moustache, when he moved to stand beside him again, were red in the candle light, flickering in shadows.

"It's show time," he whispered. "Need I remind you not to move from this spot?"

Nathan didn't reply. His captor slowly approached the Ark and knelt before it. He began to chant, the words nonsensical. Nathan wondered if this was an actual language, or sounds to help him concentrate. He'd heard of such things, even in the Christian community, with people speaking "in tongues," so lost in the rapture of prayer they involuntarily uttered sounds with meaning only to them.

Only this man was not praying to God, but to a demon from the Old Testament that most assumed had long ago faded into historical obscurity.

The dark stench in the room built to a physical level. Elizabeth tried moving beside him, but Paulson raised his hand, shook his head. A small fact occurred to Nathan, but one which he thought might be important, perhaps for later use. Neither of these men carried guns. At least, none that he could see. Quinn's voice had been weapon enough so far, controlling the only person who *was* armed: Josh.

If the police ever became involved in the murder investigation, all evidence would point to his friend.

After a few minutes, Quinn stopped his chanting and rose, slowly, to stand over his prize. He stared at it for a long time, long enough that Nathan was starting to get worried. Nathan looked at his watch. Only eleven-thirty. It seemed they'd been captives for hours. He looked around the room. The mini-mart at the end of the strip mall closed at ten. Wasn't Josh supposed to be the closer? Either way, anyone working there had already left. Maybe there was an alarm. He needed to get outside, break the window, do *something* to get the police here.

With Quinn occupied, Nathan could grab Josh's gun before Paulson had a chance to stop him.

He tensed, preparing to lunge at his friend before Quinn could realize what he was doing. From the way the man was scowling at the box, that would happen any time now.

"Mister Everson, shoot anyone who makes a move toward you. Be sure the bullet goes into their head. More efficient that way."

The internal momentum Nathan had been building almost pushed him toward Josh anyway. His friend had the gun raised and pointing directly at Nathan's face. Still, if he could cut to the side....

"Actually, Mister Everson," Quinn continued, still with his back to everyone else in the room, "shoot the woman if anyone makes a move toward you." Josh quickly moved the gun away from Nathan and toward Elizabeth's head.

Damn you, Nathan thought furiously. *How did you know? How could you know?*

Quinn turned around to face his small congregation. His smile was slight and mocking.

"Manny, if you would be so kind as to tie up Mister Dinneck, we have much to do, still." He looked at Nathan. "One doesn't need to be a psychic, Reverend, to sense when someone is planning a move against you. You wouldn't be a very good poker player." He glanced back at the Ark, the semblance of a smile dropping again. Paulson roughly tied Nathan's wrists behind his back with what looked like a blue paisley necktie. His shoulders stretched painfully in their sockets. Quinn looked from the Ark back toward him, and his smile did not return. In fact, his mouth continued down, past what could simply be called a frown or a grimace. With a hiss, he added, "Still, everyone has one good bluff in them sometimes, don't they?"

Nathan actually gasped when Quinn quickly reached out and grabbed the edge of the Ark's lid.

And nothing happened.

Chapter Fifty-Nine

"Come over here, Paulson, and help me lift this cover."

Manny moved slowly across the room. "But I thought, I mean, shouldn't we wait for that guy from Maine to get here?" He looked at his watch. "He's due any—hey, wait a second, that's not—"

The air was changing in the room. As Paulson pointed at the plain wooden box, Quinn's expression alternated between contempt, fear, and anger.

"Then stay where you are and learn something, you idiot!" He grabbed the cover with both hands and pulled. The box, in its entirety, raised up from the ground. Quinn glared over at Nathan, then slammed the Ark down onto the concrete floor.

It cracked; a wide crevice running down the middle of its face. Small splinters of wood and flecks of gold paint fluttered to the floor. He picked it back up, higher this time, and screamed like a mad man. Down came the box again. This time it shattered. Most of the pieces were large, oddly contorted. Other smaller splinters sailed back into the air to land on the altar or behind the macabre demon's statue.

Quinn roared with rage again, kicked at the remnants. Elizabeth backed against the wall. Nathan was glad to see her mouth pressed closed, not daring to call attention to herself while the man's rage exploded throughout the room.

Not knowing what else to say, Paulson muttered, "It's empty, and... it looks different."

Quinn screamed, "It's not REAL, you idiot!"

Nathan tried, with everything he had, to contain the hysteria suddenly filling him. Everything since coming to town was too far removed from normal. The nightmares, Hayden's disappearance and murder, a crypt with the Ark of the Covenant that was nothing but wood and paint, his father. All of it, insane. Nonsense.

Too much. It was all too much to expect one man to contain.

Nathan began to laugh.

A giggle at first, which he was able to stifle, but another came roaring out of him. He felt himself sliding into some uncontrolled idiocy, but he couldn't curb it. Elizabeth had done the right thing, shrinking into the background while Quinn expended his anger on the wooden chest, but he could not stop himself. With one final guffaw and eyes tearing, Nathan knew it was useless to fight this sudden burst of emotion. He simply didn't care anymore.

"Nathan," Elizabeth whispered, breaking her imposed silence, "be quiet."

Peter Quinn straightened and turned. He moved slowly but consistently to close the gap between Nathan and himself. His movements were those of a jungle animal toward its prey. Nathan knew he was about to die, but he was exhausted, pushed beyond his limits. He didn't care. He was tired of letting this lost, insane man terrorize him. He stopped laughing and straightened.

What would come, would come, whether he laughed at this man or did nothing at all.

"Something funny, you Jesus-loving freak?"

Nathan took a deep breath and forced himself to smile, though it was a weak gesture. "You," he said.

The first punch slammed into his left cheek and sent him to the floor. Since he was still bound, Nathan fell to his side and something popped in his right shoulder. In a haze, he was lifted up, punched again in the same place. He did not fall this time, tried to open his eyes to see from where the next blow would come. Before he could clear his vision, something hit him on the other side of his face. He went down again. A hard kick centered in the stomach. Air raced from his lungs. He curled his legs for protection, too intent on finding a way to take a breath to feel more pain. Something moved over him, then the pain came, sharply tearing up his back. He'd either been kicked again or shot. He screamed and spat blood from his mouth. He'd bitten down onto his tongue.

He had to move, get to his feet. He could hear Elizabeth screaming for Quinn to stop. He forced his eyes open and in his limited vision saw Paulson holding her back. Josh still held the gun toward her head, arm wavering uncertainly.

He also saw Quinn returning from his altar with a jagged piece of wood.

"Are you done laughing yet?" The man's eyes were wide with hysteria. Nathan tried to stand, to defend himself, but his muscles were too constricted. His shoulder throbbed dully where it had popped from its socket. He was helpless to stop anything that would come next.

Quinn raised the improvised wooden stake above him.

Forgive me for failing you, Lord. Accept me into Your arms, protect my friends and family.

"Peter, wait." Paulson's voice, a thin warbling in Nathan's ears. "We still need him. What if the real one's back at the cemetery?"

Nathan kept his eyes riveted to the wooden point dropping down to his chest. It stopped just shy of penetrating his skin, poking hard between his open jacket, pressing into his shirt. It was taking so long to get through. Quinn was growling and his hands shook. A line of spit dropped from the corner of his mouth onto Nathan's cheek. He pressed the point harder against his chest, but not hard enough to kill. It was painfully obvious that he wanted to, but his maddened expression was changing. His eyes turned back toward the altar. Paulson's suggestion had taken root, fighting with the blood lust.

Paulson continued, "Just long enough to go back there and see for ourselves. Just long enough for that. If there's not something else in the grave, we kill them all and leave them underground with their dead buddy. No mess, no evidence. But... not... here!"

Quinn's eyes were darting back and forth. Considering. He leaned forward until his forehead touched Nathan's, the stake pressing so hard into his chest that Nathan moaned in pain. "OK." He sighed. His breath smelled like mint gum and onions. "OK. One more trip, Dinneck, back to the graveyard. I guarantee you that you will suffer greatly before you die. But it'll happen somewhere more fitting. And you'll be the last to go, so you can watch your girlfriend die."

Then he was gone, standing up and straightening his clothes as much as possible. He tossed the stake to the floor. Nathan remained where he was, unable and unwilling to move.

"Take Dinneck's father and the girl to this boy's church. Any sign of people, just continue on and meet us at the cemetery. I'll go out front and have a word with Arthur first, make sure he cooperates. While I'm doing that, put the girl in the trunk then swing around front and pick Dinneck up. Don't linger there." He then leaned forward and whispered more instructions into Paulson's ear. Nathan vaguely wondered if he was using the Voice on him. He doubted it. Paulson didn't need much prodding. Whatever Quinn was saying must have been good, because Paulson looked excited. He nodded enthusiastically. Quinn stepped back and said loudly, "But put it in the back seat. We don't want the girl choking to death on fumes before all the fun starts."

Paulson nodded. "Why can't we just leave Art here? We've got enough to handle as it is, and—"

Quinn shoved him toward Elizabeth. "Just do what I say and stop questioning me. You were right about needing the preacher, for now," he added with a contemptuous gaze at Nathan, "but whether or not we find what we're looking for, there will be a sacrifice to Molech tonight. And for that, we need his father. Now move."

He turned back to Nathan. His composure had returned, though he was moving with more urgency, checking his watch often. "Get up, Dinneck. After I chat with your daddy we're going to pay one last visit to the cemetery. See what trick your little caretaker friend tried to put over on us, eh?"

Nathan looked across the room, to the wreckage of the Ark. Part of him wondered the very same thing.

Chapter Sixty

Nathan wished he could have seen his father, though he was certain Art Dinneck was so much under Quinn's influence that it probably would have made no difference. It was possible the reason Quinn didn't simply put Elizabeth back under was that he could only control so many people at one time. Especially in his current, near-panic state of mind. Quinn's confidence had been shattered in the back room. Even now, as he led him and Josh across the dark grass of Greenwood Street Cemetery, he walked quickly, impatiently.

Time was running out, for all of them. Quinn included.

Nathan heard a subdued *pop*; then the pain in his right arm faded. His shoulder had slipped back into its socket. The shoulder had been a constant source of hurt since he'd landed on the floor, though he hadn't realized how much until it was gone. The left side of his face, however, felt like he'd been loaded up with Novocain at the dentist's office. Swollen and misshapen. It probably looked as bad as it felt.

He limped behind Quinn, not from any injury to his legs but rather from the ache in his back where he'd been kicked. Whatever damage had been done to his kidneys wasn't high on his list of worries, since most likely he'd be dead soon.

He didn't want to go back into the crypt. Though it would be a relief to have the ropes binding his hands behind him loosened, Nathan was pretty sure that once inside, he would never come out.

But John Solomon's grave was not as they had left it.

The concrete slab was moved aside. Enough for someone to crawl in. Even as Quinn lost whatever composure he'd mustered over the past ten minutes, the implication of the scene made Nathan's mind reel.

There had been someone else. Someone waiting in the wings for Nathan and his fellow stooges to be taken away, or killed, before moving in to remove the true treasure.

Shouting curses, Quinn tossed the slab aside as easily as he'd smashed the Ark in the back of the store. He flipped the lantern's switch, bathing the area around the grave in light.

Josh stared at the angelic statues, waiting for his next order. Nathan and Quinn noticed the grass at the same time. Something had been dragged across it, glistening dark and wet in a wide, staggered path *away* from the open grave.

"Shoot Dinneck if he says one word!" Quinn forgot about the ladder and jumped into the grave with the lantern. Nathan found himself in darkness again, staring at the brightly lighted square in front of him. Quinn's shadow bounced wildly against the visible section of wall. Whoever had come in here had dragged something away, toward the woods. But what could have caused the wet.... *Tarretti. Oh Dear God*, Nathan thought. *He's still alive.*

He searched the trees beyond the bordering wall, trying to determine which way Vincent could have gone. How *could* it be? He'd been shot point blank in the chest. Lazarus rising from his tomb. Nathan shuddered, and felt the end of Josh's pistol press into his ribs. He did not move, after that.

Chapter Sixty-One

This can't be happening. Peter Quinn cursed his earlier impatience. He should have put another bullet into the caretaker before leaving. But the man hadn't breathed the entire time they'd been in this room.

Apparently, that wasn't true. A long, smeared line of red traveled from the not-so-final resting place of Vincent Tarretti to a hole in the wall which had not been there earlier, then angled back to the ladder. The lamp shook in his hands.

He was alive, and had escaped with the real prize. He followed the blood trail to the opening in the wall and gave the cinder block a push. It was heavy. This was real blood around him. If Tarretti wasn't dead, he was seriously hurt. How could he have moved something so big? Or the concrete slab above him?

There was no way. No way.

As had happened too often this night, Peter felt events slipping from his control. So long he'd waited, so joyously he'd congratulated himself at making his move at the right moment. Now everything was falling apart.

He reached into the hole at the base of the wall. It wasn't big enough to hold the true Ark of the Covenant. That, he was certain now, would have been so much larger than the forgery he'd taken from here. How could he have thought that... *sham*... was real? It had been too small. It had looked so glorious when first seen, but so fake and wooden in the back room of the club. How? Was he susceptible to the same parlor tricks he played on others? No. His mind was too well-trained, and their God too passive to intervene so dramatically.

He sat back on his haunches, focusing on the moment. There *was* no Ark hidden here. Only the Covenant itself, laid within this wall so long ago. The tablets were obviously the true source of power. All was not lost, then. If a dead man had them, he couldn't have gotten far. Not in only half an hour. Most of that time would have been burned by Tarretti simply getting out of this place. For all he knew, he was lying dead in the woods a few yards away or hiding behind another tombstone.

Even with these thoughts, Peter's stomach burned with fear. It had been in his reach and now it was gone. These disappearing acts had happened before; the caretakers never found.

Not this time, he told himself. *Not this time.*

He stood at the base of the ladder, composing his own resolve before climbing. He'd already had to release his hold on the girl. Tonight's events flustered him so badly he was surprised he still had control of Everson and Art Dinneck. He needed to focus, stay positive. All he had to do was follow the caretaker's clear path and see where it led him.

He was spared this task when his cell phone rang. He checked the caller ID: *M Paulson*. It had rung once before as he was parking in the cemetery's small lot, with the ID "unknown caller". His uncle's man from Maine, no doubt, standing in front of the Hillcrest Men's Club wondering where everyone had gone. Peter had allowed his voicemail to take that call. The phone was bound to ring again, and it would be Uncle Roger. When that happened, would he have the nerve to ignore it? Likely not. The man had as much hold on him as Peter had on these mindless locals.

He clicked the flash button. "Quinn speaking," he said. "What's wrong?"

Paulson's voice was shaking with either excitement or fear. "Um, Peter? Are you at the grave?"

Any other time, Peter would offer a short, threatening remark and hang up, but something in Paulson's voice made him say, "Yes, and it's empty. Tarretti's gone, along with what I believe is the prize we're after."

A pause, then, "Well, I'm standing in the church right now, and you might want to come over here. Now. The caretaker's here. I think he's dead. He was carrying something in a bag. Pretty big, whatever it is. Can't tell what; he's lying on top—"

"Do nothing! Touch *nothing* until we get there."

He wanted to be happy with this turn of events, but at the moment he couldn't afford the luxury. Things had been within his reach before, only to slip away. He had to be careful. He had to be fast. Disconnecting and pocketing the phone, Peter climbed the ladder. The outside air was cooler than he remembered, such a contrast to the staleness of the crypt. An autumn breeze filled him with renewed hope.

Not this time, he thought again.

Dinneck was standing where he'd left him, looking as helpless and pathetic as his father always had. His face was swollen, twin lines of blood drying along his jaw and neck. For a moment, Peter thought Everson might have shot him, but his own bruised knuckles reminded him that he himself had inflicted the damage.

"You'll never guess, Reverend, where we're going." He nodded to Everson. "Bring him back to the car, please." With that, he walked across the grounds toward the parking lot.

Not this time.

Chapter Sixty-Two

One more time. I know it hurts, but one... more... time! Elizabeth kicked with both feet against the trunk. There wasn't enough room in the cramped confines to give herself any leverage. Like the four previous attempts, her sneakers hit the inside of the trunk with an ineffectual thud. She paused, listening for any footsteps, for the man named Paulson to open the hatch and shoot her.

Nothing. She wasn't certain if the guy even *had* a gun. Still, with her hands tied behind her, he could do her plenty of damage.

Another sob worked itself up. She swallowed it back down. The psycho had tied a dirty rag around her mouth before throwing her in here, and the constant nausea she felt from its stench made her worry that crying would be the straw that sent her vomiting into the gag. God knew what would happen then.

Was she at the church? Quinn said to bring her here, but then whispered something else she couldn't hear. For all she knew, they were clear on the other side of town. The turns they'd taken felt right, though.

Not that it mattered. Quinn was seriously nuts. More than Tarretti or even Nate. And what was with Nate's dad? Hopping into the car and chatting with Paulson about a Red Sox game they were going to. Did he really think they were heading to Fenway Park at midnight? Another loony in a town *full* of loonies.

She remembered, reluctantly, that fuzzy period after Tarretti had been shot, when she drove with Paulson to the alley to meet the others. She'd *wanted* to go with him, nothing more than an evening drive with an old friend. The world had been a hazy whiteness, like she was sleepwalking, or half-awake under the sheets. Memory of that time seemed clearer now than when it actually happened.

Is that what was going on with Mister Dinneck? Did he even know where he was?

No, no, no! She kicked the truck again in her frustration, mostly with her knees. This was insane. Mad Karnak the Hypnotic Genius was *not* controlling everyone's minds. Josh was *not* a murderer. Nathan was *not* chosen by his God to—

"NNN!" she shouted through the gag and kicked the trunk again, and again, and again.

The trunk popped open.

For a full minute, she lay there, sucking the cool, beautiful air into her nostrils as it flooded into the trunk. She stared at the billion stars in the sky.

Well, she thought with a sudden calm, *this is a good sign.*

Even as she squirmed to get into a position to raise herself up, Elizabeth heard the sound of an approaching car. *Thank God. Yes, hurry.* There was no time to be dainty. She rolled out of the trunk, slammed onto the pavement and broke the fall with a sloppy half-roll. As she did, she noticed two things at once. She was, indeed, in the parking lot behind Nathan's church. And, the car she heard was pulling around the building and coming her way. Speeding up, actually.

She moaned through the gag. *Please, no.*

The car stopped a yard from her, engine running, headlights blinding her to everything but the vague shape of the driver's door opening. Someone stepped out. For the slightest of moments she thought—or hoped—the voice she heard next would belong to some concerned parishioner stopping by to check on his young pastor. But, of course, it belonged to Quinn The Magnificent. She sighed into her gag.

"Well, well, the damsel in distress tires of waiting for her—"

Elizabeth stumbled to her feet and ran toward the church. Realizing the error in this, she cut sideways and made for the woods. Quinn appeared in front of her, arms open.

"Not so fast, young lady."

"MMM NNN SS ELZZZHHH!" she screamed and sent her knee up between his legs. He closed them in time to trap her leg, then twisted his body sideways. She fell off balance onto the ground. He grabbed her bound arms and pulled her up. She squirmed, but his hands were all over her, strong, confident, assuring she could not escape. He was stronger than he looked.

"Enough," he said. "Calm down *now* or you go back into the trunk and you will never leave it again." He kept his voice low but the honesty in the threat was clear. She stopped struggling, telling herself the battle wasn't over. She wouldn't give up.

She sifted sideways, enough to get his overly curious hands to shift, then said, "WZZ NNT?"

He began to lead her toward the church door. He waved a hand toward the car and the passenger door opened. Josh got out, opened the back door and gestured to Nathan with the gun.

Quinn said, "NNT," mocking her gagged speech, "is right here. Time to play nice with your friends now—Elizabeth, was it?—or someone is going to get hurt."

Nate was tied in a similar manner as herself, though he was fortunate enough not to have a rag stuffed in his mouth. He looked at her, tried to smile but winced as his bruised cheek stretched painfully. He settled for a small nod, then focused on the sidewalk.

She glared at her captor. "WW DON OOH JZZS HHHMMMTZZ MM AGN?"

"Well," Quinn said, ushering her into the back door, which was now open with an impatient Paulson waiting for them, "I could *hypnotize* you again quite easily, as you're well aware. But then we'd have no need of the gag and I'd miss you talking in such an eloquent manner. I'm beginning to enjoy this little game of 'What is ELZZZHHH saying?'"

"FF YEW, YEW..."

"Elizabeth," Nate's voice, behind her. "Chill out. Our time'll come, I promise."

Quinn laughed. "That's the first correct thing you've said all night, Pastor."

Hearing Nate's voice brought with it a surprising calm. She was with him again. That was *something*, at least. For better or worse. They entered the darkened kitchen, then into the church hall. Things were quickly moving toward the *for worse* part, when Paulson shined his flashlight into the sanctuary.

Behind the gag, Elizabeth screamed.

Chapter Sixty-Three

As a group, they walked slowly around the sanctuary, staring at the scene in the flickering light from Paulson's unsteady hands. A man's body lay prone in front of the podium. A thin trail of blood smeared along the floor, leading back the way they'd come. Nathan had noticed the trail dotting the sidewalk, but hadn't time to consider it because of Elizabeth and Quinn's argument.

Now he understood. Vincent Tarretti, if he hadn't been dead before, had to be now. There was a jagged hole in the back of his jacket. Small puddles of blood pooled around his body, less than Nathan would have expected if the man were still alive.

"It's there," Paulson said, moving the light so the bright center of the beam shone on something half-covered by Vincent's body. "I don't know if it was already here, or if he carried the thing all the way, but—" He stopped, his voice reaching a fevered pitch as he spoke. He must have realized how he sounded and simply stopped talking.

Quinn stepped past the short railing and knelt a small distance from the body. All was silent, and then Nathan heard the sound. He looked around, unable to place its source, deciding perhaps that it was only in his head. Singing, maybe? That made no sense. Voices, yes, but distant, changing in cadence and pitch. Chants, like monks, then only wind through the trees, applause, a child crying, water, thunder, more voices, an orchestra playing one incessant note....

Peter Quinn stumbled backward until he was outside the short railing. His movements were of a man suddenly terrified. In his face, however,—even in the half light of Paulson's flashlight—was the unmistakable glow of rapturous joy. With his movement, the sound diminished, fading to nothing, coming back to linger in the back of Nathan's head.

"Turn off the light a moment," Quinn whispered.

"What?"

A little louder, "Turn it off."

With a click, they were cast in darkness, save for the glow of one streetlight shining through the stained glass windows. A glow, faint, like a child's glow-stick the day after trick-or-treat, emanated from beneath Vincent Tarretti. Nathan blinked. He struggled to find a thought that fit what he was seeing. The light wasn't really there. That made no sense.

He cleared his throat, needing to break the silence. He knew, with no more doubt, that Vincent had been telling the truth. Perhaps not the *entire* truth, as evidenced by the false Ark, but he knew what lay beneath the man's body. It was what these people had been after. At least part of it.

God, what do I do?

The flashlight lit the scene again, this time in the grip of Quinn himself. His voice was breathy, as if in the throes of passion. "Move the body, now. Carefully! Do not touch the package beneath him."

Manny Paulson looked incredulous. "You're not serious. You think I didn't see that? I can hear something, too. Something's not right here."

"Do it, or I'll have Mister Everson shoot you in the heart. Let's see if you last as long as Tarretti did."

Paulson looked over at the other three. He seemed about to say something else, perhaps suggest one of *them* do the job, but apparently decided against it. With Quinn keeping the light shining toward the podium, Paulson stepped forward.

Nathan looked away a moment, and almost jumped in surprise. Sitting in the fourth pew, a serene expression on his face, sat Art Dinneck.

Nathan whispered, "Dad?"

"Not another word, Dinneck," said Quinn, his voice losing some of its earlier awe. He kept his eyes riveted on his assistant. Paulson reached down and gripped Vincent's bloody shoulder as Quinn added, "Not another sound."

Chapter Sixty-Four

The Red Sox were down by three runs in the second inning. It was still early. The crowd eagerly cheered for the new batter. Beside Art, Paulson took a bite of his hot dog and said nothing. In the man's silence, Art felt obliged also not to speak. Manny had said something to that effect, some word or suggestion when they found their seats that told Art it was time to watch the game and keep silent.

The rookie, Baker, was up. The count was two balls, one strike. Lead runner moving from first, a bit too far. He'd better be careful. A homerun right now would bring them to within one. Art closed his eyes for a moment, letting the sun warm his face.

Dad?

Nathan loved coming to the games. Now that he was in town, he should call him. Make some amends for all the trouble lately.

He opened his eyes. Paulson took another bite of his hot dog, staring intently at the game. He'd already taken quite a few bites, but there was still a lot left to it. Maybe he'd bought two. Art looked at the cardboard tray on his friend's lap. Nope, nothing else.

That was weird.

For a moment, Fenway Park was lost in a haze. Art rubbed his eyes. Nathan was standing a few aisles down, looking back at him. This wasn't the ballpark. He was in church. Everything was dark. For some reason, he wasn't startled at finding himself first in Boston then Hillcrest. A slow understanding unraveled inside him.

"Nate?" He tried to smile and lift his hand to wave, hoping he could explain what was going on. Fenway Park returned for a moment, then the church. The only constant was Nate standing in front of him.

"Nathan is not here. Be quiet now; the batter's about to get a double. Just watch the game." Nathan blinked from existence. The park was back in its full green splendor. Art felt the excitement of the moment filling him. Wild foul ball by Baker. He was staying with it. Something nagged at him, though. Had he just seen Nate? No, of course not. He needed to get some more sleep, daydreaming like this.

He was in Fenway Park. His son was in Florida. Working with a parish there—

Nate had come home.

Just his imagination. Baker swung at a low, inside pitch (at least, Art thought that was what was pitched, it was hard to tell from these far-angle bleacher seats). *Crack!* A line drive up the middle between second and third base. Everyone screamed. The Orioles' shortstop dove, missed. The crowd went crazy. Art just smiled.

Hadn't they been playing the Yankees?

Why couldn't he just enjoy the game? Beside him, Paulson took another bite of his never-ending hot dog.

The Yankees must have been a different game. Beverly was right. They needed a vacation. He looked down at his seat. Instead of the small plastic chairs, it was wood, like a pew. No, no, these were Fenway seats.

Beverly. He did tell her about the game, didn't he?

Something was wrong. Something was wrong. Something was wrong....

Chapter Sixty-Five

Manny Paulson would gladly have run naked down Main Street rather than grab this dead man's shoulder. Tarretti's windbreaker was wet in places, stiff in others with blood in various stages of drying. He used both hands to turn the man over.

"Nate?"

The voice startled him and he turned back toward the pews to see who'd spoken. Apparently everyone else had been surprised by Art Dinneck's voice, because they were also looking back. Manny felt Tarretti's body slump away from his grip. Quinn was aiming the flashlight at Dinneck. The man was leaning forward in his seat, eyes still glazed, but he'd spoken his son's name.

"Mister Dinneck," came that creepy voice Quinn used too often for Manny's comfort, "Nathan is not here. Be quiet now; the batter's going to get a double. Just watch the game."

Art sat back against the seat, his suddenly troubled expression softening into its earlier, moronic complacency. Manny wondered, not for the first time, how often Quinn pulled that trick on Manny, himself. He assumed he'd remember it, but seeing how Art and the others had been so well-controlled all these months, maybe he wouldn't.

Quinn shined the light back toward the sacristy and said, "Let's hurry this—" and said nothing else.

Manny looked down. One hand still held loosely to Tarretti's shoulder even though the man's body lay against the front of the podium.

Tarretti's eyes were open in narrow slits. He was holding a pistol in his hands.

"God forgive me," the dead man croaked. The muzzle of the gun flashed and Manny felt a hundred pounds of fist slam into his left hip. The church spun. He forgot where he was, what he'd been doing. He hit a low railing, turned and rolled over it, tried to get out of the way of the car that had hit him.

Heshotme, heSHOTme.

The room was a strobe of light. Quinn flattened himself onto the floor, the flashlight making a narrow line on the carpet. Enough for Manny to see he'd landed away from the others, resting against the front of the first row of seats.

His hand moved instinctively to where he'd been punched—*shot, I've been shot.* It came away covered in blood, quickly followed by a river of the stuff pouring from a hole burned into him, just above his thigh. He felt a bigger hole on the side of one buttock.

Back at the podium, Tarretti was not standing up and aiming the final death shot. Instead, his eyes closed, slowly, and the gun fell from his limp hand.

"Help me, Peter," Manny whispered. "Please."

*   *   *

Vincent Tarretti felt the gun slip out of his fingers, then could feel nothing.

Lord Jesus, forgive me. I've tried to protect it. Please, let it have been enough. Forgive me for shooting that man. I didn't know what else to do. Please take me now. I can't go any farther.

For a moment, the outlines of the others in the church came into full view, cast in the afterglow of the flashlight. He saw Nathan Dinneck and focused on him for an eternal moment, then his eyes closed. He did not face the darkness of earlier in the crypt, only light. The longer he stared, the brighter it shone. He watched with eyes no longer physical. No more pain. A cotton-blanket warmth enfolded him. There were others in the light. Three figures, coming toward him. He knew them. Knew them all. He wanted to shout with joy.

And in that moment, Vincent Tarretti's mission came to an end.

Chapter Sixty-Six

This isn't happening. How could that man have lived?!?

Peter Quinn looked up from his prostrate position before the sanctuary. It was a gesture not of supplication but self-preservation. Tarretti had been packing a weapon! The fact that the caretaker might have been armed was the reason he'd originally sent Everson into the crypt first, the reason he'd told the boy to shoot the man as soon as he identified him from Peter's description. He'd been right to do so. The man had not only cheated death long enough to crawl to this place, but he still had his damned weapon.

Manny Paulson moaned against the pew beside him. Peter ignored him. He'd served his purpose and was dead to him now. Tarretti had done him a favor, actually.

Nathan Dinneck and Elizabeth were crouched awkwardly on the floor, their bound hands keeping them off balance. Josh Everson stood beside them, oblivious to what had happened. Peter was grateful he'd thought to bring the boy this far. Aside from being the only one who could be tied to any murders, he would prove useful now that Paulson was down.

Any leeway he might have had, time-wise, was gone. There weren't many neighbors close enough to hear the gunshot, but he couldn't play the odds any longer. Not when his final act of devotion to Molech was so close.

Nathan Dinneck rose up suddenly and Peter had to make a decision. Tarretti dropping his gun could only mean he was finally dead. *Had* to mean that. And now young Dinneck was going to do something stupid, or try even with his hands tied.

Peter stood just as quickly and said, "Mister Everson still answers to me, Pastor. I can have him kill your girlfriend *or* your father with one command. Do not try anything that will test my patience."

The minister said nothing. The girl still knelt beside him, unable or unwilling to lift herself up.

Peter shone the light over the caretaker's body, then looked back at

Josh Everson. The gun in the boy's hand was the only thing keeping Dinneck at bay. He couldn't risk leaving Tarretti's weapon too close to his hands. Just in case.

Only one option, unless he wanted to do it himself. He stepped toward the woman and gently helped her up. Undisguised hate poured from her. As soon as she was standing she stepped away from him.

"Such a temper you have," he said, focusing his voice toward her. Eyes widening, she muttered incoherent words through her gag. She was feeling his power already. The thought gave him the pride and impetus to continue. "I have a task for you, young lady. It will not take long, but you need to do it right away."

"Elizabeth, don't—" but Dinneck's protests were cut short by Peter's hand rising up quickly, stopping just short of slapping him across the face.

"Do I need to demonstrate how serious this moment is, Reverend?" Without turning from Nathan's stare he said, "Mister Everson." He needed to keep any panic or impatience from his voice. To keep control of these people, even for these few remaining minutes, required calm.

But he had to hurry.

When the boy looked his way, Peter repeated, "Mister Everson, please count to six, then shoot yourself in the head."

Nathan had expected Quinn to tell him to shoot *him*, or Elizabeth. He shouldn't be letting him hold their lives for ransom anymore. But Josh had killed a man tonight, if Vincent's unmoving form meant that he'd finally passed away. Intentional or not, could he take a chance his friend was prepared for death? The same was true for Elizabeth.

Josh raised the gun to his own temple.

No, he couldn't. If there was any chance, even three more seconds of a chance... "OK," Nathan said. "But stop now or forget everything." Something dark stirred within him, a horrible realization too heavy to dwell on. Not yet.

"Mister Everson," Quinn said quickly, "stop what you are doing and lower the gun. But keep it trained on the lovely Elizabeth."

Nathan felt Elizabeth move against him again as she began to come out of her funk. Her return to normalcy was short lived.

"Not to worry, young lady. After our enjoyable talk outside, I've decided to spare you, for a while. I think we can have great fun together. In the meantime, you will please go to the podium and put Mister Tarretti's gun atop the back altar so it is no longer within his reach." Elizabeth did not respond, but quietly took a step toward the sanctuary. "One moment," Quinn said, his voice losing some of the calm of earlier. Elizabeth hesitated. Quinn cursed quietly and fumbled with the knots binding her wrists.

Seeing this man touch her, even if only untying her, filled Nathan with a rage he could barely contain. He looked sideways to Josh, saw the pistol still aimed at her.

Even if only for a few seconds... he reminded himself. He did not know how much longer he could hold back. His hands were tied, but if he surged forward, perhaps knocked Quinn's head against the floor...,

God, give me patience. So many lives are at stake. Help me to know what to do.

The short prayer calmed him, if only enough to stay his ground. The darkness returned to his heart. In those brief seconds when Josh had raised the gun to his own temple, Nathan understood how much he had failed these people. All his life, the only thing he wanted for himself was ordination, a chance to share the Gospel with as many people as possible. People except, apparently, those closest to him. Nathan went out into the world, but left Elizabeth and Josh to find their own way to salvation. She never wanted to hear it, true, but Josh... for all Nathan knew, his best friend yearned to be part of Hillcrest Baptist, to follow the path Nathan walked. But in all the years they'd been friends he'd never asked, save for casual invitations. Afraid it might come between them. Now, it was too late.

Chapter Sixty-Seven

Quinn managed the knots at last and flung them away. The rope landed across Manny Paulson's shoulder. Paulson had managed to move against the pew, obviously trying to reach the side exit, but his strength seemed to be ebbing as fast as the blood from his hip.

"Peter," he gasped from his dark corner. "Peter, call an ambulance. Please help me. I can't move my leg."

Peter ignored the plea. It felt as if he'd lost an hour just untying the stupid woman. Now that she was free, he needed to maintain a steady voice. He expected to hear police sirens approaching in the distance at any minute.

"Elizabeth," he whispered into her ear. "You may now approach the man on the altar and take his weapon."

She did so, with hesitant but obedient movements. When she had the gun in her hand and Tarretti made no sign of resisting, Peter took a deep breath and let it out slowly. One less obstacle, at least. "Please lay it atop the altar and return here."

As she did, Peter stared down at the dirty sack beside the dead man. It was surprisingly free of any bloodstains. Tarretti's body had been mostly moved aside by Paulson. The long-sought-after tablets, carved by the finger of the Israelites' God, lay inside. As if this thought was the catalyst, the sounds they'd all heard earlier returned. A single note from a distant organ, voices that were nothing but wind, voices singing, chanting.

Stop it! Focus.

Elizabeth slowly returned from the back of the sanctuary and stood between Everson and the preacher. The gun lay on the altar, too far for Tarretti to reach without giving away any pretense he might be playing at. Peter moved the flashlight beam away from the prize and saw again the faint glow; felt it, electric, a tingling across his face.

"I—" Peter began, but the overwhelming significance of what he was about to say caught in his throat. So long searching. So long, and now he would be the one to bring it to fruition. Not his uncle, not some faceless follower a hundred years from now. *He* would finish it.

Tears welled in his eyes. He used the hand holding the flashlight to wipe at his face. Before he dared touch the Covenant, he needed to confirm its true ownership. It must change "hands" officially.

He walked into the sanctuary, ignoring the others, lowering his trembling hands. "I claim this prize," he said, whispering at first, then cleared his throat and continued in a louder, assertive voice, "that which once belonged to Solomon, King of Israel, devoted servant of the dark god Molech. I claim the tablets of the Covenant in Molech's name, to be taken under the care of the Ammonites, his eternally faithful servants, now..." he reached closer, "...and forever." He closed his fingers around the sackcloth and the prize within, felt its power course through his hands, up his arms. For a fleeting moment, he thought he would burst into flames, melt away, like in that absurd Hollywood movie. He did not. The power passed through him. His body was a conduit. It did not kill. It *empowered* him. Now he understood how Tarretti had survived such a long and arduous journey with his injuries.

Peter stood, wanting to laugh with sheer joy. Nathan Dinneck beat him to it. The boy laughed, a weak, pathetic attempt at indifference. Peter could hear his terror. That, too, empowered him.

"Solomon was no servant of any demon. You're fooling yourself—"

"He pledged his support to many dark gods later in his illustrious life, Reverend. You know that. Granted, it depended on which wife he was trying to coax into bed at the time." Peter walked slowly, reverently, from the sanctuary, stood as he'd done before in front of the first pew. "When one pledges devotion to Molech, even if only to ingratiate himself with a woman, such devotion is forever. Does not your God say the same of his own people?"

He glanced into the front pew and another ripple of excitement ran through him. Paulson had brought the two-gallon gasoline jug as Peter had instructed him. He'd also opened the tall stained-glass windows along the front and side of the church. The upper portions were fixed, unable to be opened. But the lower half of each was hinged to open outward at the turn of the crank. Paulson had done well. *Faithful to the end*, he mused, and the joy overflowed now. Everything had come together.

Paulson reached forward and grabbed feebly at his pant leg. Peter kicked his arm away.

Dinneck continued with his frightened half-smile. "Perhaps you've been fooled again, Quinn. If those were the true Commandments you'd be dead now. You know as well as I do that only priests of God may handle them."

How obscenely ignorant this holy man was. "If you held in your arms what I now hold, Reverend Dinneck, you would be silenced. I can feel their power, and it strengthens me. Didn't you hear my claim, just now? The Covenant no longer belongs to your God. It belongs to my master. I am now his high priest."

Dinneck shook his head. Peter suddenly realized he was stalling. Time had slowed for him, lost as he was in such rapture. But not for the rest of the world. If a neighbor had heard Tarretti's shot, the police would come soon. Dinneck knew that. The boy was too smart for his own good.

They couldn't wait any longer. It was going to be a pleasure to watch him die. Peter laid the red jug at the step leading into the sanctuary and said, "Elizabeth, would you be so kind as to pour this gasoline around and atop the podium, maybe a little on the altar as well? Be sure to cover Mister Tarretti's body. Move quickly now, girl. We have one final task to accomplish."

She did as asked, unscrewing the cap and pouring the gasoline haphazardly across the raised wooden area within the railing. Gas spilled across her slacks and shoes. She gave no reaction except to cough twice through the gag.

"That's enough, dear," Peter said. "Leave it there and come down now."

She coughed again, then stumbled, reaching out to catch the railing. The fact that she did this without any instruction from him told Peter that she might already be slipping from his control. It would not matter, if he performed the sacrifice quickly.

He began his final and long-planned task. The sense of urgency became a whirlwind in his head. The church was filling with fumes too quickly. No turning back now.

"What is burning down my church going to accomplish!" Dinneck shouted. *Good,* Peter thought, *be afraid.* He reached into his pants pocket and produced a Zippo lighter. He had purchased this particular one a long time ago, using it only for lighting the candles in the small temple behind the storefront, or other altars at other locations. It would be used tonight for the last time. For the ultimate burning. He liked this lighter. It would be missed.

"Most powerful master," he shouted, keeping his gaze steady on Nathan Dinneck, "I offer you your first sacrifice!" Stepping down the aisle past the first pew, he flicked the lighter. A small flame rose up. He was ready to toss it away if the flame grew any higher; if the gas fumes had indeed filled too far into the church. Nothing happened.

Not yet.

"It is time for the sacrifice. As is decreed by the most powerful lord, Molech the Demon of all Power and Majesty, who commands blood sacrifice of his followers, I commit you," he looked toward the pews, "Arthur Dinneck, to come forth and offer your son to him now."

Chapter Sixty-Eight

Nathan's father stood from his quiet vigil on the bench. His brow was wrinkled, as if confused by Quinn's words. Still, he stepped out of the pew and walked to stand beside him. Quinn looked at Nathan and smiled—the expression no longer calm, but one of madness. Perhaps panic, as well. He shifted the weight of the Covenant under his arms. In his other hand, the flame continued to issue forth from the Zippo.

"Come forward, Nathan Dinneck," Quinn said, then added, "and do it quickly, please."

Elizabeth moved beside him. She coughed again, and pulled the gag away from her mouth. She blinked at him with red-rimmed eyes. Eyes which seemed to be coming back into focus.

What do I do? Nathan thought with a sudden terror. *What do I do?*

"Now, Reverend!"

In her remaining confusion Elizabeth muttered something Nathan did not understand, but in this lowest hour of despair he found her inaudible comment comforting.

Nathan stepped forward until he stood in the aisle between the rows of pews.

With no further fanfare, Quinn tossed the lighter over the railing and into the sanctuary. Before it landed, the air exploded with a *whoosh*! The sanctuary glowed in a perfectly round ball of flame. Then it twisted into a vision from hell. The podium burned. A pillar of fire enveloped Tarretti's body and already reached toward the railing. A wall of heat moved before it. The first wave was weak; the second, as the gas can by the altar ignited and fuel and fire spread out in all directions was far stronger, more physical. The floor of the raised platform bubbled and blackened. Rivulets of gasoline were now rivers of fire heading toward them, reaching toward the carpet lining the aisle.

A third wall of heat poured over and through them. Now smoke was rising everywhere. Tarretti's gun jumped from the altar as a round exploded. The bullet embedded itself into the sanctuary wall. Before the gun landed another explosion spit into the air, then another. The rounds exploded from the gun's clip, tearing it apart. A projectile whizzed past Elizabeth's arm and slammed into the pew between her and Josh. Still gripping the gag at throat level, she tried to breathe, taking in only hot, acrid air. Josh received no orders to the contrary and so did not try to stop her. He took a reflexive step back from the heat, blinking away the pain growing on his face. He lowered the gun he was holding, leaned against the pew.

As Art Dinneck approached Nathan, his troubled expression was nonetheless still void of any other sign of understanding, still under Quinn's control.

"Art Dinneck," Quinn said, having to shout now above the roar of the fire spreading past the altar railing, tearing up the walls of the sanctuary and ripping into the ceiling above. Long-dry wood splintered and cracked, giving itself to the fire. "Take hold of your son, firmly, and do not let him go. He is small and could get lost." Art smiled wider and grabbed Nathan by the shoulders, his grip too strong for Nathan to simply shrug himself free.

Elizabeth looked down in time to see the carpet in the center aisle burning, reaching to where Nate and his father stood with Quinn. She couldn't hear what the latter was saying. The sprinklers sprung to life overhead, too late for any effect. She felt water drop to her face only to evaporate a second later. The inferno coming toward them was too big already, too hot to be stopped.

Her sneakers were on fire. She tried to kick away the flames, realized in time she should simply kick them off her feet. As she did so, she fell backwards into the first pew. Her socks were not burning, but they felt wet with gasoline. She pulled them off and threw them onto the bench beside her. Snippets of her short time at the podium came back to her. Had she lit the fire? No, she didn't think so.

Josh was standing in front of her, facing the approaching flame with one hand raised to his face. Elizabeth reached forward and grabbed the back of his jacket. He might turn around and shoot her, but at the moment she didn't care. He fell on top of her, a heavy, unresisting weight.

Nathan's father smiled and squeezed his shoulders. "Nate!"

Quinn cradled the wrapped tablets like a child in one arm and held Nathan's arm with the other. "Look at the flames, Art Dinneck. These are the flames of our god. He demands a sacrifice, and thus you shall give your first born unto him. Do it now! There is no more time. Do it!!"

The fire roared behind them. The heat was constant. Nathan's head felt as if it were already on fire.

"Josh!" Elizabeth screamed. "Wake up!" In the light of the fire his face looked red, sunburned. It probably *was* burned. He raised both his hands to his face.

He wasn't holding the gun any longer.

A large section of burning ceiling cracked and fell onto the lost podium. The sprinklers cut out, their feeder line severed.

The heat was too much. Elizabeth crawled into the next pew and half-dragged Josh with her. He followed, reluctantly obedient but obviously still too confused to understand the danger. From somewhere a million miles away, Quinn's crony, Paulson, was screaming. Josh looked around the church frantically, arms flailing as if coming out of a nightmare. Elizabeth figured that wasn't too far from the truth. Once he joined her in the second pew, she turned to scream at Nathan that he could run. Her gaze moved past the threesome in the aisle to the flames and roiling white and black smoke filling the church, the fire ripping the dry wood apart with flaming hands.

There was a face in the midst of the fire. Elizabeth blinked, knowing it was an illusion.

It did not go away. It twisted, became more defined. A massive bull's head with eyes of flame darker than those around it.

No no no no no no no! "Nathan!!!!!!!"

Chapter Sixty-Nine

Arthur Dinneck shouted, "Nate! Come on. We can get them if we hurry." He pushed forward, toward the creeping fire, its furthermost edges only three feet away. Nathan tried to maintain his balance, but his hands were tied behind him. All he could do was dig his left foot into the carpet, push himself against his father's chest. His ankle seared with pain from the fire crawling toward it.

Quinn laughed and shouted, "Now, Art! Now or never!!!!"

"Dad!" Nathan screamed into his father's face. "Dad, wake up!"

It was hot today, but as long as Nate was with him, Art would bear it. He held his son's hand and pointed toward the two seats that were open behind the right field wall.

"Nate! Come on! We can get them if we hurry." He was smiling, and so was Nate, but something still felt wrong.

Open your eyes, Arthur Dinneck.

It was his own voice, shouted from behind him, from *everywhere*.

The elusive nagging feeling of earlier was now an inferno in his mind. Flames roared up in front of him.

Hillcrest Baptist was on fire. He was holding Nate in his arms. Was he rescuing him? Nate, only twelve years old and already looking like a grown man. It was good to be here with him. The seats were empty. He had to hurry.

The church was burning. Something vile hovered in the air over the sanctuary.

Peter Quinn's voice commanded, "Now, Art! Now or never!!"

God, help me. What's going on? He needed to throw Nate into the fire. Into the burning mouth which loomed right behind his son. He needed to do it now.

No!

Now! He had to do it now!

Nate shouted, "Dad! Wake up!" He wasn't a boy anymore. He was grown.

Art needed to do what he was told.

Flames poured over the ceiling, ripping apart his church and his life. Beverly was in the kitchen now, waiting for him, crying. He'd left her again. Quinn worshipped a demon. He hadn't cheated on anyone; it was just a movie on a television.

I've done nothing wrong.

I've done everything wrong.

* * *

"Now, Dinneck! Now!"

Peter Quinn knew that he had to get out of this building. But the first sacrifice had to be made. To have the treasure and not offer a gift of thanksgiving was sacrilege. He sensed the demon's arrival, looming behind him. It waited impatiently for its sacrifice. Peter's soul would be wiped dead if he failed. He was so, so, so close!

The heat was too much. He had to leave. *Let them all burn, then!*

One last chance. Dinneck had his son. The heat bathing them would kill before the fire ever did.

"Now, Dinneck!" he shouted, preparing to run down the aisle. Any power in his voice was lost under his own frenzy. "Now! Now! Now! Now!"

Art looked at him, and his eyes were suddenly clear. "My dear God," he said. "What have I done?" Art grabbed his son, turned and threw him down the aisle, away from the fire. Before Peter could react, Dinneck turned back and took hold of him instead.

"Release me now!" Peter screamed, unable to focus his voice. He clutched the tablets tighter against his chest. Even with the heat surrounding him, he could feel their power. Ripping him apart. "Kill me and these go, too!"

The look of hatred and despair in Dinneck's eyes told him it didn't matter anymore. Art Dinneck wrapped his arms around him, gasping when the tablets pressed against him, then ran with Peter Quinn into the fire and the demon's waiting mouth.

Chapter Seventy

"**D**ad!" Nathan was on his back, unable to stop what we was seeing. He rolled over his bound hands until he managed to get to his knees. The flames tore down the aisle, devouring the first two rows of seats with the sound of a jet engine. The heat was a monstrous hand pushing him backward, toward the front doors. The upper section of wall separating the church from the second floor residence collapsed then fell burning along the side aisle. Two outlines danced amid the too-bright scene in front of him, bathed in a green and yellow haze more brilliant than the flames. After a few seconds, the world went white and he had to look away. The church was a vision of hell. He looked up and saw them again.

Nathan screamed and raised himself up to run into the flames, somehow *needing* to do so. His father, and the Covenant of God, the cause of all this death and horror, were lost there. When he glanced up a third time, the figures had fallen from view, the green glow was gone. Nathan heard a terrible screaming over the inferno's laughter. One of the figures rose back up like a phoenix, spun crazily, then melted away.

Something sailed out of the fire. The sackcloth and its contents slammed against the pew one row away from him. Five feet from that, the fire continued its forward crawl forward. Though it had been in the center of the inferno, the sack had not burned, was hardly singed.

Nathan fell to his knees again. The world around him was spots and flashes, his vision burned away. He was empty. His father was gone. Nathan would simply wait now for the fire to reach him.

"Nate!" Elizabeth's hands grabbed his jacket and fell beside him in a fit of coughing. "Oh, God, Nathan! Let's go!"

His throat was too dry to respond. She pulled him back a step. He didn't resist. She gave up trying to drag him and worked desperately at the knots around his wrists, as if he could not run without his hands. Josh crouched beside them. His expression was blank, but not without awareness. He looked like Nathan felt. Lost. Above them, smoke roiled like storm clouds, escaping through the open church windows. Not fast enough to keep it from filling the hall, closing down on them. Walls and pews blackened and popped, then were completely lost in the smoke.

The fire reached the bag containing the tablets. The carpet around it curled and blackened. How could his father have lived long enough in that inferno to throw them free? How could he even have known what it was?

"Ok, that's it! Let's go." His shoulders screamed in pain as his freed arms swung forward and down to the floor.

If that was the case, if his father's fall from God was not his own doing, maybe he was going to be all right. Maybe he was safe now. If he gave up now, Art Dinneck would have died for *nothing*.

Flames licked around and over the tablets but nothing of them or their shroud burned. Nor did Nathan's arm when he leaped forward and reached through the fire. He pulled the bag clear, surprised at the sheer weight of it. After making sure his jacket sleeve wasn't burning—it was melted in places—he staggered to his feet holding the bundle, turned and ran toward Elizabeth's horrified face.

She screamed, "Leave them here!"

Chapter Seventy-One

"I can't," he shouted. "You know that."

Josh's paralysis ended and he gave Elizabeth a kick. "Talk about it outside!" He ran toward the front door. Nathan and Elizabeth followed. Without slowing, and without fully understanding why, Nathan reached into his coat pocket and removed his cell phone. He threw it into the last pew.

The air outside filled with columns of escaping smoke from the windows and newly-formed holes in the roof. But it was cool and wonderful to breathe. Each of them coughed, bodies fighting to clean smoke-filled lungs.

In the distance, the sound of sirens. Nathan cursed and began to run around the building. He called back, "You two stay here, far enough back from the building." His words burned his throat as badly as the heat inside. "I don't exactly know what you'll say to them, but you need to give me time to get away."

"I don't think so!"

Elizabeth ran after him down the side driveway and into the back lot. One fact Nathan had filed into the back of his mind when they arrived here now returned. Quinn had never turned off his car. Nathan didn't believe in coincidence, especially now. He had to be gone with the Covenant before the police and firefighters pulled onto the street.

Elizabeth's bare feet slapped the pavement behind him. Quinn's car idled ahead, headlights trained on Paulson's open trunk. The sirens were closer. From inside the bag a growing vibration worked into his chest, shaking his bones. The tablets felt heavier, too. Just his imagination. He opened the back door and put them on the seat. When he let go, he was seized with an overwhelming need to touch them again.

Elizabeth finally reached him and grabbed his arm. "Where do you think you're going?" She sounded hysterical, kept looking back toward the burning church, as if afraid it would fall on them even at this distance.

"I can't explain," he said. "If there's any way at all, I'll contact you. But I have to leave, and it has to be now!" He got into the open driver's door. Josh was stumbling up to them, out of breath.

Elizabeth looked at Nathan, then the building, then pulled him out of the car. He was too surprised to resist. He landed on the pavement as she jumped in. Nathan panicked. She was going to take the keys. He scrambled up as Elizabeth slid into the passenger side, shouting, "I'm not losing you again! I'm nuts to go along with this any longer but I'm not losing you again!"

The sirens were so close that it was probably already too late. He saw the flashes of strobes on the distant trees. He got into the driver's seat and put the car in gear. Josh had caught up to them and was standing beside the car, alone. His face was lost against a silhouette of flames.

"I'm sorry, Nate," Josh whispered. "I'm so, so sorry. I don't understand what—"

"Come with us."

Josh shook his head, stepped back. "I killed someone, Nate." His voice was barely audible. Nathan wanted to argue, realizing the irony that he'd been ready to leave them *both* here a second earlier. But he was out of time. His father was dead; it couldn't be for nothing.

Nathan closed the driver's door. He wanted to comfort his friend, knew he would never be able to. He would pray for him, every day. It was all he *could* do.

"Don't tell them you saw us leave. I love you, Josh, please remember that." He took his foot off the brake and looked away, pressed the accelerator. They curved around Paulson's abandoned Oldsmobile and past the church's destruction. More strobes neared the entrance to Dreyfus Road to his right. He turned left and tried to turn off the headlights. They stayed on, a safety feature of most newer cars he hadn't thought much about until now.

With one eye on the rear view mirror and one on the road, he drove the car along a long curve until the flames were no longer in view. In the last moment, headlights turned onto the street behind him, then they were lost as he rounded the turn and continued down Dreyfus. Lights in some of the houses were on, or turning on, as they passed. He didn't notice anyone outside. The residents would be alerted to trouble more from the sound of the approaching fire trucks than the fire itself.

He slowed the car, taking every side road that presented itself to reduce the chance of a police cruiser or fire truck coming the other way. They needed to get out of Hillcrest, but there was one stop he had to make first. Tarretti's strongbox, under the bedroom floor. The caretaker had shown it to him knowing something like this might happen, or maybe Tarretti simply spent his life prepared for anything.

As they worked across town toward the main cemetery, Nathan did not think about his father, or what his mother would soon have to go through. Nor could he look beside him to acknowledge the woman he loved crying against the window. He just drove.

Chapter Seventy-Two

Beverly Dinneck had not yet gone to bed. She knew where Art had gone. When he hadn't come home as quickly as promised, she called his cell phone. No answer. He may have forgotten to turn it on, so she tried his number at work. Again, no answer, just the neutral tones of his voice telling her to leave a name, number and a brief message. He would get back to her as soon as he returned.

As soon as he returned. When would that be? Did the Hillcrest Men's Club ever close? That's where he was. She couldn't deny it. Had that been one of his new buddies who called earlier about a problem at work? When this thought first occurred to her, not long after Art left, she'd stormed into the bedroom and cried harder than ever before. A line had been crossed this time, a wall irrevocably raised between them. Briefly, tonight, Art had truly been *with* her. Something in his voice, his commitment to stay at home. There was such a sadness about him these past few months. Maybe he would finally tell her what was wrong.

But he wasn't with her now. Whenever he decided to come home, how long would he stay until the next time? Even now she tried to cling to some hope in Nate's homecoming. His role in their church might bring change for them all. There was always that hope.

She wandered into the living room and sat on the couch. It was late. She considered going back to bed and staying there. Her bout of crying had left her emotionally and physically drained. Then she heard the sirens. Close at first. The center of town was less than a mile away. The sounds faded. She moved to the recliner beside the window, opened it to better gauge the distance, and tried to guess where they might be going.

The sirens were joined by others. Different cadences, different vehicles. Police? An accident, maybe. Her stomach tightened. Simple worry, that was all. She stayed by the window, ignoring the cold air biting at her arm, and listened, and waited.

Chapter Seventy-Three

"Very well, Louis. Get out of that town as quickly as possible. Be casual about it, but *get out*. Don't call me again until you're safely back in Maine. Yes, all the way back."

After disconnecting the line, Roger Quinn laid the cell phone on the empty seat beside him. His large, thick fingers remained closed around it. He felt an urge to squeeze harder, crush the phone from existence like he would his pathetic nephew when he got hold of him.

The agent from Maine had done most of the talking. It was Roger's self-imposed rule not to say too much in public conversations, even if the people around him were more concerned with staring sleepily out the plane's windows as it taxied towards the terminal, or slowing packing up their carry-on bags.

Two others traveled with him, in different rows. He ignored them, and they did likewise. Not for any covert reasons. Roger simply hated casual conversations with anyone. Better things to do with his life than talk about the weather.

Louis Hautala's story was confusing at best. When he mentioned the hordes of police and fire apparatus at the town's small Baptist church, Roger was certain of one thing: Peter had been there. It was Chicago all over again. He hoped Lou didn't get arrested. There was too much red tape involved in assassinating someone in police custody. He would have enough to handle, dealing with whatever chaos Peter had stirred up.

Hautala had called from the cemetery. Solomon's grave had been left opened. The news gave him shivers of apprehension. Nothing left inside, but more than enough signs of violence, including "a boat-load of blood," as Hautala put it. At least he had the sense to don gloves and close the crypt before leaving. That was when he saw the flames through the trees.

No matter what his nephew might have uncovered tonight, he had made too much noise to risk leaving alive any longer.

Roger's ears were still blocked as the plain slowed to a stop. He zipped closed his overnight bag after putting the phone away. He stared ahead as people began to rise from their seats, seeing nothing, only thinking. Worrying. He was certain that the fool had gone ahead without waiting.

And something had gone wrong. His nephew never failed to answer his phone, especially when he knew it was his dear Uncle Roger calling. Twice now, Roger's calls were cut over to voice mail.

"Come on," he whispered to the plane. He was near the back of the plane. Disembarking would take fifteen minutes at least. The drive to Hillcrest over an hour. Maybe he would wait until morning. Keep a distance until things cooled down a bit.

He slammed the plastic window shade closed a bit too hard. Nothing outside interested him.

Chapter Seventy-Four

There were very few cars driving along Interstate 395 so late on a Thursday night. Actually, it had become Friday morning a few minutes ago. Most people were in bed, resting up for work the next day.

Nathan drove, not daring to speak or to break the tense veil of silence filling the car. The only sound for much of the past forty miles was the occasional *hah-hah-hah* of the dog's panting from the back seat. Johnson had been surprisingly acquiescent when Nathan pulled into Tarretti's driveway. Even as he walked into the house, crossing directly to Tarretti's bedroom, the large black Labrador simply sat, silent, on the living room rug and watched with unnerving detachment. He wondered if dogs had some special insight, as he'd lifted the floorboards and removed the strongbox. Some self-preservation mechanism, knowing when Master was gone and it was time to find a new human to care for him. When Nathan emerged from the bedroom with the box and went to the door, he'd paused and looked back at Johnson. The dog looked back with quiet expectation.

"Stay," he'd said, and went out to the car, putting the box into the trunk. He lifted the tablets from the back seat. The power was there again, filling him, vibrating. It took an effort to lay them back down into the trunk beside Tarretti's box. He ran back into the house, doing a quick search for dog food. After dropping the oversized bag beside the other items in the trunk, he returned to the house for the dog itself.

He was never much of an animal person, but he knew he could not leave Johnson here alone. Even now, driving along the dark highway, Nathan didn't know how they'd be able to care for the thing, give it any kind of home.

The next thought sent his stomach tightening in shame, no less than it would over the years and decades to come. *You can't leave the dog, but you could throw your best friend to the wolves so you could escape.* He had to remind himself that it had been Josh's choice to stay behind—an admirable, selfless act, even with only a couple of seconds to decide. If Elizabeth was meant to be here with him now, was Josh meant to play the role of tethered goat, left as the sacrifice in their place? Someday, Nathan might learn what cross they were leaving behind for him to bear.

The lane markers swished by in unrelenting flashes of white. Nathan was not tired. Not yet. Normally when things got too quiet, it would be Elizabeth who spoke. She always took the initiative. Not tonight.

They passed an exit, the one they'd taken a lifetime ago to find the old woman's quilt museum. The small sign Elizabeth had noticed back then was now gone. He thought to mention this, but decided not to. She was staring out the window, the tears long dried. As they passed under the occasional highway lamps, the dirt and ash smeared on her face came into sharp relief. He wondered how bad he looked himself, with the bruises stiffening on his cheeks.

He kept his window open a crack, trying to bring in some fresh air, clean out the stale burnt odor emanating from their bodies and clothes. It helped a little. Johnson's nose worked its way from the back seat, sniffing at things only he could smell. Nathan hit the switch for the back window, and the nose moved away to easier smelling grounds.

Both of them tried to ignore the palpable presence lying in the trunk, so close behind them; the fourth passenger.

The gas gauge was slightly past the halfway mark. They were approaching an exit for the town of Putnam, Connecticut and Route 44. They had to stay off the main highways. If anyone had seen their plate as they drove from the fire, there would be an APB out to every state and local police department. Did it matter, then, which road they took?

Whom would the police be looking for? Quinn? What about Josh? Again, and again, Nathan's thoughts returned to the friend he'd left behind. His mind had raced and over-analyzed everything else, as long as it kept him from the true source of horror gnawing at his stomach. Thoughts of Josh, who would likely be arrested for at least one murder.

Thoughts of his father. And his mother, who likely still didn't know that her family was gone forever.

"What," he began, then had to swallow. His mouth was dry. They should stop at a McDonald's somewhere, get a drink. He tried again, "What do you think Josh told them?"

Elizabeth turned her head, slowly, and Nathan braced himself for the verbal assault she'd been building up.

"I don't know," she said, softly. Looking back out the window, she continued, "Where are we going, Nate?"

He offered her a small, humorless laugh. "I don't know." The relief of her calmness made him giddy. He tried to control it, keep from laughing hysterically at their humorless predicament. The last time he'd done that, he'd been beaten almost to death. Where *were* they going? Good question.

Elizabeth turned to him again, this time twisting and bringing one knee onto the seat. "Nate, what was that, at the front of the church? What was it?"

"You mean the fire?"

She raised her voice. "The...*thing*... in the fire, Nate! Didn't you see it?"

He shook his head, slowly, not in denial but confusion. "I'm not sure; there was too much going on. You mean the Covenant? What *thing*?"

She looked at him a long time, not in anger but something else, something he had not seen in her face even when her mother had been sick, not to this degree. She looked... horror-struck. Her lips were tightly closed. He wanted to urge her on, feeling a twist in his gut from the possibility that tonight had more dimensions than even *he* had seen.

"What is it? Elizabeth, what did you see?"

She shook her head, quickly, a child's emphatic *no!* gesture, then turned in her seat until she was staring out her side window.

"Nothing," she said at last. "Nothing."

Johnson had forsaken his window during the conversation, his large head moving in the rear view mirror, back and forth between them. Sensing nothing more of interest, he turned his wet nose back to the two inches of fresh air coming in from outside.

They drove on, staying on the interstate. Nathan still felt exposed on this open road, uncertain of where to go next. He needed to listen to his instincts from now on. Go where the Spirit directed them.

When it returned fifteen minutes later, Elizabeth's voice was weak, tired.

"Nate?"

"Yeah?"

"Do you think God's going to mind me tagging along like this?"

He smiled, sensing the Old Elizabeth returning. Even her jabs at his faith were a welcome relief. "I thought you didn't believe in God," he said.

"Yeah, well, regardless, do you think he'll mind? I mean, bringing the dog wasn't one of your brightest ideas, but *me*... what about me?"

The question carried such a weight of importance, in its implication and the almost desperate way in which it was asked, Nathan took his time in answering.

"No, E," he finally said. "I don't think He'll mind. Don't take this the wrong way, but I'm beginning to think you were supposed to come with me."

He'd gone too far. His fear doubled when Elizabeth suddenly broke out in renewed sobs, at times banging her head lightly against the passenger window. He doubted she even knew she was doing it.

He wanted to take back what he'd said, then remembered something his pastor in Florida once told him. If a parishioner is crying, they do not want to hear anyone's voice. They only need to know you're there with them.

He reached out and gently touched her arm. Her sobs, after a while, lightened. She turned back to him, holding his arm with both of her hands, and leaned her head on it like a pillow.

After a while, he assumed she'd fallen asleep. Instead, she whispered, "We're going to have to eat, I suppose, and find some new clothes, a pair of shoes for me, if that's OK. Get rid of this car." She sighed. "I can't believe you brought the dog with us."

"I'm not sure how much money I've got, and I don't dare use my ATM card. Not that I have a whole lot in the bank anyway." He tapped the steering wheel with two fingers. "Not sure how we're going to trade in this car, either. I mean, technically, it's stolen."

"Well," she said, her voice fading, falling into sleep, "we could always sneak onto a train car, or something. I've got forty bucks in my pocket. Not much, but I guess if we're supposed to be where we are, like you said, something will come along."

Nathan agreed, but since he could feel Elizabeth's weight fall heavily on his arm, he didn't say so. Her breathing fell into an even rhythm of sleep.

She was right. They had no money to speak of, a car stolen from a dead psychopath, a ninety-pound orphaned dog, and objects of unlimited power and historical consequence—which could easily change the world simply by the knowledge of their existence—wrapped in a potato sack in the trunk. Something *had* to come along. They would drive until they could drive no more, and have faith that in the end, something would present itself.

They drove in silence down the empty highway, headlights

revealing only the next few yards ahead. Soon the car was only a red point of light driving into the night. Then it, and its occupants, were gone.

About the Author

Daniel G. Keohane is the Bram Stoker Award-nominated author of *Margaret's Ark* and *Plague of Darkness*, as well as the horror novels *Destroyer of Worlds* and *Nightmare in* Greasepaint (under the pseudonym G. Daniel Gunn). *Solomon's Grave* was his first published novel. His short fiction has appeared in a variety of professional magazines and anthologies over the years, including *Cemetery Dance*, *Borderlands 6*, *Shroud Magazine*, *Apex Digest*, *Fantastic Stories of the Imagination*, *Coach's Midnight Diner* and many more. You can visit Dan and keep up-to-date with prior and future work at www.dankeohane.com